THIS TOWN IS ON FIRE

Also by Pamela N. Harris
When You Look Like Us

THIS TOWN IS ON FIRE

PAMELA N. HARRIS

Quill Tree Books
An Imprint of HarperCollins Publishers

Quill Tree Books is an imprint of HarperCollins Publishers.

This Town Is on Fire
Copyright © 2023 by Pamela N. Harris

ISBN 978-0-06-321262-6

Typography by Carla Weise
23 24 25 26 27 LBC 5 4 3 2 1

First Edition

FOR ALL THE BLACK GIRLS FINDING
THEIR VOICES—I'M LISTENING.

NOW

EVEN WITH THE OXYGEN MASK ON, THE SMOKE CREEPS ITS WAY DOWN my throat and funnels through each lung. It swirls and wraps itself around the muscle that used to be my heart. Having a heart requires too much effort, too much empathy. I may have lost both traits somewhere along the way.

"You have to keep the mask on, ma'am," the EMT tells me.

Ma'am? I'm only seventeen. This is what Faith hinted at. What Cleo shouted about during almost every meeting. They try to age us to make us feel better about *their* actions.

But . . .

But this guy is only trying to help me. It's dark and there's smoke—so much smoke. He's not thinking *us* versus *them* when he's simply trying to do his job, right?

My hands tremble as I push the mask up the bridge of my nose and breathe in the clean air.

"Look, I know you're scared," the EMT says. His pale face gets painted by red and blue stripes from the light bars on top of the ambulances and police cars in the parking lot. "But we have a lot of folks here working on your friends, okay?"

Friends? That's right. This isn't just about me. It never was. My friends are the reason I came here tonight. I leap from the cot and try to jump down from the back of the ambulance, but the EMT grips my hands.

"Easy, now! I'm not sure how long you were in that building. Smoke can do a lot of damage."

"I'm fine." The words come out as a croak. I touch my neck and try to massage the words out, but I can't reach them. I swallow the little saliva I have left in my mouth and try again. "How many are hurt?"

The EMT shakes his head as he guides me to take a seat on the cot again. "Not sure." He squeezes his fingers around my wrist, checks my pulse.

Not sure isn't good enough. "What about Kylie?" Her name scratches my throat. "She . . . she was right next to me." I see her face, a blur of rage and sadness. Her eyes stabbing me, accusing me. Her fists clenched at her sides. Her blond hair puffing away from her face just as the explosion went off . . .

I pinch my eyes closed—both trying to remember and forget what happens next. The smoke, the soot. The drywall tumbling on top of me. The flashlight beams slicing through the dark as voices called for responses: *If you hear us, make a noise.* Did I see her when they pulled me out? Did I see anyone?

"Naomi?"

My mom's cries pull me back. I open my eyes.

"Ny? NAOMI!" she shrieks again.

This time, the EMT can't contain me. I snatch off the mask and jump down from the ambulance, squinting to find her face in between the streaks of blue and red.

"Ma . . ." My voice fails me. I cough and try again. "MOM!"

My mom breaks past two police officers and barrels toward me, her forehead crumpled with worry. She crashes against me, almost knocks me off my feet. I bury my face in her shoulder, and her jasmine perfume replaces the smoke in my nose. I cling to the back of her shirt. My fingernails stab my palms, but I grip even tighter. If I let go, I'll return to this nightmare, and I want to daydream a little longer.

A pair of sturdy arms envelop us both, pushing us closer together. I can tell from the stubble tickling my forehead that it's Eric. And it's that tickle, my mom's arms—the three of us locked together in a desperate huddle—that does me in. The tears start to spill, and I can't stop them. I don't even try.

My mom pulls away first. Her hands inspect my face, my shoulders, my waist. "Are you hurt?" she asks.

"What the hell happened?" Eric cuts in. He turns his head toward the rubble that used to be the entrance to King Pin's Bowling Alley. That's the first time I really take it all in. The yellow police tape tracing the edge of the building. The SWAT team circling the rubble, speaking in hushed, angry voices. The ambulances, so many ambulances. One of them holds Faith. Thank God she's okay. She sits in the back, oxygen mask on like a good patient, as her EMT wraps a bandage around her wrist. She doesn't look scared. If anything, she seems . . . confused. Her brown eyes look in my direction, but it's like she's staring off somewhere behind me. Somewhere through me, even.

Then there's Cleo.

She sits on the curb with some of the others, her minions. Not even sure when they arrived. Or have they always been here? Everything happened so fast. Her hands are pinned behind her with handcuffs; Senegalese braids are still pinned on top of her head like a crown, not a stray hair out of place. Two police officers loom over them, scribbling notes even though nobody's mouth is moving. Cleo smirks with every muscle in her face. She sees me and lobs that smirk right at me.

But I don't see Butter. He was right here. Right here with her. At least he was before. And still, I don't see Kylie.

"Are you Naomi Henry?" A police officer approaches me. His hat is tucked inside his armpit, but he looks anything but relaxed. His jaw clenches as he sizes up Eric's broad shoulders and six-foot-plus inches of Blackness.

"Who wants to know?" My mom's in front of me like a shield.

"Are you Mrs. Henry?" the police officer asks. My mom gives a stiff nod. "We have reason to believe your daughter was an accomplice to the attack at King Pin tonight."

Accomplice? *Attack?* The words plummet onto me as hard as the crumbling drywall did. I stumble and fall against Eric. If it weren't for him, I'd be flat on my back, staring up at the sky and waiting to die.

"The hell she is!" Eric barks.

The police officer shifts his eyes toward Eric, and I swear I hear them roll. "You the father?"

"Pretty much." Eric grabs my hand and puffs out his chest, like claiming me was a badge of honor. If only.

"'Pretty much' doesn't count, sir. Unless you're her lawyer or guardian, I'm going to ask you to excuse yourself from this conversation."

Something like a rumble seeps from Eric's throat as his feet twitch toward the police officer. My mom takes a step to shield Eric now, and I'm right next to her. A wall to protect him from what's bound to come next.

"If I can interject . . ." My EMT takes two timid strides

to all of us. "I haven't finished checking on Miss Henry. I'm not sure how injured she is."

His sincerity builds a knot in my throat. He's trying to save me. He's trying to save my family. I can't believe I almost made him the enemy.

The police officer glances over me. "She looks fine to me. I'll get a medic to check her out at the station." The police officer pulls a pair of handcuffs from his belt. The moonlight bounces off them, blinds me. "Naomi Henry, you're under arrest. Anything you say can and will . . ."

His words blend together in my stomach, and I hiccup, almost vomiting them back out. This can't be real. I'm stuck in a movie about someone's life I don't want. None of this was supposed to happen. I'm not supposed to be here. Neither was Kylie. . . .

Someone cries out, and my heart bangs against my rib cage between each action:

My mom's hands spread out to the police officer *(lub DUB)*.

Police officers circle my mom, guns pointed at her *(lub DUB)*.

Eric shouts, stringing curse words and threats together *(lub DUB)*.

Two officers pin Eric to the ground, his face crushing against the pavement. His arms pretzel behind his back as the cops try to cuff him *(lub DUB)*.

"You're hurting him!" my mom cries. "Please. You're hurting him!"

Eric mutters something under his breath. He moans. He gags. He can't breathe. Oh my God, he. Can't. Breathe.

My scream rips through the air, silencing the chaos around me. My knees smack against the concrete.

"Just stop!" I beg. I choke on my own tears. "Please, I'll go with you! Just stop! Just stop!" I keep repeating those words until they climb off Eric. Until I see his face lifting and gasping for air. The original cop who tried to arrest me pulls me back to my feet. Continues to read me my rights as he places my arms behind my back, clasps on the handcuffs. The coldness of the steel feels surprisingly refreshing since my whole body's on fire.

"It's okay, baby," my mom says between sobs. "It's okay. You're going to be fine." She tries to follow me as the officer shepherds me to his car, but another cop blocks her.

I'm in the back seat of a squad car. I press my forehead against the window and close my eyes. Maybe if I keep them closed long enough, I'll fall asleep and wake up the next day. I'll realize that this was all some kind of stress dream because of college applications or prom-dress shopping or some other normal shit that most high schoolers get to worry about.

"Not sure what you all were thinking," the cop says to me, refusing to allow me to dream. "But now you know bombs aren't like what you see in video games or whatever. They actually kill people."

At that, my eyelids pop open. I push myself upright in the back seat, and the world spins. "What? Who's . . . who's . . . ?" I can't even get the word out. *Dead* is too extreme. Too final. Saying it aloud will make it concrete.

But the cop doesn't respond. He drives out of the parking lot. I scan it one last time. Faith holds on to her bandaged wrist, chewing her lip like she's chewing back tears as she watches me. Eric holds up my mom as she cries into his chest, not able to look at her only child being taken away by the police. Cleo is marched to another squad car, her chin lifted toward the black sky. Still no Kylie.

I never see Kylie.

THEN: SIX WEEKS AGO
CHAPTER ONE

I PUT ANOTHER DAB OF ECO STYLE GEL ON MY FINGERTIPS AND SMOOTH it along my edges. Lay them down real good before I slip on my butterfly hair clip. I glance in my bathroom mirror again as I fluff out my coils.

"New hair, who dis?" I say to myself. Okay, waking up an extra forty-five minutes earlier than usual may have made me a bit loopy, but it did the trick. It gave me enough time to get dressed, untwist my hair, and mold it into something manageable for the first day of school.

As I put on my silver hoop earrings, I check out my profile in the mirror one last time. Hell, maybe it was more than manageable. My hair was giving me Solange Knowles vibes—though maybe not as big and bold. Yet. I had put in my last relaxer right before the end of last school year. Then I kept my hair in braids all summer to protect it from breakage. Today'll be the first day I've ever gone to school—or hell, *anywhere*, with my natural hair out for all the world to see. But Kylie said we needed to step it up for our senior year. Wait until she checks out the leap I'm making with this fluffy hair.

The sizzle of bacon greets me as I make my way to the hall closet next to the kitchen. Eric's at the stove with his back to me, head hanging low. The only way I can tell he's half-awake is because his hand jerks a little to flip over the bacon. No humming or small talk from him. At least not until he's taken a few sips of coffee.

I rummage through the piles of shoes and used gift bags on the hall-closet floor. "You seen my cheer shoes?" I ask him, then automatically shake my head. His brain is still broken from lack of sleep. He takes on a few graveyard-shift cleaning gigs, so I expected him to still be snoring. "I thought Mom washed them, but they're not in my room," I say, this time more to myself.

Eric rummages through the kitchen cabinets, more than likely searching for a mug to get his caffeine on. "Front door," he says, sleep coating his throat.

Just like he said, my white cheer shoes are chilling by the front door, right next to my backpack. A slip of paper peeks out from inside one of my shoes. I read the note written in purple marker:

You got this if you want it, gurl!

I laugh. My mom thought she was doing something with that unnecessary *u*. But she tries. That's one reason why I love her. And those eight words hit the way she intended them to. They remind me that I'm not married to cheer. That if I want to try something else, be someone else, the choice is mine. Mom has caught me one too many times copying dance moves in the mirror from hip-hop majorette videos. She's noticed how posters of Southern University's Dancing Dolls or Alabama State's Stingettes have replaced images of the cheerleading teams from Ohio State or Texas Tech on my bedroom walls. She's noticed a lot over the past year or so and puts it all into these eight words. Compact but compelling. Another reason why I love her.

"How long is practice supposed to be? You know your mom expects you to visit her after school."

Whoa, I get two sentences in a row. I turn and, just as I figured, Eric's sipping coffee from his favorite mug. *Not Today* on one side, *Nor Tomorrow* on another.

"It's not practice; it's tryouts," I correct.

Eric's whole face lifts to attention as he finally notices me. "Look at you," he says with a smile.

I roll my eyes. "Ugh. Stop." I reach up to touch my hair but second-guess it. I worked too hard to get it just the way I want it. I can't mess it up by matting down one side and making everything all lopsided.

"I mean it. Looks good." He nods with approval.

"Really? It's not too . . . *too*?"

"I have no idea what you're talking about, but I'm going to go with . . . no?" He grabs his phone off the bar top. "Here. Let me take a picture for your mama."

I don't even complain, because I get it. This is the first time Mom hasn't been able to see me off on the first day of school. Our days used to start out over at the Brookses'—her preparing a spread of fruit, eggs, and bagels for me, Kylie, and Kylie's twin, Connor, since that's what the Brookses kept in their kitchen. *White-people breakfast*, Eric used to joke when my mom tried to pull out the same menu on weekends. But my mouth grew fond of the combination, so mornings without it or Kylie and Connor felt off. Like leaving out the door without your keys. Or ending a call with a family member and not saying, "Love you."

Mom had saved up enough money to finally open her own day care center, just like she's been saying she wanted to do since she read *The Very Hungry Caterpillar* to me, Kylie, and Connor. And it was the animated way she read us stories, and how she wiped Kylie's tears when she fell in her roller skates, and even how she spent hours helping Connor make homemade glow sticks for his fifth-grade science project—I knew she had too much love in her heart just for me. She wanted to share it with other kids, and now she was getting her chance.

I place a hand on my hip and cock it toward Eric's phone. Ask him to hold his phone up a little higher like Kylie tells people every time they take her picture. Something about that angle makes you look smaller, and I need all the flattering angles I can get now that Mom likes to joke about my "junk in the trunk," which popped up sometime during last winter break.

"Got it," Eric says, snapping one last picture. "Your mama ain't name you Naomi for nothing." He tells that joke whenever he gets a chance. As if I could even compete with the Melanated Goddess that is Naomi Campbell. I would need at least five more inches and fuller lips to even be on the same page.

"Now have a seat and eat this breakfast of champions." The coffee must be working its way through his veins. He sounds more alert and, dare I say, *chipper* now.

I peek down at the bacon, eggs, and biscuit with glistening gravy sitting on a plate on the table. Calculate the number of calories in my head. Kylie and I are both going for fliers this year. I won't be flying anywhere with a whole bunch of gluten and grease weighing me down.

Eric reads my face, and I guess I have uncertainty written all over it, because he squints at me. "I'm gonna kill you. You know I could still be sleeping, right?"

"I can wrap it up and eat it when I get home," I offer. "I'm heading out soon, and we're grabbing something at school."

And because she's my best friend and knows when I need her, my phone chimes with a text message:

We're heeeeere. Bring yo ass.

I smile in relief and hold up my phone. "See? Gotta go."

"'Cause God forbid if Her Highness walked up here to greet you at the door, right?" Eric rolls his eyes. The only time Eric rolls his eyes is when he talks about Kylie—or any other Brooks, actually.

"Somebody needs a nap," I say. I hold out my fist, and Eric bumps his against it three times before slapping me a five—completing the handshake we created about a month after he and my mom became a thing. "I promise. Me and that biscuit have a date this evening. See ya."

"Not if I see you first."

I groan at the Dad Jokiness of it all as I make my way out the front door. I climb down the stairs of our apartment complex and spot Kylie's glossy blue Audi idling in one of the accessible parking spaces. She checks out her makeup in the mirror in her sun visor as Roma climbs out of the passenger seat, sunglasses perched on top of her head to keep her bobbed brown hair out of her face.

Roma spots me and smiles. "We're seniors, bitch!" she shouts at me.

Kylie turns up the volume of the hip-hop music streaming from her speakers, and Roma bends over to pop the tiny hump she calls a booty. I laugh and mimic her. We groove for a few seconds longer until Roma ends our dance break by climbing into her rightful spot in Kylie's back seat, and I take my place in the front. Kylie shimmies her shoulders to the music once I'm buckled in, but then pauses to truly take me in.

"What's going on with your hair?" she asks with a laugh.

The music stops. At least in my head. Megan Thee Stallion's lyrics get replaced by static, and I will every muscle in my hand to not reach up and touch my hair. To not draw more attention to it. I think of something witty to say to cut through the awkwardness, but my tongue feels heavy, and I want to swallow it and choke and die on the spot.

"I think it's cute." Roma's voice breaks through from behind me, and air finally releases through my nose. I've never wanted to hug her more. "It's different, you know? Kinda mature."

"I never said it wasn't cute," Kylie says. She pushes my shoulder to let me know she's joking, but my body's so rigid that it barely budges from her nudge. "I just asked what was going on. Like, how did you get it to look so curly and stuff? I'm just used to your hair either being straight or braided." She gives me a smile and then focuses behind her as she backs out of my parking lot. She doesn't break gaze for safety, though. Kylie never checks behind her when driving, overly relying on her rearview cam. But she knows that the longer she looks at me, the longer I'll know she's lying through her teeth. She hates my hair. And now I hate it too.

"Yeah, I told my mom it was too much," I say, rolling my eyes as I roll out fake news. "But she wanted me to give it a try so . . . whatever. I'll probably change it again this weekend."

Five minutes later, we're all rapping along to Megan like the conversation never happened. But every now and then, I find myself peeking in the sideview mirror, tugging at one of my coils to see how straight I can get it. At one point, my eyes meet Roma's eyes in the mirror.

She raises her eyebrows at me: *You okay?*

I shrug one shoulder back at her: *It is what it is.*

It's true. Kylie's always going to be Kylie. She's messy buns on the weekends, but layered blowouts on Mondays. She's all shade and burns online, but tears and Taylor Swift ballads IRL. She's quick fingers and scorched tongue from scalding matcha lattes. She's all-teeth smiles, but only because she's biting back pain. That's where I come in. To take away her phone and wipe away her tears while listening to Taylor's version of *Red*. To remind her to wait five minutes before gulping down piping-hot tea. To carry what's behind that smile. It's been that way for as long as I can remember. Kylie tossing away her question about my hair was only because I wasn't there to catch it before it landed. And it landed with a thud.

We turn onto Windsor Boulevard, and I try running my

fingers through my hair again. Windsor Boulevard is the last stretch before we reach Windsor Woods High, as well as the longest and busiest stretch of road in our town. Whatever anyone needs, they can find on Windsor Boulevard. Last-minute grocery items? Hit up Food Lion. Quick bite to eat? Roll through the Dairy Queen drive-through. We have the animal hospital to tend to your sick pooches, the police department to air your grievances, and even Farmers Bank to get your money right. No wonder the street bears the name of our town. The 'vard is like Walmart, if Walmart were fifty miles long. Available twenty-four seven, accepts all forms of payment, and clothing optional. There is that streaking tradition at Windsor Cemetery, after all—not that I've ever participated.

We make it to Windsor Woods, and Kylie finds one of the last spots in the senior-class parking lot. We all talked over the weekend about the perfect time to get to school. We didn't want to look too thirsty or anything, like we were dying for attention. Kylie figured a few minutes before the first bell was the sweet spot. The perfect amount of time for the right people to see us before we started our day. We climb out of her car, and I slip my arms through the straps of my JanSport backpack.

Kylie's forehead creases. "What happened to the Kate Spade I got you?" she asks, nodding to her own shoulder bag to remind me of what mine is supposed to look like.

"It's so nice that my mom didn't want me to mess it up," I say. I pretend to pick something off my shirt so Kylie won't sniff out my lie. My mom wanted me to return the bag. She's been getting weirder about the presents that Kylie gives me ever since she stopped working for the Brookses. I think Eric's starting to get in her head.

"Mess it up? What are you—five? I'll talk to her about it." She swats her hand like it's no big deal, then links her arm through mine. "One more year, Ny. One more year, and we'll be strutting down the sidewalks of Manhattan in our tutus like Sarah Jessica." Kylie's been a hardcore fan of *Sex and the City* since sixth grade, when she accidentally streamed an episode on her tablet. She got me hooked during our sleepovers, and we gave our classmates the real tea after those dry sex-education weeks in health class.

"Didn't she get pissed on in that tutu?" Roma asks.

"Ew, she got splashed by a bus. Who are you? Why don't you know this?" Kylie shakes her head at Roma, then looks at me, waiting for me to join in with her disbelief.

I give a laugh. A weak one, though, because I know Kylie's hinting at us going to NYU. That's only what we've been talking about the last hundred years. But when I wasn't binging *Sex and the City* with Kylie, I was inhaling reruns of that old nineties show *A Different World* with my mom. Even though Denise and Whitley and Dwayne Wayne all attended some fake historically Black college, everything about it felt *real*. The sororities, the step teams, the all-Black everything. I never knew that something could be so genuine but still magical at the same time. We don't have that much Black pride here in Windsor. Yeah, there are more than a handful of us who live in town, but most are like Mom and Eric. They work hard and keep their heads down, complain about the Confederate flags adorning their neighbors' yards in the privacy of their own homes. And there were a lot of those here. Confederate flags. I never thought much of them until Eric's cousin from New York came to visit us two Christmases ago: *I mean, damn, didn't the South lose?* he had asked us during dinner. *You guys are* Gone with the Wind *old-school down here.*

Frankly, my dear, Windsor didn't give a damn. My neighbors were going to rock their Confederate flag T-shirts and hug their Black friends at the same damn time. That's just the Windsor way. Maybe that's why Kylie can't quite get the appeal of *A Different World*. Last time I tried to make her watch an episode, she kept joking about the old-school fashion. Or how nobody from Richmond, Virginia, talked with as much twang as Whitley Gilbert. She talked, talked, talked and never really listened. Never really felt it.

So that was that.

We weave our way through parked cars and wave at the people we want to see, ignore the ones who've done one of us wrong at some point. Especially Jackie Sanders. She gets the coldest of shoulders after posting that Roma sounded like "Miss Piggy on crack" for belting out an Ariana Grande song at the ninth-grade talent show. I mean, yeah, Kylie and I laughed like we were on crack when we first read Jackie's post, but Roma's our girl. We hate who she hates, and vice versa.

Every now and then I get a double take—eyeballs not sure if it's really me until they notice Kylie's arm linked through mine. Nobody says anything about my hair. Not sure if that's a good thing or a bad thing, but I hate the in-between.

We get to my locker first since it's on the first floor.

"Jealous," Roma says. "You got the best location. The end of a row *and* right near a restroom?"

I give her a look. "In what world is being near a restroom ever awesome?"

Roma twists her mouth to one side to consider my question. "For more elbow room, I'd take the occasional crop-dusting."

Kylie and I exchange confused glances.

"You know? The occasional stench that wafts out of the bathroom when the door swings open?" Roma slaps her forehead at us, all: *Duh?*

"That is not a crop-dusting," I insist, opening my locker. "A crop-dusting is when someone passes gas in front of you and forces you to walk into their stink cloud."

"Okay, are we in a locker room? Why are we talking about stench and stink clouds?" Kylie asks as she leans against the locker next to me and looks through her phone. She's seeing who's posting about the first day of school before it's officially begun. "Okay, tell me why Jared's yet to like my pic but has the nerve to like Serena posing next to a damn muffin. Everyone knows that bitch doesn't eat. Like, what's the point?"

If my locker wasn't already open, I'd bang my head against it. I don't want to get sucked into the Kylie-Jared-Serena drama this year. Every time Kylie dumps him, I hope it's the last time I'll have to listen to his political name-dropping. Jared's dad interviews politicians for his right-wing podcast, so Jared likes to pretend he has clout too. Every time Jared tries to move on with Serena, Kylie gets all green and finds a way to make Jared come crawling back. And I'm stuck hearing stories about how *hilarious* Lindsey Graham really is.

"Why are you even following Serena?" I ask.

"I'm not. I'm following the hashtag she used."

"Oh, okay," Roma says with an eye roll. "Hashtag Stalker Status."

"Hashtag Jared Junkie," I add.

Roma and I laugh as Kylie pretends like she's going to throw her phone at our heads. She would never. Too many secrets in there.

"'Scuse me. You're kinda in front of my locker."

Faith Hayslett lingers in front of us. Ripped jeans, baggy sweatshirt, and wedge Timbs. Everything is cocked to her right. Her hip, her backpack—even her hair. The left side of her head showcases a buzz cut, and the rest of her hair spills over the right side of her face in loose corkscrews. Her hair type must be 3C. I researched curl patterns all summer, in hopes I'd be in the 3 category. But I'm 4C all the way. All zigzaggy with no clear direction.

We stop laughing as Kylie steps out of Faith's way.

"My bad," Kylie says to her.

Faith just gives her a nod. She doesn't smirk or frown in irritation. If anything, she seems on the verge of yawning. Like we're too silly to be on her level. She doesn't even acknowledge my new hair. Then again, Faith Hayslett hasn't acknowledged much about me for as long as I can remember. At the start of last school year, I heard rumblings about her wanting to start a dance team at Windsor Woods, and my stomach twisted with nervous energy. Finally, I'd be able to have a chance to show off everything I've learned from my online videos. I'd even found a way to sneak away from Kylie during lunch to make my way over to Faith's table. Before I even had the nerve to ask her about the dance team, Faith squinted at me like she was trying to make out who I was. I think she even asked me if I was lost.

I did the most logical thing I could think of: I asked her where the extra napkins were. I returned to Kylie with a stack of paper towels—and we tried out for the varsity cheer team later that afternoon.

"Anyway," Kylie says in dramatic fashion as she raises her eyebrows at me and Roma, bringing me back to the present. "I heard the school is offering Chick-fil-A during lunch now. Their grilled nuggets are fire. We're so getting that today."

My stomach rumbles at the mere mention of food, reminding me that I passed up Eric's feast earlier this morning. I rummage through my backpack in hopes of finding a granola bar, and one of my cheer shoes tumbles to the floor.

"Shit, that reminds me." Kylie pulls out a pair of crisp white Varsity Aeros Cheer Shoes from her bag and hands them to me. "Happy birthday."

My eyes almost fall out of my head as I inspect the shoes. I checked them out online over the summer. I wanted to ask my mom to splurge for a pair, but with her opening the day care and everything, I figured money would be even tighter than usual.

"It's not my birthday," I manage.

"Consider it an early birthday present. I knew you had your eye on them. Plus, it's about time to retire that pair, so . . ." She shrugs. No biggie.

A smile spreads across my face. I reach out to hug Kylie, but Faith slams her locker closed next to us and jolts the smile right out of me.

Faith looks our way and blinks at her damage. "My bad," she says. Her voice is flat but nasally, in the exact same tone as Kylie's from about a minute ago. She pops an Altoid into her mouth and heads down the hall. I watch after her, wondering what the hell her deal is.

"Um." Roma raises a hand. "My birthday's next month. Where are my shoes?"

"Oh. Hold on. They're right . . ." Kylie digs through her bag again and pulls out her middle finger. She smiles. Roma smacks her hand, and the two laugh as they start slapping at each other. I don't join in, because I'm still watching the back of Faith's head until she disappears into a classroom. I try to remember what in the world I did to end up on her shit list—or, even worse, her couldn't-care-less list—but come up empty. I'm not sure why I even care what list Faith would put me on, but thankfully I don't spend a second longer wondering, because Connor takes that moment to strut down the hall with some of his boys from the wrestling team.

Damn, can that boy strut.

He holds on to a towel wrapped around his neck, emphasizing his biceps, which mold into perfectly sized mounds. He's dewy from the top of his blond hair down to his thick calves. It's obvious that he and the guys just came from morning weight training—and by the way I've studied every inch of him, it's obvious that I enjoy seeing him come from weight training.

He checks me checking him out, and I don't look away. Too late for all that. So he gives me a smile and struts in my direction.

"Ky and Ny," he says, like always. Roma waves a hand in front of herself to remind him that she's also here, like always.

"Ugh, you stink." Kylie curls her lip at him, then looks at Brian and Weston, who flank him. "You all stink."

"It's called pumping iron, sis." Connor rubs his towel across his face and tosses it at Kylie. He does that kind of stuff to Kylie all the time. Rams her head into his sweaty armpit. Gives her a high five, only to leave a used wad of his chewing gum in her palm. *We shared a womb*, he'd remind her. *My germs are your germs.*

Kylie gags and hurls his towel back to him. "I'm sure you left the house with a change of clothes. Some deodorant, maybe?"

"Coach wanted us to take a quick lap around the track. But since no one's out there to monitor us, we thought we'd take a slow one down the halls. See who's here." Connor snaps his fingers and points at me. "Your hair."

I snap my fingers and point to my hair. "Is here," I add.

"I like it." He smiles and tussles his own hair. "I like it a lot. It reminds me of Nakia from *Black Panther.*"

"Well, I only did my hair like this because I knew you'd like it, Connor," I say with only a hint of sarcasm. I worried the most about what he'd say about my hair. Now that he's said it and *it* was positive, I can breathe a little smoother. I'm not sure when I started to worry about what Connor thought about me. Maybe sometime after he started to fill out his wrestling singlet or when my hand found his while watching the latest *Scream* and he rubbed tiny circles onto my knuckles to keep me calm. For the whole movie—and like five minutes after the credits ended.

"Reminds me of Childish Gambino," Brian says, nodding to my hair, and Weston laughs. Connor punches Brian in the arm, and I hear one of Brian's capillaries pop. Brian groans and the laughter stops.

"He's an ass," Connor says to me. "But you're beautiful." He turns to Roma: "You're okay." Then to Kylie: "And you're annoying."

"Bye, Connor." Kylie holds up a hand to dismiss him.

Connor laughs, and he and his friends continue their hallway tour. I smile after him. He has that effect on me. My polished nail could break, my phone battery could die, and the sky could fall, but he'd still find a way to make me smile. I remember the start of the summer. Floating in the Brookses' pool. His hand on my lower back as he teaches me how to swim. His hands grazing other parts of my body until—

"No." Kylie's finger is in my face, poking through my memory. "I told you already—bad idea. Kissing Connor is like kissing me."

I pull a disgusted face and Kylie laughs, her mission accomplished.

"Come on," she says. "Roma and I still need to get to our lockers before the bell rings."

Roma gives me a sly smile as I shove my new shoes into my locker and close the door. I wait until Kylie turns away to return the smile. Make sure it's nice and wide, since Connor thinks I'm beautiful and all.

TWO

I WALK INTO SECOND BLOCK, HONORS PHYSICS. MY ETERNAL LAB PART-ner, Drew Mize, spots me and makes a dramatic show of wiping imaginary dust off the lab stool next to him with the sleeve of his cardigan sweater. I give him a brief curtsy before taking my seat.

"Your hair is giving me my entire life," Drew says with a grin that eats up his entire face.

"Shut up. Really?" I pat at my hair, and it surprisingly still has a bit of moisture to it. Drew's opinion is almost as important to me as Connor's. Drew finds the silver lining in my dimmest days. I mean, my guy even complimented the crutches I had to use for a week after spraining my ankle from some failed tumbling move. I would've made him my boo if Phil Townsend III didn't beat me to the punch back in seventh grade. He and Phil have been off and on ever since, so I had to settle for Drew as my science boo as soon as we hit high school. We're the Kobe and Shaq of lab work—though we argue over who gets to be Kobe every other week.

"Thanks. And what about you, sir? West Coast vibes all the way."

Drew pretends to flip his auburn frosted-tipped hair over his shoulders, even though it doesn't go past his ears. "You know how I do. Idle hands, baby."

"What? No Phil this weekend?"

Drew rolls his eyes. "I don't know that man. Sorry to that man."

I laugh. So Drew and Phil are on ice, but before I can get the deets on why, Faith Hayslett strides into the classroom and looks around—trying to find an empty seat. My breath gets caught in my throat. It's rare to find other Black kids in my honors classes. It's been me, Xavier Moore, and Kennedy Bowers since forever, plus maybe some military kid weaving in and out over the years. But never Faith Hayslett. I just assumed that Faith was too chill to stress about honors classes and advanced diplomas. Like maybe she'd rather spend her energy on burning sage and clearing out negative energy. But here she is—shoulders and chin in an upright position like a gymnast about to murder a floor routine and get that gold.

"Is she lost?" Drew asks me.

At that, Faith cuts her eyes at us and I quickly look down at my lab table. She makes her way past me, her backpack hitting against my table and jostling it just a little, but enough. She makes her point.

"Shit, you think she heard me?" Drew snickers under his breath.

I can't even return a polite laugh. I don't want Faith to think I'm laughing at her, even if Drew kind of wants me to. I mean, not like *that*, but Faith won't understand that Drew's just being Drew. Cussing out Drew would be like kicking a shih tzu or some other puppy that's too adorable for its own good. Faith doesn't know that Drew's all bark and that's it.

"Girl, I love your nails!"

I look over my shoulder. Faith has found a spot next to Kennedy, and Kennedy has taken it upon herself to grab Faith's hand and inspect her polish. Faith says something in return, and their laughter scratches something inside me. All these years with pretty much the same classes, and Kennedy talks to me only to compare answers on our study guides, but in five seconds she and Faith are talking about something outside of sines and cosines. What made Faith so different from me?

The bell rings, and our teacher, Mrs. Ward, is at the whiteboard. "I don't know about you all, but I blinked and summer was gone," she says, her cheeks blooming like she ran a marathon before coming into the classroom. She waits for the timid laughter for her timid joke. Two of my classmates comply. I haven't seen her around before. Most of the teachers at Windsor Woods have been here since the Civil War—and the younger ones are from this town anyway. They put in their four years to get their teaching degree, then come back home to "make a difference." We still have a painting of Stonewall Jackson in our library, though.

Mrs. Ward claps her hands together. "I want to try something. I've been told that this group has been together for a while, so I want to shake things up. Give you all a chance to work with someone new."

Okay, she's *definitely* not from around here. The groans swim across the classroom like a wave. Drew adds to the chorus of groans, even holding both of his thumbs down to lay it on extra thick. One for him, one for me.

"Since I don't know everyone yet, we'll just pair up alphabetically for the first half of the semester," Mrs. Ward continues.

This time I groan. Seating arrangements in alphabetical order? Are we in second grade? Mrs. Ward starts going through the roster and one by one, my classmates stand to move to their new tables, some dragging their feet in protest. I try to run through the roster in my head, try to remember if there were any last names between Henry and Mize that would break up me and my Eternal Lab Partner.

". . . Faith Hayslett and Naomi Henry . . ."

My eyebrows twitch in response. I was so worried about who came after me alphabetically that I didn't consider I might get paired with someone before me. And I damn sure didn't consider being partners with Faith Hayslett.

"You getting up?"

Faith stands behind Drew, already plopping her backpack underneath the lab table. Message loud and clear. The good news is that I don't have to move. The bad news is Drew does. Drew grabs his iPad and steps over Faith's backpack.

"Miss you," he mouths to me, then proceeds to do the sister hand clap from *The Color Purple*. I let out a small laugh. I should've never told him to watch that movie.

Faith takes Drew's former seat and opens her binder to a blank sheet of paper. She then lines up two pens and a pencil next to it. She's ready to get down to business even though Mrs. Ward is still calling out names. And even with our classmates grumbling and skidding lab stools across the floor, there's a balloon of silence around me and Faith that I feel compelled to pop.

"I like your nails," I say, then bite my lip. She's heard that already. She probably knows that *I* heard her hearing that already. Which means she probably thinks I'm making fun of her. Again.

"Thanks." Faith doesn't look in my direction.

I nod. Mrs. Ward is only on the *L*s. Help. "Did you do it

yourself or . . . ?" I don't finish. Not sure why. Maybe I want her to finish for me so we can have whatever moment she and Kennedy had. *Look, we're completing each other's sentences already. How cute are we?*

Faith just stares at the whiteboard as if she's waiting for words to magically appear.

I exhale through my nose. If we were going to make any progress, I needed to make the first move. "Look, I didn't think you were lost or anything. Neither did Drew. We just never saw you in here before."

Faith finally looks at me. She has a nose ring. It's tiny and gold, and can she be any more badass? "Today's the first day of school."

I fold my hands together so I won't slap one of them on my forehead like the emoji. "No, I meant . . . usually the same people are in these classes over and over again."

Faith shrugs. "Sorry to break your monotony."

At that, I rock back on my stool. This girl's looking for a fight. I'm not trying to give her one, but I'm not about to let her clown me either. "I'm good. It takes more than a new person joining my class to knock me off-balance."

"Yeah. I noticed."

I blink at her. She noticed? Noticed what? This girl barely has said more than two words to me in all the years we've been in school together. In fact, I think our last meaningful conversation—before the awkward cafeteria encounter last year—was on a sixth-grade field trip when she asked me if I was going to eat all of my peanut butter and jelly sandwich. I gave this chick half, even though my mom made sure to cut off my crusts and use the crunchy peanut butter I love. I'm still waiting on my thank-you, but that would've required more words between us.

"Your girl earlier," Faith continues, possibly reading the confusion across my face. "Even with her playing you, you kept steady. I give you that."

My confusion has morphed into full-blown befuddlement. "What are you talking about? When did she play me?"

"I guess since you didn't get your shoes from Saks or whatever, they didn't make the cut, huh?"

Oh. Everything clicks now. She thinks I'm tripping about Kylie's gift to me. I mean, I guess someone who doesn't know us might think she was clowning me, but Kylie's always done stuff like that. She knows when I want or need something before I do. Those are the perks of seeing someone practically every day for the last decade.

"Kylie was just being nice," I say. "Just like I'm trying to do now." I give her a tight smile, let her witness all the kindness just oozing out of me. Even if I want nothing more than to shout in her face that Kylie and I aren't just best friends—we're sisters. We have matching scars on our right knees to prove it. After I skinned mine during an intense game of freeze tag, Kylie made sure to scrape her knee across the pavement so she could hurt just like me. If that wasn't sisterhood, I didn't know what was.

Faith studies me for like a second before giving me another shrug. "'Kay." With that, she turns her head to watch Mrs. Ward talk about class expectations.

I've been dismissed with one syllable. Not only that, but I've also been judged because I accepted a gift from my best friend. It's not like they were hand-me-downs. Kylie's stopped giving me her old designer clothes sometime between me growing D-cup boobs and what Beyoncé calls a "fatty" inside my jeans. This time, Kylie went out of her way to buy something that she knew I'd like. That's a true friend. No, a *sister*. I want to explain this all to Faith, but she starts jotting down notes about upcoming assignments. I chew the inside of my cheek and do the same. I just hope I can read my handwriting later because right now everything looks fuzzy.

I barely slip my small, cotton shorts over my hips before I'm running out of the locker room and onto the football field. I didn't plan on being late to cheerleading tryouts, but I also didn't want to head out there looking like Donald Glover, aka Childish Gambino, as Brian had pointed out earlier. I needed to add in more leave-in conditioner and tease my hair some to give it a little body. Nothing felt natural about this whole natural-hair thing.

I spot the rest of the girls stretching near the sidelines and take my place between Kylie and Roma. Coach Beverly looks up at me from her clipboard, and I give her a small smile as I bend over to stretch out my hamstrings. She does not smile back. I hope she doesn't hold me running like eight seconds behind everyone else against me. She has said more than once that just because we were on varsity last year doesn't guarantee that we'll make it again. It seems like she's told me maybe two times more than everyone else, like she and I both knew I was on borrowed time.

A hand slaps my ass, and I snap upright. Kylie smiles at me.

"Sorry. Couldn't help admiring your lovely lady lumps," she says with a laugh.

"Ha ha," I say.

"She's telling the truth." Roma pulls one of her feet up to her butt to stretch her quads. "Can I borrow them for a day?"

"Roma, you definitely don't need any more junk in your trunk," Kylie says flatly, like she was reading facts from a textbook.

I reach over and flick her arm.

"Ow! What? Roma knows I love her fat ass." Kylie smiles again.

"It's cool. I'm used to Kylie taking out her Daddy issues on me," Roma says, painting on an even bigger smile.

I cock an eyebrow at Kylie. "Daddy issues?"

Kylie swats a hand, knocking my words away. "Nothing.

Boring legal stuff. You know how it goes. People get jealous and want what my dad has. Tale as old as time."

My eyebrow hasn't settled. Sure, I know that Mr. Brooks has to settle cases related to workers' comp or whatever every now and then. *The price you pay for being a business owner,* he'd always say. But I haven't heard about any recent drama. Before I can probe any further, Coach Beverly blows her whistle.

"All right, ladies. Change of plans," she shouts at us. There's a megaphone by her feet, but she never needs it. Her lungs can wake the dead. "We're holding tryouts in the gym instead."

I join the other girls in a mini whine fest. The gym is the worst because the AC is unpredictable as all get-out. This many bodies in that little space, and it starts smelling like we're in a fast-food restaurant up in there.

"How come?" Kylie demands, speaking for all of us.

Coach Beverly doesn't have to answer. The pounding bass from the school's marching team does it for her. The band members spill out onto the field, the melody of Missy Elliott and Da Brat's "Sock It 2 Me" oozing out of their instruments like a lazy, but powerful, groove.

But it's not the band that I can't keep my eyes off. Sashaying out in front of them are the Windsor Woods Wolverines, also known as the dance team. Their hips rock to the drumbeat as they make their way to the center of the field. Just as the beat drops, so do they—dipping so low to the ground that their asses almost kiss it. But they all have the knees of champions, hovering above the ground just enough to make their movements push past filthy into finesse. And leading them all is Faith Hayslett with a grin on her face. Not the fake kind I and most of the squad glosses on. Hers is boundless. Wise. Hell, intoxicating. Like she knows her melanin is popping and she makes all the Black and Brown bodies behind her do the same.

Chills. Starting in my scalp and tickling their way down to my toenails. This is what I envisioned a Windsor Woods dance team would look like, *feel* like. This is why I've studied hundreds, maybe thousands, of hours of HBCU majorette and dance-team videos. This is why I sought Faith out last year. I wanted to move the way that they moved, without any care or constraints. I wanted to be part of a sisterhood. Different from the one I had with Kylie. A sisterhood where I could get advice about hair products or laugh at episodes of *A Different World*. I wanted to be as powerful as they all looked right now.

I peel my eyes away from Faith long enough to glance at the rest of my squad. To make sure that they see what I see. That they *feel* what I feel. But instead of eyebrows lifted in wonder, I'm met with pouts. A few eye rolls. Kylie has her arms folded across her chest.

"I still think Mr. Hicks was wrong," she says, referring

to our principal. Last year, he went to battle with the school board to get the dance team approved until the board finally gave in. They even featured his efforts on *Good Morning America*. "The school already has us. What's the point?"

She shakes her head and follows Coach Beverly and the rest of the girls back into the building. I take one last look at the Wolverines as they high kick and land flat on their backs in a domino effect with not so much as a grimace. Black joy instead of Black pain.

That. That's the point.

THREE

I DON'T GET KYLIE'S TEXT THE NEXT MORNING UNTIL ABOUT FIVE MIN-
utes before she is supposed to pick me up:

Sick. Might not make it to school today. Sorry!

The hell? She was fine when she left me at my mom's
day care yesterday—albeit a little salty because I stayed with
my mom instead of going on a Target run with her. I just
chalked that up to her stressing about home stuff. Taking
her Daddy issues out on me, as Roma so eloquently put it. I
didn't remember hearing a sniffle or cough from her.

I suck my teeth. "You gotta be kidding me," I say to
the screen of my phone. If it's whatever's going on with Mr.
Brooks, she could just tell me. She tells me everything.

"What's that?" Eric asks, two barstools away from me,

poking his spoon into his bowl. He took yesterday's hint. Instead of a morning feast of bacon, he opted to make oatmeal with cinnamon. He even sliced up some apples as garnishes, as he put it. At which I snapped my fingers in applause. That's the thing about Eric. He's been with my mom for over ten years, but still goes hard to make me like him. Not like he needs to try at all anymore. He won us both over.

I sigh and drop my phone into the outside pocket of my Kate Spade satchel. I, too, could take a hint. Kylie was offended that I didn't bring it to school yesterday, so I dug it out of my closet to nip the drama in the bud. I'd just have to hide it from my mom again before she came home from work.

"Can you give me a ride to school?" I ask Eric. "I think the bus already came."

"Where's Her Highness?"

"Apparently sick."

Eric raises a skeptical eyebrow. "On the second day of school? I call foul."

"Kylie wouldn't miss the first week of school just for anything. Plus, she did sound kind of hoarse yesterday." I don't know why I always find a reason to lie for her. Eric doesn't care if Kylie has a cold or a cold sore, but the story rolled across my tongue like butter. "All I know is I feel fine, so can I have a ride? Unless, you know, you want to give me your keys." I smile and wiggle my fingers at him.

Eric looks down at my hand and shakes it instead. I groan and pull away. "Fine. Grab your stuff," he says. "I need to grab me a McMuffin anyway. This oatmeal ain't hitting on nothing."

We're in the car in less than five minutes. As soon as I buckle into the front seat of his Nissan, I stab a text to Kylie.

Really??? No heads up???

I stare at the extra question marks, then sigh and type again.

You okay, tho? Need to talk?

I stare at the screen for a few seconds. Kylie's usually quick on the draw with her responses. At least for me. She even managed to give me a play-by-play of her grandfather's entire funeral last year, and her parents were none the wiser. But this time, I get nothing. Not even bubbles letting me know that Kylie's at least thinking about replying.

"So, how was practice yesterday?" Eric asks, automatically changing the station to listen to Charlamagne Tha God rant about anything and everything.

I set my phone facedown on my lap. "It was tryouts, not practice." And I'd rather not think about it. My first attempt at flying was met with a resounding two claps from Coach Beverly. Two—and I think the second one was her killing a gnat. Not that I could blame her. I had been a bit distracted, thinking about how the Wolverines were bucking with the breeze out on the field while I was perfecting split jumps in a muggy gym.

"But you're already on the team."

"You're not guaranteed a spot on varsity. And besides . . ." I remember the pulsing drums from the marching band. Faith and the other Wolverines wrecking shop along with them, their hips and arms swaying freely to the beat. Kylie had dragged me to our first cheer tryouts in middle school, too nervous to go on her own.

I HAVE to go, Kylie reminded me when I asked her why even bother if she was so nervous. She was right. Her mother was an elite cheerleader back in her day—and yes, Mrs. Brooks always uses the word *elite* to describe her years with pom-poms to make sure we know she was a big deal. That is, if the trophies she showcases on floating shelves in the Brookses' study aren't enough. Or the toe touches she'd bust out in front of me and Kylie's other friends when she had a little too much Dom Pérignon at a dinner party. Yeah, Kylie was destined to be a cheerleader as soon as Mrs. Brooks found out that she needed to buy pink for one of her embryos.

I, on the other hand, couldn't even get into those *Bring It On* movies that Mrs. Brooks insisted we watch. And when I dared to show Coach Beverly an eight count of choreography that had seven counts too many of rhythm, she stared at me like I had told her I joined the Illuminati. So I stayed with the usual staccato handclaps for Kylie. After a while, I started to somewhat tolerate cheer, and the camaraderie that came along with it. That is, until Faith formed the Wolverines and snatched off edges.

"Besides . . ." Eric waves his hand, welcoming me to continue.

"I'm trying out for a different position. A flier. They may not want me."

"Yes, they will. And if they don't, I'll get Charlamagne to go in on them." Eric turns up the radio as Charlamagne announces his Donkey of the Day.

I laugh just as my phone buzzes. About time Kylie answered me. I grab my phone to see not a text from Kylie, but an alert from my Instagram account. Great. I wonder what dance craze Roma is trying to learn now. I can wait until she shows me at lunch later.

"Does Charlamagne ever give himself Donkey of the Day?" I ask Eric.

"Careful now. Say that too loud, and Black Twitter will come for you."

"Yeah right. Black Twitter goes harder on Charlamagne than anyone else." My phone buzzes again. Another Instagram alert. Then another. And one more. What in the world?

"Who's blowing up your phone this early?" Eric asks.

Before I can answer, my phone buzzes one more time as Roma sends me a text:

OMG. Did you see it?????

Okay, that was about two question marks too many, even for Roma. I open Instagram to see what has everyone so amped up.

The first alert is from a cheerleader from Smithfield Pines, the only other high school in our county, at the opposite end. We usually give each other polite nods at games, being two of the handful of Black girls on our squads. The whole *Hey girl, heeeeyyy* with our eyes.

Yo, don't she go to your school?

Below the message is a shaky video of a white girl and some Black guy with a ball cap talking outside a store. Target, maybe? I can tell by the red shopping carts. The white girl paces as she talks into a phone, then pulls the phone away from her to flail her arms toward the Black guy. Things seem intense. The white girl flips her hair out of her face in anger to make sure the Black dude gets the full volume of her words. And that's when everything clicks: the blond hair, the skinny jeans, the shiny blue Audi sneaking into the shaky frame.

It's Kylie. Somebody recorded Kylie.

I start the video over and turn up the volume.

KYLIE: (into her phone) . . . yeah, and now they won't leave me alone. I'm just trying to leave.

BLACK DUDE: Ay, not sure who you're talking to, but like I told you before. We were just checking on you. You're the one that just flipped out.

KYLIE: (pulls away phone) I flipped out because you almost killed me!

GUY HOLDING CAMERA PHONE: Yooo, she chargin' you with attempted manslaughter, bruh!

BLACK DUDE: (smirks at camera)

KYLIE: You almost hit me with your car, then came charging at me like you were trying to rob me!

GUY HOLDING CAMERA PHONE: (laughs) She is wildin', bruh! This keeps getting better!

BLACK DUDE: We ran out to make sure you was good. Now that we see that you are, we can be on our way, but you're blocking us.

GUY HOLDING CAMERA PHONE: I don't know, you sure she's good? Sis must've hit her head or something.

KYLIE: (into phone again) Yeah. Yeah, okay. (hangs up and dials another number)

BLACK DUDE: Sooo, we good? Are you going to move out of our way so we can leave?

KYLIE: My dad told me to call the police so we can get everything sorted out.

GUY HOLDING CAMERA PHONE: YOOOO! She calling the cops, G!

BLACK DUDE: You for real right now?

KYLIE: (holds up phone to her ear and avoids eye contact)

BLACK DUDE: You for real right now? Go ahead and call

them. Let them know how we DIDN'T hit you and now you're blocking us in with your car.

KYLIE: (into phone) Hello? Yes. I'd like to report an incident.

(BLACK DUDE AND GUY HOLDING CAMERA PHONE LAUGH)

KYLIE: (into phone) I'm at the Target on Jefferson, and these two Black guys are trying to flee the scene. . . .

BLACK DUDE: WHAT? Bruh, what the fu—?

I close out of Instagram and let the phone fall into my lap. It's heavy. When did my phone get so heavy? Just the thought of lifting it right now makes my hands tremble. I squeeze my fingers and try to massage them into submission. Try to get them to calm down. Try to get *me* to calm down.

"What were you watching?" Eric asks.

Good question. I can't answer because I can't stop staring at my trembling hands. At the phone on my lap that feels like a stone.

"Ny, what's going on?"

"Kylie . . . Kylie got into an argument." I wince as the words leave my throat. An *argument* doesn't seem accurate. An *argument* means there was an equal exchange. But nothing about that video felt equal. "I mean, she got into it with some guy and called the cops."

"Some guy?" Eric stops at a red light and fully swivels toward me. "Some *Black* guy?"

I give a slight nod. That's all my head can manage at the moment. If I move it any more, too many thoughts and feelings might slip out. Deformed thoughts and feelings that hadn't taken shape yet. Like a mound of clay waiting to be pulled and pinched.

"Well . . . is he okay?"

I blink at him. "What you mean?"

Eric frowns. "What do you mean what I mean? A white girl calling the cops on a Black guy is like an automatic death sentence."

I rub my forehead. Eric does this. Too much, if you ask me. He always finds reasons to bring up the whole Black/white thing and how us Black folks have it so much harder than white folks. I remember one of the first times I hung out with him and Mom together, we all watched *Straight Outta Compton* and he kept cussing and walking out of the living room whenever there was a scene with a white cop being a bully. Which sucked, of course—but it took us twice as long to finish the movie because of his dramatics.

And maybe that's just what this is. Dramatics. People blowing something out of proportion. I know Kylie. Like "sharing the same ChapStick when one of us leaves ours at home" kind of know. If she called the cops, if Mr. Brooks told her to call the cops, there had to have been a good reason.

"Don't you think that's a little extra?" I ask Eric. "It's not like we're still out here picking cotton."

"Ny, if you really thought that, you wouldn't be sitting here looking like you were about to throw up."

I look down at my hands, still shaking, and shift in my seat. I can't move as much as I want to because my seat belt digs into my neck, strangling me. And just the idea, the fear, of being strangled by my seat belt travels to my armpits until they get all swampy. I roll down the window to let the breeze cool me off, but the air feels stale. Stagnant. Not allowing a gust of wind to blow these shapeless thoughts out of my head. If they ruminate too long up there, I'm scared what they may morph into. Too scared to think what Kylie has morphed into.

Eric and I don't speak for the rest of the drive. It's like I'm scared to say the wrong thing, and Eric's scared to tell me I'm wrong. He finally pulls into Windsor Woods High's parking lot, and I unbuckle my seat belt before he can fully shift into park. Any second longer in this car and I might implode.

"You need a ride home?" Eric asks as I unbuckle my seat belt and gasp for air.

I think I tell him that I'll catch the bus, but my eyes, my mind, are elsewhere. I'm staring out toward the school building, trying to gauge the vibe so I can prepare myself. I wish that was my superpower. Feeling a mood and camouflaging myself to match it. Or maybe just disappearing when the vibe's all wrong.

"Hey." Eric cuts into my thoughts and leans toward me. His face serious, but soft. Just like when he shared with me that he had spent some time locked up. He didn't want to tiptoe around me. If we were going to be family, he wanted me to know the truth. I think that was when I knew I loved him. "You good? You need to stay home?"

If only. Taking a day to check in with Kylie to get some answers is just what I need. But staying home would also mean I think something's wrong. I give Eric a weak smile. "So you can make me clean out the fridge or the toilet bowls? No, thank you." I initiate our handshake just to fake the funk even further, then climb out of the car. Brace myself.

I need to cannonball the hell out of this shit. Just power through until I find someone, anyone, to give me answers about what I just saw. It's starting to become clearer that Kylie's off playing hooky, but maybe Roma will have the full story. Maybe this was all some elaborate prank to stir up talk before homecoming. Maybe I shut the video off before the big dance break or gotcha moment so that Kylie could get more votes for homecoming queen. She did say she wanted to go out with a bang this year, after all.

As I enter the main hallway, you can tell everyone's hyped about the video. I pass pockets of people circling around phones, tee-hee-heeing at Kylie being Kylie to the tenth power. Every now and then, a pair of eyeballs spots me.

Not caring about my hair anymore. Eyebrows raised, smirks on mouths. Faces practically screaming: *This is who you roll with?*

I hug my arms across my chest, wishing again that I could make myself disappear. Or maybe rewind time so I could take Eric up on his offer to stay home. Kylie had the right idea about getting "sick" today. I make it to my locker with no Roma in sight. I pull out my phone to respond to her text:

Where are you? Meet me at my locker.

The thud of the locker next to me makes me just about jump out of my skin. Faith looks at me with her head tilted and her hand still flat against her locker.

"Jesus. You scared the hell out of me," I say to her.

"That seems to be a thing with you."

I can't tell if she's trying to be funny or an ass. So, I do to her what she's done to me after all these years: ignore her. I glance back and forth between my phone and the hallway, waiting for Roma to either respond via text or in person. I try to remember if there were any cues from yesterday that would've set Kylie off like that. I think about my mom watching Kylie storming out of the Itsy Bitsy Academy after I told Kylie I was getting a ride home with my mom. That there was no point in me wasting money at Target if I didn't need anything.

"She's on one today," my mom had said as we sprayed

down toys with disinfectant. But then a second later: "I'm sure she'll call you later. She always does."

But she didn't. And I didn't call her either. I knew that something was off with her, something about her dad. But I got home so late from Itsy Bitsy that all I could think about was scarfing down Eric's biscuit and the fried chicken Mom picked up from Popeyes on the way home. Then I climbed into bed and cyberstalked Connor. I'm an awful friend. If I had just gone with her—hell, even just called her—this video wouldn't have existed.

I don't spot Roma coming down the hall, but I get a better visual: Connor. This time he's not strutting straight from a workout with his boys. He walks with purpose, the zipper from his fleece jacket grazing the bottom of his clenched jaw. He almost doesn't hear me when I call his name. Twice.

"What's up, Ny?" He glances down at his shoes, like he's thinking twice about slowing them down to chat with me. But he does—for me. He even tries to give me a smile, but I know him too well. The smile never reaches his eyes.

"What's up?" I need something to do with my hands, so I hug my Kate Spade bag. "Kylie texted me this morning. Is she okay?"

Connor's mouth twitches, the smile fading. He's chewing on something and doesn't want to share, not even with me. "What do you mean?"

Oh no. He thinks I'm asking him about the video. Of

course, I want to, but not yet. Not until I know that he's good. That we're good. Connor and I only recently learned this new dance between us, and it doesn't have a name yet. A tricky two-step of finding our own rhythm without Kylie pounding the percussion.

I shake my head like I'm fanning away the awkward. "No. She said she was sick. What's wrong?"

Connor exhales through his mouth. Relief. "Yeah, she has one of those headaches she gets sometimes. You know how she is. A headache's a migraine, and a paper cut is a gouging wound. . . ."

"Careful. He might call the cops on you for blocking the hallway," Jaxson Fields says as he smirks his way past us. He tugs at his skinny jeans, trying to pull them over his narrow hips. Jaxson's the only Black guy at our school still rocking the skater boi look.

Connor spins around in Jaxson's direction, and his face darkens. "The fuck you say to me?"

Jaxson turns to face Connor and one eyebrow lifts, clearly amused. "Naw, son. What the fuck you just say to *me*?"

I hug my bag tighter to keep my stomach from falling to the floor. Connor's always been steady. I've seen him mad only a handful of times, mostly as kids when someone joked about his "hot" mother. When his face gets dark like this, all cloudy with a chance of thunderstorms, it never ends well.

"I don't care for all the back-and-forth. If you got

something to say, dude, just say it." Connor takes a step toward Jaxson.

I place a hand on Connor's arm to ground him. To help him feel something familiar before all hell breaks loose. "Connor, the bell's about to ring," I say. I try to rub my thumb across his elbow to soothe him, to turn down his rage. But his fleece jacket is too thick. I can't reach him.

"Okay, fine." Jaxson takes two steps toward Connor, completely ignoring me. "Let your sister try pulling that shit on me."

"Or what?" Connor's nostrils flare, and my hand slips off him.

"You want to find out?" Jaxson asks.

I don't know who pushed who first. But the next thing I see is a tornado of limbs crashing against each other in the center of the hall. Others rush over to *ooh* and *ahh* and record. The bodies seem to multiply at such a quick rate that I have to squeeze myself against my locker to not catch a fist or an elbow.

The school resource officer runs over about a minute too late and pries Connor and Jaxson apart. A male teacher decides now is a good time to step in to help de-escalate, but to no avail. My classmates are on one hundred, laughing and jumping like we just won the homecoming game.

I manage to peel myself from my locker. Several teachers begin herding us and telling us it's over. It's done. Get to wherever we need to be. Before I push my way into the crowd, my eyes land on Faith across the hall. She watches as Connor gets escorted toward the main office. She shakes her head before looking back at me. The cock of her head says it all:

The teachers are wrong. This is only the beginning.

NOW

EXT. KING'S PIN BOWLING ALLEY—TWILIGHT

A FEMALE NEWS REPORTER, CASSIDY EDWARDS, WITH A FACE FULL OF MAKEUP, STANDS IN FRONT OF YELLOW TAPE SURROUNDING THE BLACKENED ENTRANCE TO THE BOWLING ALLEY. ORLANDO JONES STANDS NEXT TO HER, A BANDAGE ON HIS FOREHEAD AND HIS SHIRT COVERED WITH SOOT. FIRST RESPONDERS MOVE IN AND OUT OF THE FRAME.

CASSIDY: Cassidy Edwards here, reporting live from the King's Pin Bowling Alley on Highway 17. First responders rushed to the scene after reports of an explosion. The cause of the explosion has not been confirmed, though early accounts indicate foul play. I'm standing here now with a firsthand witness, Mr. Orlando Jones. Orlando, you were in the parking lot when the explosion happened. Can you share what you saw?

ORLANDO: Yeah. I'll try. I didn't see much, but I heard it. It sounded like thunder. Like the sky was about to crack open and hail. Then I saw the smoke coming from the building. Saw some of the building get swallowed up. It was some scary shit. My bad, I can't say *shit* on air, right?

CASSIDY: I understand you must be quite shaken still, Orlando. Last week, you were involved in a protest here at this very location. Is that right?

ORLANDO: Yes. With my organization, Don't Attack Blacks. Our goal was to stand up for the voiceless. As you know, the owner of King's Pin, Scott Brooks, is being accused of discriminatory practices. We wanted to shed light on that and stand up for the victims.

CASSIDY: Is that why you were here early this morning? Were you holding another protest?

ORLANDO: (pauses) Listen, I can't get into much without my attorney present. What I can say is that I heard rumors that something awful was going down tonight, and I came here to try to stop it. As you can see . . . I was too late.

CASSIDY: Now when you say rumors, did you hear that—?

REPORTERS (O.S.): Is that Scott Brooks? Scott Brooks is here! Mr. Brooks, Mr. Brooks! Can I get a statement?

CASSIDY: (to camera operator) Come on!

CASSIDY RUNS TO THE PERIMETER OF THE PARKING LOT, WHERE SCOTT BROOKS CLIMBS OUT OF HIS CAR. HE WEARS PAJAMA BOTTOMS WITH A WILLIAM & MARY SWEATSHIRT. HE PUSHES PAST A SWARM OF REPORTERS.

CASSIDY: Mr. Brooks! What are your thoughts that this was a targeted attack? Mr. Brooks, do you think this has anything to do with your pending lawsuits?

SCOTT IGNORES THE QUESTIONS AND RUNS RIGHT TO A MALE, UNIFORMED POLICE OFFICER.

SCOTT: I'm looking for my children. I heard that my kids were here.

POLICE OFFICER: Yes, sir. There was a gathering of high school students present in the facility when the explosion occurred. All individuals have been escorted either to the hospital or the precinct for further questioning.

SCOTT: Is everyone okay?

THE POLICE OFFICER HESITATES TO RESPOND.

SCOTT: Is anyone hurt?

POLICE OFFICER: I'm sorry to report that there is one fatality. . . .

SCOTT CRIES OUT AND FALLS TO HIS KNEES. FIRST RESPONDERS RUSH TO HIS SIDE. CASSIDY TURNS TO THE CAMERA AND SIGNALS "CUT" WITH ONE HAND.

FOUR

I KEEP MY HEAD DOWN.

That's the only way I'm getting through today. I stare down at my hands. Keep my eyes on my paper. Find an interesting stain on the laminate floors of the classroom. Anything and everything to ignore the incessant hum of drama in the hallways or avoid the scrutinizing gaze of my classmates. If I lock eyes with them, they'll have questions. I do too. So many of them. But the one with all the answers is the one home. "Sick." Too sick to pick up her damn phone, because I haven't heard a word from Kylie. Hell, I'd take even an incomprehensible mumble at this point. Even that might make the fogginess of this day a little clearer.

"Still nothing?" Roma clunks her tray onto the table

across from me, its heaviness temporarily overpowering the buzz in the cafeteria. I scope out her lunch: waffle fries. A bottle of Cran-Apple juice. Fried nuggets from Chick-fil-A, not the rubbery grilled ones we shovel down to watch our waistlines. She tops it off with a huge chocolate-chunk cookie. When Kylie's not around, Roma loads up on carbs like she's prepping for a wrestling match.

I peek down at my phone, pretty much the only thing on my tray aside from a water bottle and a plastic bowl of prepackaged garden salad. Even with Kylie gone, I eat like a rabbit—but Roma's cookie sure looks appealing. Just enough sugar to help me speed through the rest of the day.

"Nothing," I answer. "Just like when you asked me five minutes ago."

"Here, let me try." Roma snatches my phone, stabbing her chocolatey fingertips into the screen.

"How do you even know my passcode?"

Roma scoffs out a laugh. "Are we going to act like you and Kylie don't use each other's birth dates for everything?"

"Lies." I grab my phone back from her. My passcode happens to be *Connor's* birth date. Sure, it's the exact same as Kylie's, the laws of twindom and all, but Connor is three minutes older, so he's had the date longer. I think about Connor in the hall again, throwing away his golden-boy reputation at school to defend his sister. In fact, Connor is the only reason why I've lifted my head at all today, searching for signs that he's okay. But I haven't seen him since the scuffle this morning. He's not even here for lunch. I waited about an hour after the fight to text him—figured that would be enough time for him to find out whatever his punishment might be. So far, nothing. Now two Brookses are ghosting me.

"If Kylie's not answering either of our texts, what makes you think she'll answer your texts from *my* phone?" I ask Roma.

"Because I was going to pretend to be you, but edgy," Roma explains. "Replace all your 'Where are you?' texts with 'The fuck you at?' That would've made her ass hit Reply."

"I don't know about that," Shauna Silverstein says, taking a seat at the table with some of the other girls who I've been on the squad with since freshman year. "I'd stay at home forever if I were her. You see what they're saying now?"

"Who's *they*?" Brittany Akers asks, remnants of her protein bar flying out her mouth. She still hasn't gotten used to the braces she had to get over the summer. Neither has Kylie. Yesterday, Kylie told Brittany she should've gotten Invisalign, as if her parents had thousands in extra cash to throw away. Brittany just laughed and changed the topic. I still caught her rubbing her tongue across her teeth throughout the rest of the lunch period. Kylie's words have that effect on people. She could make a Kardashian-Jenner second-guess their wardrobe.

"I don't know, like everyone." Shauna turns her phone

screen around so that the whole table sees, but whatever she was looking at has gone to sleep and we stare back at blurry reflections of ourselves. "They're calling her Parking Lot Becky now."

A loud snort rolls over our table. I look over at Roma, and her hand is covering her mouth, Cran-Apple juice leaking through her fingers. "My bad," she says behind her hand. She takes a napkin and tries to clean up the crime scene on the table. "But a nickname already? Is what she did even that serious?"

She turns to me for validation, and I jab at my lettuce with my fork. Make it look like I'm hard at work doing whatever I'm doing with this salad. Anything to not have the conversation my friends want me to have. Not because I don't want to—I'm just not sure how. It's like I'm walking across a bed of nails. If I linger too long or make a jerk reaction, I'm a fucking kebab.

"Right? And to be called a Becky? That's like the ultimate offense," Shauna says, pushing her thick, frizzy hair out of her face so she has a clearer path to her banana.

"I thought that was being a Karen." Brittany again. "Who wants to be the clueless lady calling the cops on Black people at a block party?" She looks at me. Why do they keep looking at me?

This time, they wait for an answer, almost like they want to see me impaled. I'm not ready to sacrifice myself, so I shrug.

"I don't know. The cops never came to break up one of my mom's get-togethers." Not that my mom throws too many parties at our apartment. I always thought it was because of the lack of space, but maybe Mrs. Anderson downstairs has something to do with it. She always stares a little too long and hard at me at the mailboxes if she hears even a hint of music from my earbuds.

"Isn't a Becky someone who breaks girl code and sleeps with someone else's dude? That's what Beyoncé says, at least," Brittany continues. This time, it's me who tries to hold in a snort. It kills me how Brittany or some other girl from the squad think they're experts on Beyoncé's music.

"I thought Becky was code for blow jobs," Roma adds.

"Becky is just like a Karen, but younger." Ava Marks looks up from the graphic novel she's reading to join our conversation. "A Karen is a middle-aged white woman, and a Becky is like her annoying little sister. Unmarried, unaware, and unbothered as long as she has her Starbucks, Uggs, and a selfie stick." She looks at me, exasperated. All, *Why is it always up to* us *to school these girls?* Ava's the only other girl with melanin on the squad besides me, even though her mom is white. Her dad's half-white, too, but has enough Black in his bloodline to give Ava's skin a "fresh from tanning in the Maldives" sun-kissed tint. Mostly, though, she passes, which is why the quiet look she gives me almost knocks me out of my seat.

"Well, shit, that's Kylie with a capital *B-E-C-K-Y*," Roma says with a small chuckle. "Why are people tripping about it now?"

"Because she tried to get those guys in trouble for a dumb reason," Ava says. "They didn't even hit her or her car, so they didn't even need to check on her. I'm sure they wish they didn't now."

"Yes, we all know Kylie can be Team Too Much, but it's not like we saw what happened before homeboy started recording," Shauna says.

My face crumples at her use of *homeboy*, like I took a bite out of an underripe banana. Since when did Shauna talk like that? And of course, she gets all hood on me just as two girls—one Black and one South Asian—walk past our table, their faces chopped and screwed at Shauna before giving each other a look. Something quiet to me but full of exclamation points between them. The Black girl catches me looking at them and gives me a smirk. I slouch in my seat. I knew coming to the cafeteria was a bad idea, but Roma told me I didn't need to hide, because I didn't do anything wrong.

So why did I feel like crawling under the table?

"My dad says these days, everyone feels like they have to record everything," Brittany says. "Almost like nothing ever really happens if we can't see it, you know?"

"Yeah, well, my dad says even with a camera, people will see what they want to see. It took George Floyd dying for most of us to get on the same page. But before him, we also saw Philando Castille. Alton Sterling. Even Rodney King. Nobody even got in trouble for what happened to them." Ava looks at me again and cocks an eyebrow, begging for me to join the discussion. This is the most passionate I've seen her about anything outside of a sale at H&M. But the louder she gets, the smaller I feel. I'm slouching so much that my chin almost touches the table.

Shauna scoffs. "I hardly think a disagreement about a not-really-accident incident is on the same level as a Black guy getting into an altercation with the police."

"Well, do you know what happened when the police got there?" Ava asks. At that, Shauna takes a sip of her Diet Pepsi. Like her mouth needed to keep busy since it didn't have an answer.

"I'm sure if anything bad happened, we would've seen it on the news, right?" Brittany looks at me. Everyone at this table keeps looking at me. Like I'm supposed to speak for Kylie. Like I'm supposed to speak for all Black people. But how am I supposed to do both?

And it's not just this table. It's every table. Eyeballs finding their way to me, expecting me to say or do something. Two tables in particular filled with mainly Black students keep staring over at us. Staring over at me. Staring over at me at a table filled with white cheerleaders when my white best friend tried to get two Black guys arrested.

They hate me.

I leap to my feet, the pressure getting too thick to breathe. "I'm going to try her again." I grab the rest of Roma's cookie and hold up my phone. "Out there, where I can hear better." I don't wait for the squad to answer. I just dart out of the cafeteria and head to a bathroom stall. Eat Roma's chocolate-chunk cookie in peace.

I don't leave the bathroom until the final bell of the day rings.

FIVE

"BABY, YOU'RE RUINING MY LEAVES," MOM SAYS TO ME FROM ACROSS the kitchen table. "You still not feeling well?"

I had skipped out on cheer tryouts this afternoon and hopped on the bus home instead. I made sure to stay in the back with my earbuds in to drown out the chatter. I had heard so much of it throughout the day that I was full of *Did you hear?* and *Can you believe?* My stomach was going to burst from all the speculation if I didn't get home. I hid out in my bedroom until Mom came home and asked for help with decorations for the day care center. So now she, Eric, and I are cutting out leaves from construction paper and stringing them, in between bites of pizza. I'm already on my third slice. I'd rather be stuffed with cheese and Italian sausage than drama.

I look down at my sheet of construction paper and realize that I cut into my leaf outline instead of around it. "My bad," I say. "I could tape it together."

My mom studies me as she threads a string of yarn through some of her paper leaves. The ultimate multitasker. "You want me to grab you some Excedrin? Should knock your headache right out."

"No, I'm good. I think I just needed to put something on my stomach." I take another bite of my pizza and wait for the buttery crust to do its magic. To make everything better.

Mom twists her mouth, face full of suspicion. "Somebody from the squad say something to you?"

"More like somebody from the squad acted a fool," Eric chimes in before I can respond. I give him a look, and he shrugs while adding a new leaf to his pile.

"What's that, now?" Mom asks, glancing back and forth between Eric and me.

I raise my eyebrows at him: *Really, though?*

Eric raises his back: *Yep. Really.*

"Okay, one of y'all better speak." Mom puts down her string of leaves and folds her arms.

I sigh. Might as well get this over with. Mrs. Brooks might say something to her about it anyway; then Mom might get mad at me for not giving her a heads-up. "Kylie never came to school today because somebody posted a video of her."

"What kind of video?" Mom asks, then covers her mouth

with her hand. "Oh my God. Kylie, no." From the way she shakes her head over and over, Mom thinks Kylie got caught facedown and ass up.

"Ugh, no. Nothing like that." I wave my hand to wave the thought out of her head. "She just called the cops on some dudes."

"Some *Black* dudes," Eric makes sure to add.

Mom's hands slip from her face. "She did?"

"It didn't matter that they were Black," I say, because that's what I do. Protect Kylie. That's what sisters do. I'm sure she'd do the same for me. No, I *know* she'd do the same for me. "She felt scared, and that's what we're told to do when we're scared, right? Call the cops."

"Were they threatening her?" Mom asks.

I start cutting out another leaf, not answering. I wasn't there. A two-minute video clip doesn't tell the whole story. There were so many moments before that guy decided to press Record. Anything could've happened. But saying all of that to Mom would put it out there, and it would be hard to walk anything back if there's a small, ant-sized chance that Kylie was in the wrong. And what if she was wrong? I hate to think about that as an option. Hate to think about choices I'd have to make then. So, I don't think about it. Instead, I grab another slice of pizza.

"What do you think, Naomi?" Eric asks. "Did those guys seem threatening?"

I dab a napkin over my new slice. If I blot away most of the grease, it shouldn't matter if I'm on my fourth slice. "E, you're just looking for a reason to not like her."

"Kylie's a child. How do I look not liking her? I don't like her actions—like calling the cops on two kids because they wanted to help her."

"They tried to help her? What in the world was she thinking?" Mom asks, wide-eyed. She seems like she wants to laugh, but something stops her. "Wait, are the boys okay?"

"You sound like Eric," I say. They were so quick to think the worst. I don't understand when asking for help became such a controversial thing. And Kylie's never asked for help. She's always been so certain, so diligent. When she speaks, you can almost hear the period when she's done. That's how confident she's always been. So if she called her dad, then the cops, there had to be a good reason. At least, that's what I'd like to believe.

"I sound like a human," Mom says. "Not all cops are bad, but things like that tend to escalate."

"All I know is that Kylie didn't come to school and I can't reach her, so I'm sorry if I'm a little more worried about her right now. You know, the other girl you practically raised?"

"That's why I'm surprised. Kylie knows better than to abuse 911 like that."

Eric scrunches his nose. "Does she, though?" Mom plucks his arm. "No shade. Yes, baby, you've done a fantastic job taking care of her. But you know who her parents are. Not enough nannying in the world going to erase all that privilege."

I shake my head. Eric was making assumptions about Kylie and the Brookses, just like Kylie made about those guys. So why does Kylie have to be the only villain? "It wasn't like Mr. Brooks was just handed all his bowling alleys," I say. "Plus, he took a hit with the pandemic. Ky said business only just started picking back up. And now he's dealing with some legal drama. Kylie just had a lot on her mind."

Mom and Eric exchange a look. So quick that I'd have missed it if I had blinked, but it was right there. Thick and silent between them. Before I can press them about it, Mom jerks her head: *No.*

Eric sighs and scratches his chin. "Yet, both his kids were able to get new cars for their last birthday. Interesting."

"Because they invest and stuff. Maybe if we knew how to save and invest money around here, we could . . ." The words drown in my throat when I catch Mom cocking her head at me. Shit, I've done it now. I turn to Eric for help, but he leans forward, daring me to continue.

"I'm sorry, are the accommodations here not to your liking?" Mom asks.

I dig deep for the right words. Something that would get the foot out my mouth without admitting that I was wrong about the Brookses. Thankfully, I'm saved by a knock on the door.

"I'll get it." I jump out my seat like there's a wasp on my chair. I scurry over to the front door and peek out of the peephole. Kylie stands on the other side of the door, looking very un-Kylie-like. Her hair is slicked back into a low ponytail, and her whole body seems to be swimming in an oversize sweatsuit. She hugs herself and looks down at her feet, like the embarrassment of everything is sitting on her shoulders.

I swing the door open, and Kylie peeks up at me.

"Hey," she says. Her voice is hoarse. Raw. "I hope it's okay that I popped by unannounced. I didn't know where else to go."

I grab Kylie's hand and pull her to me for a hug. She rests her head on my shoulder and pretty much melts into me, transferring the weight from her shoulders over to mine. I plant my feet into the carpet to keep us both steady.

"Of course it's okay," I say in her ear. I pull away and smile. "Come in."

Kylie follows me inside, and the buzzing between Mom and Eric switches to a loud hush. The silence in the room is so thick that I hear Kylie's breath whistle through her nostrils.

"If it's cool, Ky and me are going to head into my room," I say, my voice bouncing off the walls.

Mom snaps out of it and gives Kylie a smile. "Sure. Y'all make sure to take some pizza in there with you."

"That's okay, Mama Nina. I don't have much of an appe-
tite," Kylie says.

"Well, it'll be out here for you if you change your mind,
baby."

Kylie gives her a soft smile as we head back toward my
bedroom. Eric nods at her. That's the most he can do, but at
least it's something. I can't close my bedroom door behind
us fast enough. Kylie plops right onto my bed and curls up
with my oversize stuffed Tigger. This furry dude has gotten
us through so many childhood heartaches, like the time the
Brookses took a vacation to the Cayman Islands and my mom
refused to let me go with them. Even though Mr. Brooks was
going to pay for everything. Mom said something about not
wanting to owe that man any more than she already did. I
never questioned what she meant by that, because I was too
busy giving her the silent treatment. But her words float back
to me at the most random times, like a phantom scent that
takes you to a forgotten memory.

"Girl," I say, sitting next to Kylie. "What in the actual
what?"

Kylie hugs Tigger so hard that I wait for him to gasp for
air. "The way that everyone's talking about me, Naomi. You
know that's not me. You know I'm not that kind of person."

"Of course, I know." I reach out to touch her shoulder, but
something stops me. Something invisible but nagging, like an
itch. "What happened, though? Before the recording?"

"I'm leaving Target. By myself, you know, because you had to stay with Mama Nina or whatever." She makes sure to give me a look. Brief, but pointed enough so I'd catch it. "I'm backing out just as this other car comes barreling through the parking lot like a maniac. Like they thought they were on the interstate instead of a parking lot, you know? I hate people who drive like that."

I wonder if Kylie bothered to look behind her to back out. Knowing her, probably not. She always expects others to stop for her. For the world to stand still and the seas to part, just like Connor always jokes. But I nod along and give Kylie time to finish her story.

"So I slam on brakes so the idiot wouldn't hit me. I get out of my car, check my bumper to see if they actually got me. My dad would kill me if I got a scratch on that car already. Next thing I know, these . . . *guys* come running up behind me. Just hovering over me. And I'm by myself, you know?"

I couldn't help but notice the pause before Kylie said *guys*. There was an adjective that she didn't include, whether intentional or not. She's scared to say the word *Black* in front of me—her *Black* best friend. And even though she doesn't say it, it's all I can hear.

"Were they just checking on you?" I ask. I need more clarity. Something to make sense of it all.

"I mean, they claimed they were, but how am I supposed to take it? I didn't know them. I had so much on my mind, and . . . I don't know. You would've been just as scared, Ny."

Her dad. She was still stressing about her dad. She didn't want to add a fender bender on top of whatever troubles he has now, no matter how small that fender bender might be. And she's right. I've listened to enough true-crime podcasts to know that murders and kidnappings start with the most mundane circumstance, like a minor car accident. I'd like to think that the skin color of the guys wouldn't dial up my fear, but I think about those moments when I cross the street after noticing a guy walking behind me. Or hold my purse a little closer when a guy squeezes onto an elevator with me. What did those guys look like? Did it matter?

I shake my head and return to Kylie. Next to her, like I should be. "Did the cops show up?"

"No. I mean, not really. There was a security guard patrolling the area, so he came over to mediate or whatever. Wanted me to move my car so I could let the guys leave. I backed in front of their car . . . just to be sure they weren't up to anything and then tried to leave because I wasn't an easy victim."

I try to follow her story. Put myself in her shoes, feel her same fear. And I am there, with her . . . except I'd probably just let the guys go on about their day. Especially if they didn't touch me or anything. But at least there were no sirens. No cops. No huge scene.

"Good. That's good," I say. "And everything was cool

after that? Did the guys just leave?"

"Yeah. Not before talking more shit to me and exchanging words with the guard."

The relief bubbling up inside me dissipates. I see faces smashed to the pavement. Knees pressed to the backs of necks. Hear muffled screams. Pretty much every image, every clip, that's penetrated my social media feed for the past few years. "Did the guard have to force them out of the parking lot? Did he put his hands on them?" My hands start to sweat, so I slide them under my thighs.

Kylie looks at me like I just slapped her across the face. "What is this? Why are you worried about them? They're not the ones being called racist and other crap that isn't true. You're supposed to be *my* best friend." Tears well up in her eyes, and I feel like shit. I just made this moment about everyone else but her. I pull her in for another hug before the tears spill.

"You're right. You're right. I'm sorry." I rub her back as she sniffles over my shoulder. What was I doing? I was sounding like everyone else. I'm supposed to have her back. "What can I do?"

Kylie pulls away and wipes her face with her sleeve. "My dad said I need to go to school tomorrow. That I shouldn't hide out, because I didn't do anything wrong. He was hoping you'd be by my side."

I frown. "Why wouldn't I be?" Kylie and I always went to

school together. What would make tomorrow any different? The way Kylie said it, though, made it seem like Mr. Brooks wanted Kylie to parade me around like some trophy Black friend. My stomach clenches at the thought, fighting against the pound of pizza I just devoured.

Kylie simply nods, oblivious to my confusion. "I was also thinking about making a video. Something where I could tell my side, you know?"

I shrug with one shoulder—to tell her that I'm somewhat with her, but not all in. Maybe I'm scared to hear her side. "Sure. If that's what you feel like you need to do," I push out.

"I figured a video would be more sincere than typing up a statement on the Notes app and posting it. I don't want to be a celebrity apologizing for something stupid a thousand years too late. But if I'm too serious, everyone will scroll past. I figured I'd do something to poke fun at myself while making a statement."

I'm not really sure what the hell Kylie's talking about, but my job right now is to be the supportive best friend. To give her the space she needs to process this mess she's in. I can ask questions another time.

"So . . . you'll help me?" Kylie asks.

"What, like hold your phone and record you?"

"No. Be in the video with me."

I frown again, trying to read her, but something's redacted. "Why would I be in the video?"

"Because . . . I can't make fun of myself by myself. I need you there to call me out. And you're my best friend. I mean, I could ask Roma but she's . . . you know." She smiles at me.

Not Black? I want to ask, but Kylie's been through enough for the day. She doesn't need me of all people to accuse her of being something she's not. Because she couldn't be what everyone said she was. I mean, I would've seen it after all this time. Besides, I'm sure I know what she means. Roma's our girl, but *I'm* Kylie's best friend. We're sisters. It makes sense she'd ask me to help her.

My mouth tries to form the word *yes*, but it catches on my tongue. I take that as a sign. Kylie's not the only one who needs to process this mess. I need time too.

I paint on a smile. "I'll think about it."

Kylie raises her eyebrows, as if she wasn't expecting my response. But she keeps the smile on her face. "Promise?" She holds out her pinkie finger.

I link my pinkie through hers but can't promise her out loud. That would lock me in too much—and I don't want to feel caged.

SIX

I'M STUCK IN KYLIE'S CAR. I PEER OUT THE WINDOW AS THE WORLD moves on without me. Everyone laughing and airy, no drama weighing them down. No deep questions to ask about relationships or life. Everyone else moves through their day as carefree as a breeze. I blow a fog of breath onto the glass, then smear a happy face onto it. Maybe if I project it, it'll reach me.

"By the time we leave the car, it'll be our ten-year reunion," Roma complains from the back seat. We're in the high school parking lot. We got here a little earlier than Kylie wanted us to, so she's killing time by redoing her makeup in the rearview mirror.

"If you want to get to school all bright and early, go

ahead. Be desperate," Kylie says as she fans her eyelashes with mascara.

"And what are we calling this?" Roma asks under her breath. Too low for Kylie to catch it. A laugh gets caught in my throat. She has a good point. Kylie was so eager about putting on a united front that she asked us to color coordinate our outfits. Blue jeans on the bottom, red T-shirts on top. White Chucks on our feet. Patriotic as all get-out.

"But why?" I asked Kylie on our group FaceTime with Roma after Kylie had left my apartment last night. "Are we starting a folk band?"

Roma laughed, which set Kylie off.

"So I have to explain fashion to you guys now?" she sniffed. "I figured you both wanted to support me. If I would've chosen something extra with a designer label, I would've been the asshole, right? It would've been my fault that my parents buy me nice things."

"Whoa, shots fired," Roma said, still laughing.

But Kylie didn't even crack a smile. She just rubbed a red face with her sleeve, the tears ready to make their grand entrance again. My hands had started to sweat again. Kylie Brooks had pissed me off. I knew she was pulling some passive-aggressive shit about my mom being broke, and I couldn't even set her straight, because *she* had a bad day. And her bad day superseded my pride, at least for the moment.

"It's fine," I said, working overtime to not let my jaws

clench as I spoke. "I have a red shirt."

As I looked myself over in the mirror this morning, I kept in mind that I was close to wearing Howard University's colors—one of the HBCUs I wanted to apply to this fall. Whatever statement Kylie was trying to make, I'm sure that wasn't it. But having that piece of knowledge, that small connection to a cultural phenomenon, made me a little less angry at Kylie. It gave me something that was just mine for the day.

"Okay." Kylie puts away her makeup bag and raises her eyebrows at me, still waiting patiently in the front seat of her car.

I give her a thumbs-up. "You look great."

Kylie nods a thank-you and takes a breath. "You guys ready?"

"Duh," Roma says.

"Ready," I say, and add a reassuring smile.

Kylie climbs out of her car, and we follow suit. I hold my breath and wait for the stares, the finger-pointing. The sky to fall. But everyone's so busy rushing into the building or chatting with their own friends that the walk thus far is anticlimactic. Good. I'll take boring over drama this morning. I shouldn't be this surprised. This is the Windsor Woods way. In seventh grade, this kid named Jimmy Frazier scrawled the letters *KKK* on the sleeve of his beat-up red hoodie just to get a rise out of our Black math teacher. She dared to give him a failing grade on our first test. He wore that hoodie every day. Every. Day. Nobody said anything. Faith had been the one to finally ask Mrs. Butler about it, on a day when Jimmy was absent (or maybe even suspended).

"He just wants attention," she told the whole class. "Let's not give him any." She gave a smile so sharp that it could've sliced concrete.

And that was that.

Kylie pinches my arm during our walk to the school building to get my attention. When I look at her, she smiles. She's never been so happy to be from a town this unbothered, ever. I use every muscle in my face to return her smile.

"Oh, I emailed Coach Beverly last night," she says. "I told her that we both had bad sushi and that's why we missed try-outs yesterday. She tried to sass back, but even through email, I could tell it was half-hearted. We're good."

"Thanks," I say, though I lose what little pep in my step that I could muster. I had thought, maybe even hoped, that skipping out on practice yesterday would be the last straw for Coach Beverly. That she'd accuse me of not giving my all, and I could reluctantly admit she was right. Then I could tell Kylie and Roma and the rest of the girls that I'd have to try out for the Wolverines. "To keep up with my extracurriculars for college applications," I'd say. I had it all worked out with diagrams and everything in my head.

Before we can make it to the front steps, we're blocked

by Nevaeh Bridges and two of her friends. *Nevaeh* is *heaven* spelled backward, she told me back in sixth grade when I signed her yearbook. But standing here in front of me, with her face all pinched up and her hip cocked to one side, she looks anything but angelic.

"You serious right now?" Nevaeh says to Kylie. One of her hands is balled into a fist at her side. The other grips a Frappuccino. She squeezes the plastic cup so hard that whipped cream trickles its way down to her knuckles. It's like she's picturing Kylie's neck. "You strutting up to the school like we want you here?"

Kylie shrinks next to me as the air rushes out of her body. "Anybody could come to this school. It's public. And I'm not about the drama today, okay? We just want to get to class."

"Oh. *We?*" Nevaeh raises an eyebrow at me, all: *Really, bitch?*

My feet take a tiny step back. I didn't tell them to. They move barely an inch, but somehow Kylie notices. She glances at me, her eyes filled with questions.

"Yes, we," Roma says. She gets annoyed with Kylie as much as anyone, but you can't say she isn't loyal. "Now, if you'll excuse us . . ."

Neither Nevaeh nor her friends move. One of them even widens her stance, squaring herself. Daring us to take one more step. I grip the strap of my shoulder bag to keep my hand from trembling. I try to think of a way to get myself out of this. I mean, us. All of us, including Kylie. But I don't know Nevaeh that well. I don't know what to use against her. Yeah, we've gone to school together since forever, but Kylie's always been attached to my side. Since Kylie never found a reason to talk to her, neither did I. Not outside the usual pleasantries.

Nevaeh's far removed from pleasant right now, so changing the subject to ask about her summer might get met with a smirk—or something worse.

"Whoa, is there a problem here?" Jared Crews walks up, all polo shirt and chino pants and parted hair and smug grin. Kylie looks happier than usual to see him, but his presence makes my stomach tug. If you look up *Basic White Dude* in the dictionary, you'd find a picture of Kylie's ex. He's the last guy who needs to interfere right now.

"Nobody's talking to you," one of Nevaeh's friends says.

"Doesn't look like they want to talk to you either," Jared says, nodding toward Kylie, Roma, and me. He includes *me*, makes it known that it's us against them. How did I get here? Volun-told to take a side. I never verbalized my consent to be on either team, but silence speaks volumes. Even now, my stillness shouts at both Kylie and Nevaeh, and they're both hearing opposite things.

"And since nobody wants to talk, how about we break this whole thing up?" Jared continues. He bobs a fist up and down while he speaks. Not in a threatening way. More like he's holding a buzzer for a quiz show. He wants to show his sincerity through gentle, affirming gestures. I'm sure he's learned this from the politicians his dad interviews for his podcast.

"Jared?" Serena Warren now. Tall and slim in her high-waisted jeans, like she just stepped off the cover of *Teen Vogue*. She glares at all of us from the outskirts of our angry bubble, but soon focuses on Jared. On Jared next to Kylie. "What the fuck? Don't get mixed up in all her bullshit."

Any other time, Kylie would've told Serena where to stick her input. Now, though, Kylie shuffles closer to Roma and Jared. Using them as a shield. Or a cloak to help her disappear. I wonder if there's any room for me to join her.

Jared sighs and runs a hand through his hair. "Not now, Serena."

"Yeah, not now, Serena," Nevaeh says. "Unless you want in on this too."

"Hey." Jared releases his invisible buzzer and extends his whole hand toward Nevaeh, piercing it through the air like a karate chop. "There's no need to make threats."

"Or what?" Nevaeh asks. "You gonna call the cops? Or is Becky going to do that for you?" She jerks her head at Kylie, as if we didn't know who she could possibly be talking about.

"Careful, we're in the parking lot. You know this is where she gets her power," Nevaeh's other friend, who has a buzz cut, says with an actual snort.

Kylie rolls her eyes, getting bolder with the presence of Jared. "You weren't even there to know what really happened."

"We saw what really happened. Two Black guys were being chivalrous, and you tried getting them arrested for it." Nevaeh's eyes are so narrow, I can barely see the whites in them. This is only going to get worse. I feel the static in the air and it nips at my skin, causing the hairs on my arm to rise. Still, I can't find my voice. Can't find the words that'll put both Kylie and Nevaeh at peace. I'm not even sure if those words exist.

"I didn't try to get them arrested."

"Oh, because you tried to get them killed?"

Kylie's mouth drops open, and it seems like her voice gets stuck too. She blinks out of it and shakes her head to start over. "Don't be dramatic."

I wince. *No, Kylie. No, no, no.*

The smirk on Nevaeh's face is gone, boiling into gnashing teeth and pointy eyebrows and flaming eyes. Just red, red, red coursing through her whole body and working its way out.

"Bitch, I'll show you dramatic." It happens in a flash. One second the Frappuccino is being strangled in Nevaeh's hand; the next it's hurling toward Kylie. The cup smacks against Kylie's chest with a thud, then a splat. I jump back to avoid the ricochet of whipped cream and mocha swirl, but it's a bloodbath. No one in a two-foot radius is completely unscathed.

I pat myself to assess for any damage when I hear a strained whimper. Kylie. She looks down at her shirt, her arms sticking out from her sides like a stick figure. Her shirt looks like a crime scene, swirls of red and white and chocolate brown bleeding together. Definitely not the aesthetic that Kylie was going for. She stands there, frozen, like a victim.

"What the hell is wrong with you?" Roma asks, her voice on the edge of shrieking.

Nevaeh shrugs. "She looked thirsty." Her friends laugh, and all three of them strut up to the building. Their job is done. They humiliated Kylie in front of a crowd. Just like she did to those guys at Target.

My heart knocks against my ribs. I feel like I just ran a 5K, even though I stood there. I can't believe I just stood there. I didn't even make a peep. Kylie and I learned how to tie our shoelaces at the same time. We camped out in the same bathroom for at least an hour when we first learned how to use tampons. I've seen sides of Kylie that only her gynecologist has seen, and I couldn't say one word to defend her. No, not couldn't. I didn't *want* to. I wanted to hear what Kylie had to say for herself. To give Nevaeh and her friends a reason not to hate her. To give me a reason to defend her. Wow. Roma could've very well been speaking to me: *What the hell is wrong with you?*

"Come on. I have an extra shirt in my car," Jared says to Kylie. He wraps his arms around her and guides her back toward the parking lot. It's only then that I notice that Kylie's crying.

"Really, Jared?" Serena shouts to the backs of their heads. Jared gives her a look over his shoulder, all *Sorry, but she needs me more.* Serena's jaws clench together before she storms toward the school building, her shoulder giving mine a harsher-than-necessary bump.

It's only then that I snap out of it. I swallow to try to wet my throat. "Kylie," I squeak. I clear my throat and try again. "Kylie? You okay?" But she's still walking away with Jared. I start after them, but Roma grabs my arm.

"Let him take care of her right now," Roma says. "That's probably what she wants anyway."

"I didn't say anything." I watch Kylie and Jared as they reach his car. She buries her face into his chest, and he rubs the back of her hair. "I didn't say anything." I repeat the words, almost like I needed to hear them to believe them. To document this moment because it felt different. New.

"Look at us." Roma points at our matching outfits. "We've said enough. Let's get to class. Stop by the bathroom first, though. You got Frap on your shoe."

I peek down at my shoe. There's a droplet of chocolate near the toe. Oblong-shaped, just like a teardrop.

SEVEN

BY THE TIME I GET TO SECOND BLOCK, THE WHOLE SCHOOL HAS GOTTEN wind of what went down in the parking lot. Before I can sit down at my lab table, Drew's on me like an ant on a crumb.

"You okay? Are you bleeding?" He leans over and inspects my face.

I frown at him. "Why would I be bleeding?"

"Some baristas don't know how to work a blender, and ice can be deadly. My uncle from Buffalo got sixteen stitches from an icicle gone rogue."

"No ER trips for me," I say, spreading my arms so he can survey the rest of me. I stop short of telling him nobody got hurt. Even though Nevaeh's morning coffee didn't leave any scrapes or bruises, Kylie's pride took a beating. Sometimes it's the invisible scars that take longer to heal. "And can you do me a favor and not add to the gossip? The less lips flapping about it, the quicker it'll go away."

"Bae, I don't think this is going away anytime soon."

His words ring in my ears like a warning. I hate to admit it, but he's probably right. Nevaeh did more than show her ass this morning. She also made a statement. The Black students weren't going to go through the usual Windsor rituals to deal with Kylie. Being quiet was no longer an option, especially after spending a pandemic with nothing to do but watch Black folks be disrespected on the World Wide Web. So where did that leave me? I had drawn a line in the sand ever since I played in the sandbox with Kylie and Connor, choosing to spend their and my birthdays at Busch Gardens or Water Country USA—or day trips to Sandbridge in Virginia Beach. Whereas Faith and Nevaeh and all their friends were just as keen to celebrate at the local Chuck E. Cheese or backyard barbecues. They no longer sent me invites, and I no longer expected them. I had my circle, my people.

Now, though, Kylie's probably pissed at me for not defending her honor. Instead of having a serious heart-to-heart, Roma would laugh everything off with a reference to the old Michael Jackson song "Black or White." And Connor? I haven't seen Connor since his fight yesterday, nor has he responded to any of my texts. That hadn't stopped me from searching for him through the crowded halls. No luck so far.

"OMG." Drew again. "Do you think that means Kylie has to move? Could you imagine? Being uprooted during your senior year? Isn't that the start of all those teen horror movies?" His eyes shift to the right and he stands upright, pinching his mouth closed. Drew clamming up can mean only one thing: Faith is here.

She reaches our table and raises her eyebrows at Drew, dismissing him without a single word. Drew takes the hint. He makes a heart with both hands right against his chest to me before heading to his seat. I don't look at Faith, and she doesn't look at me. It's like we both know that our eyes will say something we don't want them to about what happened this morning. And neither of us is in a listening mood.

"Morning, ladies." Mrs. Ward shimmies over to us, breezing through our fog of silence. "I just got this in my email and thought you both might be interested." She places a black-and-white flyer on our table. The school doesn't have that much coin for colored printer ink. I examine the paper, and a small smile escapes me. The flyer doesn't need color to grab my attention. It's about a scholarship for Hampton University, a local HBCU. Something about money for STEM majors. I'm not sure if I want to major in science or technology when I get to college, but I am sure that I need a scholarship. And HU was appealing. Not THE HU in DC, but close enough to Mom and Eric to come home on weekends. During the week, I'd be immersed in Black history,

Black culture. Black pride.

Mrs. Ward smiles at me, amused by my amusement. "A representative from Hampton will be at the college fair tomorrow. Maybe you could ask them about this." She returns to her desk, and I slide the paper closer to me and review the details. How much money, GPA requirements, deadlines. All of it. For the first time, applying to an HBCU feels like a real possibility. Like the stars or some other higher power saw what I needed and landed it right on my desk. Now the ball is in my court.

Faith clicks her tongue next to me. Subtle, but loud. She wanted me to hear it, but she didn't want to seem like she was picking a fight. Too late.

"I was going to pass it to you when I was done," I say.

"I didn't expect you to be so into the idea of going to an HBCU." She looks me up and down, as if surprised I had the audacity to read anything about Hampton University.

"I'm Black, aren't I?"

"Being Black doesn't give you a free pass to take a scholarship out of a deserving Black person's hands." She looks me over again, all decked out in my red, white, and blue. The top of one of my Chucks is still a little damp from scrubbing off the residue from Frap-Gate.

"And why am I not one of those deserving Black people?"

Faith crinkles her forehead like I just asked her to tell me the meaning of life. "Your friend did what she did, and you just sashay into the school behind her like the Kelly Rowland to her Beyoncé. You can't just pull the Black card when it's convenient for you."

She slaps open her notebook and makes our table shake. Or maybe I'm just shaking. If we were in a rap battle, I would've been booed off the stage while the crowd carried Faith on their shoulders. She stated facts. I did show up to the school looking like Kylie's tanner doppelgänger. Doing that on any other day is tacky enough, but I chose to coordinate with her just one day after her video went viral. A video of her calling the cops on two Black guys who didn't put a hand on her, but she was scared enough to think they might. Those guys could've been my cousins. One of them could've been Eric.

Mrs. Ward glances over her shoulder at us from the whiteboard. Her eyes bounce between me and Faith. Back to me. I give a half smile and open my notebook, ready to work. The sooner class begins, the sooner it can end. The sooner I can get away from Faith and her facts. Mrs. Ward gets back to the whiteboard as if nothing has happened at all. She starts her lecture on force and motion, and the classroom spins around me.

Everything's moving too fast, and I can't keep up.

I will my left leg to keep steady as I pull my right leg up behind me. I wobble for a second, but my hands find each other and guide my leg up toward my head. I hold my breath and hold the pose for a couple of beats, just like a true scorpion. My squad's palms are under my shoe, keeping me balanced. Coach Beverly blows her whistle and I release my foot, dropping down to the safety of Chloe Johnson's and Shauna's arms.

"Yeah, bitch," Shauna says, slapping me on the butt. Her mane of hair is piled up on top of her head, more of a boulder than a bun.

I nod a thank-you to her and glance over at Coach. She scribbles something onto her clipboard for what feels like an eternity. Finally, she looks up at me. "Looking good out there, Henry."

Now I feel like I have permission to smile. I peek over at Kylie, who's stretching near the bleachers with some of the other girls. She gives me a wink, letting me know that she saw everything. I do a quick dance with my shoulders, and she laughs. I've been trying to do that all practice—get her to smile, laugh. Anything jovial to push out what happened this morning. Jared took her off campus for lunch, so I didn't get a chance to apologize for not standing up for her earlier. But Kylie's all about fun versus feelings. If I keep her smiling, I'll keep her from crying. And maybe that'll keep her from asking me why I didn't say anything in the first place.

"Get some water and stretch. We'll try some basket tosses in five," Coach Beverly says to me.

I nod and run over to grab my water bottle from next to the wall. As soon as I take my first sip, a door slams near the coaches' wing of the gym—this small hallway that used to house utility closets that they fashioned into micro-offices for the women coaches. Talk about sexism. Faith, Nevaeh, and two more Wolverines spill out of one of the offices. Nevaeh's face is streaked with tears, and her cheeks puff as she blows out a breath. Anger. Not the rage I saw on her face this morning, but a different kind of anger. Something blue and devastating. Faith reaches out for her shoulder, but Nevaeh shrugs her away. Her arms flail as she shouts something I can't quite hear, but that I feel. The whole gym feels it as most of the squad quiets down and watches her. Nevaeh continues to rant until her eyes land on Kylie. Kylie's on the floor, contorted into a butterfly stretch. She's the only one not looking in Nevaeh's direction. Not because she can't hear her, but because she's choosing not to. Brittany leans over and says something in Kylie's ear, and Kylie throws her head back and laughs. Louder than she's laughed all practice. Her giggles reverberate off the bleachers and walls.

That does it for Nevaeh. Nevaeh charges toward Kylie as Faith and her teammates try to hold her back. The Wolverines' coach, Ms. Denita, stomps out of her office just in time.

"Hey!" she barks, one hand on her hip, the other pointed directly at Nevaeh. "E-nough! Go on home, Nevaeh."

Nevaeh's jaw clenches as she snatches herself away from

Faith, her sneakers pounding against hardwood as she leaves the gym. Faith and the other two Wolverines trail behind Nevaeh, arms crossed, heads down. Anything to avoid eye contact with their spectators. I wait for Faith to spot me but she's out the door without a single glance. Ms. Denita and Coach Beverly look at each other from across the gym. Ms. Denita nods before returning to her office. Kylie and Brittany laugh again, their timing like a jackhammer during a baby's nap time.

I frown at them, even though they can't see me. I frown *because* they can't see me. Kylie's never found Brittany that funny. If anything, Kylie's more likely to laugh *at* Brittany than *with* her. She was proving a point, which Nevaeh received. Yeah, throwing a drink on someone is pretty foul, but whatever this is that Kylie's doing feels . . . childish.

Ava jogs over to me to retrieve her water bottle.

"What the hell was that all about?" I ask her. After lunch yesterday, it seems like the two of us have formed an unspoken alliance. Bonding over things we chose to ignore before.

Ava squirts some of her water onto her curly hair and shakes it out like a puppy. "The Wolverines have a week suspension from activities. Coach Beverly talked to Ms. Denita about the whole Frappuccino thing."

I frown again. I've been doing that a lot lately. "But that was just Nevaeh's actions. Why does their whole team get a consequence?"

Ava shrugs. "All I know is that Coach Beverly was pissed. I don't think she was even happy with the suspension only being a week. But you know how she gets about Kylie. She can give Kylie a hard time, but nobody else can." Ava shrugs again, this time her shoulders barely lifting. Like she didn't have the energy to explain. It's Kylie's world, and we're all just living in it. Nothing can change that.

Coach Beverly blows her whistle. "Henry! Brooks! Side-by-side basket tosses!"

I exhale and jog back to the center of the gym, and Kylie joins me. Her spotters are in place quicker than mine, and I watch as they throw her in the air. Kylie's arms stretch from her sides just like wings. She soars above us all. And she can't stop smiling.

NOW

POLICE INTERROGATION TRANSCRIPT
ON OCTOBER 13, DETECTIVE ROBERT SUMMERS INTERVIEWED
JUVENILE NAOMI HENRY IN INTERROGATION ROOM 4 AT THE
WINDSOR POLICE DEPARTMENT. NO OTHER PERSON WAS IN
THE ROOM.

RS: It is presently 0353 hours on Thursday, October 19. Detective Summers here speaking with a Miss Naomi Henry. Naomi, would you please answer a few logistical questions for me first? You are presently seventeen years old, correct?

NH: Yes.

RS: And your first name is spelled *N-A-O-M-I*?

NH: Yes.

RS: And for the record, you've granted me permission to speak to you without the presence of a legal guardian or legal counsel, correct?

NH: (silence)

RS: I need a verbal answer for the recording.

NH: (clears throat) Yes. I didn't do anything wrong. Did someone say I did anything wrong?

RS: I'm not obligated to respond to that.

NH: So then why am I here? Why am I arrested if nobody said anything?

RS: Great question. Why were you at the King's Pin Bowling Alley earlier this morning?

NH: (long pause) One of my best friends was having a birthday party there.

RS: After-hours?

NH: I guess so. We did that sometimes. I mean, not we. Kylie and Connor. They let us into the bowling alley after-hours. Their dad owns it.

RS: And you were aware of this party?

NH: Yeah. I mean, I was there.

RS: And yet you showed up hours after everyone else. You and a . . . (papers rustle) . . . a Mr. Aidan Graham?

NH: Is he . . . is he okay? I didn't see him when—

RS: Was Mr. Graham invited too?

NH: Yes. I mean, no. No. He came with me.

RS: He came with you? Did he know anyone at the party?

NH: I mean, he knows me, so . . .

RS: So . . . you brought him with you? Along with Miss Cleo Hayslett and Mr. Orlando Jones?

NH: I didn't come to the party with Cleo or Orlando.

RS: Yet you were all there. Interesting. Just as interesting as the fact you showed up to a party with people you no longer associated with.

NH: That's . . . that's not true.

RS: It's not true that you quit cheerleading? That you had a falling-out with Miss Kylie Brooks? That your mother no longer was employed by the Brooks family?

NH: (long pause) Yeah, but . . .

RS: But what? Did I say anything false?

NH: No, but it didn't happen like you're trying to make it sound.

RS: I'm just listing facts, Naomi. How about you help me with a little more? Like you didn't arrive to the King's Pin to party with your former friends. You knew there was a bomb there, and you wanted to see everything through.

NH: No . . .

RS: Okay, so you felt guilty. Ran there to remove the bomb then—(loud thud)—boom!

NH: No! That's not true either!

RS: But bombs have consequences, Naomi. Bombs destroy property. Bombs leave bodies.

NH: I'm done. I want to see my mom.

RS: You weren't thinking about Mom when you planted that bomb.

NH: I said I'm done. I don't want to say anything else until my mom gets here with a lawyer. Please.

RS: Fair enough. Until your mom gets here, how about some light reading?

NH: What's that?

RS: You want to know who was killed, right? (papers rustle)

NH: (lets out a loud wail)

(RECORDING ENDS)

EIGHT

I GO TO KYLIE'S HOUSE AFTER TRYOUTS. SHE SAID HER PARENTS insisted. That it's been "forever" since they've seen me. Of course, I agree to go. I learned my lesson after ditching Kylie two days ago. Who knows what other video might surface if I leave her to her own devices again? Besides, Mr. and Mrs. Brooks are like another set of parents. They cheered just as loud for me as they did their own children at eighth-grade graduation. They never forget my birthday, and Mrs. Brooks has wiped a few of my tears whenever Mom and I fought about random things.

But a formal dinner invitation felt . . . different. Odd, even. I usually just pop up, and they pull out more plates and silverware. No questions asked and no fuss made. Tonight, though, seems like a lot of fuss. The formal dining room is decked out with a lace-trimmed tablecloth and the shiny silver cutlery from their curio cabinet. The same silverware that Mrs. Brooks hires a cleaning service to polish every few weeks. There's even a damn candelabra at the center of the table.

I stand in the entrance of the dining room and peek down at my baggy sweats, Adidas slides, and *Good Vibes Only* T-shirt. "I'm drastically underdressed," I say to my boobs.

"Stop it. You know you're home." Kylie nudges my arm. "How many times have you walked around here in pj's and gopher slippers?"

"They were chipmunks," I correct.

"They were ugly." Kylie smiles at me and drops into one of the chairs. She changed into a T-shirt dress after practice, but she prances in it like it's an evening gown. Kylie could make worn jogging pants look like something straight from a Paris runway.

"Language, Kylie." Mrs. Brooks enters the dining room carrying a bread basket with varying shades of brown dinner rolls. The Brookses are the only family I know that uses an actual bread basket—as well as the only family that considers *ugly* a bad word.

"What else would you call those god-awful rodent shoes that were attached to Ny's feet for like two years?"

"Adorable, just like her." Mrs. Brooks sets the basket next

to the candelabra, then turns to take me in. "Look at you." She smiles and spreads her arms toward me. I smile back and spill into them. Mrs. Brooks smells and feels like a cup of cocoa on a snow day. No matter how cold and frigid the world was outside, she was there to keep me safe and warm.

She pecks me on the cheek and then pulls away, still holding my arms with her hands. "Kylie told me you did something different to your hair. I love it."

"You do?"

"Absolutely." At that, she takes her hand and tries to rake it through my coils. My whole body tenses. I had been meticulous in moisturizing it after practice, getting the curl pattern to fall the way I wanted it to. And here's Mrs. Brooks, fluffing and pulling my hair like she's the one that spends hours detangling it after a wash. "How long have you been hiding these curls?"

"Too long, probably." I smile again, step back from her hand, and make my way over to the table. I'll look less rude if I move with intention. "You guys expecting anyone?" I take a seat across from Kylie.

"No, honey. Just the family. Speaking of which . . ." Mrs. Brooks turns to Kylie. "Where's your brother?"

A breath catches in my throat. Connor. I still haven't seen or heard from him since yesterday morning. Though it's been almost thirty-six hours, it felt more like thirty-six years. Each minute stretching like putty. I hadn't realized how much I relied on those daily exchanges between us. A slick smile, a stolen touch. Tiny acts to show we're thinking about each other.

Kylie shrugs as she texts on her phone. "I'm not his babysitter."

"Thank goodness, what with how attentive you are." Mrs. Brooks gives me a smirk.

"Was he suspended from school?" I ask.

Mrs. Brooks's eyebrows hitch for a second, caught off guard from the directness of my question. The Brookses have spoken in codes and riddles for as long as I can remember. Kylie and Connor wouldn't get time-outs but "independent time." If someone had to use the bathroom, they'd have to "make a delivery." And if Mr. and Mrs. Brooks wanted some intimate time, they were "off to visit friends." I was grateful for the last code, in particular.

The shock fades from Mrs. Brooks's face and gets replaced by a full grin. "Goodness, no," she says with a laugh. "Whatever for?"

I try not to frown as I remember the fight. The fists flying in the air and Connor's red face once he and the other guy were pried apart. Just as I open my mouth to explain, I feel a broad hand on my shoulder.

Mr. Brooks beams down at me, his teeth as straight and shiny as his hair. Kylie jokes that her dad spends more time getting ready than her mom does. I believe it. I've never seen him with a single hair out of place.

"I didn't know we were inviting supermodels to dinner tonight," he says.

I roll my eyes and laugh. "Far from it."

He pecks my hand like a gentleman, then takes his seat at the head of the table. "Well, everything is in alignment in the universe because we've got the family all together again."

"Not quite." Mrs. Brooks nods to Connor's empty chair.

Mr. Brooks shakes his head but laughs, just as jolly and corny as a dad from one of those old black-and-white TV shows. "I can never keep up with that boy. Kylie, where's your brother?"

Kylie looks up from her phone and groans. "Ugh, why does everyone keep asking me that?"

We hear the front door open and shut and the thump of someone tossing a bag on the floor. At least I think it's a bag. It could very well be my heart.

"Ah, and here's the man of the hour." Mr. Brooks stands and claps for Connor as he enters the dining room, his ball cap swiveled to the back of his head and his blond hairs curling against his forehead. Kylie stands and joins her dad in the round of applause.

Connor rolls his eyes but gives a dramatic bow. When he lifts his head, his eyes land on mine. He smiles at me, and everyone else disappears. It's just me and him in a room with only the flames of the candelabra reflecting from our faces. I force myself to smile back and not just ogle him like a dessert menu.

He takes a seat at the table. Right. Next. To me. It's not the first time I've eaten next to Connor, but it's the first time I've eaten next to him since our moment over the summer. Where he stared at me in his pool like he was seeing me for the first time. When he leaned in to kiss me, we got interrupted by his friend Weston cannonballing into the water a few inches away from us—washing away my hopes of sharing my first kiss with Connor. I always knew I didn't like Weston.

"And you choose to be here," he says to me. His foot bumps against mine and doesn't move. I swallow a sigh.

"Please. Naomi knows she doesn't have a choice. She's one of us." Mr. Brooks gives me a wink as he settles back into his seat. "Which reminds me . . . thank you for supporting Kylie at school today. A lot of people wouldn't consider marching into that school with her. And that's why you're family, not just a friend." Mr. Brooks's knife scratches against his plate as he cuts into his steak. Mrs. Brooks rests her chin into her hand and smiles at me like a not-so-secret admirer. The way they both look at me makes me feel like Mr. Brooks didn't just suddenly remember to have this conversation. They've written the script and are now reciting their lines.

I reach for my glass of water. Not to drink it, just to press the coolness of it against my palm. It feels like someone has turned on the heat, and the vent's right over my head. My eyes roam across the faces at the table, and I have the sudden urge to call my mom and ask her to come over. Not for comfort, but to level the playing field. I had never felt so Black around the Brookses. I had never even thought about being Black when I was around them.

I keep my eyes on Kylie, hoping for some kind of reassurance. She pokes at her green beans with her knife and doesn't look up at me. I'm drowning, and she doesn't even toss me a life jacket.

"Well, the plan was to march into the school with her, but—"

Kylie kicks at my foot underneath the table. Oh, so now she looks at me, her eyes pleading. I raise my eyebrows back at her: *What did I say wrong?*

"But Jared wanted to talk to me," Kylie continues for me. "Ny and Roma went in before me."

I purse my lips together so I won't say anything else wrong. Kylie doesn't want her parents to know about Nevaeh, even though what happened wasn't her fault. Nevaeh was the one who stepped to us, not the other way around. The only thing Kylie did to provoke her had nothing to do with Nevaeh.

Right?

"You two back together?" Mrs. Brooks asks, thankfully interrupting the questions swirling in my head.

Mr. Brooks groans. "God, I hope not."

"Dad!"

Connor laughs at Kylie, and Kylie narrows her eyes at him.

"I thought you guys liked Jared," Kylie continues.

"I do, just not for you. No guy is good enough for my girl. For either of my girls." Mr. Brooks nods over to me. "Can't I convince you both to not date until you're thirty-five?"

At that, Connor shifts his eyes to me and raises his eyebrows, all: *You down for that?* I squirm in my seat as my cheeks get hot. I'm so glad my complexion can't reveal when I'm blushing.

"How were cheer tryouts? You two officially make the team again this year?" Mrs. Brooks asks, graciously changing the subject.

"Not yet," Kylie says, setting her phone down on the table. "But it's only a matter of time. Coach was practically drooling over Ny's stunts today."

I scrunch my nose at her. "Ugh. No, she wasn't."

"Oh, please. 'Nice form, Henry.'" She drops her voice down a few octaves and takes on Coach Beverly's southern drawl. "'Strong legs, Henry. Carry my firstborn child, Henry.'"

I raise my dinner roll over my shoulder as if I'm about to hoist it at her. Kylie throws her head back and cackles. Just like she did when Nevaeh was upset about the Wolverines' suspension. I return the dinner roll to my plate, suddenly not in a playful mood anymore.

"I'm just glad you guys are doing this together again. Nothing like family having your back, especially after this week." Mr. Brooks reaches his hand across the table to grab Kylie's, but she's too busy adding pepper to her scalloped potatoes. "All that fuss over a little video." He snorts under his breath. I could only imagine the daggers Eric's eyes would throw at Mr. Brooks if he were here. Hell, the daggers that would fly out Eric's mouth and land right in Mr. Brooks's chest.

"What did you make out of all that, Naomi?" Mr. Brooks watches me as he sips his wine. Once again, my face gets hot, but not because Connor keeps finding reasons to graze up against my leg or arm. Mrs. Brooks leans forward in her seat, waiting for my response. I glance over at Kylie to get me out of this, but she cradles her chin in her hand, watching me. I even feel Connor's eyes on me.

I take a sip of my water to buy more time. I take three gulps too many, and my hand trembles as I set my glass back down. I want to peel off my skin and use it as a blanket to hide. Funny, I've never felt the need to hide here before. This place has always been my second home.

"All of what?" I finally ask.

"All the to-do about a young girl doing what she had to do to protect herself when confronted by two men." Mr. Brooks's forehead crinkles, as if he's trying to explain himself to someone who's speaking another language. Maybe we are speaking different languages, because there are things that he said that are a little confusing. Like how Kylie was "confronted by" instead of "checked on." Like how Kylie was a "young girl," but the guys were "men," even though they both looked like they were a minute after their own high school graduation.

But he's a father protecting his daughter. He would feel the same way if it were me in that video. At least, I think he would.

"I think it's because people didn't know the full story," I say, treading lightly. Making sure that I walked the fine line between what the Brookses want to hear, and what Eric would hope I'd say. "Everyone doesn't know Kylie like we do." I give a small smile to Kylie, and she doesn't return it. She just chews on her potatoes, moving her jaw slowly and deliberately like it's the toughest potato she's ever eaten in her life.

"I just think people are so quick to make things about race," Mrs. Brooks says. "This would hardly be a blip if those guys were white. It would just be another disagreement in a parking lot. You can't have a different opinion from someone who looks differently than you without being racist or sexist or homophobic. Makes you just want to stay home." She leans back in her seat as if the very thought of it all makes her exhausted. "Little do those trolls saying all those vile things about Kylie know that we make donations to the NAACP every year. We give to the Angel Tree program every holiday season."

A laugh rips out of Connor's mouth. "Not every kid on the Angel Tree list is Black, Mom," he says in between snickers.

Mrs. Brooks sighs and shakes her head at him. "You know what I mean, Connor." She turns to look at me. "Naomi, you understand what I'm saying. You of all people should know that we're not racist."

I want to nod, but it feels like the ceiling is pressing down on me. The rafters are pushing onto my shoulders and cutting off my air supply. I try to take a breath, but it comes out like a hiccup. It's funny how breathing, something that feels so natural to you, can suddenly take so much effort.

Something squeezes around my hand. I look down and Connor is cradling it into his, using his thumb to stroke my knuckles.

"Who's ready for dessert?" he asks. He gives my hand another squeeze, and I squeeze back: *Thank you.*

The only thing that could make this evening worse is watching Jared Crews beat on his chest like Tarzan before flipping into the Brookses' pool. Kylie lets out a whoop and applauds for him as if he did an Olympic-worthy dive. She was texting him throughout dinner. Apparently, it had been her plan all along to make him dessert instead of the pineapple flan Mrs.

Brooks prepared. He returns to the surface and grabs Kylie in a bear hug before flinging her back into the water. Kylie lets out a louder-than-necessary scream, and I roll my eyes. She's always so extra around him, as if she has to work hard to prove to him that he's funny and brilliant when really he's as bland as a Wheat Thin. But Kylie wants what Kylie wants.

I take a seat on the steps leading down to pool and tug at the bikini bottom she let me borrow. Once upon a time we wore the same size, but now Kylie's Brazilian cut was more of a thong for me. I wiggle again to get the fabric out of my butt when Connor's feet appear on the steps next to me.

"Don't tell me you're still afraid of the water." He takes a seat beside me on the middle step. "I thought you'd be a little braver after our lesson this summer." If I wasn't squirming before, I'll really start shimmying now. This is the first time Connor has referenced our almost moment over the summer. His silence made me think that he regretted it or something. He leans back, resting his elbows on the top step. The water ebbs and flows against that trail of muscle that leads down into his swim trunks. He smiles as if he knows simply relaxing, simply being, makes my heart and everything under it dance.

"I just didn't want to go in and interrupt the lovebirds," I say, remembering how to speak again. Kylie squeals again as Jared lifts her in the air. She falls on top of him, and they giggle like hyenas before the kissing begins.

Connor frowns in disgust. "Yeah, they're annoying. And that idiot doesn't realize that Kylie's using him because she's having a bad week."

I throw my hands up in agreement, water splashing on both of us. "Thank you. I knew it wasn't just me." I reach over and wipe off the droplet of water I left on his forehead from my enthusiasm.

"You know you're only getting me wetter, right?"

I laugh. "Sorry." I start to remove my hand, but he grabs it and presses it against his chest.

"But I didn't want you to stay after dinner to talk about my sister and her doofus."

"Really?" I try to keep my voice steady, even. "Why'd you want me to stay?"

Connor leans forward and kisses the back of my hand, and Jesus, is he trying to kill me? "I haven't gotten to see you as much as I've been wanting to."

I take in a shaky breath. "I know. I didn't even think you'd be in school for the rest of the week after that . . ." I let the words linger. He didn't want to talk about Kylie—and bringing up his fight was definitely talking about Kylie. He wouldn't have even gotten into a fight if it wasn't for her.

He tosses his hand, dismissing it all. "That was nothing."

"Neither one of y'all got in trouble?" I ask. I don't know why I keep asking. The more my mouth moves, the more I'm stalling what Connor and I could be doing right now instead.

"Nah, my dad took care of that."

Of course he did. "And . . . the other guy?"

Connor lets out a small laugh. "Yeah, they threw the book at old boy. Think it was like his eighth offense at the school. Fights, thefts, the whole nine. Classic thug in training."

I snatch my hand away from him before I know what I'm doing. This conversation, his interesting choice of words . . . Everything felt dirty, and not in a good way. And I wanted my hands to be clean. To be free. "Connor," I say, disappointment dripping from each syllable.

"Whoa, you know what I mean." Connor reaches for my hand again, squeezes it like he's trying to grab for whatever we had like a minute ago. "He's just a frequent flier in Principal Hicks's office, that's all. Dad said the guy's uncle used to work for him years ago. Maintenance or something. All the good tools used to go missing anytime he left his shift, so Dad had to get rid of him. Dad says the apple doesn't fall far from the tree, or some corny shit like that. You know my dad. Never met a proverb he didn't like."

Connor laughs, and I search hard for the joke. But the more Connor talks about his dad, the more I'm seeing things about Mr. Brooks that I didn't notice before. Cracks behind the shiny presentation. Or like those lottery scratchers Mom and Eric love so much. Scratching away for a prize but ending up with a dud.

"Your dad had time to deal with your school drama? I heard he was dealing with his own issues." I don't know why I say it as a dig, but I do. As if I want Connor to see the cracks too.

Connor gives a slow, tentative nod. "Yeah. Somebody always wants to sue my dad for something. It's like a rite of passage in Windsor." He looks down at our fingers intertwined together, studying the pattern. "I felt pretty bad I had to add on top of his pile of bullshit. That he needs to do damage control for Kylie's bullshit. But at least you're helping her with that apology video. That should ease up some of this mess."

I blink. "Kylie told you I was doing the video with her?"

"She said you were thinking about it, which means you're doing it. Ky and Ny, right?" He smiles at me—and I'm sure he didn't need Mr. Brooks's help to get him out of trouble. Connor's smile could make a judge let him off the hook for murder, even if he came to the courthouse with a bloody knife.

"But we're doing it again," he says before I answer. "No more Kylie talk. Let's continue our swim lesson instead." He takes my other hand and leads me deeper into the water. "Remember, just like you're on a cloud." He rests his hand against my lower back, and I tilt away from him, lifting my legs from the floor of the pool until it's only him holding me above the water.

"Relax," he says, all soft and warm. Gentle enough to make me forget the awkward shit that just happened between us. "I got you."

I take a breath and close my eyes. Feel the water tickling at my scalp and the backs of my knees. Feel Connor's fingertips keeping me afloat. I spread my arms a little farther, as if I'm inviting the stars to hug me. On a cloud, just like Connor said. It takes me a few moments to notice I no longer feel Connor's hands.

"Connor?" I open my eyes, and Connor is a few inches away, his hands bobbing above the water next to him and definitely not on me. I'm floating. By myself. With nothing to support me. My arms and legs panic before the rest of me does. I flail and search for the edge of the pool to grip onto. Connor's next to me again in under a second, before I can even think about drowning.

"It's okay." He grabs my waist and steadies me back on my feet. "I told you. I got you."

I laugh the nerves out of me and shake my head. "Sorry about that."

"You don't need to apologize." His hand is on my chest. "Your heart's beating fast."

My laughter melts into a weak smile. "It's not from the water," I say.

Connor nods as if he understands, and of course he does. He gets me and I get him. He steps closer to me, hands still on my waist. He's leading me in a dance, and we keep grooving until my back is against the wall of the pool. His face is so close that I smell the Altoid he chewed on after dessert. His mouth inches closer to mine, but he pauses before they meet. He raises his eyebrows: *Can I?*

I mumble something that's part yes, part moan, and our lips tangle together. It's not until I allow my arms to wrap behind his neck that it hits me: Connor is kissing me. I'm kissing Connor. We're kissing each other. I've thought about this moment so many times over the past year. Wondered if it would feel strange, like kissing a brother. But there's nothing brotherly in the way Connor's holding me. Kissing me. If anything, our mouths and hands know what to do—as if this moment has always been endgame. We just had to sketch out the rest of the story first. Soon my legs are wrapped around his hips like they belong there.

Connor pulls away and smiles, his mouth all pink from our heat. "You've thought about this before, huh?"

I smile back. "So have you."

Connor buries his head into my neck and kisses on it. I want to close my eyes, but I don't want to miss anything. Instead, I tilt my head back and stare up at the stars. They wink back at me.

NINE

WHEN I GET TO SCHOOL ON FRIDAY, READING, WRITING, AND RATIOS ARE
the last things I want to think about. Connor lives rent-free
in my mind. His laugh, his lips. His fingers . . .

I half listen to Kylie and Roma debate the lyrics to an
Ariana Grande song on the drive to school. There's been nervous energy in the car since they've picked me up, and the
chatter has been nonstop. I get it, though. We're all thinking
about Frap-Gate even though none of us wants to talk about
it. None of us wants to think about what might be waiting
for us when we roll up to the school. And I want to join Distraction Drive with them, but . . . Connor. I trace the edges
of my mouth. Remember what this mouth was doing the
night before. And will myself not to giggle at the memory.

"Sad bitch!"

Kylie plods her way through my daydream. I blink and she's staring at me. One hand on the steering wheel and one eyebrow raised.

"'Scuse me?" I ask.

"Ariana should be a 'sad bitch' and not a 'savage.' Isn't *savage* one of those banned words we're not allowed to say anymore?"

"Oh, and *bitch* is still okay?" Roma asks from the back seat. "Plus, Megan Thee Stallion made millions off the word *savage*. Can't be that bad."

Kylie peeks over at me again, more concerned about being right than about getting us to school safely.

"Google it," I suggest. I lean back in my seat and close my eyes, and I'm back in the pool with Connor all over again.

Thankfully, first block doesn't require much brainpower. The senior class gets to head to the cafeteria to attend a college fair. And the fuss of it all makes the walk to the building seamless. More staff and teachers are out and about than usual, guiding representatives into the school while also making sure their best and brightest don't do anything to embarrass them. Local and state colleges, plus a few select schools from across the country, litter the space with their tables of pens, brochures, hand sanitizer, and lofty goals. My first stop is the NYU table with Kylie, even though Kylie knows everything there is to know about the school. She asks questions as a raggedy-veiled attempt to impress the representative, who's probably some grad student working admissions to pay for tuition.

"I'm really looking for a culturally inclusive learning environment. Is it true NYU has one of the largest numbers of international students compared with most other schools in the US?" Kylie bats her eyelashes. Honestly. I pinch my lips together so I won't laugh.

The rep, with his Jupiter-sized Adam's apple pointing at us, nods once. "Sure," he says. "Care for another stress ball?"

We fill our bags with NYU stress balls, water bottles, and ChapSticks until we're asked to move along by a teacher who's earning their paycheck today. Kylie groans and nods over to the Columbia University table. "I told my dad I'd go talk to at least one Ivy League this morning. Come with?"

"Just give me the Wikipedia rundown." I spot Drew yawning as some lady from Liberty University flaps her arms in the air, possibly preaching the merits of attending an evangelical institution. "I'm going to make sure Drew doesn't sin this morning."

"Good luck with that." Kylie tugs at my hand before heading over to the Columbia table. I spot two Black girls scoping her out as she walks past. I remember seeing them on the field with the rest of the Wolverines. They give her a look that would feel like a punch if Kylie were paying attention, but she flits past them like a leaf swirling in the wind.

I think that only pisses them off more. One of them opens her mouth to say something, but the other nudges her in the ribs. Nods to a teacher leaning against one of the walls. I'd never been so relieved at the presence of my former geometry teacher.

As I let out a thankful sigh, someone pinches at my shoulder from behind. My body responds before I see him, cheeks flushed and knees wobbly. Connor struts in front of me and smiles that certain smile of his.

"Hey, you," he says.

"Hey, you." I smile back.

"Making your plans to leave me next summer?"

I shrug. "You can always make my rom-com dreams come true and chase after me in the airport." I'm somewhat surprised by how casual I am with him.

"Why do you think I've been going so hard in the gym? Have to get my cardio right for that very moment." He moves closer, and I think he's going to kiss me, right here. Right now. In front of the entire senior class. "I could've driven you to school today, you know."

I lift an eyebrow. "Just today?"

Connor laughs, then bends over to tap his forehead against mine. A smooch between the two. I'll take it. "Long-term plans like that need a label, don't you think?"

My heart hiccups at even the joke of Connor becoming my boyfriend. Of becoming something official. We could both apply to colleges in DC. Me to Howard, him to Georgetown. Hell, maybe he could come to Howard with me. Stranger things have happened.

He must notice the shock across my face, because he gives a small laugh and takes my hand. "Call me later?"

I breathe in his question. "Sure," I exhale.

He rubs his thumb across the back of my hand before catching up with some of the guys from the wrestling team, making sure to give me one last look over his shoulder. I hate to see him leave, but I love to watch him go. And yes, I'll be as clichéd as I want to be if it means watching the way his jeans hang off his hips.

"What. The. Fuck?" I don't have to catch up with Drew. Suddenly, he's three inches away from my face.

I pout at him for blocking my view. "What?"

"You and Junior over there." He hitches his head in Connor's direction. "You two were dry-humping each other with your eyes. Are you two . . . ?" He claps his hands together three times.

It takes me three more beats to catch what he's tossing. He thinks Connor and I have done the deed. "What? No?" My voice gets pitchy. I clear my throat and try again. "No," I say, my tone deeper. Firmer.

Drew cocks his head at me. "Then why you sounding like he's seen your O face?"

Leave it to Drew to talk about dry-humping and orgasms

first thing in the morning. I bite my lip, at a loss for words. Connor and I didn't have sex in the pool. But he's great with his hands. So great that he caused these tiny earthquakes in my body that I've felt only once before, and that was by myself after reading a *Teen Vogue* article on . . . self-exploration.

"Biiiiiitch," Drew says with a smile when I'm silent for too long.

I grab his hand and pull him to a quiet corner in the caf-eteria. "Will you stop?" I peek around the room and search for Kylie. It was bad enough that I felt what I felt with Kylie's brother when she was like ten feet away from me. I damn sure didn't want her to have to hear about it in a room full of people who think she's a Karen-in-training. Thankfully, she's nowhere to be seen.

"It wasn't on purpose," I say to Drew under my breath.

He studies me. "Did you consent, though?" he asks with-out a hint of sarcasm on his face.

"Absolutely."

The smile returns. "So . . . it was a *happy* accident?"

I don't say anything, which Drew takes as permission to continue.

"Did he have a happy accident too?"

I laugh and slap his arm. "You're bad."

"Um, like you can talk. What are you guys going to do now, though? It has to be awkward with Kylie. Especially with all that drama going on with her."

Just like that, I go from floating to sinking. Connor made me forget about viral videos and parking lots and Beckys. It was just me and him and what colors we'd wear to prom. It was all happily ever after. Why did I have to deal with the plot twists before reaching that?

"That'll probably be over soon," I say, more wishful thinking than actual belief.

Drew's mouth twists to the side, like there's a secret rolling around on his tongue that he's trying to hold in.

I sigh. "What?"

"Some folks are a little salty after Kylie ran her mouth about Nevaeh. They're pissed that the Wolverines aren't going to perform at the game next week. I'm hearing talks of retaliation."

Dread rises to the pit of my throat and settles there, like bile. I try my best to swallow it down. "Like what? Like they want to hurt Kylie?"

"I don't know all the deets. I'm neutral, but I can't hide all of this." He flings his hand across his body, referencing his white skin, I assume. "But don't worry," he adds, because I'm pretty sure I look like I'm about to throw up. "There's always a lot of talk and very little follow-up. You know our classmates have the attention span of squirrels."

I sigh again, but this time it comes out like a groan. I miss when all I was worried about was debuting my new 'do and completing college applications. This fair was supposed to help me solidify my choices. Come up with a plan of where I'll apply and when. But now Kylie and I have to figure out a way to get her out of this whole mess. I have to do more than just stand by her—I have to speak up for her. If I can vouch that she isn't racist, then everyone would have to believe it. Connor's right—it's always been Ky and Ny.

"And hey, at least you look cute today." Drew pulls at the sleeve of my cropped hoodie. "Does Connor like it?" He claps his hands together in that vulgar way again and laughs at himself.

I pull back to swat at him again when something catches my eye. There, sandwiched between the University of Virginia and Old Dominion University, is a table for Howard University. The Hilltop. The Mecca. The institution that molded Chadwick Boseman and Thurgood Marshall and Kamala Harris. The premier HBCU actually sent someone to my little school in my little town to recruit students. If this isn't a sign that things will get better, that I can still have my dream of living with Connor in Georgetown while visiting Kylie in New York, then I don't know anything else.

"I'll talk to you later, weirdo," I say to Drew, and make a beeline to the Howard table before he can even say goodbye. A Black girl with Bantu knots hands a brochure to a pair of students as I approach her. I take in the banner draped in front of the table. The deep blue and red and white. The determined bison peering back at me, ready to kick ass and take names. Hell yeah.

"Dope, right?" the girl says to me. "A lot of people just see bison as these calm, peaceful animals, but best believe they're a force to be reckoned with. Just like our students."

"They persevere," I say, nodding in awe. "I love it."

She tilts her head at me, as if she didn't expect to find someone like me somewhere like here. "I'm Sonequa," she says. "You interested in learning more?" She glances over my shoulder. "Are both of you interested?"

I look behind me, and Faith walks up to the table, hugging herself as her oversize cardigan hangs off her shoulders.

"Yeah," Faith answers, not looking at me.

Sonequa gives her prepared spiel on all Howard has to offer, and I remember some of the facts from their website, which I've looked at only a hundred thousand times. She hands me and Faith some HU goodies before repeating her pitch to another group of students who stop by. Faith stands off to the side of the table, flipping through the school's guidebook. I don't move either. I have just as much of a right to be here as she does, so I read through the same book. Even nod like I'm learning something new.

"I read that Jasmine Guy thinks that Hillman College in *A Different World* is based off both Howard and Hampton."

I almost drop the guidebook from my hands. I look up and Faith is staring at me. She's talking to me. She raises an eyebrow and waits for me to respond.

"Y-yeah," I say like an idiot. "I read that too." *Groundbreaking, Naomi.* I tuck the book under my armpit to give Faith my full attention. Moments like these come once every never, so I need to show her I appreciate it.

"My cousin's not buying it, though," she continues. "Hampton University is *thee* HU to her. And since both Hillman and Hampton are in Virginia, she says it's the end of story."

I smile. "She went to Hampton, I take it?"

"Goes to. She's a sophomore there now."

Hundreds of questions swirl in my head, but I don't want to bombard Faith with them. I can't scare her off when she just got rolling. I stick with one: "Is that why you were interested in the scholarship Mrs. Ward showed us?" And I wished I picked a different question. Nice job bringing up the tension from class yesterday. I don't want to remind Faith that she hates me.

Faith just shakes her head. "No. I mean, it's not the only reason. Hampton's definitely in my top five choices, but it's a private university. Private universities cost more money, no matter if it's in state or not. Ebony Fire's pretty lit, though."

I nod, all too eager at the mention of Hampton's dance team. Their routines are some of my go-tos on YouTube. Those girls have skills—most of them are actual trained dancers. And all that talent is only an hour's drive away from me. Might as well be the moon, though. I mainly only left

Windsor when I took trips with the Brookses—and Hampton University has never been on their itinerary. "Have you seen them live?"

"Not yet, but Cleo invited me and the girls to come to campus after our game next . . ." At that, Faith's voice drowns out. The game. The game where the Wolverines were supposed to dance but now can't, because Kylie got embarrassed and took everyone down with her. Nevaeh was wrong, but it's not fair that Faith and the other Wolverines had to pay the price.

I tug at my fingers and try to pull out the right words. "Yeah, I'm really sorry about—"

"Hey, Ny."

No, no, no. I'm usually thrilled at the sound of Kylie's voice, but right now she has the timing of a period on a wedding day.

Kylie prances over to me and Faith, and her eyes dance between us. "What's up?" she says, though she sounds like she has other questions to ask.

"Nothing," I say. "We were just—"

Faith turns on her heel and walks to the Old Dominion display table before I can finish. She can't stand to even be around Kylie. I wonder if she was part of that retaliation chatter that Drew heard, but I can't imagine. Faith's always been so indifferent.

"I met my Ivy quota," Kylie says, oblivious to the tension.

Or maybe not caring. "Let's cut out of here. I have some ideas about our video."

The apology video. The video that even Connor thinks I should help with. And maybe after the vanishing act that Faith just pulled when Kylie showed up, this apology video needed to happen, like, yesterday. The sooner we can get it out, the sooner we can cease all talk of revenge. And maybe Faith and I can have conversations without avoiding land mines.

Kylie links her arm through mine and steers me away from the Howard University table. Away from Faith. Away from the prying eyes. Soon it's just me and her in a stairwell, plotting out an apology. Ky and Ny. Like always.

TEN

THE WEEKEND GOES BY NOT IN A BLUR, BUT A BREEZE. KYLIE AND I
knocked out her video after cheer on Friday, but Saturday
was all about me and Connor. Connor and me. We drove
an hour to Yorktown Beach and spent the afternoon laughing, lounging, and lobbing water at each other. In between,
though, there was kissing. Lots of kissing. Lots of catching
our breath in between all the kissing. And while I'd love to
stitch Connor's lips against mine, my favorite parts of the day
were the quiet moments between us. Rubbing suntan lotion
on each other's backs. Pressing my cheek against his chest
and listening to the steady *beat, beat, beat* of his heart while
he snoozed. Or him resting his head on my lap while I read
for English class, *Pygmalion* in one hand, his sandy curls in

my other. At one point, he caught me looking down at him.

"What's wrong?" he asked, staring up at me.

I let out a slow breath. "I don't want today to end." His hair slipped through my fingers.

He smiled and rolled over to his side, so that his lips were mere centimeters from my navel. "So stay here, in the moment. With me." He made it sound so easy. And it was. I refused to check the clock on my phone while I was with him, just let the sinking sun in the sky tell me the time.

The bad part about staying in the present with Connor is that when the future comes, all I want to do is revisit the past. Revisit my Saturday with him. So when Monday hits, I can't muster up any enthusiasm when Mrs. Ward announces our first lab assignment. Something about shooting tennis balls at a monkey. Mrs. Ward says it'll help us learn about gravity or acceleration or whatever, but I'd much rather focus on my chemistry with Connor.

Mrs. Ward walks past and sets a stuffed monkey on my lab table. It smiles blankly at me.

"No monkeys were harmed in the making of this lab," Faith says under her breath.

I laugh. They're the first words she's said to me today, and they were golden. "I don't know. These tennis balls look dense," I say, squeezing one.

"Who's out here shooting monkeys anyway? How does this lab make any sense?"

I shrug. "I think Mrs. Ward just wanted an excuse to charge twenty stuffed monkeys to the school's account."

Faith scoffs as she packs our tennis ball into the tube attached to the edge of our lab table. "Well, if they're giving out bank like that, Mrs. Ward should've had us shooting at Apple Watches."

My laughter is intersected by the bloop of a TikTok alert on someone's phone.

"Excuse me? You all know my policy about phones being on in class. Whoever it is, turn it off or it's mine," Mrs. Ward warns from the back of the class.

Faith widens her eyes, impressed. "Okay, Mrs. Ward got a little bit of Black mama in her. Much respect."

"I did catch her watching an episode of *Real Housewives of Atlanta* before class last Friday," I say.

"See, that's where our roads diverge. It's *Potomac* for me all day."

My mouth drops open as if Faith has strung together the most poetic words. "Right? Aren't those ladies the perfect balance of boug-ghetto?"

"Yasss. A glass of champagne in one hand and a shot of Henny in the other," Faith says.

I laugh again and get our monkey into position, stringing him up on a wooden pole at the opposite end of our table. The pole is supposed to be a tree, but this is Windsor Woods and not West Beverly. We weren't shelling out money for shrubbery. I don't know why I was so worried about not having Drew as a lab partner this year. Drew and I could always laugh and take care of business at the same time, but it felt good not to pause our kiki-ing to explain that *boug-ghetto* is another way of calling someone ghetto fabulous. Or the many reasons why him saying anything is ghetto is not a good look.

"The hell is this?" Kennedy storms over to us and slaps a manicured hand on our lab table, right in the path between our tennis ball and monkey.

"What's up?" Faith asks.

Kennedy shifts so that her back is facing Mrs. Ward and shows us her phone. "You a TikToker now?" she asks me.

The video. My and Kylie's video. Kylie said that she'd probably upload it tonight, not in the middle of the school day. Guess she was eager to put this whole Parking Lot Becky thing to bed. So was I. That way I can walk the halls with her without feeling like there's a bull's-eye on our backs. Or hold Connor's hand in front of everyone without them wondering if he's racist too.

"I don't think one video makes me a TikToker, but okay," I say with a shrug.

Kennedy rolls her eyes so hard that I think the whole room tilts. "Your lab partner's cosigning what Becky did," she tells Faith. "She thinks it's funny as hell."

It's my turn to roll my eyes. "I'm not cosigning anything.

We made a joke video—like millions of people do every day."
I look at Faith for support, but Faith's eyes are on Kennedy's
phone as the video restarts:

PARKING LOT BECKY TO THE RESCUE

INT. GROCERY STORE CEREAL AISLE—DAY

NAOMI PERUSES THE CEREAL AISLE AND GRABS A BOX OF LUCKY CHARMS. KYLIE WALKS UP, HER MOUTH AGAPE.

KYLIE: 'Scuse me, did you just grab the last box of Lucky Charms?

NAOMI: Yeah, looks like it.

KYLIE: (into phone) Hello? Police?

EXT. BROOKS FAMILY POOL—DAY

NAOMI AND KYLIE LIE NEXT TO EACH OTHER ON LOUNGE CHAIRS. NAOMI RUBS ON SUNSCREEN, AND KYLIE PEEKS AT HER OVER HER SUNGLASSES.

KYLIE: 'Scuse me, is that SPF fifty or higher?

NAOMI: (glances at bottle) No, it's SPF thirty. Why?

KYLIE: (into phone) Hello? Police?

INT. KYLIE'S CAR—DAY

NAOMI AND KYLIE ARE IN THE FRONT SEAT OF KYLIE'S CAR, SINGING ALONG TO A RAP SONG WHILE KYLIE DRIVES. AT ONE POINT, NAOMI RAPS ALONG TO THE WORD *NIGGA* **WITH THE ARTIST. KYLIE CUTS DOWN THE MUSIC.**

KYLIE: 'Scuse me, but did you just say what I think you said?

NAOMI: What? *Nigga?*

KYLIE: Isn't that word illegal?

NAOMI: Maybe for you . . .

KYLIE: (shakes head) Not cool. (into phone) Hello? Police?

[END SCENE]

I give a tiny laugh once the video ends and restarts itself. Not because anything was funny. I rehearsed it too many times to laugh at anything at this point. But what else are you supposed to do when you watch yourself trying to act?

"What you think? Should I create one of those 'for your consideration' ads for the Oscars?" I ask, just to break the wall of ice that forms around us.

"The hell?" Faith looks down at Kennedy's phone, watching my video even after Kennedy put it on mute. The images reflect on her eyes, and she has yet to blink. Just takes it all in like she's under hypnosis.

"I was joking. I'm not giving Viola Davis a run for her money," I say, knowing damn well that Faith wasn't confused about my joke. She's referring to the video. My and Kylie's video. Ny and Ky.

"What's funny about a white person calling the cops on a Black person?" Faith asks, finally blinking before looking at me. Burning a hole through me.

"Thank you!" Kennedy throws both hands in the air.

Faith and I were joking like five minutes ago. But now, she looks at me like she did before. No, worse. Faith never really looked at me before. Now it's like I stepped on something foul, and the stench hasn't left me yet.

"Nothing's funny about it," I say, making sure I emphasize the right words. "We were just highlighting the ridiculousness of when white people do it." I use the same phrasing that Kylie said to me each time I asked: *Should we? What if? How come?* They made sense to me then, but Faith and Kennedy stare at me like I'm speaking Mandarin.

"But it's more than ridiculous," Kennedy says. "It's dangerous—*and* deadly."

"We weren't joking about anyone dying," I insist. "I would never do that."

"Bitch, you. Just. Did." Kennedy claps her hands between each word, each clap like a slap to my face.

"Wait, who are you calling a bitch?" I ask. Kennedy might not have beat me down physically, but I wasn't going to take a verbal smackdown either.

"Ladies." Mrs. Ward is in between us. Faith and Kennedy on one side, and me by myself on the other. The line was drawn over the course of two minutes. "Is there a problem over here?"

Kennedy folds her arms and pokes her lips out at me,

challenging me to open my mouth and snitch. Just like Kylie did with Nevaeh. Mrs. Ward looks at her, then at me. Her eyebrows lifted, ready to pounce with a discipline referral with even the slightest of nods.

"No," I say, staring right back at Kennedy. Letting her know I wasn't backing down, whatever this was. "Kennedy just came over to help us with the lab."

"Well, Kennedy has her own partner to help. Isn't that right, Kennedy?" Mrs. Ward extends her hand back toward Kennedy's lab table, where her partner is using his backpack as a pillow.

Kennedy and Faith exchange a look before Kennedy nods and treks back to her table. Like they've made an agreement that I'm not privy to. To make matters worse, Mrs. Ward pats my arm before making her way back to her desk. Just me.

I inch my way back to the table. Faith returns to getting our monkey into position, almost like Kennedy and I didn't just come to blows over a dumb thirty-second video. Maybe that means she wants to move on and we can get back to joking about Bravo reality shows.

"If you want, I can type up our findings when we finish." I offer an olive branch. Not sure if we were beefing, but I wanted to squash anything just in case.

"Ma'Khia Bryant," Faith says.

I blink. "Who?"

Faith looks at me. "Somebody called the cops on her. Now she's dead. I have more examples if you want material for your next video."

I wince. "Faith, I didn't mean—"

"Let's just get this done before the bell rings." Faith shoots the tennis ball at the monkey, and I jump like I'm the one who takes the hit. Maybe I can use that, this twinge deep in my gut. I could end my misery now and be excused to the nurse.

I glance up at the clock to gauge if I need to make a break for it. I catch Drew looking between me and Faith, me and Faith. "The fuck?" he mouths.

"The fuck?" Drew asks me as soon as we step into the hallway.

"Apparently, I'm a racist," I say just as Faith and Kennedy brush past me. Kennedy gives me a sneer over her shoulder before turning back around and whispering something to Faith. Faith doesn't bother to look back at me as they disappear farther down the hall. Once again, I'm invisible.

"Because of your and Kylie's TikTok?"

I stop in my tracks. "You saw it too? Damn, am I the only one who follows Mrs. Ward's no-phone policy?"

"Please. I've watched two episodes of *grown-ish* on my phone during her lecture on Newton's laws of motion."

I take a breath to prepare myself. "And . . . ?"

"Yara Shahidi's gorgeous, per *uge*. Oh, and I think I'm still Team Luca. . . ."

I slap his arm. "Drew. What did you think about the TikTok?"

"Oh." Drew shrugs. "Some of the jokes were more Tyler Perry than Issa Rae, but Tyler Perry's a billionaire, so kudos to you. Xavier wasn't doing much applauding, though."

I sigh and start walking again. "So, he thinks I'm a racist too?" Great, so all the Black kids in my honors classes were back to hating me again. This video has done the exact opposite of what I hoped. Instead of everyone forgiving Kylie, they've now added me to their shit list.

"I don't know. He didn't do much talking, mainly just grumbled. But Xavier never really does much talking. I didn't know until a week ago that his voice had dropped three octaves. He said my name, and I thought God was talking to me. I was shook."

I peek around the hall to look out for any nasty glances. That way, I'll know which set of eyes to avoid for the rest of the day. But mostly everyone is doing their own thing. Walking to class, checking their phone, shooting the shit. Maybe everyone else knew the intent behind my and Kylie's video. That we weren't cosigning; we were calling out.

"It couldn't have gotten a lot of views already, right?" I pull out my phone to text Kylie. I could get her to pull the video before anyone else gets wind of it. I can already picture her reply: *It's not our fault people can't take a joke.*

"Maybe. Usually, Kylie only gets a ton of likes when she's shaking her ass to trap music, so you're probably—oh, shit." Drew stops so abruptly in his tracks that I collide with his arm and almost drop my phone.

"Jesus, Drew. What the hell?"

He doesn't respond. Just stares straight ahead like he's seen a ghost. I follow his gaze, and my eyes land on my locker. There, scrawled across it in bright orange marker, are the words *AUNT JEMIMA*. Whoever wrote it was angry. Pissed, even. They traced over the letters so many times that each of them is bloated and blurry, like their hand was clenched into a fist while writing. Several people form a small semicircle around my locker, mouths frozen in mid gasp or laugh.

My feet move before the rest of me can respond. I'm at my locker, limbs shaking as I use my sleeve to try to scrub away the words. The anger. But they are permanent. I'm sure the person wishes they could tattoo the words on my forehead. Still, I scrub harder. What the hell else could I do? Someone laughs. I turn and phones are pointed at me, taking pictures. Recording me. Probably making me a meme.

"Stop," I say. To no one and all of them. I just want them to stop.

"Excuse me? Don't you all have a test to fail or something?" Roma's next to me, glaring at my spectators. She links her arm through one of mine as if she knows I might crumple to the floor. I look at her and thank her with my eyes. She gives my arm a squeeze.

"Half of them probably can't even read." Drew's on my other side. Real close. I get it. They're making a wall between my locker and everyone's phones. It's probably a little too late now, but still. They're trying, and I want to cry. But I won't. I can't. They'll make that a meme too.

"Funny how your girl wasn't camera shy when she posted that pathetic-ass video," a Black girl with large hoop earrings says. Sheree. We had PE the same block our freshman year. We sat on the bleachers together whenever one of us had our periods to keep the other company. We'd pretend we were sports commentators while we watched everyone else play basketball. Now she glares at me like she wishes she could hurl a basketball right at my face.

"The only thing pathetic is that you don't have anything better to do right now," Roma says.

"I am. I'm watching your friend get what she deserves."

I rock back on my heels. Good thing Roma's still holding on to me, or I would've fallen right against my defaced locker. What I *deserve*? All I did was try to show everyone how silly Kylie had been about the whole parking-lot thing. We were calling her out. How did I become the villain in all of this?

"And what did the rest of us do to deserve being subjected to your bad breath right now?" Drew asks Sheree.

"They have an invention for that. It's called Colgate."

Some of the spectators laugh. Unless they're still laughing at me. I can't really look at any of them anymore. I breathe through my nose and stare at my shoes as much as I can. If I zone out enough, maybe I'll wake up and still be in Mrs. Ward's class. I didn't get much sleep last night. It's perfectly reasonable that I dozed off in class and none of this is happening right now.

"Bitch, you don't know me!" Sheree again.

"No, but I met your breath like five minutes ago."

"Drew," I say. Or I try to say. I lean more against Roma as the insults continue to lob across the hall. Drew then Sheree. Roma then someone else. Back to Drew. The insults start to bleed into each other until it's one large wound in the hall. No one waits for an opening. They shout over each other. And in the midst of this bloodbath, I notice something jarring. Drew and Roma are on my side, and everyone they yell at for me . . . happens to look like me.

What in the actual hell?

"Enough!" Our assistant principal, Ms. Guy, marches in between us with two school resource officers. Her hair is pulled up into a tight bun, which makes the corners of her eyes angrier than usual. "Whoever is still in this hall in the next five seconds is getting detention. Move it!"

Just like that, the crowd disperses. Not without a few angry rumblings, though. Drew shrugs at me with one shoulder before heading to his next class. He's not one for goodbyes, but I know how he feels. He's shown his loyalty to me. Roma hasn't let me go yet.

"Walk you to class?" she asks me.

"That won't be necessary. Ms. Henry's coming with me," Ms. Guy says.

I bite the inside of my cheek and it screams at me, reminding me I'm still very much awake. This is all still real.

ELEVEN

MS. GUY'S OFFICE LOOKS AND SMELLS LIKE THE WAITING ROOM AT A spa. On one side of her desk, she has a small tray with sand and a tiny rake. On the other side, one of those miniature rock waterfalls with perpetual running water. She refuses to use the embedded fluorescent ceiling lights and instead has a standing lamp on dim. Soft, ambient music pours out of a hidden speaker, and somewhere there's a plug-in that makes the whole room smell like clean laundry.

I guess her goal is to make first-time visitors like me feel welcomed before she sends them off to clean the toilets in the clinic—or whatever she dishes out as punishment. The whole vibe is enough to make me roll my eyes. Usually, Kylie and I would've exchanged the same smirk of annoyance with each other, but she hasn't glanced at me once since one of the school resource officers escorted her into the office to join me. She's been putting me on ice since the car ride this morning. Tossing me a nod instead of her usual smile. Even telling Roma that she didn't have to move to the back seat.

"Is there a problem?" I had asked Kylie, fastening my seat belt in my rightful spot on the passenger's side.

Kylie just shrugged. "Not like you would know. I hadn't seen you all weekend."

I groaned, then pulled a face at Roma in the side-view mirror. Roma smiled and shook her head. Not only did Connor and I spend all of Saturday together, but we also FaceTimed most of Sunday, streaming episodes of *90 Day Fiancé* together. Kylie didn't know what to do with that—with me spending so much time with a Brooks that wasn't her. I figured we'd have to talk about it at some point, but she wasn't in the talking mood this morning. And by the way she leans away from me in Ms. Guy's office, she's still feeling some type of way.

"I'm sure you both probably have an idea of why I called you into my office," Ms. Guy says, rubbing hand lotion between each of her knuckles. If she starts taking off her earrings, we're in for an ass whooping.

"Actually, I don't," Kylie says, raising her hand. "And I have a chem test this period, so . . ."

I look at Kylie with my eyes wide. I'd never seen her with

this attitude toward Ms. Guy. She didn't even respond to Ms. Guy's greeting before taking a seat.

"While I appreciate your commitment to your academics, Ms. Brooks, I'd like to talk about your and Ms. Henry's social skills."

I turn back to Ms. Guy and frown. I talk only to people who talk to me at this school. And I still nod at the people who haven't said a word to me. Not to mention I say my pleases and thank-yous to any adult in this building. My social skills are on point.

"I treat everyone here with respect," Kylie says, speaking what's on my mind. "So does Naomi." She nods in my direction, even though she still doesn't look at me. Petty with a capital *P*.

"Well, your social media suggests otherwise," Ms. Guy says.

Kylie frowns. "Isn't what we do outside of the school building our business?"

"Not when what you do trickles into this building. And I'd suggest you watch that tone before you're taking your chem test in ISS, if you catch my drift."

At that, Kylie slumps in her seat and folds her hands in her lap. There's no way that Kylie would want in-school suspension. We all know that's the place where students who come to school too stoned to function end up—and spending time with druggies doesn't look too good on college apps.

But Ms. Guy had to let Kylie know what happens when you give lip to a Black woman. Kylie was used to being as sassy as she wanted to be with her own mom. I've never even seen Mrs. Brooks give Kylie so much as the stink eye when Kylie's broken curfew.

"I've seen the videos," Ms. Guy continues. "Both of them. And I'm concerned that it's causing a lot of tension here at Windsor Woods."

"With all due respect," Kylie begins in her best good-girl voice, "I didn't release that video of me at Target. In fact, I was filmed without my permission, so my dad is dealing with that on the legal side of things."

Kylie's words hit me like a rock thrown at the back of my head. The Brookses planned on suing those two guys? I figured everyone would take the L—no harm, no foul. No cars were damaged, and no laws were broken. If Kylie wanted to end the drama here at school, taking legal action doesn't seem to be the way to go. I want to tell her that with my eyes, but this chick still refuses to turn my way.

"Then me and Naomi wanted to address the travesty of white people calling the cops for silly reasons. At the time I did it, I truly felt like my safety was at risk. But I can also understand why I might have been another white girl abusing her power. The edit of that first video certainly made it seem like that was the case."

I grip the arms of my chair, my nails digging so deep into

the wood that they almost break. It takes every muscle in my body to not smirk at everything Kylie just said. To not throw back my head and cackle at its stupidity. When did Kylie become so . . . clueless?

The twist of Ms. Guy's mouth tells me that she finds this conversation just as ludicrous as I do. "Regardless of your intentions, your efforts were not well received. And when something causes a disturbance of this magnitude, I need to intervene. I'll be calling to speak with your parents."

My parents? As if my mom didn't have enough going on with the opening of her day care. "I don't understand," I say. "I'm the one that had my locker vandalized. Shouldn't whoever did that be the one to get in trouble?"

"Rest assured, Ms. Henry, that we will be doing a thorough investigation to find out who damaged your locker, and they'll face the appropriate consequences." Ms. Guy extends a hand on her desk, as if she's patting my hand from afar. Somehow, I feel it. "And calling your parents isn't a punishment. We always find it best practice to inform parents when there have been actions that have impacted several students."

"Well, are you calling *everyone's* parents? Like the chick who used her coffee as a weapon against me?" Kylie asks with a sneer.

Ms. Guy cocks her head at Kylie. "I know how to do my job, Ms. Brooks," she says. "How about you just make better decisions with your social media. If it causes any more disturbances at this school, you'll be chatting with me again. And next time I might not be so accommodating, okay?"

"This is some bullshit," Kylie says when we leave the main office. "People have sued whole districts for trying to control what students do on their social media. Let her come after us if she wants to." She finally looks at me, waiting for me to nod along or say yes or do whatever else I've been doing this past week. For her.

"Or what?" I ask, digging my hands into my pockets. I have to keep them hidden or I can't be responsible for what they might do. "You're going to give her even more attitude?"

Kylie frowns at me. "If it's necessary. You saw her in there. She barely gave a damn about your locker. She was all eye and neck rolls. I thought her head was going to tumble onto the floor at one point."

I clench my fists inside my pockets. "Are you serious right now? Not all Black women roll their necks when making a point. Even with all the smack you were talking, she kept her composure. But I guess it didn't matter, because you saw what you wanted to see."

"Hold up." Kylie grabs my arm to get me to stop walking. "What the hell's your problem? You're acting like I'm the one who tagged your locker."

I shrug. "Might as well. You got me looking like a clown

online. I knew it didn't feel right, but nooo. I figured my *best* friend would have my *best* interests in mind."

"I'm sorry, but I didn't point a gun at your back to make that video. You could've said no. Or is it that hard for you to say no to my brother?" She spits the last word out, and I'm right. God, I know this girl like the back of my hand. I can't believe she's still finding time to be jealous in the midst of all this.

"Really, Ky? I can't even pick a different place to eat than you without you getting pissed. And if I put my foot down, you might accuse me of rolling my neck in an aggressive way." I snatch my arm away from her. Kylie jerks back like I just tried to stab her. That's okay, though, because she cut me somewhere deeper back in Ms. Guy's office.

"Who even are you right now?" she asks me. "Since when are you in love with Ms. Guy?"

"Kylie . . ." I take a deep breath. I shouldn't have to finish my sentence. But even if I did, something tells me she still wouldn't get it. "Just take down the video. Okay?" I don't wait for her to finish. I walk toward my next class and feel her eyes on the back of my head.

"What the hell were you thinking?" Mom throws her hands up in the air. She hadn't even bothered to take off her shoes after a long day at work before she started laying into me. Ms. Guy wasn't lying about calling our parents. I can imagine the embarrassment my mom felt getting her first call from Ms. Guy about me in between diaper changes.

"She wasn't. That's the point," Eric says.

I swivel my head to Eric, who sits next to me on the couch: *You too?*

Eric shrugs back: *Wrong is wrong.*

"When your friend does something wrong, you're supposed to call them out! Not give them a pass," Mom continues.

"I wasn't giving her a pass," I say. "I was calling her out even more by highlighting the stupidity of it all." I sound like a broken record, constantly explaining my intentions. But if I had to tell the same thing to different people, then maybe *they* aren't the problem. That video was more insensitive than I had feared. So much for listening to Kylie.

Mom scoffs. "The only person that was looking ridiculous in that video . . . was . . ." She stops herself and pinches the bridge of her nose. But it's too late. I read in between the ellipses, and I want to close the book. I slump farther into the couch, wishing I could melt into the fabric.

"I'm sorry, baby," Mom says, studying my face. "I'm not mad at you. I'm just disappointed about the situation. Ms. Guy said the video is causing a disturbance at the school."

"My vandalized locker is causing a disturbance at the school," I insist.

"Oh, best believe, we're going to get that person's ass," Eric says.

"Baby." Mom pokes her lips at him. It's Eric's turn to slump in his seat. "What he means is that we're going to make sure the school finds out who did that to you, but that doesn't take away from the fact that you need a consequence too."

"Mom," I protest.

Mom holds up her hand. "I can't take away your phone, because you need it to stay in touch with me. So instead," she says, sighing, "I want you to take some time away from Kylie. Just for a little bit. You can catch the bus to school, and Eric can pick you up after cheer practice."

My mouth doesn't even move to protest. If this were a week ago, Mom and I would be arguing until the sun came up. How dare she try to keep me away from Kylie? But something about her decision today feels kinda right.

Mom hitches her head toward the back of the apartment. "Go to your room. I'll call you when dinner is ready."

Eric gives me a reassuring pat on my back as I climb to my feet and head to my bedroom. I barely have a chance to close the door behind me before he and my mom start going in on me.

"I just thought she knew better," Mom says, disappointment dripping out of her mouth.

"I always warned you about those Brookses. That sense of entitlement is no joke. And you heard all that talk about everyone suing him. Of course his kids are going to turn out like that."

"Maybe it's my fault. I raised them like they were all siblings. I didn't want Naomi to feel different, but maybe I should've made sure that she did."

I back away from the door and throw my hood over my head to block out the conversation. I didn't want to hear any more. Of course, I knew I was different. I could never put my hair in a high ponytail like Kylie unless I got a weave. I never cared as much about tanning as Connor. And every time I left the Brookses' house, my apartment felt small enough to suffocate me. The thing is, though, I hated being reminded about being different. Kylie and Connor never reminded me—at least not on purpose. They made me feel like I belonged in their home, even if my mom was the help.

I plop onto my bed and pull out my phone. I prepare to text Kylie, like I always do around dinnertime if we aren't eating together, but my thumb lingers above the screen. Time away from Kylie meant virtually too. Plus, I didn't have anything to say to her until she took down that damn video. Speaking of which . . .

I open TikTok and search for Kylie's profile. Not only is the video still up, but it has even more views and comments. Even with dread tugging at my stomach, I click on the speech bubble to see the comments:

Are they serious?

It's the Black girl cosigning for me. . . .

Yooo—homegirl's in the sunken place.

Who wanna bet that the sista bleaches her skin???

Like 80 percent of the comments are about me. And like 100 percent of the comments about me are negative. They all hate me . . . and Kylie still hasn't taken down the video. Even with my hands sweating, I can't stop scrolling. It's like I'm searching for someone, anyone, who has my back. And then I see it:

ConMann19: Chill. Ky's dope and Ny's doper. If you can't take a joke, then keep scrolling.

Connor. He's been reading through the comments too. If I can't get to Kylie, maybe I can get to him. Especially since he sees what everyone's saying about me. I FaceTime him, and he picks up quicker than I expected. He's outside somewhere. Maybe by his pool. He's lounging shirtless with his baseball cap swiveled backward, and his tiny blond curls sprout out against his forehead.

"There she is," he says to me. "I've been waiting to see that face all day. What you doing?" He speaks so calmly, so cavalierly. Almost like he didn't see my locker. Which is impossible because everyone's seen my locker.

"Nothing. Just being the most hated girl on the internet," I say, leaning back against my headboard.

He raises his eyebrows. "I thought that was Ky."

"Not this week. I'm the Black girl high-fiving Becky for calling the cops. Otherwise known as Aunt Jemima."

Connor smirks. "That was bullshit. I was so pissed when

I saw it. I've already rallied up the guys to find out who did it. You can't trust Hicks and Guy to take care of it."

In Connor's world, rounding up his crew to roam the streets like a gang in *West Side Story* is romantic, but all I needed him to do was call me. Check on me. Not make things worse by starting a turf war.

"The delivery was obnoxious, but the message was received," I say. "People have a right to be mad at me. And your sister's not exactly doing me any favors."

"That video was hil-arious, Ny."

I frown. "Not really."

"Please, that suntanning bit? Perfect."

"Connor." I push away from my headboard and get closer to the phone so Connor can see how serious I am. "You see what they're saying about me."

"Since when do you care about what people think?"

What the hell? Since always. He's supposed to know me. "Well, when everyone's saying the same thing, it hits a little differently."

"Not everyone." Connor sits up from his lounge chair, like he wants me to see his seriousness too. "Not me."

I sigh through my nose. Okay, maybe he does know me. "And I appreciate that, but even you telling everyone that I'm dope or whatever won't change their minds. Not when they see me standing by smiling when Kylie's pretending to call the cops or whatever. I told her to take it down, and she hasn't. Can you talk to her?"

Connor groans and throws his head back. "You know I hate getting in the middle of you guys' stuff. She's already pissed at us about this weekend."

"Connor, this isn't arguing over which Barbie we get to play with. Ms. Guy already gave us a warning, and my mom—"

"Is cool as hell," Connor says. "She knows a joke when she sees one."

"She's disappointed." I look away from the phone so I can't see myself saying the words. That would make them too real.

Connor takes off his hat and tousles his damp hair with his free hand, in deep-thinking mode. "I'll say something. But I can't make any promises. Kylie does her own thing; you know that. Besides—this whole thing will blow over in like a week."

A week? I'm not sure if I can take a week of being the Black community's biggest sellout since Lil Wayne went hard for Donald Trump. But that's the thing—Connor doesn't get it. I've always been Black, but lately it's felt like something I wanted to shout about. Like finding a beautiful vintage dress in the back of my mom's closet and realizing it fits me perfectly. I wanted to throw flowers at myself when I looked in a mirror now, praising my thick curls and round nose and sepia complexion—no filter needed. I wanted to be around people who basked in their Blackness, future leaders of the world. Innovators. Groundbreakers. But to now have that stripped away from me, to have those same people hate me . . . I don't know. It feels pretty lonely.

"I'm not hanging up until you give me a smile," Connor says, oblivious written all over his face.

I flash him a little teeth, but even that takes too much effort. When he hangs up, it seems like our weekend in the sun happened a thousand years ago.

NOW

I'M STILL ALONE. JUST ME AND A COLD, STEEL TABLE AND THE HUMMING from the fluorescent lights above me. Detective Summers made sure to leave the file folder. One of the photos peeks out from it, just a corner of the image that's now seared into my brain. I can't stand to be alone with it, but I'm also not brave enough to reach out and tuck the photo back in. Instead, I hug myself and rock. Imagine my mom's arms around me as she lulls me to sleep, just like when I was a kid. Why can't I be a kid again?

The door opens and I jump, eager. Hoping to see Mom's face as she rushes into the room and scoops me up like I'm still her baby. But it's not Mom. Instead, it's a white woman with long brown hair tucked neatly behind both ears. She strolls in carrying an array of snacks in her arms, and she smiles down at me and closes the door behind her with her foot. I sink back into my seat at the sound of the door clicking shut.

"I tried to remember what I loved to snack on when I was your age, so I went to the vending machine and got a little trigger-happy." She dumps the snacks onto the table. "These were my go-tos." She slides a pack of Twizzlers and a can of Sprite toward me, then lifts her eyebrows like she's expecting me to sob with gratitude.

"Thanks," I mumble. "But I'm not really hungry." Lie. All I can think about is eating right now. Stuffing my face enough to push tonight out of my head. But eating this lady's snacks seems like I'd be taking a bribe.

The lady shrugs. "Suit yourself." She sits across from me and tears into the package of Twizzlers. She takes a bite out of one and dances in her seat, like she just tasted ambrosia from the gods. "Detective Mary Kate Stretch. You can call me MK, though."

I don't want to call her anything. "I asked that other detective for my mom. I don't want to say anything else until she gets here."

"Oh, you don't have to tell me anything, sweetie. I'm not even recording our chat. I just came in here to check on you. And to sneak in a quick snack break for myself." Detective Stretch takes another bite of her Twizzler and glances over at the file folder. "Goodness. He left this in here with you?" She grabs the folder and tucks the dangling photo back inside.

I let out a sigh, relieved that the physical reminder is at least out of sight. The memory of it, though, is still fresh. Painful. I hug myself tighter.

Detective Stretch looks down at the closed folder and shakes her head. "Such a tragedy. This was your friend, right?"

I bite down on my bottom lip and look down at my lap. *Just go away*, I think. *Just take your snacks and leave.* I'm not ready to talk about it. Any of it.

"I lost a friend in high school, too," she continues, unable to read my thoughts. "Car accident. I was there . . . in the car. He was driving, but . . ." She rubs the heel of her hand across her forehead, as if she's trying to push the memory back into her brain. Remember it correctly. "I couldn't help but feel like it was my fault. He'd been drinking. Not a lot. Two beers, tops. And I'd seen him guzzle down way more than that at other parties. I thought he was fine. I thought . . ." She lets out a shaky breath. "It just happened so fast, you know? One minute we're rapping along with Limp Bizkit, and the next . . . ugh, I was there. I could've driven the car. I hadn't had anything to drink. I wanted to stay sharp for my volleyball the next day. Of course, I didn't end up going. I was waking up in a hospital, with my dad telling me that Ben was gone. He was just here, but then he was gone."

She shakes her head like she can't believe what she's saying, then lets out a small laugh. "I still can't listen to 'Nookie' without wanting to vomit now. But I guess I'm not unique with that sentiment." She looks at me and waits for me to laugh with her, but I keep chewing on my lip. Keep wishing for her to disappear.

She leans toward me. "You're always, *always* going to think about the what-ifs. But that's never helpful. What is helpful, though, are the things you tell us right now. Help us. Help your friend. It won't bring them back, but—"

I curl into myself, pushing my forehead against my knees. The finality of her words, knowing that someone isn't coming back from tonight, it's all too much for me to handle right now. So, I scream instead. I let out a wail that spills out of this room and gusts into the night wind beyond these walls.

TWELVE

I FORGOT HOW QUIET THE HALLS OF WINDSOR WOODS CAN BE WHEN you're there in time for the breakfast shuffle. Per my mom's orders, I caught the bus to school Tuesday morning and entered the building around the same time the teachers showed up for work. Don't get me wrong, the halls were still bustling with students—mainly freshmen and sophomores—going wherever students went when they had this much time before first block began. I didn't know what to do with myself. I didn't want to wait by my locker until Kylie and Roma made it to school. The janitors tried their best to scrub away the orange letters, but all they were able to do was make it a blush tint, as if the softness of the color would take the sting away. It did not.

I go to the cafeteria to grab a bite to eat and settle for a yogurt parfait and a bottle of water. I scan the room for a safe space, but there are too many eyes, none too willing to invite me to their table. I still have the scarlet letter across my chest: S for *sellout*. I find a small, empty table tucked near the back corner and make a beeline for it.

"What's up, Beck-eisha?" a Black guy with a goatee of acne shouts to me. Freshman, probably, especially with that pathetic attempt at a burn. Regardless, the punch line works well for his gangly group of friends, and they snicker and howl something else in my direction that I can't quite make out. Mainly because I choose not to.

I take my seat and keep my eyes on my parfait, as if spooning it takes all the mental power I can muster. My phone buzzes on the table next to me. Kylie. She's been trying to hit me all morning. I sent her an abrupt text late last night:

Catching bus.

No emojis. No explanation. Just enough so she wouldn't burn any gas driving to my apartment for no reason. She took her sweet time answering me—not texting me back until six thirty this morning. So I kept her on unread.

A loud cackle erupts in the cafeteria, and I almost don't look up, figuring it's someone else trying to clown me. My curiosity gets the best of me, though, and I spot Faith, Nevaeh, and two other girls from the Wolverines entering the cafeteria, laughing and carrying on about something. Nevaeh throws up her arms and starts to pop her booty to a song that only those four seem to hear. The girls hype her up and laugh again. Faith laughs so hard that she claps her hands, and I watch her in awe. I've never seen her so light before. In physics or at the locker, she's always down to business. Hell-bent on doing whatever she needs to do so she can go about her day and leave me to mine. Even those brief moments of joking with her yesterday seemed a little heavy. Faith kept Bubble Wrap around her to keep me from getting too close. Not with her Wolverines, though. With them, the plastic was off, and she was close to floating.

Faith's laughter fades, and her eyes fall onto me. I quickly look back down at my parfait. Damn. Now she thinks I was mean mugging her or something. It's bad enough that I'm Public Enemy Number One with Black Windsor Woods.

"Pathetic, table for one." Serena Warren sashays past my table flanked by two friends who are equally blond, equally tall, and equally annoying. Serena's the blondest of them all, though. Her hair's almost the color of milk. Anyone else would look like a White Walker from *Game of Thrones*, but Serena passes for an ice princess from a Pixar movie, which makes her all the more frustrating. Somebody that beautiful should be using her powers for good. Instead, she and her girls peek back at me and giggle like I'm wearing mismatched shoes.

Okay, the Black kids mocking me is one thing, but I'm not about to be played by Serena "Backup Plan" Warren and her two Warren-ettes.

"Still salty that Jared kicked you to the curb once again, I see," I say, glaring right back at them. "Did he let you down easy this time, or did he just ghost you?"

The giggles come to a screeching halt. Serena spins around and props one hand on her hip. "Care to say that again?"

"I said . . ." I drop my spoon onto the table to keep both hands free. To stay ready. "Jared dropped you for Kylie. Again. For like the eighteenth time."

Serena purses her lips, her cheeks growing pinker than her lip gloss. "For the record, I ditched Jared because he's an ignorant idiot. Which explains why he rolls with Kylie." She looks me over. "And why she rolls with you."

I jump up from my chair. If a table weren't between us, Lord only knows what I'd do to knock that stupid smirk from her mouth. But Serena doesn't even flinch. If anything, she arches her back and grows an inch.

"Careful. My name isn't Becky or Karen. Try me and you get these hands—not a call to the cops." She points her finger to every other word, as if she's been studying rap videos all her life for this moment. And it's everything—the poking of her finger, the slur of her words, the accusations—that leaves my head swirling and me standing here blinking at Serena like a fool. It's almost like Serena thinks she's Blacker than me. Come to think of it, she's always kind of been this way. She tried to teach me the art of twerking at our final fifth-grade dance. Taught me the words to a Migos song during a seventh-grade field trip. She even looked at me like I had two heads when I mentioned in ninth grade that I hadn't worn cornrows in my hair before that point. Serena's the palest chick I know, yet, somehow, had been my unwelcome guide to Black culture. What in the actual what?

"What's so scary about your hands?" Faith steps up to my table, Nevaeh and the other two Wolverines in tow. They form a line between me and Serena, and I can hardly believe what's happening. Is Faith . . . *sticking up* for me? "They look a little mild to me."

"They look a little *pale* to me," Nevaeh adds with a click of her tongue. One of the other Wolverines laughs.

Serena looks them up and down. "I don't remember inviting you to this conversation," she says.

"I don't remember needing an invite," Faith shoots back, then takes a giant step toward Serena. "But you can try sending us away if you want."

"Please try," Nevaeh says. "I'm looking for a reason to get sent home today."

Faith and her friends stare down Serena and her friends. I hold my breath, waiting to see who'll break first. Finally, Serena scoffs and turns her glare to me. "You're not worth all this drama," she says. Then back to the Wolverines: "Keep in mind that this is the friend of the heifer that benched you guys."

My whole body feels flushed, heat rising from my toes and settling in my chest. Leave it to Serena to remind Faith and Nevaeh why they should hate me.

"Girl, just bye." Nevaeh shoos Serena away with a flick of her wrist.

Serena mumbles something to her friends, and they march out of the cafeteria, off to harass someone else. Faith and the Wolverines look at each other, then start cracking up.

"Is she for real?" Faith asks them.

"Sis thinks she's Black cuz she listens to Drake," the shorter friend says.

"You mean *Aubrey*?" Nevaeh corrects, which sends them howling even more.

Faith turns back to me. "You cool?"

I blink and look down at my clothes for some reason. Like Serena's words somehow dirtied them. "Yeah. Yeah, I'm cool."

Faith nods at me, and she and the girls start to walk away. Wait, that's it? They come to my rescue, then just disappear? This isn't some superhero movie, and I wasn't trying to be a damsel in distress.

"Hold up," I call out. All four of them turn back around. I swallow down anything right I could possibly say in the moment. Faith lifts an eyebrow, expecting something.

"Thank you?" The words come out like a question. I wish I would've kept my mouth closed.

Faith nods again and waits to see if I have anything else.

"I'm Naomi," I say to the two girls I don't know, holding my hand against my chest in case they couldn't see me.

"We know," the short friend says with a grimace.

Faith elbows the short girl on her side. "This is Amari," she says, nodding to the short girl. Then she points to her friend with the honey-blond Brazilian weave. "And that's Mercedes. I think you already know Nevaeh."

I nod. "Yeah, we both had Mrs. Flythe for sixth-grade English, right?"

"Mm-hmm," Nevaeh says, staring down at her nails like she'd much rather be filing them than talking to me.

"She stayed coasting on Dizzy Drive," I say, trying to jog Nevaeh's memory. "Remember how she'd always lose her pencil in her hair? She'd be all, 'Where did I put it? I know I just had it.'" I give a weak laugh at my impression. Faith and her friends just stare at me. I try to think of something else flighty Mrs. Flythe did, but Faith's phone buzzes and saves me from making an even bigger ass of myself.

Faith smiles into her phone. "Cleo says we're good, y'all. She got us in."

"Yasss!" Mercedes says as she and the others do a syncopated shoulder dance.

Faith catches me watching them. "My cousin," she says, holding up her phone. "She's letting us roll with her to this social-justice event on her campus. Ebony Fire's performing there and everything."

My eyes get wide. "You get to see Ebony Fire in person?"

"Yeah, well, when your whole dance team is on suspension, you seem to have more free time on your hands," Nevaeh says with an eye roll.

"True that," Amari adds with her mouth cocked to one side.

Ten seconds ago, they were ready to throw hands for me, but now they're back to treating me like the annoying cousin at a cookout. I guess it's okay for people to talk shit about me when they don't look like Serena. I nod and take my seat again. They had a right to be pissed at Kylie and, by proxy, me too.

"Have fun," I say to Faith. I stir the granola into my yogurt, wishing I'd grabbed the chocolate-chip muffin I'd been eyeing instead.

"We will," Nevaeh says as she turns to walk away. Amari and Mercedes follow her, but not Faith. Faith scratches at the back of her head.

"Did you want to come or something?" she asks.

My heart stops. Did she mean it, or did she just notice how pathetic I was looking? Did I care? This was my chance to see an actual HBCU dance team in action. Up close and personal and not hunched over my phone or laptop watching recorded performances.

"Nuh-uh!" Amari shakes her head as she and the others stop in their tracks. "There ain't enough tickets."

"Girl, you know we don't need tickets," Faith says to her. Back to me: "Did you? We rolling through there right after school."

My mouth stretches to form the word *yes* just as my phone buzzes. Kylie. Again. And then it hits me.

"I have cheer practice." My shoulders deflate as I say the words out loud.

Amari and Nevaeh throw up their hands in annoyance and walk away. Mercedes laughs and follows them.

Faith shrugs at me. "Thought I'd offer." She jogs after her friends, who give her a mouthful. I don't have to hear them to know what they're saying. It's all in the wild gestures they aim back toward me as they head to the breakfast line to grab their food: *Why the hell would you even invite her?* As I swallow down my parfait alone, I wonder the same thing.

I get to my locker a few minutes before the first bell rings, and Kylie and Roma wait for me there. Roma taps at an invisible watch on her wrist.

"Where have you been?" Roma asks me.

"Breakfast," I mumble. I wait for Kylie to give me a tiny

wave or smile, but she leans against my locker and texts on her phone.

Roma scrunches her nose. "Ew." Then her eyebrows rise and iron out the wrinkle between her eyes. "Wait, did they have any of those sausage-stuffed-in-pancake things? My God, I could eat those every day."

"Because you're five," Kylie says. She stuffs her phone into her back pocket and graces me with eye contact. "Your phone dead? I texted you like a hundred times."

"That's a lot of texts." I motion my head at her to ask her to let me get in my locker. Kylie smirks and pushes herself off it.

"Did they ever find who did that?" Roma asks as I enter my combination.

"Nope," I say, grabbing what I need for first block. "But maybe I can make a TikTok about it. Wrap a handkerchief around my head, flip some pancakes. Maybe I could even serve Kylie breakfast in bed." Okay, maybe I was going harder than necessary this morning, but breakfast put me in a hard mood. Serena coming after me, the Wolverines inviting me to chill with them out of pity . . . And all for one reason: Kylie.

Kylie slams my locker door closed just as I grab the last book. I want to cuss her out for almost maiming my fingers, but she stares at me like she has never stared at me before.

Her face is flushed. Her eyes pinch at the corners. Her bottom lip trembles like she's about to go into a rage, but she isn't angry. Kylie gets still and cold when she's angry. She only gets this red, this wobbly, when she's about to cry. And I'm the one bringing her close to tears.

"For the record," she says, her jaw tight and controlled, "I took down that stupid video. That's what I've been trying to tell you all morning." She barely finishes her sentence before storming off toward the bathroom. And I know it's because she doesn't want anyone to see her cry. She doesn't want *me* to see her cry. Not when I'm the one who caused it.

"Look." Roma eclipses my view of the girls' bathroom door. "I don't know what's going on with you two, but fix it. Hanging out with only one of you is like sitting on a barstool with a shaky leg. You need all three of them to feel balanced."

I sigh, too tired to be the bigger person this time. "A lot of barstools have four legs."

"Bitch, you know what I mean." She pinches my arm. "Just do me a favor and make up by practice. You can't be a cheerleader if you're not cheery." She smiles at me before bopping toward her first class of the day. But her words trail behind her like the fumes from an exhaust pipe. Maybe I didn't feel like being cheery. Maybe I felt like setting everything on fire.

THIRTEEN

FAITH LOOKS JUST AS SURPRISED AS I DO WHEN I CATCH UP WITH HER after school in the parking lot. I didn't mention anything about going to Hampton University with her during physics class. Truth is, I didn't know I was going until about five minutes ago. I opened my locker to get my cheer shoes for practice, but my arms wouldn't lift to grab them. They *couldn't* lift. Just the thought of raising my arms seemed like a monumental task, like I had spent all day hoisting cement blocks over my shoulders and adding any more weight to them would rip me apart at the seams.

I wanted to feel whole.

"You have any room for me?" I ask, out of breath. I raced around the parking lot in a panic, fearing I wouldn't be able to find her in time.

Faith inspects me, and the corner of her mouth quirks a little, like she's trying not to smile. "Nevaeh and 'em are going to make you squeeze in the middle," she warns.

"That's fine. That's more than fine." I chew my top lip to keep it from moving and saying anything that'll make me sound too thirsty.

I follow Faith through the rows of departing cars until we reach an older white Chevrolet Cavalier. Mercedes is in the driver's seat, and Nevaeh and Amari are in the back, arguing over which song to stream from Mercedes's phone. They settle on a mid-tempo groove from Fousheé and sing along to it.

Faith opens the passenger's door and leans inside the car. "Ay, she's rolling with us."

Mercedes looks from Faith to me, then shrugs. "'Kay," she says.

"Nuh-uh!" Amari hollers from the back. "Ain't no room!"

"Girl, you acting like you got ass or something," Mercedes says to her.

Amari just crosses her arms across her chest and pouts. Faith folds the passenger seat forward, then raises her eyebrows at Nevaeh. Nevaeh stares back at Faith. Faith snaps her fingers at Nevaeh, all: *Get a move on.* Nevaeh lets out a groan to end all groans as she climbs out of the back seat.

"Thank you," I say to her.

Nevaeh looks away as I squeeze into the back seat next to Amari. I give Amari a smile. Amari sighs, then looks out the window. I nod and hug my shoulder bag against my lap as Nevaeh spills back into the car on the other side of me. Her hip stabs against mine, but she doesn't bother to scoot away. She takes up as much space as she wants to prove a point.

"Play nice back there, or Mercedes will turn this car around," Faith says with a smile as she gets into the car.

Nevaeh and Amari roll their eyes in unison. Mercedes peels out of the parking lot, and I watch as Windsor Woods High gets smaller and smaller in her rearview mirror.

There's this feeling you get when you spend time with a group of people who know each other well, but couldn't pick you out of a lineup. Even though we've lived in the same town since I can remember, Faith and her friends speak a different language than I do. Their inside jokes are buried deep in a capsule that only they have access to. But that's more on me than it is on them. My world has always consisted of Kylie and Connor. They were all I saw and all I needed. At least, I used to think so. There was a time back in sixth grade when Nevaeh tried to let me in. She wanted me to dance with her and some other girls for the Windsor Middle talent show.

"I be seeing you dance and stuff during PE," she told me. "You can keep up with me." She added that part with a smile. Even back then, her confidence could move mountains.

Kylie and I had already made plans to sing a Taylor Swift

song for the talent show. I never wanted to be a singer; neither did Kylie. But everyone back then was posting cover songs online, so we both figured: Why not? I told Nevaeh no without even thinking twice about it. Nevaeh didn't think twice about asking me to dance with her again. Not even at those middle school dances when everyone piled up in a big group to copy moves we found online. My group always included Kylie and Connor and Roma, and Nevaeh's included her people. Her people who were also my people, but I never joined. And now here I am, trying to make up for lost time. Like a duckling searching for a new mother after losing theirs.

In Mercedes's car, the most I can do is smile and nod as they trade barbs—not that anyone's speaking directly to me anyway. Every now and then, Faith looks back in my direction and I think she's going to smile or ask me a question, but then her eyes shift to one of her girls and they start kiki-ing without me again.

I stare straight ahead, watching Mercedes navigate through the traffic on 64. We'd survived being stuck behind a truck carrying pigs to slaughter on a one-way road before hitting the interstate, flecks of pig shit splattering her windshield like gnats. Once we hit the interstate, the scenery changed. Just like when Dorothy visits Oz and suddenly everything's in color. The traffic is thicker, the buildings are taller, and the drivers are more pressed to get to where they need to go. I lost count of how many times Mercedes shouted at someone who cut her off or honked a horn at her for driving the speed limit. It's ten miles per hour over the speed limit or more in the city. Us country girls take note.

When we reach the Hampton University campus, all the pig shit and road rage seem worth it. We aren't more than an hour away from Windsor but feel like we've traveled to a different world. Now I get the name of the TV show. The grass is greener. The buildings have cracks and character, like they're bursting at the seams with thousands and thousands of stories. And the people. Man, the people. They're every shade of brown under the rainbow. For once, I'm in a place where I'm not counting how many Black and Brown faces I see. I don't have enough fingers and toes for that here. And it's all just an hour away. That's it. It takes everything in me to not bump into a student or a piece of architecture as I try to digest as much as I can while we trek across campus, looking for the event we've been invited to. Or they've been invited to. I'm an all-too-eager party crasher.

"There's Cleo," Faith says, pointing at a group of students near the edge of the courtyard in the middle of campus. I almost ask which one she is, but somehow, I already know. At the center of the group is a girl with Senegalese braids that are pulled back into a faux-hawk. She wears a T-shirt with only the first names of boss-ass Black women: *Harriet. Ida. Rosa. Coretta.* And everyone gravitates around her as if one day, they wouldn't be surprised if her name was added to the shirt. She stands with her shoulders back and chin up as if she knows this.

The girl who I assume is Cleo looks in our direction and then waves us over. Faith and the rest of us push through the crowd until we reach her.

"Hey, big head," Cleo says to Faith. "Took your ass long enough."

"We left right after school," Faith insists. "Why didn't you tell me it would be so hard to find a place to park?"

Cleo clasps her hand to her chest. "Nowhere to park on a college campus? Who would've guessed?" Her eyes land on me. "Who you?"

My name gets lodged in my throat for some reason. Like I haven't learned how to talk to people in college yet.

"This is Naomi," Faith answers for me. "She's cool."

I try not to blink in shock. Did Faith really just call me *cool*? From how she ignored me during the whole drive here, I'd figure I was the complete opposite of that. So opposite I was boiling.

Cleo looks like she's about to say something else to me when a guy whose Afro is so voluminous that it rivals Colin Kaepernick's taps her on the arm. "They starting," he says.

Cleo pats the air, directing the group around her to shut up and sit. So we do, shuffling around and taking seats on the pavement, the grass, the stone benches. Somehow I find myself on the bench squeezed between Cleo and the dude with the Kaepernick 'fro.

A light-skinned guy with a shaved head stands in the center of the courtyard holding a megaphone. "We know why we're here!" he shouts into the megaphone. Just like Coach Beverly, he doesn't need the extra volume. The megaphone pops and sizzles from the impact of his voice. "For far too long, they've tried to keep the Black man down!"

Everyone claps and hollers in response, as if they all know who the "they" is the guy's referring to.

"But as I stare out at all these beautiful, melanated faces with these brilliant, melanated minds, I understand. John Anderson is scared of us. He knows what we can do, what we can be! Guess what? He *should* be scared. They all should be!"

Everyone cheers again, so I raise my hands to clap, too, even though I have no clue who this John Anderson person is.

Cleo leans over to me. "Anderson's the teacher in Newport News who cut his seventh-grade student's dreadlocks," she says in my ear. I guess I wasn't hiding my confusion as well as I thought. "It's been all over the news this week."

"Oh yeah," I say, as if I suddenly remembered. Truth is, I've been avoiding social media as much as possible for the past few days.

The guy with the megaphone goes on and on about this

teacher. How we all need to march to the next Newport News school board meeting and demand that the teacher be fired. The crowd continues to gas him up, cheering each time he shouts something in dramatic fashion. I keep clapping too. A part of me gets it. Nobody has the right to put their hands on someone else's hair. I think about Mrs. Brooks's fingers on my curls. She's family, but even that tiny gesture felt intrusive, like she walked in on me as I was stepping out of the shower. But then there's this small part of me, the size of a tick and buried under layers of empathy, that wonders about the full story. This teacher couldn't be just walking around with a pair of scissors ready to butcher any hairstyle he hated.

Right?

". . . and now, I want to thank our lovely sisters of Ebony Fire for joining us tonight and bringing attention to the cause. Let's give it up for them, y'all!"

The women of Ebony Fire strut out into the center of the courtyard as Kendrick Lamar's "Humble" bangs out of a large speaker. The crowd cheers again, but the volume, the *energy*, feels different. A switch has been flipped and turns all the electricity in the air from static into something dynamic. Something that weaves through all the whooping and hollering and sizzles into a battle cry. And it reaches me too. As Ebony Fire throws their bodies around to the *boom, boom, boom* of the speakers, the bass line scratches at my fingers, my spine. Until I'm remembering their movements from all the YouTube videos and completing the choreography in my head—every now and then a move escaping into my hands and shoulders.

I hardly notice that I'm dancing a little until I catch Cleo watching me, her eyebrows lifted in amusement.

"Sorry," I mutter, folding my hands across my lap to keep them still.

Cleo shakes her head. "Never apologize for shining, queen," she says to me.

She turns back to watch the dance team, but the word *queen* flutters over my head like a crown. I raise my chin to keep the crown steady.

Everyone's still buzzing after the rally as we crush into two booths at a Wingstop near campus. Cleo, a light-skinned girl with freckles across her cheeks, and the dude with the epic 'fro who I heard Cleo call Butter sit across from me, Faith, and Nevaeh. Amari and Mercedes are at the other booth with the rest of Cleo's friends. Most of the guys, actually, with their HU hoodies and peach fuzz and college IDs. Amari and Mercedes grin and giggle like they're front row at a Giveon concert.

A waiter comes over and places our order on the table. Good thing, because I'm starving. It's like I was the one out in the courtyard, flinging my body around and working up a sweat. Nevaeh pokes at one of her wings and smirks.

"Why couldn't we eat on campus? I already know what Wingstop tastes like," she complains.

"You not missing much," Cleo says as she swirls sugar into her iced tea with her straw. She then pokes at her ice cubes, making them bob up and down in the tan liquid. I realize that I'm watching her about three seconds past awkward and drizzle some sauce onto my wings. She makes the most mundane tasks seem extraordinary. I bet she even folds laundry with a little bit of swag.

"Lies. You know our sloppy joes go hard," the girl with the freckles says.

"What you need to do is invite your cousin to the student center on Friday afternoons," Butter says. He's already going to town on his wings. He even licks one of his thumbs, not even bothering to impress any of us.

"Why? What's Friday afternoons?" Faith asks.

"We throw a party there from twelve to two. The place gets turnt. We're all pregaming for the weekend."

"That's what's up," Faith says. She and Nevaeh slap each other a five, all giddy.

Cleo cocks her head at Faith. "The only thing that's 'up' on Friday afternoons is high school for you, big head. You have to graduate first before you can party with the grown folk."

Faith rolls her eyes and sinks into the booth, her joy officially deflated.

Cleo smiles at Faith's dramatics. "So . . . what did you think about this afternoon?" It takes me a moment to realize that she's talking to me. The quiet girl pouring way too much honey mustard on her wings.

"They were amazing," I say, wiping my hands on a napkin. "They were flawless and rugged at the same time. They all moved like they loved what they were doing. They loved the eyes on them. You can tell a lot of them trained all their lives just to be part of Ebony Fire. It probably feels like winning the lottery to make the team."

I lean back in my seat, out of breath from all my fangirling. Cleo and her friends glance at each other, then start snickering. Faith and Nevaeh shift in the booth next to me, the awkwardness at the table enough to make them itch. I pat a napkin against my mouth, making sure there was no honey mustard on my face, even though I haven't even taken a bite of my wing yet.

"We were talking about the rally in general," Butter says to me. "The cause. Ebony Fire are always on point, but they were there for a reason. The same reason we all were there. At least, most of us." He raises a skeptical eyebrow at me, and I hold on to the edge of the table to stop myself from crawling underneath the booth until it's time to go.

"You can't fault the girl for showing love to EF," Cleo says, then turns to me. "It looked like you wanted to run out there and join them. Was I tripping, or did you actually know some of the moves?"

I give a sheepish shrug. "I've been studying them online. Some of their eight counts are the same, but they hit them differently depending on the song they dance to."

"What you mean?"

"Sometimes they're flirty; sometimes they're aggressive. It all depends on the bass line and lyrics. A hip swirl for Rihanna is a buck for J. Cole." I pick up a wing to take a bite when I notice that eyes are on me. Everyone at the table. Staring at me with varying shades of curiosity. I tend to do that when I talk about dance. The motions make more sense in my head and my body than they do in my mouth. I drop my chicken and pull out my phone. "I can show you better than tell you."

I go to my Photos app to find my Dance folder. The one where I store all the clips of me strutting like a Dancing Doll or bucking like a J-Sette. My fingers twitch as I find one of my better dancing clips, as if they're trying to stop me from embarrassing myself. The only people who have ever laid eyes on my dancing videos are me, myself, and I. Yet here I am, about to peel off my skin and bare my soul to a table filled with strangers. But something about Cleo's vibe and curiosity makes me want to take that leap.

I find one of the routines that I did to a Playboi Carti song and press Play. Think about leaving my phone on the table and running off to the bathroom until it's over.

"Yo, is that 'Magnolia'?" the girl with the freckles asks over the music.

Cleo nudges her. "Quiet, Neesa. Just watch."

I swallow and turn up the volume on the video. Watch as my hips sway back and forth to the beat like a pendulum, my arms rocking with them. Watch as I dip lower, hips now thrusting back and forth to the beat. Arms pumping like I am ready to knock down doors. My eyes close for a few beats, getting lost in the rhythm as I buck like my life depends on it. As the melody shifts, my arms pour out of me like milk as my booty popping evolves into slow body rolls. Video Me copies the fluid movements of the Dancing Dolls from Southern University, smooth and graceful like a ballerina. I made sure to end my routine on a high note, stretching my right leg up to my ear and holding the pose for a few seconds. Then, in the most dramatic fashion, I fall from the frame into a death drop.

"Yooo!" Neesa and her freckles slap her hands together hard, over and over. More applause above my head. I look up and notice that the group from other booth had made its way over to scope out my video as well. Whooping and hollering. For me. I even see Mercedes giving me snaps. I give a small smile and squeeze the phone back into my pocket.

"Not bad," Cleo says. But her smile's so wide and saying more than just "not bad." I don't push, though. Something tells me that a "not bad" is impressive from Cleo. "You all must keep her in the front for everything."

"She's not a Wolverine," Faith says, eyeballing me like I've just grown two heads. "Naomi's a cheerleader."

"Cheerleader?" Butter repeats, his face a huge question mark.

"Yeah," I say. I think about running off to hide out in the bathroom again. *Cheerleader* sounds like a dirty word in their mouths. Almost as bad as *sellout*. "I've only been doing it for a few years." Six, actually. I still feel Kylie's hand squeezing mine as we showed up to our first tryouts in sixth grade. Sweat sealing them together and her nails digging into my palm. I still hear the squelching noise when our hands separated after being glued together for so long.

"Too bad that's not the video you uploaded onto Tik-Tok," Nevaeh says, sipping on her lemonade. Might as well have been tea. Faith cocks her head at her, disapproving.

Neesa snaps her fingers and points at me. "I knew you looked familiar! You're that girl clowning around with Parking Lot Becky." Her realization seems to bounce off the walls of the restaurant and slap me right in the face. I slink farther into the seat.

Butter looks at me and lets out one of those laughs that come out like a quick cough, all self-righteous and judgy. It's only then that I notice he has dimples. It would be cute if he didn't flash them to mock me. Nevaeh side-eyes Faith. Even though I still don't speak their language, her message is loud and clear: *Told you not to invite her.*

I don't speak for the rest of dinner. I barely even hear what everyone's talking about. There's a lot of laughter and shouting over each other in the way Black folks do when we all get together. The Black joy spreads throughout the entire restaurant, but somehow, I'm immune to it.

I linger next to Mercedes's car in the parking lot as everyone says their goodbyes to each other. Amari and Mercedes try to get the guys' numbers, and Faith and Nevaeh hug Cleo goodbye. Finally, Faith and her friends pour into Mercedes's white car, and I take a breath, preparing for the uncomfortable ride back home. I text my mom that I'll be home in about an hour. I hope she texts back soon so I can spend the whole way home engaging in small talk with her. Anything's better than silence.

I wait my turn to climb into the car when Cleo walks over to me.

"CleoWarrior29," she says to me. I blink, confused. "I don't do TikTok, but I'm on IG a lot. Holler at me if you want to know more about HU."

"Oh. Th-thank you," I stammer.

She holds up a fist to me, all Black power, before strolling to her car. I squeeze back into Mercedes's back seat and hug my shoulder bag against me again. My mom texts me back:

MOM: *Have a good time?*

ME: *YES.*

I rest my head on the seat behind me. Everything's tight back here, but as Mercedes bumps music from her speaker, all I want to do is swing my hips. Get lost in the music again.

FOURTEEN

BY THE TIME FRIDAY ROLLS AROUND, I STILL CAN'T GET MY TIME AT HU—
my time with Cleo—out of my mind. I followed her on
Instagram as soon as I got home. I would've followed her as
soon as I got into Mercedes's car, but I didn't want to come
across *that* thirsty. It took her two days, but Cleo followed me
back. To say her pictures were inspiring would be an under-
statement. Every picture she posted was a slice of a larger
theme. There was a black-and-white image of the backs of
Black guys' heads, showing a variation of hairstyles: fades,
locs, and Afro puffs. A colorful close-up of her T-shirt fea-
turing a Black woman's face with words scribbled across it:
Innovative. Powerful. Unapologetic. A reposting of a Black
mother embracing her son, tears streaming down both their

cheeks as if they've just survived the unimaginable. All her pictures were about Black pain. Black joy. Black magic.

But she posted my favorite picture on Thursday night. An image of the ladies of Ebony Fire, their eyes closed and arms stretched wide, frozen in the thrill of a dance move. Even when they weren't in motion, they were breathtaking. And Cleo must've known I would feel this way, because she tagged me in her post. She tagged *me*.

That's what did it. What gave me the last push to do something I've wanted to for months. Hell, probably since Nevaeh asked me to dance with her back in sixth grade, but my default mode was Kylie. On Friday morning, I tell Connor he doesn't have to pick me up for school. He'd been driving me a lot this week, especially since Kylie and me weren't a Kylie and me for the moment. But I wanted to get to school early and alone so I wouldn't back out of what I was about to do.

I wait at my locker for her. About five minutes before the first bell rings, Faith makes her way down the hall. She takes her time getting to her locker, adjusting her earbuds and scrolling through her phone, probably searching for the perfect song to get her ready for the day. She pauses when she spots me spotting her, takes out an earbud, and raises an eyebrow: *Yeah?*

"I want to try out for the Wolverines," I say to her.

Now she takes out her other earbud. "Come again?"

"Good morning," I say. Rinse, repeat. "I want to try out for the Wolverines."

"That's what I thought you said. But you know we haven't been able to practice all week, right?"

I wait for her to give me a look. A smirk to remind me that it's my best friend's fault that they haven't been able to dance. But she just opens her locker and rummages through it like she does every morning.

"Plus, our tryouts were cut short from the suspension. I don't even know if Ms. Denita is looking for anyone else to join."

I had a feeling that might be the case, but I remember the script I rehearsed in my head and push forward. "I was hoping that maybe you could mention me to her. You know, since you were able to see what I could do."

Faith's face scrunches up. "I saw a short clip of you do some booty popping and body rolls. It was cute, but Wolverines aren't just cute. We're fierce."

"I can be fierce." My voice comes out as a whine. The antithesis of fierce.

The side of Faith's mouth rises in skepticism.

"Look, I'm just asking for a chance. Just get me in front of Ms. Denita and the girls. I could even be an alternate or whatever."

Two thin Black guys I recognize in passing start snickering a few steps away from me. From the way they sneer at me,

I already know what's coming.

"Massa let you in the house today, mammy?" one of them says to me.

I look down at my feet, pretend I don't hear him. Even though Kylie took the video down, there were still memes—both online and in the minds of my classmates. The school had finally repainted my locker, but now the color was so striking that my blue looked radioactive compared with the lockers surrounding mine. A constant reminder that it had been defaced. A constant reminder that I was different.

"We're in a school, not a house. Maybe you need a mammy to tell you the difference," Faith snaps to the boys.

The guy who made the comment smirks and grabs at his crotch, the laziest of rebuttals.

"But what you grabbing, though?" Faith taunts.

The other guy cackles and points at his friend as they ease down the hall. I exhale a little once they're out of sight. I can't let out a complete sigh. Even if Faith stood up for me, once again she was reminded that I was a pariah. Who would want to be on a team with the Black girl all the other Black students here hated?

Faith pushes her locker closed. "I'll see what I can do," she says, then walks to class and doesn't look back at me. I hug one of my textbooks against my chest and smile. It wasn't a yes, but I'll take it.

✳ ✳ ✳

I try not to grit my teeth as Kylie pushes through the dresses on one of the racks at Macy's. I never realized how grating the sound of plastic hangers against metal rods truly is, but Kylie filters through the dresses with such force I'm sure everyone in the store's teeth are tingling.

"What about that red fit and flare?" Roma tries, placing her hand on the rack to stop Kylie's aggressive hunt.

Kylie shakes her head. "Jared doesn't look good in red." She throws her head back and lets out a groan. "Why do all these dresses *suck*? What about you? Have you and Connor decided what colors you're wearing for homecoming?"

It takes me a few seconds to register that she's speaking to me. The car ride to Macy's was filled with prolonged pauses and loud music to drown out the prolonged pauses. Roma had texted me the night before to remind me of our dress-shopping date. Without our car rides to school and the space that Mom wanted between me and Kylie, my interactions with Kylie consisted only of tiny waves in the hallway when one of us caught the other one staring. My skipping out on cheer tryouts this week didn't do us any favors. I told Coach Beverly that I had the worst menstrual cramps ever, and the look Coach gave me in return seemed to ask why I dared to even have a uterus. But at least Coach wanted answers. Kylie didn't even have the right questions for me all week.

"Oh. We haven't really talked about it," I say to her. I rub my fingers across the glittery mesh of one of the dresses on the rack just to give them something to do. Kylie and I didn't do awkward, so navigating it felt as bumpy and out of place as . . . the glittery mesh on this dress.

"Really? Hasn't he been escorting you to school for the past few days?"

"He hasn't been escorting me. He volunteered to give me rides," I correct.

"So, what? You guys didn't talk about anything?"

"Maybe they didn't do much talking at all?" Roma's eyebrows dance up and down, and Kylie pretends to gag.

I laugh and give her a small push. "We just didn't talk about homecoming," I say. We talked about everything else. Like the charley horse he got after practice on Wednesday and the new Dua Lipa song that I hated but couldn't get out of my head. And deeper stuff like what summer might look like before we go off to college—and the summers after that. He was leaning toward Princeton or Duke because of their strong wrestling programs. I didn't tell him about my Howard or Hampton plans. I could see the miles between our schools as he spoke, and I didn't want to put any more distance between us until we needed to.

"Well, he hasn't been talking to or about anyone else," Kylie continues.

I bump into a clothing rack. "He talks about me? To *you*?"

Kylie pinches her lips together like she's thinking carefully about how to answer my questions, then shrugs because she remembers she's still kind of salty at me. "Not really. But he doesn't talk about anyone else to me either, so . . ."

I blink. "That doesn't sound like a ringing endorsement." Connor stopped talking to Kylie about girls five years ago, right after Kylie and I tagged along on his "date" with Emma Huff at Mr. Brooks's bowling alley. We spent the night telling Emma how Connor used to have a booger wall next to his bed.

"Maybe if you weren't making yourself so scarce, you two would have a chance to talk about it," Kylie says. She takes a lavender dress and holds it against her. "What do you guys think?"

"It's purple," Roma says. "I thought purple reminded you of eggplants. You hate eggplants."

Kylie groans again. "Ugh, you're right. I can't walk around the whole night looking like a hard-on." She tries to put the dress back on the rack, but I step in her way. She's not getting off that easily.

"What do you mean I've been scarce?" I ask.

"I mean your presence has been lacking. Isn't that the definition of scarce?" She strolls around me and returns the dress to the rack. She's so unbothered that a meteor could crack through the ceiling and she wouldn't even flinch. Her calmness makes me want a meteor to fall right on her head.

"Just because I haven't been around you doesn't mean I've

been scarce. It means I have a life."

"Really? What have you been up to?" She steps away from the dresses and folds her arms across her chest, challenging me. I hate how well she still knows me. Excluding my Tuesday night at Hampton University, I've spent my time getting through school or skipping out on cheer practice. Aside from stalking Cleo on Instagram, my car rides and phone calls with Connor were the highlights of my day. But spending time with her twin isn't the most riveting thing to Kylie.

I fold my arms across my chest too. "I don't have to tell you anything. Just like you didn't tell me about your adventure in the Target parking lot until the whole world found out." If she wants to play dirty, so can I.

Kylie narrows her eyes at me. I know that look. She's plotting the ruin of both me and my firstborn child. Being on the receiving end of it is a little chilling, actually, but I don't dare let Kylie see me shiver. I stand up straighter, wait for Kylie to flinch first.

"Insufficient to satisfy a need or demand."

Kylie and I peel our eyes away from each other to look at Roma. She holds her phone up to us.

"The definition of *scarce*. I googled it," she says.

I shrug at her: *Really? Now?*

Kylie huffs and snatches an emerald dress off the rack. "I'm trying this on," she says. More to herself than to us, since she's already walking toward the dressing rooms.

Once she's fully out of sight, Roma tugs at my arm. "This is supposed to be fun. It's our last homecoming dance of high school. We've only been talking about this since forever."

I return to reviewing the dresses, even though my heart isn't into it anymore. It hasn't been into it this whole afternoon, actually. There's a space there for Kylie that's turned the beating in my chest into a murmur, and it needs to be repaired before I can fully put my heart into anything around her.

"Lots has changed since forever," I say.

"But why?" Roma asks. "Kylie messed up. You messed up. That's what we're supposed to do right now. My mom says that high school is the time for fucking up. You guys are doing it right, so let's just kiss, make up, and move on to the next fuckup. Please." She clasps both hands together, like she's grabbing onto what she can of our friendship.

I sigh and continue to lazily push through the dresses. Any other time, I would take that olive branch without any hesitation, but what Kylie and I were experiencing was more than just a usual high school fuckup. There was a wedge between us, and we needed a forklift to remove it.

"Seriously, Naomi. It's not the same without you around. And she's too stubborn to admit it, but Kylie misses you too. She brings you up all the time."

"What? To talk shit?" I ask.

"Talking shit is still talking, right?" She tugs my arm

again. This time, gentler—like a shy kid trying to get their parent's attention. "But don't you miss us too? Miss *her*? Just a little bit?"

All I can do is look down at the dress I happen to have my hands on. Of course, I missed them. I missed Kylie. Even though I had the time of life seeing Ebony Fire earlier this week, the first thing I thought about doing was FaceTiming Kylie about it. There was so much joy rumbling inside me that I needed to let out, even if I didn't have the right words for it. But with Kylie, I never really needed words. I could look at her with wide eyes and a stupid grin, and she'd feel exactly what I felt. Without her around this week, I had to attach words to my feelings—and I had a limited vocabulary.

Thankfully, I don't have to admit any of this to Roma. My phone chimes, and I get a new text message from Faith:

Ms. Denita wants to see you dance on Monday. Be ready.

My heart pounds at the message. Is this an official tryout? Do I get to pick my own music? My own choreography? Just as I'm typing in some of these questions, Faith shoots another text:

But you need to check your fam.

She sends a link underneath her last message.

"Who's that?" Roma asks.

I don't answer. I click on the link, and it leads me to a TikTok. Connor and Weston pop up on my screen. Connor's hair is longer, so this must've been filmed two years ago when he went through his brief emo period. Connor and Weston are laughing like crazy, as if they started recording mid-joke.

"Say it again," someone says off-screen. Brian, more than likely. The three of them are usually attached at the hip.

CONNOR: Why is it when I'm around Black people, I start speaking all ghetto?
WESTON: I don't know, mane.
CONNOR: Fo sho, shawty.
WESTON: Fo shizzle, my nizzle.
CONNOR: Deez nuts, yo!
WESTON: Hands up, don't shoot!

Connor and Weston crack up laughing again. The video pauses, then replays on its own, as if I need to see it again with my own eyes to believe it. I want to stop it. I need to stop it. But every muscle in my hand, my whole body, tenses, and I can't even raise my thumb to close the window.

"The hell is that?" Roma asks, next to me. She snatches the phone from my hand and glares at the screen, her face hardening as the video continues. "This is fucking disgusting." She turns to me to cosign her sentiments, but I'm still frozen. Still clenched. Was that really Connor? *My* Connor? The one who loves watching Jordan Peele movies with me. The one who calls my mom Mama Nina. The one who couldn't stop telling me I was beautiful last Saturday as he cupped my face and kissed my lips. There he was on my phone, mocking people who look like me. My people. Even after Roma stops the video, his laughter still lingers in my ears. Taunting me for being such a fool.

Roma places her hand on my back, and I flinch. "You okay?" she asks.

My response gets lodged in my chest, burning a hole that no amount of antacid could fix right now.

"Okay, what do y'all think?" Kylie struts out the dressing room with her emerald dress and pink lips and blond hair and clueless twin brother. She blinks at Roma and me when we don't immediately fawn over her. "What happened?"

That's what I'd like to know.

FIFTEEN

IF LAST WEEKEND FELT LIKE A DREAM, THIS WEEKEND IS A NONSTOP
night terror. Screams and cold sweats and restlessness. Instead
of kissing Connor on a beach, this Saturday I huddle in my
room under the covers, scrolling through tweets and memes
and GIFs going in on Connor. Local Black Twitter wasn't
playing any games, digging up more dirt and finding long-
buried tweets from Connor that hadn't aged well:

Lizzo > Skinny Adele #badbitchoclock #thickthirty

I love me some Popeyes chicken. Does that make me
black???

On the real, if you didn't know who Obama was and he
called you up, you'd think he was some white dude from
Montana. #BigFacts

Each reveal makes me want to throw up, but I keep sifting through them. Keep scrolling. I. Can't. Stop. It's almost a need. The more I search, the more I'd hoped I'd find a loophole. Proof to all the haters that someone hacked Connor's account. That the stuff I was reading wasn't coming from the same guy I used to eat dinner with almost every night. He was an imposter. A poorly drawn sketch, when the Connor I knew was smart and funny and multidimensional. I mean, I'd have noticed these questionable tweets before, right? Unless . . . unless I'd been too blinded to slap on glasses and really see them. I'd probably been too quick to toss them aside as playful banter. That's how everyone talked in Windsor Woods. We take cheap shots, and then it's all kumbaya and grabbing a bite to eat at Dairy Queen. Me and Kylie and the rest of the squad. Mom and Mrs. Brooks and Mrs. Brooks's sorority sisters, when they were in town. There couldn't be a divide if we were all blended together, breaking bread.

But Connor's tweets hit differently post–Target parking lot. And folks online are hinting that maybe something's rotten in the Brooks abode. It's enough to make me want to grab Connor by the shoulders and shake him. Scream at him like a Tyra Banks GIF: *I was rooting for you. We were all rooting for you!*

My sleuthing is interrupted only by Connor himself. He tries calling me on Saturday. Multiple times. Like fifty-six-missed-calls amount of times. And then there are the string of texts:

I've been trying to reach you. Can you hit me up?

Is your phone working?

Okay, I think you're pissed at me. If you pick up, I can explain.

Ny, please . . . talk to me.

On Sunday, he actually rolls up to my apartment. Eric does his customary three knocks and a pause before cracking my door open. He finds me, leaning against my headboard with my laptop balanced on top of my thighs. I chew on a Snickers Ice Cream Bar for lunch, caramel and cream dripping down to my knuckles.

"Connor's out there," Eric tells me.

I blink and jolt upright, almost knocking my laptop to the floor. "Where? In the living room?"

Eric gives me a look, all: *Yeah, right.* "Your mom's talking to him at the front door. She asked me to see if you're available."

I didn't give Mom the full story about Connor, but she gathered a summary. Mainly from my clipped responses when she asked whether I was hanging with him again this weekend. My pinched face as I jerked my head no was enough to tell her that she couldn't be inviting Connor in all willy-nilly per usual.

I almost glance in my vanity mirror to give myself a quick

once-over, to make sure I look presentable enough to flirt. But the tweets and TikToks come flooding back, almost like they're right there on my computer screen again.

I settle back against my headboard. "I'm not," I say, then lick ice cream from my fingertips.

Eric gives me a nod, impressed. "You want me to get rid of him?" I knew what he meant by that, but I didn't want Connor to find out what Eric meant by that. I hadn't reached the point of wanting to scare Connor. Not until I heard the full story. But I didn't want to hear his side today.

"Just let Mom handle it, please," I say to Eric.

Eric pretends to snap his fingers in disappointment, then gives me a wink. I listen as Eric relays the news. Mom's gentle voice as she says something kind and motherly to Connor. Connor's muffled voice right before he retreats. I climb off my bed and pull back the curtains on my window. Watch as Connor walks to his silver Audi, hands stuffed into the pockets of his jeans. He pauses at his car door, and for a moment I think he's about to look up and spot me. But he just tousles his hair, almost like he's pissed at it for daring growing on top of his head, then spills into the driver's seat. I watch as he drives away.

I was this close to playing sick so I wouldn't have to see the fallout in school on Monday. Online was torture, but walking the school halls would be Dante's inferno. I could already imagine the shade, the smirks. The . . . fights?

But then I remembered the Wolverines. Faith said Ms. Denita was giving me a chance, and I wasn't about to give that up. Not when I saw the amazing things dance teams could do at the college level. The Wolverines were the only thing to get me out of bed that weekend. In between my incessant scrolling, I choreographed a two-minute piece to show some of my best moves. At least I hope they're my best.

I survive breakfast by taking a muffin to the school counseling office. It's probably time to get started on these college applications, so what other time to start them than when I'm trying to avoid all things Brooks and bias? I talk to my school counselor, Mrs. Song, all relaxed smiles and bright optimism because she's fresh from her maternity leave. A chunky beige baby smiles at me from the framed picture on her desk.

"He just turned four months," she explains when she catches me eyeballing the cherub. "I swear to you, I'm seeing his personality already. I tripped after putting him in his stroller the other day, and I kid you not, that little guy laughed at me. I have a jokester on my hands."

I smile, even though I'm guessing he probably just had gas. Mom says that about the little ones when I catch one of them giving me a toothless grin. But still, it must be neat to not have a care in the world other than sleeping and eating and pooping. Squeezing in moments to laugh at your mom. Not worrying about tweets or TikTok or turmoil. Good vibes only. Lucky kid.

We come up with a timeline to get all my applications done. Mrs. Song is "thrilled" about my decision to apply to a few HBCUs. "My husband is a graduate from North Carolina A&T," she told me. "Go Aggies!" I never knew Mrs. Song's husband was Black—just assumed she'd married someone Korean like her, especially because of her last name and all. Then again, I've never asked her about her personal life. I haven't been asking questions for a long time, period.

I ask Mrs. Song if I can come back during my lunch period to research scholarship opportunities. "Absolutely!" she sings, just like someone who's had only an infant to talk to for months. "But I'll also see you in a few minutes."

When I get to first block, I find out what Mrs. Song means. We're all instructed to go to the gym for an assembly. Each class level is squeezed into its respective section on the bleachers. The senior class has the fewest students, so at least we're not sweating on top of each other. We have attrition to thank for that. Principal Hicks and Ms. Guy stand in the center of the humid gym and preach to us the merits of community and acceptance.

"You can't spell *Windsor* without *W-I-N*," Principal Hicks shouts into a microphone. "And you know how we win? By fighting bigotry and engaging in anti-racist efforts."

Fuuck, kill me now.

I try not to, but I find myself searching for familiar faces. Drew, Phil. The girls from the squad. The twins. Dammit, I still look for the twins. I can't find Connor, and I can't help but wonder if that's on purpose. This assembly seems to be triggered by his past actions, so he probably got a heads-up to steer clear. Hang out in the clinic or something. I find Kylie sandwiched between Jared and Roma two rows above me. Kylie keeps her head down, texting on her phone like her life depends on it. Anything to avoid the scrutinizing eyes of people who know that she, also, is to blame for this hour of torture.

Ms. Guy introduces Serena Warren to sing a cover of Christina Aguilera's "Beautiful." Serena struts to the microphone in leather shorts and a shimmery blouse. She came to school prepared. She sways side to side during the musical intro, then moves into power stance to begin belting out the lyrics. She doesn't even give the song time to warm up. She goes full throttle on the first chord. I groan and look back at Kylie and Roma. I can't help it. I need to see Kylie's face during this completely affected and completely inorganic performance. Kylie's still staring down at her phone, chewing her thumbnail like she's reading something important. Jared, though, leans forward, mouthing the words along with Serena like a stage dad. Good thing Kylie's preoccupied. Roma catches me looking at them. She makes a stabbing motion at one of her ears.

I laugh and turn back around.

Somehow, I make it to the final bell of the day, and my

stomach flip-flops for a good reason. It's time for my tryout for the Wolverines. I didn't have time to stress about it during the day, too nervous to cross any invisible lines that have been formed within the school that the assembly did nothing to erase. I made it through the day unscathed by keeping my head buried in a book and my own business minded.

Needless to say, I let out a silent groan when I spot Kylie waiting for me at my locker.

She looks down at a novel she's holding as students push past her; a few linger to shake their heads and suck their teeth in her direction. Kylie seems to have read the same survival guidebook as I did, because everyone knows that Kylie prefers to watch the movie rather than complete the assigned reading. She senses my presence and lifts her head.

"Hey," she says to me, her voice so tiny that I read her lips to follow what she's saying.

"Hey," I say back, just as quiet.

"Connor's been trying to reach you."

I lean against my locker and let out a breath. He even tried to reach me at school today. Calling my name down the hall as I beelined it to my next class or the school counseling office. I'm still not ready to talk to him—especially in front of so many judging eyes. "He sent you to tell me that?"

"No, he doesn't know I'm talking to you."

Someone coughs something in Kylie's direction. I can't

make out what they say, and she probably can't either, but she presses herself against the locker next to mine as if she wants to hide in it.

"Coach Beverly told me you quit cheer," she says once her nerves return.

I nod, remembering me drafting the email this morning as I sat on the curb and waited for the school bus. My fingers moving like they were on fire because if I slowed down, I'd lose my nerve. I rewrote the last few lines at least five times:

I want to thank you—for believing in me these past three years. For challenging me when I thought I couldn't. For warning me when I thought I could. You have played a seminal role in the girl I am, and the woman I've become. I hope you understand my decision to say goodbye at this time, but I know you have an amazing squad of ladies who'll do right by you this year.

All the best,

Naomi Henry

I hit Send and shoved my phone into my bag so I wouldn't have to look at it anymore. But I stared at my bag. Studied it. I had just smuggled a bomb in there, and I waited for my world to explode. After a few seconds, my phone chimed and I jumped. A yelp even escaped my mouth. Coach Beverly had already sent me a response: *Got it.*

Got it. That's it. The whole email had to be three paragraphs long. I probably even included a thesis statement. There's no way she read the whole thing in that brief amount of time. Yet, she got it. She got it, and I laughed. I laughed until the bus finally rolled up, and the driver gave me the side-eye, probably wondering what I was on. I didn't care, though. I was better than high. I was free.

"Are you sure, though?" Kylie moves closer to me in the hallway. "She told me we both made varsity. Even with you flaking all last week, she knew what you were capable of."

"I didn't flake. I just . . ." I think about summarizing the reasons I gave to Coach Beverly, but I couldn't. Not to Kylie. She'd smell the bullshit on them before I got my sentence out. So, I keep it real. "I didn't want it anymore."

Kylie's forehead crumples. "Is it because of me? Is it because of Connor?"

No. Yes. All of the above. "It's because of me," I say instead. "That's all."

Kylie's mouth opens and closes so quickly it's like her lips blink. I wait for her to say whatever she's dying to say, but she just nods. She turns to walk away, then looks over her shoulder. "It won't be the same without you." She doesn't wait for my response, just scurries away like a draft is carrying her off.

I almost drift with her . . . then remember I have somewhere to be.

✳ ✳ ✳

"Okay, let us know when to cue the music," Ms. Denita tells me as she joins the other Wolverines on the bleachers in the gym.

I take a deep breath and shake out my arms, my legs. If I shake them hard enough, maybe some of these nerves can dance away. It's a good thing that today the cheer squad has the football field. I couldn't handle their squinted eyes toward me, murmuring things about me being a traitor. It's bad enough that the Wolverines glare at me for taking away a few minutes of their practice time. Practice time taken away from them for the past week because of my best friend. I scan the crossed arms, the curled lips, and even the occasional eye roll to find at least one inviting face. I spot Faith leaning against the bottom bleacher, her legs crossed at the ankles. She gives me a tiny nod, though she must be hiding a smile in her pocket or something. But a nod is close enough.

I give a thumbs-up, and Ms. Denita's assistant, Rico, presses something on his phone. Michael Jackson's "Wanna Be Startin' Somethin'" starts bumping out of the Bluetooth speaker and immediately reaches my feet. The choreography I've practiced all weekend seeps through me, and I pour it all out on the gym floor. I make sure to kick my feet a little higher, pop my back a little harder. If my hair actually bounced, I would've whipped it sharp enough to take an eye out. I make sure to dance more gracefully, but also tougher than I've ever danced in my life. These two minutes are worth a lifetime. When I end with a split, I make sure to throw my body so hard against the floor that deep-sea divers could feel it.

I pull myself back up to my feet, and I hear the pitter-patter of light applause. Mercedes is in the center of the bottom bleacher, hands slapping together with enthusiasm. She looks around and notices that she's the only one applauding, so stops and pushes her hands under her thighs.

I try to swallow, but my throat is dry. My water bottle calls me from the sidelines, but I'm not sure if it's okay for me to grab it yet. I keep standing where I am and fold my hands behind my back so the girls won't see me fidgeting. Ms. Denita gets up and strolls over to me.

"Can you do a grand jeté?" she asks me.

"Yeah," I say, nodding more than I intend to. "I mean, a little."

"A little?" She raises an eyebrow at me. "Then that ain't grand, baby."

"I mean, yes. Yes, I can."

She just stares at me for a second. Two seconds. Three.

"Oh!" She wants to me to show her. I back up to give myself a running start, then prance toward the bleachers and give a leap, my legs extending in opposite directions. I land softly on feet and then return to where I was standing.

"Hmm," Ms. Denita mutters. Not like she's pondering something but snorting through her nose. "Thank you. We'll take it from here." She scribbles something into the small notebook she's holding.

I blink at her. She looks up at me. "Thank you," she repeats, then hitches her head toward the exit.

"You want me to leave?" I ask. "Like, for the rest of the afternoon?" I figured she wanted me to stay for the rest of practice. Not necessarily to join, but to see what I'm missing. What could be.

"Yes. Now, if you don't mind, baby, we need to get to work."

"Yeah. Because *somebody* made us miss a whole ass week," Nevaeh calls out. The girls respond in agreement:

"Facts!"

"I know that's right!"

"Sis got some nerve coming up in here."

"Um, excuse me." Ms. Denita bugs her eyes out toward her team. "I don't remember asking for nobody's opinion." She turns her gaze directly to Nevaeh. "And last I checked, you were Nevaeh Mariah Bridges, not Pinocchio. Nobody's pulling strings to make you do anything."

Nevaeh pouts and tucks her chin into her hand. I don't know how Ms. Denita does it. She's tiny, reaching only my chin, with eyeglasses so thick she could store water inside the lenses. She comes across as a shy librarian, but you know within the first five minutes of speaking to her that she's a ball of fire. And she's the only person I've met with a Mute button for Nevaeh.

Ms. Denita turns back to me and does a double take, probably wondering why the hell I'm still here.

"Thank you," I say to her, then grab my water bottle and head for the locker room. Ms. Denita calls the Wolverines into formation for their warm-up. Rico blasts Aaliyah's "More Than a Woman" through the speaker, and the girls melt into a synchronized warm-up routine, filled with shoulder rolls and calf stretches. Faith's eyes land on me, and she gives me a small wave. I smile and wave back. Maybe this means I can reach out to Faith later tonight—ask her what happens next. I don't dwell any longer, though, or Ms. Denita might blow a gasket about me still being in the gym.

I grab my shoulder bag out of the locker room. No point in changing back into my school outfit. I left no crumbs on the floor with my routine, but I'm not sweaty enough to earn a shower. I have another hour until the after-school bus leaves, and I can't call Eric, because he was out installing satellite dishes for people all day. I plop down at one of the tables outside the library. The school designed this area like a mini coffee shop to appeal to the hipster parents who had moved into our small town to take advantage of the lower cost of living. Needless to say, this area didn't get a lot of traction in a school where locals and lifers are the vast majority. Especially now, since everybody is off at a practice or tutoring in a classroom or chilling at home. I pull out one of my textbooks and a notebook and start knocking out some of my homework.

I'm on only my second math problem when a shadow casts onto my notebook. I look up and Connor's there, face and arms flushed and damp. He's in sweat shorts and a tank top, so he must've stepped out of wrestling practice. There was a time when I knew his schedule by heart. There was a time when I knew *him* by heart.

"Hey. I've been trying to get at you all weekend," he says in between breaths. Like he sprinted just to be here, in front of me, at this very moment.

So, this is it. What I've been trying to avoid since Friday. I look down at my books and pens and papers spread across the table. It's obvious I'm not in a rush. I can't scurry my way out of this conversation now. "Yeah. I've been busy," I say, tapping my pencil onto my notebook. "I had to get ready for . . . tryouts." I guess that's what I would call it. I don't know why I feel a need to give Connor a reason, but I do.

Connor nods and uses the bottom of his tank top to wipe his face. A week ago, this small act would've made my lady parts dance. Today, though, my whole body's on ice. "Ky told me you quit cheer. Why? I'm sure you were good enough."

I blink. "I *am* good enough. I just outgrew it." *I outgrew a lot of things*, I want to add. But just because my outside's chilly doesn't mean my heart is.

"That's what's up," he says.

And his video with Weston flickers through my head again. *Fo sho, shawty.* Okay, maybe I can't have this conversation right now. I slam my textbook closed. "I have to catch the after-school bus." That bus isn't rolling up for another forty-five minutes. Connor doesn't know, though. The only time he has to ride mass transportation is for field trips or away matches.

"Wait, I can take you home."

"That's okay. You have practice, and I told my mom I'd help out at Itsy Bitsy today." I gather all my things and head toward the bus ramp at the back of the school. Connor jogs to catch up with me, and again, I want to shake him so hard. All year, I would've died for this moment. For Connor to want my attention. But why couldn't he want to spend time with me *before* I found out he was the antagonist in my story?

"Okay, wait. Wait." He grabs my hand to get me to stop walking. "I know you're upset about the video. . . ."

"Connor, I—"

"I never posted it, Ny. I would never post something like that. I don't even remember recording it. Brian doesn't even know how somebody got it off his phone."

"Is that supposed to make me feel better?" I snatch my hand away. He wanted to have this conversation, so let's have it. "That you didn't *remember* being racist? Does stuff like that happen so much that it's hard to remember *that* time?"

Connor's bottom lip quivers, and he's seven years old all

over again. Falling from his bike and skinning his knee and running to my mom to fix him up. "You know me, Naomi. You know I'm not racist."

"I saw the video, Connor! Read the tweets!"

"I know!" He pauses and takes a breath. "I didn't . . . I didn't mean anything by them. I know better now. And I promise, I *promise*, that I'll never do anything like that again."

I shake my head. "Yeah, because you got caught."

"No. Because I see the way you're looking at me now, and I don't want you to ever have to look at me that way again." He takes a deep breath and takes my hand again. "This isn't the way I wanted this to go down, but Brian spotted you here and ran to tell me before it was too late, so . . ." He drops down to one knee, and I'm so caught off guard that I don't even think to snatch my hand away again. My eyes get so wide that I'm sure eyebrows disappear under my headband. I know this boy ain't about to do what I think he's about to do.

"Naomi Cherie Henry . . ."

Oh, God.

"Will you do me the honor of going to homecoming with me?" He does that thing he knows that I love—rubs the back of my hand with this thumb. "I had a poster in my car. Even got the hookup with the strings section in band to serenade you after cheer practice, but . . ." He stretches out his empty arms. "This is all I got right now."

Wow. My heart keeps betraying me and pounds against my rib cage, looking for an escape. He wanted to go all-out. For me. For a dance that's not even senior prom. But still, I can't ignore everything that I've read. Everything that I've seen over the last few days. I feel split in two. One half of me wants to have a magical night with Connor, but the other half wants to force him to read a copy of *Stamped*.

Connor smiles that bold smile of his, full of teeth and high cheekbones and . . . privilege. I draw my hand away from him.

"Why now?" I ask.

He blinks and gets to his feet. "Because homecoming is in like two weeks."

"No. I mean, why are you asking *me* now? After all this time?"

Connor frowns, and I can see the question mark between his eyebrows. "Because me and you haven't been a me and you until this past summer. Before, it was you and Kylie . . . and me when you two got bored. But I like this new equation." He reaches for my hand again, and dammit, I let him take it. Again. "I like that there's a me and you."

Connor sounds like a romance novel. No doubt, I would've underlined the words he just delivered to me at least three times. Maybe even doodled a few hearts by them too. I think about all the girls at Windsor Woods who would kill for this moment. Hell, I was one of them. But that was before his skeletons were yanked out the closet. I look down at our interlocked fingers, a weaving of onyx and pearl, and think about the things he tells Brian and Weston about me when I'm not around. If he said what he said online, I can only imagine what happens when someone isn't pressing Record.

"Let me think about it." The words just tumble out of my mouth, but I don't rush to pick them back up. I want Connor to stare at them. Sit with them. Like I've been doing with all his tweets and posts.

This time, Connor's the one to pull away. "*Think* about it?"

"Yeah, we probably shouldn't rush . . . this." My finger swirls around in the space between us.

Connor watches my finger, then shoves his hands in the pockets of his shorts. "Sure, Ny. I get it." His temple throbs as he bites down on the inside of his cheek, definitely not getting it. "Coach is probably looking for me."

I nod. "And I have the bus. But I'll call you."

"You do that." Connor turns and heads toward the weight room without a second glance. He walks farther and farther away, the space between us as wide as an ocean. And I still can't swim.

NOW

I CAN'T BE ALONE RIGHT NOW. DETECTIVE STRETCH TRIES TO LEAVE ME, give me a moment to get all my tears out. But I don't want to be alone again. It'll be just like being trapped underneath all that drywall and plaster. Just darkness, searching for a light to escape. I don't want to be in the dark again.

Detective Stretch sits there, occasionally resting a hand on my back as my cries devolve into whimpers. I don't know how long it takes, but I'm all cried out. The pain is there, right behind my eyes, but the well is dry. I've cried enough for a lifetime, and I'm not sure if my body's capable of forming another teardrop.

"I'm . . . I'm thirsty." The words come out hoarsely.

Detective Stretch nods and tries to pass me the can of

Sprite she brought in earlier. I shake my head, frowning at the thought of trying to swallow anything fizzy.

"Just water, please."

"Okay." Detective Stretch stands and I leap to my feet, so abruptly that it startles her and she flinches.

"Don't," I say, wanting to grab her hand and pull her close to me. The fear of the darkness crawling up my back. "Don't leave, please. Can I come with you?"

Detective Stretch sighs and looks over my shoulder, at the mirror behind me. I wonder if someone's behind there. Watching me, waiting for me to share something crucial between all the sobs. "Yes, but stay right next to me, okay? Don't speak to anyone." She opens the door, and I welcome the gust of air. The feeling of new air across my skin, not the stale air that's been keeping me company in the tiny interrogation room.

Detective Stretch slips her hand through the crook of my arm and leads me down a tight corridor lined with closed doors. Maybe other interrogation rooms. I wonder if some of my friends are in there. Suck in a sharp breath at the thought of the one friend who isn't. We turn right, and two vending machines wait for us, one for snacks and one for drinks. The detective leads me to the drink machine and inserts a card.

"You good with Dasani, right?" she asks. "Hope so. That's all we got."

My eyes float to the door next to the machines. A small outline of a person in a triangle dress in the center. "Can I go to the bathroom?" I ask. I didn't need to pee. At least I didn't think I did. Strange, because I don't remember the last time I went. I just wanted to wash my face, my hands. Get the stains from the explosion off them. The soot on my fingers is a constant reminder of what I couldn't stop.

Detective Stretch lets out a small sigh. "Five minutes. I'll wait for you out here."

I wiggle away from her grasp just as the door across from us swings open. The guys' bathroom. Detective Summers walks out and spots me. His eyes bounce between me and Detective Stretch, and a smirk crawls up his face.

"Really, MK? No heads-up?" he asks.

Before Detective Stretch can respond, someone follows Summers outside the door. He stops in his tracks when he notices the small huddle in the hallway. My breath catches in my throat as I take him in. There are still traces of soot on his clothes, on his face. But his cheeks and eyes are red like he's just spent ten minutes trying to scrub off as much as he could. They might be red from something else too. I know they are, even if he wouldn't admit it to me right now.

"Connor," I cry out, and my feet rush over to him before they know any better. Detective Summers throws his meaty arm up in front of Connor, creating a barricade.

"Don't even think about it," Detective Summers snaps, his eyes small and beady. Full of hatred, and it's all directed at me. "MK, control your girl." He barks it in a way that makes me shudder. Almost like Detective Stretch owns me and I need to get taken out back and whipped into submission.

I feel Detective Stretch's hand on the small of my back. Soft. Kind. "Come on, Naomi," she says. "I got your water."

I'm not ready to go back into that tight, cold room. Alone with the snacks and the buzzing lights . . . and the photos. Those horrible photos. I can tell that Connor isn't ready to go back to wherever they've been keeping him too. His hands are balled into fists that he tucks under his armpits, wrapping himself like a straitjacket. He hasn't looked at me yet. Just looks down at his smoky shoes as he shifts his weight from foot to foot.

Detective Stretch presses into my back, urging me to move along. Not yet.

"Connor," I say again, my voice still raw and ragged from the tears. "I'm sorry. I'm so sorry." To my surprise, my eyes get damp. I'm not undergoing a drought from grief.

Connor finally looks up at me, his face red and harsh and crumpled. He's not just distraught; he's pissed. "Are you, though?" he asks, his throat full of phlegm.

What? Of course I am. *Of course.* He has to know that. He has to know me. Even after everything, I'm still me. But my words stay lodged in my chest, flaming like heartburn. Detective Summers grumbles something and pulls Connor down the hall, away from me. He becomes a blur before the tears fall again.

SIXTEEN

IT'S STRANGE. CLEO AND I BARELY KNOW EACH OTHER ASIDE FROM OUR DMing, but it's like she knows when I need a life raft. I'd been underwater after my confrontation with Connor, chewing through dinner without really eating. Nodding along to conversations with Eric and Mom without really listening. By the time I make it to my bedroom Monday night, I'm drowning. But then Cleo sent me a message:

We showin up and showin out at the NNPS board meeting Tues night. You in?

ME: Hell YEAH. But . . . I need a ride.

I bit my lip while I waited for Cleo to respond. I already looked desperate from my too-quick reply. And now I had to throw in needy. Cleo responded two minutes later:

I got you.

She picks me up Tuesday afternoon, right from the school parking lot. She drives an older-model Nissan Rogue, with zebra-print seat covers and a tiger-print steering wheel. Inconsistency never looked cooler. She sings along to some neo-soul song I've never heard before while she drives, stopping her harmony only to vape out her window. She doesn't have the best voice, sharp when the singer is subtle. But she doesn't care. She sings like she recorded the song herself.

It's only when we reach Hampton city limits that Cleo turns down her stereo to chat with me. "This your first protest?"

"Yes. Wait, no. I mean . . . maybe?"

Cleo glances at me with an eyebrow cocked.

"I did this thing in tenth grade to get the school cafeteria to incorporate Meatless Mondays. A few of us passed around a petition and boycotted the cafeteria for like a week." That was one of the longest weeks in my life. I still remember sneaking pretzels and granola bars in the bathroom stall just to stop my stomach from rumbling.

"Well . . . did you get your Meatless Monday?"

"We did, actually."

"Cool. You a vegan?"

"I was for like a minute." I crack my knuckles just to have something to do. "But then my mom's boyfriend brought home Five Guys for dinner one night and . . ." I just shrug.

Embarrassed that I'm telling Cleo about my weakness for bacon cheeseburgers.

"And you tore that motherfucker up. I get it. Five Guys be lacing their patties with crack or something." She takes another hit from her vape pen. "But there are other vegans and vegetarians at your school. Good for them. Good for you."

I lean back in my seat and smile. Yeah, good for me.

We make it to campus and head straight for Cleo's dorm, where a group is already in the residents' lounge getting their signs ready. A few faces I remember from Wingstop, but most of them are new to me. Faith and her friends didn't come, because they had Wolverine things to do, and since I hadn't heard from any of them, I assumed I didn't make the cut. Being here, with Cleo, feeling like a grown-ass woman doing important things, takes some of the sting out of Faith and Ms. Denita's silence. It also keeps me from spending another night dissecting Connor's homecoming proposal over and over in my head.

Cleo abandoned me once we entered the lounge, so I float around the room until I find a blank poster board to use. I automatically go for the red marker. People have no choice but to notice red. It's loud, bold. Attention-grabbing. It'll get the job done. I keep the message simple: *RESPECT OUR CROWNS*. I almost draw a crown on top of one of the letters, but I don't want to overdo it. Less is more.

"Yo, you tryna scare off the white folk?" Butter stops at my table and frowns at my poster. His Afro is tamed with skinny cornrows zigzagging across his scalp. "Looks like you're shouting at them in their pets' blood."

I look down at my letters. Damn, he's right. I wanted my sign to have an impact, but the edges of each letter are sharp. Angry. Just like the bloated letters on my locker.

"Boy, get out here with all that Stephen King bullshit," Cleo says, taking a seat across from me. "Don't hate because you needed help spelling *respect*. There's a song about it and everything, bruh."

Butter pretends to laugh before playfully pulling at one of Cleo's braids and joining a group of guys at another table. I look down at my poster and think of how I could make it less murder-y.

"It's fine," Cleo says, reading my mind. "You have a great message, and people are damn sure going to see it. *Periodt.*" She stabs at the air with her marker.

I smile just as Butter's table start cracking up at something. On instinct, I look over and expect them to be looking at me. But they're all engrossed in something on Butter's phone. I blow out a breath in relief.

"You know he was just messing with you, right?" Cleo says. I don't know her major, but she needs to look into a career in therapy. This girl knows how to read a feeling.

"Seems like he likes messing with me." I work on my last

letter on my poster and add curves to the *N* to make it more delightful and less demented.

"Don't take it personal. He tries to roast everyone, but sometimes he can't read a room. But most guys are like that. Clueless."

"It's not right," I say. More to myself, but loud enough for Cleo to hear. "They get to say what they want, do what they want. And we're supposed to smile and bat our eyelashes just because they all of a sudden give us the time of day. Like, where are the consequences, man?"

Cleo blinks at me. "Something tells me we're not talking about Butter anymore."

I drop my marker and lean back in my chair, thinking of Connor. "Tell me college guys are different. That they understand cause and effect. They get more mature, right?"

The laughter at Butter's table reaches a fever pitch. One of the guys even jumps from his seat and jogs away, as if he needed air from whatever joke they were all in on. Cleo shakes her head at them, then turns back to me.

"You were saying?" she asks.

I smile at her. "Never mind."

"Did I tell you about my first boo?"

Outside of our DMs about dance teams and demonstrations, Cleo hasn't told me much of anything about herself. I shake my head.

"Girl." Cleo smiles and leans back in her seat, as if she has to get comfortable for this story. "Clyde Pernell Barker." I pull a face and Cleo laughs. "Yeah, I know. Family name. Couldn't be anything modern like Justin or Omari, but thankfully we all just called him CP. So, CP and I got together my junior year in high school. He was a senior, new to the school. And fine. I'm talking Larenz Tate in *Love Jones* fine."

I raise my eyebrows, impressed. I've seen that movie a few times with my mom, mainly because of the fineness of Larenz Tate. So fine, in fact, that Mom and I used him as a barometer to gauge handsomeness. *He's like a two on the Larenz Scale. Definitely not a seven.*

"He's actually the person who introduced me to activism," Cleo says. "I went to my first rally with him. My first sit-in with him. We even climbed a flagpole together to pull down an old Confederate flag in front of a courthouse in Richmond. Of course, we got tased together as soon as we got down."

"Whoa," I say. She must've been in love. I don't know if I'd follow anybody anywhere if I knew I could possibly get zapped with electricity. "So . . . what happened with him?"

Cleo pokes her lips out and accompanies it with a loud smirk. "He dumped me a week before my senior prom. He told me that he wanted to travel up the East Coast to fight for social justice, and that it wasn't fair to me to try the long-distance thing. Child, I found out that he was following this big-shot activist who'd he been sleeping with for months.

Apparently, she saw footage of our Confederate flag incident and got all hot and bothered. I think they're engaged now or whatever. Basically, thanks to me."

I curl my lip. "Ugh. What an asshole."

"No. Not ugh. Look, guys are flawed like the rest of us. Sometimes they can be the best thing on this earth since satin bonnets; other times you want to cut them out like dead ends in your hair. You can't control them, so don't even bother."

I nod in agreement. I wanted Connor to be the Connor I pictured in my head. The Connor from the beach two weekends ago. But he wasn't perfect. If I had realized that sooner, maybe those videos and posts from him wouldn't hurt as much as they did. Maybe.

"You know what you can control, though?" Cleo continues as she picks up my poster from the table. "Being a boss bitch. A trailblazer. A supernova who's ready to snatch edges and wake people's asses up. So . . . you ready to be *that* bitch?" She stands and holds out her hand to me.

I take her hand and push out of my seat. Something shifts in me. Like that stomach tickle that happens at the top of a roller coaster, right before the first dip. Scared of the drop but looking forward to the ride. I arch my back, and I'm not just standing next to Cleo in a student lounge. We're standing side by side on top of a damn mountain.

"All right, Black people," Cleo says to the room while still holding my hand. I give her hand a squeeze. "Let's roll out."

I've never attended a school board meeting before, but it looks pretty much how I'd expect it to. An auditorium just like in a high school. The stage has a long bench with all the members from the school board seated and facing us. A podium with a microphone in the center of the aisles to let the people talk. Or at least give the illusion that the school board wanted the people to talk.

We post up in the back row of the auditorium, posters tucked away under our seats. Cleo told us not to come in guns blazing or they'd find a reason for us to leave before the meeting even got started. If someone popped their gum too loudly, we could get kicked out for disorderly conduct. So, we waited until Cleo's signal. But as the minutes inched on and the school board discussed expenditures and infrastructure and other multisyllable words that went in one ear and out the other, my legs bounced with anticipation. I tried to keep them still, but they did their own thing.

Once again, I get stuck next to Butter, and he bumps his knee up against mine. I look up at him, ready to meet his smirk with one of my own, but instead he pats the air between us and takes a breath: *Relax. Just breathe.* I bite at my lip but take a deep breath through my nose, and let it seep out through my mouth. He nods and gives me a small smile. My legs go from frenetic jazz to smooth R&B. I keep up this measured breathing until it happens:

"And now we'll open the floor for new business," the chair of the board, Mr. Copper, whose skin is pale and flaky and the exact opposite of his surname, announces.

Cleo stands from her aisle seat and marches straight down to the podium. A middle-aged white guy with a stack of notes also makes his way to the mic, but Cleo bypasses like she's going around a slow car in the left lane.

"Name, please," Mr. Copper says, looking at the papers on his desk instead of up at Cleo.

"My name is Cleo Hayslett, sir, and a conversation tends to go better when you're looking a person in their eyes—unless you have a condition that warrants otherwise."

The vice chair, a petite brunette with a nameplate that says *Mrs. Drummond*, jerks her shoulders as she covers her mouth, smothering a laugh from deep inside.

Mr. Copper's head snaps upright, and his face reddens. The sudden action jostles his eyeglasses, and he uses his middle finger to adjust them. "Okay, Ms. Hayslett, what new business would you like to bring forth?"

"I would like to call for the immediate and just termination of John Anderson's teaching contract."

At that, the rest of the back row and I stand and raise our signs over our heads. The school board members squirm in their seats and glance at each other. The crowd in front of us swivels their heads to see what all the commotion is. A few of them shake their heads in annoyance. The nerve of us for exercising our First Amendment rights.

"The employment status of employees is not up for public discussion," Mr. Copper says.

"Why not?" Cleo asks. "Aren't hirings, promotions, and contract renewals brought up at school board meetings all the time? And the actual incident was up for public consumption through the media. Channel Three released the student's name, even though he's a minor."

A few of Cleo's friends clap and hype her up.

"Left-wing nonsense," an older white woman shouts to her friend next to her so that we all can hear.

Her friend nods and turns her head toward Cleo. "Go home," she barks.

"You go home!" Neesa snaps back. The woman clutches at her chest like she's trying to digest some bad Chinese food.

"Order!" Mr. Copper bangs his gavel. The back-and-forths continue, so he bangs it even louder. Finally, the arguments go from a boil to a simmer. Cleo stands patiently with her head held high during all the chaos, like a true queen.

"No offense, Ms. Hayslett," Mr. Copper continues, "but you don't seem much older than most of our students. Do you have a child who attends Newport News Public Schools?"

Cleo cocks her head. "Do *you*?"

Mr. Copper pushes aside the paperwork on his desk and leans right into his microphone. "My point is that you do not seem to have a personal stake in this matter." Every syllable that leaves his mouth clashes against the frequency of the microphone, and every breath and grunt he makes is amplified for the whole audience to hear.

"Personal stake?" Cleo repeats, then gives a tiny laugh. "Sir, do you realize that 54 percent of your student population identifies as Black and or African American, but you consistently struggle to retain faculty members of color? Moreover, Black students make up 62 percent of short-term suspensions compared with 15 for your white students. So, if you really need to know, my *personal stake*, sir, is that you clearly do not have enough qualified individuals to mold Black minds. To listen to them. Validate them. Empower them. Let alone respect them enough to not put their grubby paws on their goddamn heads!"

The back row explodes with cheers, and I join the frenzy. The air is electric. Cleo's electric. The energy hums through my veins as I hold my sign up higher. Cheer louder. Catching the Holy Spirit, as Mom would say.

Most of the other attendees don't find a reason to rejoice and dance in the aisles. They cuss, shout. Rebuttals and expletives spray out of their mouths like venom, but their poison can't reach us. We have virtue on our side.

Mr. Copper bangs his gavel over and over, trying to regain some control of the meeting. But he's powerless. His face contorts into something vicious, predatory. Reminds me of a recent DM from Cleo: *There's no one scarier than a white man who thinks he's lost power.*

"Get rid of her," Mr. Copper growls into the microphone, baring his teeth and ready to take a bite out of someone. Two uniformed officers leave their posts alongside the walls and come barreling toward Cleo. One even has his hand on top of his baton, fingers curled and ready to pull it out of his belt if needed.

Fear travels through me. "No!" The desperation in my voice surprises even me. I drop the poster and start toward Cleo before I can even wrap my mind around what'll happen next. I just reach the aisle when someone grabs me around the waist from behind.

"Don't," Butter says to me. His voice is firm, but his grip is soft. He pulls me behind him as he and some of the other guys with us race down the aisle. More screams. Chaos. What the hell did I get myself into?

"You don't have a right to put your hand on my body," Cleo says. No, she commands. Even without shouting, her voice has substance. She raises both hands to show the officers and the school board and the angry parents in the crowd that she's not a danger. She turns to look at Butter and her other friends and, just like that, they calm down and back away.

Cleo nods at them, then turns back to the school board members. "Don't touch!"

"My crown!" the HU crew responds.

"I'm Black!"

"And proud!"

The chant ping-pongs back and forth like we're in a sermon, and Cleo leads the charge as our fiery pastor. She keeps her hands up, but not to surrender. To summon. The voices behind the chants are so powerful that the floors rumble beneath us. I raise my poster high over my head and shout my response until my tonsils bleed:

"Don't touch!"

"My crown!"

"I'm Black!"

"And proud!"

Mr. Copper bangs that damn gavel so consistently, so hard, that I wait for the handle to snap off. Might as well, because that gavel is as useless as Mr. Copper himself. He's no longer in control. We are. And that's a scary thing.

SEVENTEEN

CLEO PULLS INTO AN EMPTY PARKING SPACE IN FRONT OF MY APART-
ment building and puts her car into park. The energy from
the protest still buzzes through my limbs, and it takes me
a couple of seconds to realize we've stopped moving. I lean
back on the headrest to take it all in. I peek over at Cleo and
catch her doing the same thing. A laugh seeps out of both our
mouths, a joke told only with our eyes.

"Like, *what*?" I ask, once most of the snickers have
escaped. "What was that? What is this?" I place my hand on
top of my chest, not sure how else to describe what I'm feeling but to touch it.

"That's living, boo," Cleo says, because of course she gets

it. She *is* it. "That's not asking to be heard but insisting on it. Demanding it."

"Wow." My hand drops back to my lap. Had I known social justice felt like this, I would've started attending rallies last summer instead of sneaking glances at Connor in his swim trunks. Both made my heart flutter, but Connor caused a rumble. Tonight, though? Tonight felt like thunder. "And now I just go home and go back to normal?"

"Naomi, something tells me you were never *just* anything."

I smile. Not because I'm flattered, but because I believe her.

"But if you loved tonight, you should roll with us to the rally on the first. Some heavy hitters are going to be in town. There's this guy named Orlando who's going to be like the next Ibram X. Kendi, and he's basically from our own backyard. Seven-five-seven all day." She holds up a fist to put some respect on our area code. "You might get a real kick out of it."

I want to say, even scream, yes. I've physically been around Cleo only two times, but I already feel older. Seasoned. She's handed me a magnifying glass, and now I want to see everything amplified. All the cracks and crevices, so that I know how to fill them in. She's a force, someone who sees something in me. I'm not a means to an end to her, a comfort blanket to take along with her to Target or tryouts or New York City. Cleo believes in my meanings. In my dreams.

But these dreams have to get through high school first. "You mean October first?"

Cleo nods. "Yeah, in downtown Hampton. I'm talking spoken word, live music, and some local leaders in the Don't Attack Blacks movement. That guy Orlando's one of them."

I sigh. "That's the same night as homecoming. I mean, I want to go, but I already told my friends that . . ." I don't even know what else to say. Kylie, Roma, and I have talked about the homecoming dance all summer. My last one before I left Windsor Woods in my rearview mirror. But Kylie and Roma feel like a world away. And I still can't think about Connor without my heart breaking just a little. I live in this strange intersection of dread and obligation, and my guilt is pulling me in the latter direction.

"Say no more," Cleo says. "You know how to reach me if you change your mind." She holds up her fist again: *Black power.* I hold mine up in return and feel like I've just been initiated into her circle.

Cleo's headlights peel away as soon as I unlock and open my front door. She taps her horn goodbye. I take a breath to prepare for the barrage of complaints I'm about to receive from Mom and Eric for showing up one minute after curfew. On school nights, I can't stay out past ten, which Kylie helped me negotiate up from nine thirty with a couple of pouts and *pleases.* But when I enter the living room, Mom isn't standing there waiting for me with her hands on her hips. Instead, she and Eric sit on the couch with their eyes glued to the TV.

I blink. "Um, hey, y'all."

"Hey, baby," Mom says, her eyes not leaving the TV.

I frown and look to see what has them so distracted. The ten o' clock news is on, and a reporter looks poised and serious as she reads from her teleprompter. At the top corner of the screen is Mr. Brooks's latest professional headshot. The top button of his shirt collar unbuttoned to come across as more approachable. His hair parted and swooped to the right. *Young Bieber hair*, Kylie joked.

"Why is Mr. Brooks on . . . ?"

Mom holds up her hand and shushes me. I take a seat on the arm of the couch to catch the tail end of the report:

"*. . . and this is the third former employee that has joined the civil lawsuit against Scott Brooks for discriminatory practices. Legal representatives for these employees indicate that Brooks paid them less due to their racial background and made stereotypical comments in their presence. In one example listed, Brooks allegedly referred to his Black employees as 'the help' and told one of his employees that he's lucky that he has a 'white-sounding name.'*"

Eric smirks and throws himself back against the couch. "What did I say?" He tosses a hand toward the TV. "I told you something was off with that man, Nina."

Mom shakes her head and mutes the TV. The screen now shows a family picture of the Brookses, only Kylie's and

Connor's faces are blurred out. I know that picture. They took it three years ago during a visit to a Busch Gardens Christmas Town event.

"Not now, Eric," Mom pleads.

"He's not getting out of this one, babe. They're taking his ass to court. You know that means they got something solid on him."

The television switches to footage of Kylie at the Target parking lot. They blur her face, even though everyone in town's already seen it. Without thinking, I shush Mom and Eric. I have to hear what they're saying about Kylie. And, without thinking, Mom and Eric quiet down instead of giving me lip for being bold enough to shush them.

"*. . . Brooks's daughter recently had a controversial viral video that appears to show Scott Brooks directing his daughter to call the cops on two unarmed Black men. Over the weekend, Brooks's son had videos and social media posts surface in which he makes some insensitive comments about individuals of color. . . .*"

Some of Connor's tweets pop up on the screen over a blurred-out picture of Connor in his wrestling singlet, putting Quentin Tynes into a headlock. Quentin's one of two Black guys on the team with Connor. Connor's not as tight with Quentin as he is with Brian and Weston, but they're cool. They were goofing off in that picture—it had made the yearbook last year. Seeing it now at the same time as Connor's dumbass tweets distorted the picture more than the blurs the reporters added over their faces. Now there was something twisted about the image. Sinister, even. A chill travels up my spine, and I hug myself to keep warm.

"Okay, we've heard enough." Mom mutes the TV and tosses the remote control onto the coffee table. "Now they're dragging the kids into this? I have to call Kristen—"

"Nina, don't you pick up that phone," Eric says.

"I just need to know if they're okay. If the babies are okay . . ."

"They're not babies anymore. The sooner you realize that, the sooner you can let them go. Let that whole damn family go."

Mom drops her head and stares at her hands, clinging them together as if she's still clinging onto Kylie and Connor. They weren't babies anymore, but she still felt like they were *her* babies. Still saw their chubby cheeks and wide, blue eyes and floppy hair that slipped through Mom's fingers like silk whenever she tried to brush it into a style.

I remember it like it was yesterday. The day Mom first told me that I was going to see more of Kylie and Connor outside of Mrs. Hart's kindergarten class. Mom waiting for me next to Mrs. Brooks's BMW. "Come on, baby. We're riding with them. We're going to be spending more time at Kylie and Connor's house." Me wedged in the back seat between the twins as Mom and Mrs. Brooks peeked back and smiled at us from time to time. After minutes of silence.

Kylie's fingers touching a plastic barrette at the end of one of my plaits. "I like your hair," she whispered to me. I glanced at her blond curls, pulled back into one fishtail braid. "I like yours better," I whispered back. Something about that tickled Kylie, and she laughed and laughed. It was contagious. Soon, I was laughing too. Connor had cupped the sides of his face and cried out, "My ears!"—which only made Kylie and me laugh harder. That was that. The bond had been formed.

"As soon as you call them to talk about this case, they're going to pull you into this mess," Eric warns Mom in our living room. He takes both my mom's hands into his, Kylie and Connor slipping right through her fingertips. "You can't get involved with this, baby. Think about how hard you've worked, how much you put up with, just to get your business up and running. I don't want you do anything to jeopardize that, you hear me?"

Mom sighs, and our eyes find each other's. Locked in, going through the same grieving process of saying goodbye to such a huge part of our lives. She breaks eye contact before I do and leans into Eric. "Okay," she mumbles, and cuts off the TV.

Eric wraps his arm around her, then kisses Mom on the temple. He looks over at me. "You need to start getting ready for bed, don't you?"

I stare at the TV screen, our hazy reflections staring back at us. I still find my eyes, though. Wide. Searching. I've never felt more awake.

EIGHTEEN

I DRAG MY FEET AS I WALK TO THE BUS STOP THE NEXT MORNING. I'D spent last night Googling more about Mr. Brooks and this lawsuit against him. Three of his former employees at one of his bowling-alley locations were involved. There was also a former housekeeper to vouch for some of the claims. She must've worked for the Brookses before my mom did, because I don't remember a housekeeper there. My mom did everything—took care of Kylie and Connor, washed the clothes and dishes, mopped the kitchen floor. She even prepared meals for them sometimes. There were times when I sat at the table with the Brookses and my mom served me too. Sitting alongside the Brookses like a bastard child dining with the royal family, while Mom stayed on her feet. Refilling our glasses, clearing our plates. I can't even remember when she ate her own meals while we were at the Brookses'—and that hole in my memory aches my chest.

Even still, the things claimed in that lawsuit didn't sound like the Mr. Brooks I grew up with. Or around. He was rarely in the house, but when he was there, he was high fives and bear hugs and big laughs. One of the claims in the lawsuit alleges that Mr. Brooks compared his employee's newborn to a "little monkey." I paused at that one. Remembered how Mr. Brooks went through a period of calling me Curious Ny. *Just like Curious George but cuter*, he would say. The need to vomit overcame me, and the pinch and pull of my stomach could be cured only by Oreos. I grabbed a sleeve of them from the kitchen and took them to bed with me.

When I reach the school bus stop, a car is idling at the curb next to the entrance sign of my apartment complex. Not just any car—a sleek blue Audi. Some of the other kids I ride the bus with scope out the car and nod at each other, impressed. I take a breath and approach the car just as the passenger window rolls down. Kylie's behind the steering wheel. She peers at me over her square sunglasses and smiles.

"Hey," she says.

I scan the car, but there's no Roma in sight.

"She got another ride today," Kylie says, reading my mind like always.

"You two in a fight?" I ask.

"No. I told her I had plans today. *We* have plans today."
She waves a finger between me and her. I give her a look, and
she smiles even wider. I know what she's about to say before
she says it. "Ky and Ny Fun Day!"

I shake my head. "I need to get to school."

"Ugh. Why? Have you even missed a day yet this year?"

"We've only been back for two weeks, Kylie."

"Then you definitely need a break. Get in."

I look back at my bus stop, and my fellow riders stare at
me in anticipation, just as invested in my decision as Kylie.
I turn back to her, and she clasps her hands together against
her mouth.

"Please," she begs behind her fists. "Our senior year has
been so fucked up. I just want to have fun again. Like we
used to."

I sigh through my nose. I haven't thought of *fun* and
Kylie in the same sentence since forever. And with good
reason. Eric had a point last night—it was time to let the
Brookses go. His words were directed at Mom, but a part of
me knew he wanted me to receive it as well. But . . . it was
my senior year. So far, this year has been tossed into a blender
and mixed into a hot-mess smoothie. There's no way I could
survive the rest of the school year with this much daily stress.

I open the passenger side's door and slip inside. "Where
are we going?"

Kylie heads toward Windsor Castle Park, which, oddly enough, isn't even in Windsor but a neighboring town in the county. We used to go there all the time when we were kids. It was a place where people could jog along trails or rent out canoes or even attend the county fair. It's basically the hub of the county, even though it used to be a plantation. Nobody ever talks about that, though. *I* never talk about that. After my first protest last night, though, I felt like shouting.

"Isn't it funny how the whole town has so much fun at a place where Black people picked cotton or whatever?" I ask Kylie.

Kylie blinks a few times. "What?" she asks with a laugh.

"The park," I continue. I Google it on my phone and scan the reviews. "Four-point-five out of five stars. 'I love this park. It has everything!' Yeah . . . including the bloody soil of slaves."

Kylie turns her head away from the road and scans me, as if she's trying to figure out where all my breaks and bruises are. She lets out a heavy sigh and looks back in front of her. "This is Virginia, boo. You can't take two steps without treading on tragic history."

Can't argue with her there, and so I don't. To fill the quiet, Kylie cuts up her radio and the low rumbling of Post Malone pours out the speakers. It's an album we used to listen to all the time in middle school, back when we couldn't wait to get to high school and be free. Or so we thought. Kylie's setting the mood for Ky and Ny Fun Day.

She parks, and we set out for the natural playscape. We don't even discuss it; the playscape is always our first, and sometimes only, destination. Not Your Run-of-the-Mill Playground, the wooden sign at the entrance says. And it isn't. It's basically like if cartoon woodland creatures came together to design a jungle gym. Every apparatus is made of trees or stone or other organic materials. The playscape had its grand opening when we were ten years old. Mom took us the first weekend it opened while Mr. and Mrs. Brooks attended some fancy luncheon. Kylie, Connor, and I oohed and aahed over the pieces of fancy equipment and didn't want to leave until we tried every single one of them. Some, more than once.

Now Kylie and I stand at the bottom of the small rock-climbing wall made of wooden planks. "Race you to the top," Kylie says. "Just like old times?"

I look at Kylie, and she's ten years old again, her blond hair pulled into two French braids leaving tails down her back. She's young and light—and it's contagious. "You ready to lose, just like old times?"

Kylie tucks her chin close to her chest. "Challenge accepted." We both stretch our limbs, then crouch into a runner's lunge to get ready. "One. Two—"

I take off running to the wall before she finishes, and Kylie screams at me.

"Cheater!" she cries out, her voice high-pitched and squeaky, not yet reaching puberty.

My shoe is already on the first foothold on the wall. I pull myself up and reach the third foothold by the time Kylie even touches the wall.

"Don't hate me 'cause you're slow!" I call down to her, my voice hijacked by ten-year-old me. I reach the top of the wall and slap the rail above it. "Ha!" I look down to rub my victory in Kylie's face, but she's no longer on the wall. I catch her sprinting toward the heart of the playscape—the thirty-foot slide.

"Bitch!" I call out to her as I hop down to the ground. Kylie cackles like the evil genius she is. She knows whoever won rock climbing always got to be the first one down the slide. She's playing dirty, but I can't be mad at her. Not when her laughter dances in the air and breathes life into the otherwise empty play yard. I chase after her, but she has too much of a lead. By the time I catch up, she's halfway up the rock path that leads to the top of the slide.

"I hate you!" I shout at her back.

"Hey, you threw the first stone," she calls back with a shrug. She makes it to the top of the slide and places one hand behind her head. Her other arm extends away for her and jerks like a water sprinkler, recreating our old-school celebratory dance. I boo her, but she's not fazed. She ends her dance with a hair flip, then pushes down the slide, lying flat on her back like we always did. On your back, you can see the whole sky so that you're flying instead of sliding back down to earth.

I don't waste time with a dance once I reach the top. I'm on my back and gliding through the air. I close my eyes for a few seconds so that I'm weightless. No drama holding me down. Just me and the smooth slide on my back, pulling at my shirt as the breeze glides across me. I open my eyes just as my feet collide against Kylie's lower back. She didn't get a chance to climb off before I took off after her.

"Ow," she hollers, then erupts into laughter. I do too. We laugh at nothing, but everything. The silence between us. The tension between us. We release it and let it waltz through the air along with our giggles. We go down the slide three more times before moving on to other areas of the playscape. Crawling through tunnels and balancing on logs and cart-wheeling across patches of grass. I don't remember the last time I've laughed this much, and I don't try to remember. I want to be present, with Kylie, even though we're reliving our youth. Treading a fine line between then and now. Finally, when we're sweaty and drained, we take off our shoes and let our toes sink into the sandbox.

"Wow," Kylie says, walking an imaginary tightrope through the box. "I don't know what they do to the sand in children's sandboxes, but it feels like fairy dust."

I trace my big toe in the sand and make a giant *N*. "I

think it's from all the tears and snot," I say.

Kylie stops walking and curls her lip at me. "Do you want me to run out and get a tetanus shot?"

"You can't get tetanus from tears and snot. Maybe just a little bit of scabies. A small ringworm or two."

Kylie gags and I laugh at her.

"You think the school already called our parents?" she asks once she recovers.

I sigh and take a seat on one of the tree stumps circling the sandbox. "Probably."

"What are you going to say?" She takes a seat across from me on another tree stump.

I shrug. "I was thinking of playing dumb. All *I don't know why they you sent you that automatic message. Must be a glitch.*"

Kylie gives me a soft smile, but I can tell that I lost her about two seconds ago. Something else is on her mind, and it brings a cloud to our sunny day. "I probably won't have to lie to my parents. They've been kind of busy lately—they might not even notice the phone call." The French braids and hot-pink biking shorts are replaced by a loose topknot and skinny jeans. Kylie's seventeen again. So am I.

I bury my toes deep in the sand until they're eaten alive. I knew this would have to come up, the whole thing about Mr. Brooks. I just didn't know that Kylie was going to be the one to mention it first.

"Those people are mad at my dad because he couldn't give them raises," Kylie continues. The words come out quickly, like she had them bottled up and fizzing inside her for so long that they erupt. "But he couldn't give anyone raises around that time. Nobody was taking their families out bowling during the pandemic. And then when he slowly started opening up his spots again, he lost more business because of the mask mandates. People were angry that they had to be reminded about all the bullshit in the world when they just wanted to escape for an hour or two with their family. So they didn't want to stay. Ny, my dad was paying employees out of his own pocket."

She has a lot of excuses for her dad. And it makes sense. If someone was accusing my mom of saying and doing awful things, my immediate response would be to go hard for her. But my mom also never had more than one person accusing her of saying and doing the same awful things. "But what about that housekeeper?" I ask. "Wasn't she working for your parents way before the pandemic?"

Kylie rolls her eyes. "Gloria stole from my parents. They could never really prove it, but every week, my mom couldn't find a ring, or a wristlet handbag, or a pair of designer shades. It was all too coincidental, so they had to let her go. Gloria never got over that. And she was even more salty that she was the one who introduced your mom to my parents, and Mama

Nina worked for us . . . I mean, for my parents, forever. She's just jealous."

I frown. I don't remember this Gloria lady. But apparently, she's the reason why the Brookses are in my life. She's the reason why Kylie's more than my best friend. My sister from another mister is what we always say about each other. Though lately, we were more like cousins five times removed.

"What is your dad going to do?" I ask.

Kylie shrugs. "I don't know. There's this and then the whole thing with me and Connor. . . ." The whole thing. She doesn't directly talk about the still-trending Parking Lot Becky video, or Connor's bigoted posts. She wraps it all up in ambiguity and puts a vague bow on top. "It's just been really overwhelming to be at home, to be honest with you. That's why I can't wait for us to leave for New York next year."

She beams at me, and all her hope shoots tiny holes into my conscience. She's hoping that I'll be part of the answer to her problems, but I checked out of her life plans for us a while ago without giving notice. "I don't know if I want to apply to NYU," I say in a hurry.

The smile fades from Kylie's face. "But . . . that's all we've talked about."

"I know. And I wanted to tell you, but you just get so happy and certain about it. There was never any room for a rebuttal."

Kylie's face continues to slacken, and I think her cheeks might land on her lap. "Is it because of me? What everyone thinks about me? What . . . you think about me?" Her voice breaks at the last question, and my heart follows suit.

"Kylie," I say. I'm up on my feet and next to her before I even remember my feet moving. "Kylie, no. This has nothing to do with you and the messiness of the last few weeks. This is all me. I want to apply to an HBCU."

Kylie eyes are watery as she frowns in confusion.

"A historically Black college or university," I explain. "I've been reading about Howard, and they're like the highest producers of Black doctors and dentists and lawyers and pharmacists. It's usually ranked in the top five of the best HBCUs—and their dance team is amazing."

"NYU has a dance team," Kylie counters. "And it's super diverse."

I nod. "I know. But . . ." I take a breath and try to collect the words the right way in my mouth. "I've been in Windsor all my life. And most of the time, I'm one of a handful of Black people in my class. I'm one of a handful of Black people when we go eat at Olive Garden. Or catch a movie at Harbour View. Or buy a homecoming dress at Macy's. I thought for the longest time that this was okay. That this was the norm. But then I watched *A Different World*, and *School Daze* after that. Then *Drumline*. Then *Stomp the Yard*. And suddenly I realized I didn't have to be one of a handful. I could be one of a legion."

I remember the energy at the school board meeting. The electricity I felt being part of a team. A culture. A movement. I want to feel like that every day.

The tears spill from Kylie's eyes, and she swipes them away with the back of her hand. But she doesn't seem sad anymore. She sat and listened to every word I had to say like a mother listening to her child talk about their first day of school. She was happy that I was happy, but kind of worried to let me go.

"New York's not that far away from DC, right?" she asks with a small smile.

"There's about four hours between NYU and Howard." I've looked this up so many times over the summer, it's saved in my search engine. I give her a smile in return. "But probably less than that with the way you drive."

Kylie laughs, then wipes her face again. "Good. Then, bitch, stop crying and let's go get some Rita's."

We stuffed our faces with two cups of Italian ice each from Rita's. We rationalized it because we had to bide our time to make it look like we spent the whole day at school, but honestly, it's because Rita's has the best strawberry-mango Italian ice in the universe. When Kylie pulls into the parking lot of my apartment complex, I smear on crimson lip gloss to hide my strawberry-stained mouth.

"And what are you going to do about your red tongue?" Kylie asks.

"I'm just going to mumble when I talk. But I think my mom's still—" I spot my mom's car in the parking lot. There goes my hope of not having to bump into her or Eric until later. "What in the world is she doing home?"

"My dad's here too." Kylie pulls into an empty space next to a black Lexus with the license plate that reads *KINGPIN*. Mr. Brooks likes people to know it's him when he drives around town. We both climb out of her car, ready to get answers, when we see Mr. Brooks making a beeline out of my building and toward his car.

"Dad?" Kylie calls out.

Mr. Brooks stops like he ran into an invisible brick wall when he notices Kylie and me. Kylie spreads out her arms in confusion.

"Hello, Mr. Brooks," I say. *Hello?* Since when was I so formal with him? I guess right around the time I found out he was potentially racist.

Mr. Brooks's face softens into a smile. "Hi there, Naomi. Beautiful as always. How was school?"

"What's going on?" Kylie asks, avoiding his question with a question of her own. "Are you okay? Is Mama Nina okay?"

My heart pounds at the thought of something being

wrong with my mom. I peer up at our living room window, as if I could see potential signs of distress.

"Nina's fine," Mr. Brooks says, a certain staleness to his voice. "Get in your car, Kylie. We're having an early family dinner." He nods at me. "You take care, Naomi."

I frown. If I thought my hello was odd, Mr. Brooks just gave me a brush-off like I was some random weirdo on the street asking him for spare change.

"Dad, what the hell?" Kylie demands, sensing the weirdness too.

"Kylie, get in your damn car." He doesn't wait for her to respond. He just slides into his car and waits for her to do the same with his jaw clenched tight.

"What the hell?" she mouths to me.

I shrug in return. Once Kylie's back in her car, Mr. Brooks peels out of the parking lot with Kylie close behind. I run up to my apartment, taking two steps at a time. There was something off about the way that Mr. Brooks left. He never really comes to our apartment. And the rare times he has, my mom has always walked him down to his car. Always. Whether it was to make sure he took a plate of food home with him or to give him another hug. They were more than an employer and his nanny. They were more than friends. They were family. We all were.

I push the front door open, and the force of it knocks the knob into the wall behind it. Mom doesn't flinch. She's leaning forward against the peninsula of our kitchen, her fists clenched like she's ready to kick someone's ass.

"Mom?" My voice is small. Scared. "What's wrong? What was up with Mr. Brooks?"

Mom peels her eyes away from the granite of the peninsula and looks at me, her eyes burning with rage. "That man wasn't Scott Brooks." She points a trembling finger toward the living room window, toward the parking lot. "That was the monster that just threatened to take away my day care center."

NINETEEN

BLACKMAIL. THAT'S THE WORD I HEARD ERIC TOSSING AROUND WITH
Mom when he came home from work. Mom gave him the
whole rundown of her talk with Mr. Brooks but made sure
to send me to my room first. This was grown folks' business,
and she already felt guilty she vented even a little of it to me.
But through my closed bedroom door, I gathered enough
brushstrokes to paint a full picture:

Mr. Brooks wanted Mom to talk to this Gloria lady and
ask her to back down from corroborating the lawsuit.

Mom didn't feel comfortable intervening in matters she
didn't know much about.

Mr. Brooks politely reminded Mom about the loan he
gave her to start the day care center. A loan he could easily

pull. A loan I didn't know anything about.

Eric politely reminded Mom that he could drive to the Brooks house at that moment and kick Mr. Brooks's ass.

They went back and forth until dinnertime, Mom pleading with Eric to not do anything that would get him locked up again. I never knew exactly what Eric did to wind up in prison years before he reunited with my mom. They were high school sweethearts, and my mom got with my dad while Eric was locked up. By the time Eric got released, my dad was out, and Eric was in. My dad lives in North Carolina. Greensboro, I think . . . or maybe it's Asheboro. One of the 'boros. I never paid attention to the return address when he sent my birthday cards, keener to see how much money he'd stuffed into it. Outside of those yearly deposits, we don't talk much about my dad. I never felt the need to—I always had Eric.

When Mom called me out to get my plate for dinner, her eyes and cheeks were puffy, and Eric was stewing in the corner of the living room. Staring at the front door as if he was trying to conjure up a way to escape and give Mr. Brooks those hands.

"Are y'all okay?" I asked, knowing damn well they weren't.

Mom gave me a soft smile. "We will be." She handed me my plate and kissed me on the forehead. I didn't think that was completely true, but I took my plate and my kiss and the surface-level conversations about what came on TV that night. But I had this lingering headache as I tried to wrap my mind around the Mr. Brooks I knew, and the monster that said those nasty things to his employees. That threatened my mom.

The headache is still here when I get to school on Thursday morning. Sitting right behind my eyes and wrapping its way around my skull until it feels like I'm wearing a helmet of pain. And it's so consuming that I barely notice that Faith is speaking until I feel her eyes on me.

"Hmm," I say to her.

"What are you doing after school today?" she asks.

I shake my head and look at her, too tired to probe any further.

"Ms. Denita wants you to practice with us today."

My eyes try to widen, but my headache pushes back. I still get a rush of energy that sends my fingers tapping against our lab table. "Really? I made the team?"

Faith shrugs. "She didn't say all that. She probably just wants to see more of what you can do." She scans my face, as if my headache has somehow spilled to the surface. "You up for it?"

I nod way too many times. "I'm up for anything."

Cheesy, but facts. If anything was going to get me through this dumpster fire of a day—of a school year, actually—it would be even the smallest of chances that I get to end my senior year being a Wolverine. Or at least being near them.

When the last bell rings, I pop two Advil, grab a pair of extra sweats I kept in my locker for cheer, and rush to the gym. The Wolverines are on the right, stretching, scrolling through phones, and shooting the shit as they wait for practice to begin. On the other side of the gym, right across from them, is my cheer squad. My *former* cheer squad. They also goof around while waiting for Coach Beverly. The excitement in my stomach has now churned into dread. It's raining outside. One of those Virginia storms that alternate between sunshine and downpour every five minutes. Neither team could practice on the field, so we all had to squeeze in here and make do. Perfect.

"What up, bitch!" Roma hollers to me, and waves like a maniac. As if I could miss her. Ava, Shauna, and Brittany notice me, too, and hop up and down like I'm a soldier who's just returned home from active duty. Their faces full of anticipation, expecting me to skip on over and join practice like usual.

I lift one hand at the wrist to give a tiny wave. Hope that the small movement conveys everything: *Great to see you guys, but I'm not here for you.* Faith and some of the other Wolverines stop their small talk and watch me, also waiting to see what I'll do. They don't have the same wide smiles as my former squad. They're crossed arms and pursed lips and cocked hips.

I take a breath and sidestep over to them, the Wolverines. Roma's and the others' faces drop. Hard, like one of those carnival rides that send you plummeting down without warning. Not Kylie's, though. She looks up at me from her V sit and reach. Her eyes bounce between me and the Wolverines before giving me a small nod and smile. She's resigned to it all, but that doesn't mean she has to be overly thrilled about my decision. I return her greeting and catch up with Faith.

"Hey," I say to her. "I'm here."

"No shit," Nevaeh scoffs, who just had to come over and join us at that exact moment.

"You should get changed before Ms. Denita comes out," Faith says as she stretches out her arms and shoulders.

I give her a thumbs-up and scurry to the locker room, trying to ignore the eyes from the squad burning a hole in my back. As I slip out of my jeans and into my sweats, a folded-up newspaper on the bench sandwiched between the rows of lockers catches my eye. The only time I see a newspaper is when Mom uses them to make crafts for her day care center. There's red scribbling on a section of it that gives me extra pause. I walk closer to get a better look, and an article about Mr. Brooks's case is on display for the whole locker room to see. The picture of Mr. Brooks that accompanies the article has been defaced. He's been given a red nose, and his mouth has been doodled over. There's an arrow pointed to him, and at the other end is the word *CLOWN* in all caps. A breath gets caught in my throat, and I look around me. There's a tickle at the nape of my neck that I usually get when I'm being watched. Someone wanted me to see this, and I can't help but wonder if they wanted to see me seeing this. But after a thorough scan of the room, the only other person here is Mr. Brooks's scribbled-on face. I turn the newspaper over so he can no longer glare at me, then rush back out to the gym.

Aaliyah purrs through the speaker and the Wolverines are in formation, going through their warm-up routine. Ms. Denita sits on the bottom bleacher next to Rico, both whispering comments to each other as they watch the girls sway and stretch. Faith's in the front. She looks at me and hitches her head behind her while she dances. Crap. I'm supposed to be doing this too. I scurry to the back of the formation and watch them for a few seconds before joining. I'm always a move behind. I rock my hips when they stretch their calves. I stretch my calves as they spin. I spin, and they're crouched down in a sumo stretch. I spot Shauna and Brittany gazing over at me in between their own stretches. Their faces are crumpled up in uncertainty, probably wondering what the hell I'm doing over here when I can't keep up with a simple warm-up routine. But I keep moving, dammit. I hope that counts for something.

The song ends, and I'm already out of breath. Being clueless burns a lot of energy.

"All right, we're tweaking the end of our homecoming routine," Ms. Denita announces. "We needed more oomph for our last two eight counts, so I tasked Faith to come up with something new. And . . ." She nods at Faith. Something tells me that's the closest you'll get to a compliment from her. "She delivered. Rico, cue up the music."

Rico's black-polished fingers tap and scroll through his phone. He seems like he has both the easiest and most difficult job in the world. Essentially, he's just playing music and taking a few notes for Ms. Denita. But I don't think Ms. Denita takes too kindly to mistakes, so that music and those notes probably always have to be on point.

Rihanna's "Don't Stop the Music" streams through the speakers, and I try to hide my smile. Rihanna sampled the music from "Wanna Be Startin' Somethin'" for this track, and MJ's early hit was my audition song for the Wolverines. I know this beat well, so maybe it'll do me some favors in picking up this routine. We all move to the sidelines as Faith remains at her position. She strut-walks toward us to the beat, her hands alternating and extending to the sides as she glides across the floor. The beat drops, and so does she into a front roll. As soon as she's back on her feet, she leaps up into a toe touch, then crouches low to do some bucking. Her hair whips and floats as she contorts her limbs and rocks to the beat. Just when it seems like she's given us everything, she plummets into a death drop with both feet and lands on her back, her whole body sharp and rigid like a bullet.

The Wolverines and I whoop and cheer for Faith as she climbs back up to her feet. Faith just gives a sheepish grin, like what she did wasn't really a big deal.

"You understood the assignment!" Amari says to Faith, and slaps her on the butt.

"Okay, ladies. I want you to run through these changes in small groups while Faith and I—" Ms. Denita's voice is intersected by the cheer squad across the gym going into one of their chants and formations:

"The S is for Super,
The U is for United,
The P is for Perfection and you know that we're
excited . . ."

I crack my knuckles to keep them from clasping in sync with the ladies. Ms. Denita glances at them, then turns back to us and continues with her orders. But she's in a battle for airtime, and this doesn't go unnoticed by the Wolverines.

"Are you serious? Are they even usually this loud?" Nevaeh asks.

"I barely be hearing them at the games. You need a stethoscope to make out anything they're saying," another girl says.

The snippy murmurs continue, and I just look down at my feet and wait for it to end. I'm not a cheerleader anymore, but I'm not about to dog the cheerleaders either. They were . . . I mean *are*, my friends.

"Hey!" Ms. Denita snaps her fingers to get our attention. "Whose practice are you at? Focus on nailing this routine. Now get into your groups."

We scatter into small pods, and of course I end up with Nevaeh and two other girls I recognize from the school halls but never had a class with. One of them, Jordan, is a transfer student from Georgia. I know the dance teams down there are lit, so she probably made the team after Ms. Denita only saw her strut.

"That's not the foot she led with," Nevaeh snaps at me after I finish a spin.

I frown. "She turned to the right. So, I led with my right foot."

Nevaeh rolls her eyes. "She turned to the right but did a left sidestep first. Like this." She thrusts her hip to the left before spinning on her right foot. "But, you know, if you want to pay more attention to your girls across the way, you could high kick it right over to them."

"That was easy to miss," Jordan says. "I forgot the step to the left until you mentioned it." She gives me a reassuring nod, and I could hug her so hard that she'd gasp for air.

"Whatever," Nevaeh mutters as she tries the spin again.

I shake out my limbs and do the move again myself, making sure to pop my hip so hard to the left that I hope Nevaeh feels it. We run through the routine a few times, once in front of Faith as she and Ms. Denita float in between the groups.

Faith tweaks one or two of our moves but says we're doing okay overall. I'll take an okay from Faith.

Across the gym, the cheer squad is working on pyramids. Kylie is at the top of one of them. She extends her left leg, and Ava, on top of the other pyramid, grabs onto it. That was supposed to be me. I was supposed to be the one towering over everyone next to Kylie. But I chose to be here, having Nevaeh and other Wolverines give me attitudes and eye rolls.

"Don't fall from grace like your dad," one of the Wolverines call out toward Kylie. Some of the girls laugh, and I search for the girl who said it. I don't know if I'm going to confront them, but I'll at least give them a heated glare. I wonder if it's the same girl who left the newspaper in the locker room for me to see.

Kylie hears whoever it was. The painted smile on her face stiffens before she falls into the arms of her base. The squad gathers around Kylie to comfort her and shoot nasty glares across the gym at us.

"Who said that?" Ms. Denita demands. I search, wanting to know too. But nobody speaks up. "Okay. Since suddenly no one remembers how to speak, give me ten laps around the gym. Everyone. Now!"

The Wolverines groan and start jogging along the sidelines of the gym. I join them, jogging next to Jordan.

"Do you know who said it?" I ask her as our sneakers squeak on the floor.

She shrugs. "I don't know, but I kinda hate her right now."

We reach the cheer squad's side of the gym. As I run past, Roma hugs Kylie while most of the other girls still hover around them. Kylie looks at me over Roma's shoulder, hurt brimming at her eyelids. I want to be the one hugging her, comforting her. I want to apologize on behalf of the Wolverines. But I can't apologize on behalf a group I don't officially belong to. And from the looks of the rest of the squad, glaring at me as I parade around the gym with the enemy, I wouldn't be too welcomed waltzing over there. Kylie's face pinches up in betrayal as I run past. She doesn't even try to look at me during my remaining laps.

When we're all out of breath and guzzling down water, Ms. Denita makes us get right into showing what we learned from Faith's new choreography. We stay in our small groups, each of us getting a chance to move into the center of the gym to practice the moves in front of everyone. I slap my hands against my lap in anticipation. We ran through the steps so much, they were a part of me now. Still, I have a bull's-eye on my back. Not just from the Wolverines, but also from my former squad members, who keep stealing glares in my direction. I have more to prove than just my place on the team. I need to show why I deserted cheer to become a Wolverine. To show that this is what gave me the joy that cheer alone couldn't tap into.

My group is called up last. We race to the center of the

gym, then strut-walk toward the sidelines on our cue. We move through Faith's routine with the power of a whole team behind us, even though there are only four of us dancing. Despite all the lip Nevaeh gave me while we practiced, we speak the same language on the dance floor. We both know what our bodies can do, and we know just how to unleash it. For these few seconds, I imagine what it would've been like if I had joined her for that middle school talent show. We could've been magic together. We *are* magic together. By the time we finish with our death drop, we're all heaving for air on our backs. I hear cheers as I stare up at the fluorescent lights in the ceiling.

When I peel myself off the floor, the Wolverines are clapping and stomping their feet. For us. For me. I jog back over to the sidelines, and someone taps the back of my arm. I turn, and Faith nods at me.

"Good job," she mouths.

I pat my chest in return: *Thank you.*

Ms. Denita's going through a string of announcements. I try to follow along, but I'm still buzzing. If I could find a way to bottle what I'm feeling at this moment, I would store it in the back of my closet and release it when I'm my lowest so that I can buzz again. Over Ms. Denita's shoulder, Shauna whispers something into Brittany's ear. Brittany smirks and nods as they both stare at me. Glare at me. Bubble officially burst.

"Nice work today, ladies. I'll see you tomorrow," Ms. Denita wraps up. We all begin walking toward the locker room. "Hang back for a bit, Naomi."

My heart does a death drop. The others push past me as I wait for Ms. Denita and Rico to finish up whatever they're chatting about. Finally, Ms. Denita slaps Rico on the back, and he heads to the exit.

"Nice moves," he calls out to me.

I blink. I'm not sure if I've ever heard Rico say anything aside from his hushed conversations with Ms. Denita.

"Thanks," I say, still in shock.

He smiles and pulls his twisted locs into a ponytail before leaving the gym.

"You picked up the choreography pretty quickly today," Ms. Denita says to me.

I shrug. "I could've been a little quicker, but I tried my best."

Ms. Denita smirks. "If you're going to be a Wolverine, you need to learn how to take a compliment. Don't dim your own shine. Lift your head up in the spotlight."

"Am . . . am I a Wolverine?" My eyebrows rise along with my hopes.

Ms. Denita chews on her gum for what feels like an hour before speaking again. "I want to put you on as an alternate."

A squeal spurts out of me as I hop up and down.

"But don't think that means you can get lazy. If any of

my girls go down, that means you have to be ready to step in for them. If anything, you have the toughest job."

My hopping simmers into a shuffle from foot to foot. I haven't figured out how to contain my excitement. "I won't let you down."

"I wouldn't have chosen you if I thought that you would." Her mouth pinches at the corners as she gives me a small smile. "Now get out of here."

I practically skip to the locker room. I know becoming an alternate is not necessarily being part of the team, but it also means that I'll be at their practices and attend all the same games and events and wear the uniform and walk around the school with my head high because, dammit, I am *almost* a Wolverine. I even give myself a little spin through the doors when I hear it:

"The fuck is this?"

Kylie. She gets squeaky when she's irritated, and her voice is as high-pitched as a teakettle right now. I run farther into the room, and Kylie's holding up the newspaper, waving it toward some of the Wolverines. I was so caught up in my happy news that I didn't even notice that the squad had finished practice at the same time. With all of us in here, it's all the ingredients for a homemade bomb that was about to go boom.

The Wolverines just snicker and go about changing out of their practice sweats.

"I said, what. The fuck. Is this?" Kylie's teeth are gritted now. Her eyes dart around the room, trying to find the culprit. She lands on me and scowls. I throw up both hands, showing her there is no newsprint on my fingertips.

"It looks like an article about your racist-ass daddy," Amari answers, and some of the Wolverines howl with laughter.

Kylie's face reddens as she rips the newspaper in half and slams it into the trash bin. "Thought you guys were smart enough not to fall for fake news."

"Fake news?" Amari cocks an eyebrow. "I wonder where you heard that from. Your Lord and savior Trump?"

I bite on my lip. Where's Coach Beverly? Ms. Denita? Any adult? Someone needed to stop this before we all went down.

"Just because her family's white doesn't mean they voted for Trump," Shauna snaps. "Plus, a lot of Black people voted for him too."

"Bitch, we don't need you to tell us what Black people do." Nevaeh throws her T-shirt onto the floor and bosses up to them in nothing but her leggings and a sports bra. *Tick, tick, tick . . .*

"How about let's calm down?" I inch my way into the middle. My former squad to my left, my new team to my right. "The newspaper is gone. No harm. No foul."

Kylie scowls so hard that I can barely see her eyes

anymore. "No harm? Someone left that so I could see them defacing not only my dad's face, but his reputation. And you say there's no harm?" She shakes her head at me: *Who are you?*

Great question. All this time I had thought the newspaper was a message for me; I didn't even consider it was meant for Kylie. I didn't even bother throwing it away. If I'd done that, I wouldn't be in the middle of this turf war right now.

"Nobody cares about your white girl tears, Becky," Nevaeh says. "You worried about your dad's picture and reputation? Heifer, there are people out there without a job because he's racist."

"Guess one bad apple does spoil the whole bunch," Amari adds.

"Oh, my whole family is racist now?" Kylie cuts her eyes at me. "You hear that? You're going to let them talk about all of us?"

I take a deep breath, try to breathe in the right thing to say. Of course, I wanted to defend Kylie. But I couldn't defend Connor's comment about Black people being ghetto. And I damn sure couldn't defend Mr. Brooks trying to steal away something my mom worked so hard for. I needed answers before I talked out of the side of my mouth. "Well, if the lawsuit gets settled, then—"

Kylie lets out a loud groan. "Oh, *fuck* you, Naomi." Spit flies out her mouth like shrapnel, piercing my skin.

"Hey! Relax! Come on." Roma yanks Kylie by the arm

and tries to lead her out of the locker room.

Kylie breaks free and keeps glaring at me. "These your girls now? Well, ask your *girls* why they defaced your locker!"

I almost gasp. Almost. The breath gets stuck in my chest, and I'm too numb to continue the response. I've heard about this before. Someone getting shot or stabbed but being too much in shock to feel anything. If what Kylie's saying is true, then I'm gutted.

"Yeah." Kylie nods and smiles, clearly taking delight in my astonishment. "Connor found out before admin could. You think your girl, Ms. Guy, gonna have your back?"

"Enough!" Roma snatches Kylie's arm again and drags her to the door. Roma glances back at me and frowns. I don't know if her frown is out of confusion or disappointment. I don't know anything anymore.

The squad storms out behind them, and Nevaeh and Amari break out into a fit of giggles. Just carrying on like Kylie didn't just drop a huge bomb before she left. If they really had something to do with my locker, they didn't care that I found out. Even though I stayed behind with the Wolverines, I'm clearly not one of them. I'm alone.

"OMG, fuck you, Naomi," Nevaeh mocks, sticking her middle finger up and sounding like a Valley girl. Amari laughs even harder.

Faith slams her duffel bag onto the middle of the floor, and the laughter comes to a screeching halt. "You serious right now?" Her glare bounces between Nevaeh and Amari. "We're just getting our shit together after all your foolishness. Now you want to sacrifice it again, for what?"

Nevaeh doesn't answer, just pulls a toiletry bag out of her locker.

"Y'all think this shit is cute, but you giving that white girl all your power. She's living in your heads, rent-free, when what you need to be doing is showing up and showing out on the field." Faith stands with her hands on her hips and surveys the Wolverines like an irate teacher after getting a bad report from a substitute. "Enough with this bullshit."

She snatches her bag back up from the floor and stomps toward the showers. The rest of the Wolverines don't make another peep. They either head to the showers, too, or make their way out of the locker room in general. Except for Jordan. She cradles her rubber shower caddy against her chest and chews on her bottom lip.

"You okay?" she manages to ask me.

Great question. I look down at my feet like the answer is buried somewhere between my toes. "Is it true?" When Jordan doesn't answer, I glance up at her. My eyes get thick and misty, and she's only a blur. "Did you all really mess with my locker?" I remember Drew. Remember him talking about the Wolverines seeking revenge. Was that it? Was I the casualty?

Jordan finally gives me a shrug. "I'm new. They don't tell me anything." She walks over and rests a hand on my shoulder. I barely feel her fingertips. The numbness hasn't worn off. "But you did good today. Everyone saw it." She smiles at me before heading toward the showers.

I plop down on the bench, in the same spot I found that newspaper. I don't know where I should go. My cheer squad doesn't want me, and it's obvious that the Wolverines don't either. I bury my face into my hands, unattached. Unwanted. Alone.

NOW

I press the bottle of Dasani against my forehead and let the coolness thaw my headache. I haven't taken a sip of water yet—just use the bottle as a compress. Momentary relief in a night filled with pain.

Detective Stretch sits across from me in the interrogation room again. *My* interrogation room. She rests her chin in her palm and studies me, as if watching me tend to my headache is something worth noting. "That was rough," she says finally. "Boyfriend?"

It takes me three seconds to realize she's talking about Connor. I see his face again, all flushed and fury. "No. We never made it that far." I untwist my bottle and take a gulp, hoping to swallow down the tears before they bubble up again.

"Hmm. Could've fooled me." Detective Stretch leans back in her chair and laces her fingers across her nonexistent belly. "He looked pretty hurt for someone who was never your boyfriend. It's almost like . . . he blamed you for everything."

And there it is. In a few words, she changes from ally to authority. She has a purpose here, and it's not just to give me snacks and Kleenex. She wants a confession that hasn't been earned.

"That's because he doesn't know the full story," I say.

"And what is that, Naomi?"

I drink more water and let the seconds stretch. I'll drink the whole damn bottle now if I have to. "Where's my mom?" I slam the almost empty bottle back onto the table.

"She's coming."

"She's been coming forever."

"There's a process for everything, Naomi." She takes my bottle and starts to peel off the label. "But we can talk in the meantime. Fill up time. We don't have to talk about last night, but we can talk about how we got there."

I fold my arms across my chest and tuck my hands in my armpits. I have nothing to do with them now that she's taken my water.

"You seem to have a lot of anger toward the Brookses. I

saw you when they brought you in. The TV was on behind the front desk, and I watched you watching Scott Brooks when he found out about the body. Your jaw kept clenching like you were gnawing something. Like you wanted to cry with him but tried to chew it down. Do you hate him that much? You can't even grieve with the man?"

My eyes dart up to her. I expect to see her judging me, but her head tilts in curiosity. Like she wishes there were a way to crack my head open just to understand what's happening inside. She's not alone.

"I never said I hated him."

"So, it's just his children that you hate? That's strange, because he made them."

"I never said I hate any of the Brookses." My voice comes out louder than I meant it to, but she needs to hear me. "I just . . . I hate what they do. I hate what they represent."

"And what's that?"

"Power," I say without even pausing. There's no reason to—it's so obvious. "Unearned power."

"We live in America, sweetie." Detective Stretch has succeeded in peeling off the label and wraps it around her fingers. "Every white person has some kind of power. That doesn't make them special."

"They're *not* special."

"Then it's not fair to punish them because you suddenly just woke up and smelled the privilege—especially when it seems like you've been benefiting from it for years."

"That's not *true*." I slap my hand on the table to punctuate the final word. Detective Stretch doesn't flinch from the noise, just continues to twirl that label around her fingers until the tips are paler than the rest of her skin. I wait for some guys in badges to storm in and slam my face against the table for daring to raise my voice and hand at this white woman. But nothing happens. It's just Detective Stretch and me and the empty space between us that she wants me to fill with words. But I don't want to.

I don't want to, I don't want to, I don't want to.

The fear fills my lungs again, and it's not because I'm scared that my words will keep me locked up. It's the detective's words that leave me shook. If this is how she sees me after just a few minutes, how do the people who know me best see me? As a girl coming to terms with who she is, or as someone who turns her back on people who were like family because being "woke" is on trend? And it's that latter image that's chilling.

"What part?" Detective Stretch asks. "What part's not true?"

"I loved the Brookses. I mean, I . . ." My tongue trips over which tense to use, but if I dwell too long on that, the tears will start up again. "Have you heard of the saying to never meet your heroes?" I try instead.

Detective Stretch nods. "Yeah. I bumped into my favorite

author at an airport. He posed for a selfie with me and every-thing, and I posted that pic on Facebook. Two days later, he goes viral for complaining how hard it is for white men to find work now. Talk about egg on my face." She shakes her head in disgust, as if she's reliving the moment when she saw her hero fall.

"Imagine if you basically lived with that author. That you shared meals with him. Secrets with him. That for some of the happiest times in your life, he was right there. Next to you." I'm in the Brookses' backyard, running through sprinklers while their pool gets cleaned. I hear the shrieks of our childish laughter. I smell the hot dogs charring on Mr. Brooks's grill. See Mom and Mrs. Brooks sitting under umbrellas, smiling at us. Mrs. Brooks leaning toward Mom and squeezing Mom's hand before turning the smiles onto each other. The memory is right there, soft and delicate—so close that if I reach out it'll brush across my fingertips like a cloud.

But you can't really touch clouds. And like most delicate things, the memory crumbles inside my palm. "That would make the news about your author more devastating, right? Remembering all the times he smiled in your face while he destroyed things behind your back. It's scarier when the monster's been under your roof the whole time."

"True." Detective Stretch finally balls up the label in her hand. "But I still miss reading his novels. It's almost like

I'm angrier at myself for falling for that misogynistic prick's words in the first place. Like, what does that say about me?" She tosses the label in the trash can next to her and shrugs. "Just like I'm sure you're worried what loving the Brookses says about you."

I tuck my hands deeper into my armpits, my arms crushing against my chest. Like maybe if I smother my heart enough her words and their sentiment won't reach it. But it keeps beating. If anything, it beats faster at the mere mention of their name. So fast that my breath tries to keep up with it. And then I see Kylie and her hair and the way it whipped around her face during the explosion. . . .

I'm gasping now. I try to take breaths, but I can only catch them in sips, puffing through a cocktail straw when I need an exhaust pipe. "I can't . . . breathe. . . ."

"Naomi." Detective Stretch's hand is on my lap. "Naomi, you're having a panic attack. It's okay. Here, breathe with me. I'll count for us. In—one, two, three, four, five. Out—one, two, three, four, five . . ." She keeps guiding me. Keeps her hand on my lap and makes me take these slow, deliberate breaths. I follow her lead and after a few rounds, my pulse steadies. My chest is lighter. I breathe again without thinking too much about it.

Detective Stretch hands me my naked water bottle. I gulp down the rest of its contents, then wipe my mouth with the back of my hand.

"Sorry," I say. "That's never happened to me before."

"I get it. You lost a lot tonight."

I nod. That's all I'm able to do. I want to tell her that I've lost a lot before tonight. That the grieving process started as soon as Kylie's Target video went viral. That since the start of this school year, every one of the Brookses has broken my heart. And maybe I'm scared that it'll always be a bit fractured. But saying all of that might bring the panic back, and I just figured out how to breathe again.

TWENTY

THE NEXT TWO WEEKS ARE AN ENDLESS BLUR OF SCHOOL, DANCE PRAC-
tice, and helping Mom out at Itsy Bitsy. The fear of Mr.
Brooks taking it all away is getting to her. I can see it in her
shoulders, her walk, her tight smile. Still, she cares for those
babies like they're her own. She wipes away every tear and
makes sure to high-five every tiny hand. It's almost like she
needs to enjoy every moment she can before it's all taken
away from her. I relieve some of that pressure when I can. I
clean out diaper pails and disinfect dolls and answer phones,
all so Mom can do what she really wants to do: take care of
the kiddos.

And I don't just do it for her. The day care is a good
distraction from my own shit. The more I'm there, the less

I'm in my own head. Reading updates on Mr. Brooks's legal issues, avoiding Kylie and Connor in the school halls. Wondering if the girls I'm dancing next to have it out for me. Not that any of them would admit it. I asked Faith about it once during physics class, away from the stink eyes of the rest of the Wolverines. Faith sighed and peeled her eyes away from the lab report she was typing up for us:

"And if they did?" she asked.

My head jerked back from the response. I had gotten used to sassiness from Nevaeh and Amari during practices and games. She'd always steered clear of it up to this point. "What?" I managed to ask.

"What happens if you find out they tagged your locker?" Faith continued. "You report them. They get in trouble. The team gets benched again, and you never get a chance to join us on the field. Is that what you want?"

"I mean, no . . ." My eyes wouldn't stop blinking while my brain rebooted, trying to understand what Faith was getting at. "But they deserve some kind of consequence, right? It's not okay what they did."

Faith twisted in her stool and turned her whole body to me. "Do you know how long Ms. Denita and I had to fight to get this team started? You think anyone wanted to listen to a quiet Black girl and the secretary from the school counseling office?"

I had forgotten about Ms. Denita's actual day job. How

she's the one who deals with class-schedule changes and new-student registration and all the other miscellaneous things the school counselors were too busy for. She's such a presence with the Wolverines that it's easy to forget that her day job requires her to stay in the shadows.

"And even with all the accolades and media we got during our first year as a team, we were a footnote in the yearbook. We get slotted during the bathroom breaks at games and other events. We had to raise our own money just to get costumes. And before they came, our moms and aunties and whoever had to sew random shit together." Faith paused and closed her eyes, as if she was back there at the beginning of it all. Squeezing her hips into ill-fitting leotards and tights.

"We're walking consequences," Faith continued as she opened her eyes. "All of us in the Wolverines. Every Black or person of color here at Windsor Woods. We're an afterthought. But we make it work. And you can too. Just keep showing up and showing out. That'll tell Nevaeh and 'em."

I swallowed, digesting every word Faith just shared. More words than she's ever shared in such a short amount of time. "Tell them what?" I asked.

"That you belong with us." Faith turned back to her laptop and typed up our notes. Our conversation was done. But I wasn't. I listened to Faith and threw my whole body into practices. My whole soul. And I stood up and cheered for the Wolverines at games from my spot on the sidelines to make them see: I was with them.

The thing about throwing your all into something is that at the end of the day, you're wrecked. Too exhausted to peel the clothes off your skin, so you just climb into bed—jeans, sneakers, and all. The same goes for tonight. I'm facedown on my bed, tennis shoes and hoodie still on, when my phone bloops to alert me of a DM. I inch my head up just enough to see a message from Cleo:

This is that kid Orlando I was telling you about the other day. Check it out. He's going IN!

I press Play on the corresponding message, and a stocky Black guy with twists edged up into a high fade is dancing along to Childish Gambino's "This Is America." He has the choreography from the iconic music video down pat, everything from the intricate body rolls to the playful shoulder jerks. Above his head, random facts about Black people pop onto the screen:

Almost 20 percent of Black people live below the poverty line, the most of any ethnic group in the US.
Only one in three Black people who need mental health care receive it.
Over 40 percent of people on death row are Black.

The video is strange, but riveting. Absurd, but grounded. Much like the original music video, I can't take my eyes off it. Cleo FaceTimes me before I can finish watching it all. I climb on my knees and fluff out my coils. I don't need to look picture ready for Cleo, but I also don't need to look like some slacker high school student who's too lazy to unmat their hair for a call.

Once my hair gets the volume I want, I answer the call. "Hey!" I wince. That came out way too loud.

Cleo's chilling. Lying in what looks like her bed in the dorms, with a silk scarf wrapped around her head and tortoiseshell eyeglasses perched low on her nose. She clearly didn't feel the need to dress to the nines for me, but she doesn't have to. Cleo could walk into a store with bedroom slippers on, and everyone would ask where she got them from.

"What you up to?" she asks with a yawn, like we shoot the shit all the time. She has reached out to me since the school board protest, DMing updates (*That clown John Anderson resigned. About damn time!*), dropping recommendations (*Listen to that new Kodak Black. Dude's the next Nas. Yes, I said it. Ion care!!!*), and sharing food for thought (*If penguins can't fly, why are they considered birds? Can't we all just be birds, then?*). Cleo's messages were as sporadic as lightning, but just as thrilling.

I look around my room, trying to find something clever to say so she won't regret actually calling me. Then remember that real recognizes real, and Cleo seems like someone who can smell bullshit from a mile away. "Recovering from the day," I admit.

"Yeah. Faith told me that you've been going hard during

practice. Getting ready for the homecoming game and every-thing."

I almost choke from gasping. Maybe it's the surprise of Faith saying something nice about me. Or maybe just that Faith says anything about me at all. "I try—" I cut myself off as I think about Ms. Denita's words from my first full practice: *Lift your head up in the spotlight.* "Yeah, I've been putting in work."

Cleo nods, impressed. "That's what's up. So, what you think about Orlando's video?"

"You were right. Dude was on fire."

Cleo points to me through the phone, as if I nailed it exactly. "And that's just his more artsy shit. He did this pod-cast interview a while back where he broke down how society treats Black athletes like modern-day slaves. Chills for days, I'm telling you."

I nod along and squint my eyes like I'm in deep thought. If this guy gave Cleo chills, there is nothing remotely pro-found I can say right now to follow that.

"You know he's going to be at that event I was telling you about this Saturday night," Cleo says, filling the space for me. "I remember high school dances being kinda lit, but Faith also told me you weren't kicking it with your usual friends. So if you wanted to roll through to the Don't Attack Blacks event, the offer still stands."

That's right. Cleo had invited me to the DAB event weeks

ago, right after the protest. That feels like a million years ago, and my life has changed in a million ways since then. The dance isn't on my list of priorities anymore. I planned to spend Saturday recovering from the homecoming game the night before. From the awkwardness of watching both my former squad and current dance team go head-to-head during halftime. So even though I have my Hulu queued up and ready to go for Saturday night, there's still a tiny, nagging part of me that thought I might change my mind. It is going to be my last homecoming dance after all, and I did have a dress waiting for me in my closet. I even had this vision of possibly working things out with Connor and giving him one dance. Maybe that one dance could lead to something else. . . .

"Is Faith going?" I ask.

"Yeah, she mentioned it. You can ride with her people if you're interested. Unless you need me to come and get you."

Cleo has been lying down the whole time we've been talking, as if she doesn't have a care in the world. But when she talks about Orlando and this event, and whether I'm coming or not, there's an urgency in her voice. Like she really wants me to be there, but she can't show it. All this time I thought I had to impress her, and she's almost begging for my company. I chew on my lip to hide my smile.

"Sounds great," I say. "Let me check with my mom first."

"Cool." Cleo holds up her fist, then hangs up without

saying goodbye. But it didn't feel rude. Cleo seems like a person with intention, and once she made her point, there was no need to dwell. I respect that.

I lie back in bed and think about how different my homecoming weekend will be compared with what I planned over the summer. It was supposed to be pom-poms on Friday, then limo rides on Saturday. Laughing and putting on makeup with Kylie and Roma, and slow dancing with Connor under dim lights. Now, though, I'm spending Friday night on the sidelines. But at least on Saturday, I'll feel like I have a purpose. A voice.

Windsor Woods High is known for two things: attendance leniency during hunting season, and Principal Hicks's famous pork ribs that he'd bring to every open house. Far from that list of notables is our football team. We usually win two games a season—three if the opposing team's coach falls asleep during the game (which has happened more than once before). So, when we enter halftime for our homecoming game on the losing end of 14–0, nobody's surprised. If anything, we all know the halftime show is about to be a lit-uation. As usual, the cheerleaders will go out and get everyone hyped and the homecoming court will make its appearance. But the part I'm most excited about, especially this year, is when the Wolverines tear up the field with the marching band.

We sit in a reserved section in the stands, a few rows below the members of the marching band. Some of the girls have windbreaker jackets over their sparkly unitards, but I shed mine sometime during the second quarter. The energy of the night, plus the possibility of the halftime show, has my heart pumping like there's a generator in my chest. I know I'm not performing tonight, but the Wolverines, these girls, they are my team, whether they want to be or not. And I want them to kick ass. I plan on whooping and hollering from the sidelines so loudly that they'll feel like I'm out in the field with them.

"There go your girls," Nevaeh says next to me, as the cheerleaders bounce out onto the field. There's a laugh tickling at her throat, as if the notion of me being friends with any of them is hilarious. And maybe it is. I haven't heard much of anything from my former team, not even Roma. But she did like a comment I left on one of her Instagram posts. It was a picture of her in front of a Harry Styles wall calendar, counting down the days until her birthday.

Mr. Styles is warming up his vocals, ready to serenade Happy Bday to you, I wrote. I edited my comment at least five times before sending it. It usually took me two seconds to write a comment to Roma, but things were so murky between me and the squad that I didn't want to leave anything that could be considered passive-aggressive. But she liked it three minutes later. That had to count for something—that maybe the door of our friendship was cracked open just a little.

Faith leans forward from her seat on the other side of me and smirks at Nevaeh. "Don't even," she says. "Ms. Denita doesn't want any drama tonight."

She's referring to last week's football game. Nevaeh, Amari, and a few others mocked the squad's routine, moving their bodies on the sidelines in stilted efforts that was more robot than cheerful human. They had gotten laughs and cheers for half of the routine before Ms. Denita marched over and gave them the business. It was too late, though. Kylie and the rest of the cheerleaders had already seen them and made sure to give all the Wolverines the evil eye as they pranced back to the sidelines.

Nevaeh throws up both hands in annoyance at Faith and sits back, watches the cheer squad's routine with a pronounced smirk on her face. She probably has to dig deep for that hate, because the cheerleaders are throwing down. Everything's on point, from their syncopated hand clasps to their transitions to their heel stretches. Kylie stands out the most, like she always does. But tonight, she's on fire. She shows no weakness as she lands on her feet from a backflip, and when she's tossed in the air into a pyramid, she's fierce and weightless all at once. It's like she knows everyone wants her to fail tonight, and she puts everything on the line to shut the haters down. It takes everything in me to not stand up and cheer her on. I don't know what kind of mixed messages that would send to my teammates, or to Kylie.

Jordan looks back at me from the bleacher below me, her mouth parted as if she just finished saying *wow*. I'm not alone—she feels it too.

An EDM song begins to blare through the speakers, and the crowd goes ballistic as the squad gets into the dance portion of the routine. Amari and Mercedes sit in the row below us next to Jordan. Amari swivels around to give Nevaeh a look.

"Girl," Amari says, and Nevaeh cracks up laughing.

I sigh under my breath. I can't figure out all the hate. It seems to go beyond Mr. Brooks, beyond all the Parking Lot Becky mess. The cheerleading squad is talented, dammit. I've been a part of them. I know how much work goes into these routines. I can't help but wonder if Nevaeh and Amari would still have jokes if Kylie never became Parking Lot Becky. If I were still on the squad. If maybe there was something deeper, buried under the soil of this town. I think about Kylie's words on our last Ky and Ny Fun Day: *You can't take two steps without treading on tragic history.* Damn if that wasn't the gospel.

Faith bumps me with her elbow. "Someone's trying to get your attention."

I peel my eyes away from the field, and Connor stands on the sidelines just below our section. He's wearing his homecoming tux already since he's part of the homecoming court, as if he wouldn't be. His admirers outweighed his haters. I hate to admit it, but damn, he looks good. He has a cobalt-blue vest under his jacket that brings out his eyes, and his hair is slicked back so we can all be in awe of his jawline. When he sees me seeing him, he smiles and waves me down. I almost look behind me to make sure he's gesturing toward me. I've pretty much ghosted him ever since he asked me to the dance. Our encounters in the halls have been down-graded to shy nods and hesitant smiles, and I've hit Ignore so many times on his calls that, eventually, they stopped com-ing. But who else would he be trying to speak to from the Wolverines?

I shake my head. "I can't," I mouth, then wave my finger around to remind him that my team is about to perform.

He clasps his hands together. "Please," he mouths back.

I glance over at Ms. Denita and expect to see her eyes throwing darts at me. But she and Rico are speaking to the band director, possibly working out logistics about the per-formance. I might have a minute before she realizes I'm gone.

"'Scuse me," I say to Faith as I climb over her legs.

Faith just lets out a loud sigh. Knowing that I'm making a huge mistake, but also knowing that she couldn't stop me right now. I reach him, and his eyes get even bluer. How is that even possible? How is that even *legal*?

"Wow." He looks over my asymmetrical unitard, one

arm bare, the other arm hugged by a tight, glittery sleeve. "You look . . . wow."

I would've blushed before, but it's hard to gauge his sincerity now. I could be just a fetish to him. The Black girl he might bang and brag about to his friends. I hug my chest with both arms. "I'm really not supposed to be talking to you right now."

It's not until Connor rocks back on his heels that I realize all the translations that one sentence could have. "I won't keep you long," he says. "I know that we haven't talked much in a while—"

"At all," I correct. "We haven't talked at all."

"That's not on me, though." He presses his hand to his chest, right where his heart should be. Almost like he wants to protect it. "All my friends have been trying to hype me up tonight. They all think I'm going to win homecoming king despite everything, you know?" He scratches at the back of his head, like just the thought of him being a bigot makes him itchy. "But I can't get excited about it. Because when I was getting ready tonight, something felt like it was missing. And that something was you." He reaches for one of my hands, but I keep them both tucked inside my arms, cradled tight against my chest.

"Ny," he says. He pleads.

I sigh and release one of my hands. He pulls a corsage out

of his tuxedo pocket and slips it onto my wrist. The petals are icy blue and matches his vest and the handkerchief in his front pocket. Hell, it even matches my unitard. It's like this moment between us was meant to be.

"I know you kinda gave me an answer, but I can't imagine going to my final homecoming dance without you on my arm." He does that thing I love with his thumb and the back of my hand. My knees get a little wobbly, no matter how much I try to plant my feet into the ground. "So . . . what do you think?"

I stare down at the corsage on my wrist, and dammit, it belongs there. I still have so many questions about Mr. Brooks, so many questions about Connor. But I can't lie and think that my heart is thumping only from the excitement of the Wolverines' performance. Being this close to him, after all this time, stirs up memories and feelings that I've tried to keep a lid on all these weeks. I hate him . . . but I miss him. I hate that I miss him.

"I hate you," I say.

He smiles. "I'll take it if that means you're thinking about me."

My mouth gets the best of me, and a small smile escapes.

"There we go!" Connor pumps his free hand, triumphant. "So . . . it's a date?"

I sigh. "Maybe we'll see each other there. And maybe

before, we'll happen to ride together and enter the dance at the same exact time."

"I'll take it," he says again. He closes the space between us and leans in like he wants to kiss me.

I almost give in. Almost. But I feel the eyes of the Wolverines on me. Feel the eyes of the Black community in the stands. They've read about the Brookses. You can't walk down Windsor Boulevard without rumblings of how wicked and twisted the family is ("I heard they let their kids whip the nanny themselves!"). And there were just as many townsfolk going hard for all things Brooks ("That Scott Brooks is a good man. Delivered my baby with his own hands, he did."). And even though 99 percent of the chatter was borderline wild, it's 100 percent clear that everyone had an opinion. If Connor and I were going to do this, we'd have to take baby steps—and kissing in front of the entire school and town is the exact opposite of that. It's a Shaquille O'Neal leap.

I pull back. "I'll see you later."

Connor nods like he understands. He's heard the chatter too. "Can't wait." He walks backward to return to the section where the rest of the homecoming court waits, but he keeps his eyes on me until he bumps into some guy tossing T-shirts into the crowd. He apologizes to the guy, then looks back at me, pulls an embarrassed face. I laugh and turn back to my section.

"Henry!"

I flinch. Ms. Denita. Ready to read me the riot act for leaving my spot without permission. I inch over to her, my hands folded in front of me so they won't fidget.

"What's that?" she asks, pointing to the corsage on my wrist.

"It's a corsage. My friend just—"

"I know what it is. What's it doing on your wrist?"

"Oh. My bad." I pull the corsage off my wrist and loop the band through one of the bobby pins in my hair. Pause to see if that meets uniform protocol.

"How are you feeling?" Ms. Denita asks, the corsage now a distant memory.

I blink. "Good?"

"Is that an answer or a question?"

I swallow and nod. "Good," I say, more certain.

She pops her gum. "All right. You're joining us on the field tonight."

I cough from gasping. I pat my chest and lean forward. "What?" Clearly, I heard her wrong. Then: "Is somebody hurt?"

"No. You've been working hard, and there's a space for you in the formation. Just don't embarrass me out there."

I clap my hands repeatedly, applauding her decision. "I won't. Thank you. Thank you so much!"

Ms. Denita turns to say something to Rico instead of

responding to me. She does a double take when she sees me still standing there. "Can I help you?"

I shake my head and scurry back up the bleachers before she changes her mind. As soon as I return to my space next to Faith, I reach for my phone in the pocket of my jacket. I have to let Mom know I get to perform tonight. I told her not to come, that I hadn't gotten a chance to perform yet, but she and Eric still wanted to come out to support me. Now they had a reason to be here instead of watching our team get their asses whooped.

"Everything good?" Faith asks me.

"More than good. I get to perform with you all tonight." I do a shoulder shimmy.

She smiles, amused. "That's what I'm talking about. And . . . the other thing?" She hitches her head toward the homecoming court in the next section of bleachers. Connor says something to one of the other tuxedoed guys sitting with him. He spots me again and waves at me.

I wave back and truly take in the homecoming court. I recognize most of the faces. All of them popular, all of them beautiful. All of them white. Has our homecoming court always been so white? "Yeah, that's good, too," I say to Faith, though I'm not sure if I believe it. I try to picture myself standing next to Connor with the rest of the court, smiling and leaning my head against his shoulder. I'd be a smudge in an otherwise pale, but perfect, picture.

Rico waves us to attention. His nails are shimmery and blue tonight to coordinate with our costumes. It's showtime. Mr. Pryor, the band director, flourishes his hands, and the band stands on the risers behind us. We cross our legs and arch our backs, serving looks before we get down to business. The percussion section begins pounding a beat, getting the crowd amped up. I take a breath and let it out slowly through my mouth. Try to slow down my heartbeat. I know this routine like the back of my hand. There's no reason to be nervous. I got this.

The guy on the snare finishes his solo, and Faith nods. It's on. "Don't Stop the Music" pours from the brass section, and we roll our bodies and climb to our feet. We sway and twist our hips right there in the bleachers. The unsuspecting crowd next to us begins to cheer, which only makes me flick my hands and rock my hips harder. Wider. We reach the part of the song when we freeze with our hands locked together in the air. Now it's Faith's time to shine. She bucks like it's nobody's business, then flicks her hair like she's using it as a whip. She beats the crowd into submission. She then prances down the bleachers with the marching band right behind her. They line the field in their designated spots as Faith pops and locks in the center of them. I've seen her do this solo a hundred times, but I wouldn't mind seeing it a hundred more. The certainty in the way she moves her body is the stuff of legend. She front flips into a jump split and then flicks her wrist, beckoning us to join her.

We do. We unlock our hands and strut our way down to the center of the field in time with the music. When we get into our formation behind Faith, we let loose. Leaping, spinning, and rocking out like this crowd has never seen before. In between one of my head rolls, I spot Mom and Eric in the center of one of the risers. Mom jumps up and down, screaming something at the top of her lungs that I can't hear, but I can feel. She's gassing me up, ordering me to get down. Eric smiles and dances next to her, just like a proud, but embarrassing, father. I'm not doing this dance just for me or the Wolverines. This is for them.

We do our two-legged death drop and end flat on our backs. My chest heaves as I stare up at the stars. Last time I did this, I was having the time of my life with Connor. Somehow, though, this is even better. The sky cracks, and there's thunder. As we ease back onto our feet to sashay off the field, I realize that the weather isn't churning on us. It's the audience. Their feet. Their roars. They make the whole field shake. Mom and Eric are right there in the fray, hopping up and down. Mom makes sure to blow me kisses. I want to smile and catch them, but I'm still in character.

Then it begins. Faint as a tickle. Something humming in my ear that might not be there. Gradually, the humming gets louder until I hear it with clarity:

"Booooo!"

I blink and search for the source. We received so much love—anything other than that had to be a mistake. Then my eyes land on the cheerleaders on the sidelines. Shauna's hand is cupped around her mouth, her lips curled into an O as the boos seep out of her. Brittany joins her. Then a few others. But the one that truly gets me, the one who turns my stomach, is when Ava joins. Ava. The one that wanted me to side with her when all this Parking Lot Becky stuff began. The one who was secretly woke. Now here she was, joining our fairer-skinned classmates in dimming my shine. All for what? Because the Wolverines teased their routine last week?

Kylie's lips are sealed. She stands with her hands on her lips, but there's something about her face. Her eyes, her mouth, that's twisted in something that I've seen before: satisfaction. She notices me looking in her direction and shrugs.

She just shrugs.

I'm supposed to be pissed, but I can't. You need a heart to care that deeply about something. But Kylie, with that simple, nonchalant gesture, just took mine and stomped on it with her crisp, white Varsity Aeros.

The jeering is contagious. Soon it curls through the crowd like a wave. Booing. Hissing. Threats for us to get off the field. As I scan the audience to see who could be so awful, so rude, there's one thing they all have in common.

They're white.

They're the friends and families of my classmates who

306

started the booing. And instead of correcting them, these grown-ass folks hop on the bandwagon. We stand in our formation, our hips cocked. Fierce as all hell. Inside I'm falling apart. My muscles ache for how much work it takes me to remain fierce. Confident. Ms. Denita and Mr. Pryor wave their hands at us, try to get us off the field. The marching band begins playing our walking-off music, and we sashay behind them. It's hard to keep the rhythm because the melody is overpowered by all the jeering. They're so loud I'm going to hear them in my sleep. They're going to haunt my dreams until I wake up in a cold sweat. Except I won't feel relieved. All this chaos really happened. Is still happening.

"Nice job," Brittany says with a sneer as we try to continue our sashay pass the sidelines. Some girls on the squad cackle. When I look at them, all I see is red. I don't recognize any of them anymore.

Mercedes, who the team nicknamed Beauty Queen because of her immaculate blond weaves and polished nails and prim mannerisms, takes the first swing. She gives a backhand and it connects right with Brittany's nose. That's when all hell breaks loose. Limbs flailing, hair pulling, piercing screams. It's a cyclone of madness. I'm pushed onto the ground, so I press up as close as I can to a set of bleachers, hugging my knees tight to my chest like a shield. I wait for the adults to intervene, but as I peek up at the crowd, some of them are jostling at each other too. Pushing, shoving, screaming. It's like the whole audience got attacked by rabid dogs and everyone's gone mad. Oh, God, where's Mom? Where's Eric?

Ms. Denita and Coach Beverly pry most of their girls away from each other. While the hitting stops, the screams continue. The cuss words. The threats. I cover my ears to drown them out. As the squad and the Wolverines part, it gives way to a clearer view of the homecoming court. None of them are fighting, but what they're doing is just as gross. Connor and a few others have their phones up, recording the chaos. Laughing. High-fiving. Having the time of their lives. Right as mine is falling apart.

Something boils inside me, scalding away my fear and cooking it into scorching-hot rage. I rise to my feet, both fists clenched to my sides. Ignoring the fray around me because I want him to look at me. To see my face. To see me seeing him. Finally.

Connor spots me, and his laughter dies. We spend a second just staring at each other. Two seconds. Three. His Adam's apple bobs up and down. He knows I've figured him out, but what he doesn't know is what I'll do about it. Connor shakes his head and gives me that lazy smile of his. The smile that usually saves him: *Can you believe this?*

No. I can't.

I rip the corsage out of my hair, keeping my eyes on Connor the whole time. His smile fades, as if he's watching a car wreck right before it happens. I throw the corsage to the ground, yelling like I'm trying to stab a hole in the ground with it. And when that's not enough, I crush it under my foot. Twisting my shoe on top of it so that the petals split apart. Connor chews on this thumbnail, his expression unreadable. Mine isn't. I even shoot him a middle finger as an exclamation point. Make sure he reads it loud and clear.

TWENTY-ONE

What time are you coming home?

It's the latest in a series of texts from my mom. I sigh and text back: *11*. It was eleven this morning when I asked my mom for permission to attend the DAB event. Eleven this afternoon while we folded laundry in front of the television. Eleven when Faith showed up to my apartment to give me a ride to Hampton. Mom and I both know my curfew, but I humor her anyway. She has a right to be on edge after the halftime rumble last night. The referees canceled the rest of the game since it was difficult to get the crowd under control. The adults were worse than the students. The fighting tumbled into the parking lot. Cops had to be called in to clear everyone out before it was deemed safe enough for students to exit. And all for what? Because the Wolverines put on a killer performance?

Mom and Eric got out unscathed, for the most part. Eric did have to knock down a few people that tussled a bit too closely to my mom. Almost fought a school resource officer for blocking his way back into the school to make sure I was okay. I was—at least physically. All of us were. But the ride back home was steeped in exhaustion and grief. Sad for the Wolverines, who didn't get to celebrate an epic performance. Sad for the football players who didn't get to finish their final homecoming game. Mostly, though, sad for the town. Our town. Mom and Eric didn't say it aloud, but it was in the way Mom pressed her head against the car window and stared out into the dark streets. In the way Eric turned off the radio as soon as a DJ cut in to talk about the halftime fight. In the way that we hugged and held on to each other as soon as we entered our living room, safe at home but scared, nonetheless. Terrified, even.

"You all right?"

I look up from my phone, and Butter stands over me holding two bottled waters. He offers me one and takes a seat next to me. We're all holed up in a Black-owned coffee shop in downtown Hampton. The small stage in the back of the store serves as an open-mic night for talent as we mix and mingle with members and allies of the Don't Attack Blacks movement.

"No," Mom had said over breakfast this morning, almost

spitting out her coffee when I asked if I could attend.

"Hell to the no," Eric added. "You saw firsthand how crazy folks can get out here. You're not getting in the middle of that again."

"Folks went crazy because there's not enough of us in the middle," I told them. "Someone needs to put some common sense in their heads. Help them see the world from somebody else's eyes. I figured you, of all people, would want me to go and learn more about the cause." I gave Eric a pointed look. One that reminded him of all our discussions and debates on privilege and oppression. On Black and white. Haves and have-nots. And it worked. Eric convinced Mom to let me go—with the reassurance that I'd text them every thirty minutes. Mom was on overkill, though. It's like her nerves and fingers are on fire tonight.

"Yeah," I say now to Butter, and flip my phone over on the table. "Just checking in with my mom." I wince as soon as my mouth closes. I did not just tell some college dude that I had to update my mommy.

But he nods and takes it in stride. "Faith told me about that melee that happened at the game. Shit was bizarre."

I look over at Faith. She's at the table next to me with Nevaeh, Amari, Mercedes, and some dude I haven't met yet. She nods along to whatever he's saying. By the way he's stabbing his hands in the air, he must be dropping some deep knowledge. Or at least he thinks he is. Faith sits there, but her eyes are somewhere else. She was like that the whole car ride to the coffee shop. Like she still needed to process everything that went down last night. We all did.

"Know what's even weirder?" I ask. "They canceled the game but are still holding the homecoming dance tonight. Weirdest of all is that they told *us*"—I point to Faith's table, then think about the Wolverines who aren't here—"that we weren't allowed to attend since the fight hasn't been fully investigated. Just us. Like we incited a riot with our bomb-ass dance moves. As if we wanted to attend anyway." I rip the top off my bottle. I take a sip even though I don't want it. But I need to close my mouth to stop venting. If I keep going, I'll dissolve into one of those angry cries that I hate, and I can't cry in front of Butter. He doesn't even like me.

Butter twists the end of one of his cornrows and stares down at the table, like he's in deep thought. Finally, he looks up at me. "That's not weird. That's fucked up. But, you know, crackers gonna cracker." He shrugs.

I look at him, and before I know it, I'm laughing. Butter watches me, amused, and then joins me. Soon, we're cackling like idiots and everyone's staring, but I don't care. It feels like I released a sneeze that's been building all day, and now I can finally breathe.

"Wow," I manage. "I can't believe you just said that."

"I'm full of catchphrases. Starting my own T-shirt line with all of them."

"Tees By B? Oh, wait, Butter Threads?"

Butter snaps his finger and points at me. "That part. I might hire you to be my creative director."

My phone buzzes on the table next to me, but I don't feel like talking to Mom again. I just hollered at her like a minute ago. She knows I'm alive, so now she needs to let me live. "You come to a lot of these events?"

Butter leans back into his chair, like he wants to settle in for the night right here. Next to me. "Nah. All this shit is a kinda buffoonery to me. All razzle-dazzle with no substance. Homeboy up there didn't even take the time to tune his guitar. Like he knows ain't nobody taking his ass seriously." He nods back toward the stage. A guy with a pick sticking out of his 'fro croons into the mic while plucking strings on his acoustic guitar. Yeah, he's terrible. He tries to hit vocal runs like Luther Vandross, but he ran out of stamina as soon as he started. I just didn't know we were allowed to admit that he sucks.

I raise an eyebrow to Butter. "Not a fan of open-mic nights?"

"I'm not a fan of no talent. Like, let yourself be great so we can all go home."

He says it so deadpan, without a care in the world, that I can't help but laugh again. That's twice in one night. He's good. "So, you must be a fan of DAB if you're sitting through this."

Butter glances around the room, then leans toward me and waves a hand for me to come closer. I do. "Can I let you in on a secret?"

His eyes are a rich, golden brown. Amber. I can see myself clearly through them. "Yeah." I nod.

Butter sighs, and I almost join him. Not sure why. "DAB is a major part of the buffoonery I hate about tonight."

I wait for him to crack a smile, but it never comes. This isn't part of his sarcasm bit. "Wait, seriously? You don't care about the cause?"

"Yeah. Just more than they do." He must notice the confusion on my face, so he continues. "You ever notice that they always seem to show up when there's drama? Always coming through with a sound bite or a gimmick. They're like the ambulance chasers of the advocacy world."

"I don't get it," I say, shaking my head. "Aren't we supposed to make noise? Isn't that how change is supposed to happen? Make good trouble and all of that?"

Butter gives me a soft look, like he doesn't want to kill my dream by telling me that the tooth fairy isn't real. "There's a difference between making trouble and being trouble."

That's true. That's exactly what I've been wrapping my mind about last night. Wondering if there was anything that I could've done differently to prevent the madness at the game. Stopped Nevaeh teasing the cheerleaders last week, or throwing away the newspaper in the locker room. Or just going with Kylie to that damn Target. Trouble just seemed to follow me wherever I went, or didn't go. I couldn't help but think: What if it's me? What if *I'm* the trouble?

"Why did you come tonight, then?" I ask Butter, more as a way to get out of my own head. Staying too long in there feels dangerous.

Butter scans the room again, then tilts his head somewhere toward the front. I already know what he's referring to. More like who. The same person who lit a fire under me. The same person who pulled me out of my funk about missing my last homecoming dance ever because there are more important things in the world. Cleo. She's in a deep conversation with two other Black guys. Her hands aren't stabbing the air with passion. Instead, one rubs onto the peace sign pendant on her necklace as her head bobs for every other syllable. She isn't talking. She's dancing, and she's leading it.

"Yeah. She seems to have that effect on people," I say.

Butter lets out a small laugh. "Say less."

I lean away from Butter and hug my arms across my chest. An icky feeling crawls over me, like I just walked in on two strangers getting it on. I need to remove myself from the awkwardness, so I change the subject. "So . . . are you going to tell me why they call you Butter?"

He cocks an eyebrow. "Guess."

I groan. "Please don't tell me it's because you're as smooth as butter or something."

"Hey, you said it." He brushes imaginary dust off his shoulder.

I shake my head but smile anyway. "If you're letting people call you Butter, your real name has to be pretty tragic. Chauncy?"

Butter scrunches his nose at me, but I'm on a roll.

"Eugene?"

He just takes a sip of his water. The suspense is killing me.

"That's not fair. You know my real name," I say.

"Not my fault that you can't get a nickname from Nell."

My mouth drops open.

He flashes a smile. "I'm playing with you, *Naomi*. I wouldn't forget your name."

I twist and untwist the cap of my water bottle. We were riffing in our own jam session, but now I've lost the beat. Butter didn't say he *didn't* forget my name. He said he *wouldn't* forget my name. Like he wouldn't allow it. Like he cared enough to remember. He's still tilting toward me like he wants to tell me another secret. Or maybe even kiss me. I study his lips. Full, but not pouty. Just like two pillows you broke in real nice until they fit under your head perfectly. I wonder what Butter's bed looks like. Then I wonder why I'm wondering about Butter's bed. . . .

"What's up, Black people." Cleo walks up to our table, and Butter leans back into his chair. The moment, whatever it was, is gone. Cleo's none the wiser. She reaches over and wipes something off my cheek. "You got glitter all over your face."

I rub my cheek, and my fingertips twinkle when I pull them away. Mercedes didn't hold back with our makeup for the halftime performance. Two Cetaphil washes later, and I'm still shimmering.

"Do I need to check you for glitter, B?" Cleo gives a slick smile to Butter.

Butter swats his hand at Cleo and gulps on his water. He doesn't look in my direction. I rub my fingertips together over and over to try to get the glitter off. At least it gives me something to do besides sit in the uneasiness. Maybe my and Butter's moment wasn't a moment, just a nanosecond.

"Naomi, I want you to meet someone." She nods toward the heavyset guy with a flattop of twists in his hair and a faded Bone Thugs-N-Harmony T-shirt. "This is Orlando, the one I've been telling you about. He's been running things for the local Don't Attack Blacks movement."

"DAB on them. All day." Orlando bobs his head into the cuff of his arm, and I recognize his slick moves from the "This Is America" parody. He holds out his fist to me, and I give him a pound. "My profound sis here tells me that you once were lost but now are found."

My forehead crinkles in confusion.

"I told him about your video with Becky," Cleo fills me

in. "But now you're applying to HBCUs and doing hip-hop majorette. All Black, e'erything."

"Oh. Yeah, I guess."

"Welcome to the fold, queen. Happy to get you back from the sunken place." He crosses his arms across his chest, Wakanda Forever. Looks like we're combining our Black movie references, but okay. He turns back to Cleo. "I'm about to go do my thing in a minute. But you and your people mingle, eat. Be merry. Stella Ramos is reading one of her pieces right after me. Shit's fire." He knocks fists with Cleo and moves on to the next group of his adoring fans.

"Yeah, nice meeting you, too," Butter calls out after him, then looks at me and shrugs. I laugh, relieved that the clumsiness between us has dissipated.

My phone buzzes again. Mom won't let up. I reach to answer her and let her know I'm okay, but Cleo grabs my hand and pulls me from my chair.

"Come on. There's two more people I want you to meet," she says, steering me toward the other side of the room. I plead with Butter over my shoulder, and he smiles and shrugs: *You're on your own.*

Cleo slows down when we reach two Black guys near the stage, the same ones she was speaking to earlier, watching someone singing and playing acoustic guitar. One is light-skinned with a low-cut fade and peach fuzz; the other's skin is bronzer and he wears a ball cap twisted to the side of his head.

"Glad y'all can make it," Cleo says to them. "Naomi, this is Noah." She gestures toward the one with the peach fuzz. "And this is Damon." She points to the dude with the ball cap.

"What up, though," Damon says to me. I open my mouth to respond, then pause. Something about him, his face, his voice, seems so dang familiar to me. Like maybe I ran into him at a store—or maybe I met him my first night at Hampton University.

It's not until Damon pats on his face that I realize I'm just staring at him.

"My bad." I blink. "I just thought we met before already."

"Yeah, I have one of those faces," Damon says. Noah snickers under his breath, and Damon joins in with him. Okay. I guess I missed the joke.

"Are you part of DAB?" I ask, changing the subject. Cleo brought me over here for a reason, so I figured they'd wanted to tell me more about the movement.

"Not quite," Noah answers once he stops laughing. And he sounds familiar too. Maybe a morning show DJ I listen to on the way to school, but he seems too young for a prolific radio career.

"But they're doing great things for the movement. Damon and Noah are going to bring about change," Cleo says. "In fact, let's bring it all in. I want to get a pic with you guys before you blow up." She flags me to come closer to her. "Come on. You too."

"Um, okay."

I move under Cleo's arm while Noah and Damon squeeze in on the other side of her. We pose for Cleo's phone as she takes a selfie. Once the phone flashes, we break from our huddle.

"We look good. They don't be lying when they say Black is beautiful," Cleo says, checking out the picture.

I smile just as my phone buzzes again. My mom's going to kill me. I finally pull out my phone to respond again. Only I'm not getting texts from my mom. I've been tagged in comments on Instagram. I frown and click on the alert. Not a second later, a picture of Connor at the homecoming dance pops up on my screen. A crown tilts on top of his head. He won—no surprise. And he isn't alone in the picture. He sticks his tongue out like Miley Cyrus back when she went through her Black phase. Someone else's tongue touches his. Her eyes closed. Her dark blond hair pinned up. A strapless red dress basically pasted around her torso.

Serena Warren.

Connor captions the photo: *The King has found his new Queen. #LoveAt100thSight*

I clutch the phone in my hand, blood leaving my fingertips. I want to throw up. I want to scream. I want to cry. But if I do any of those things, it'll only mean that I care. And I don't want Connor to think that I care, whether he's here or not.

His followers are the ones who tag me in the comments:

@NaomiTheHomey gonna be maaaaad!

Ha! Bet @NaomiTheHomey wishes she was here

Thank U. Next. @NaomiTheHomey

"What's wrong?" Faith's next to me, out of the blue, and I flinch. But I don't drop my phone. I wish it would've slipped from my hand. She glances at my screen and curls her lip. "Guess we're missing a lot at the dance, huh?"

I swipe out of the app and stuff my phone back in my pocket. "Not really." I look at the stage and keep my eyes glued there so Faith can get the hint that I don't want to talk about it. I refuse to talk about it. This jackhole has been begging me to go to the dance with him, and now he's moved on to Serena Fucking Warren. The same chick who even Jared Crews couldn't be bothered with anymore. The same chick who tried to come after me for my TikTok with Kylie. And why? Because I got pissed that he laughed during a race war at the homecoming game? What a fucking idiot. He and Serena deserve each other.

I just now realize that the singing has stopped and Orlando's on the stage, getting the crowd riled up. I haven't been following what he's saying, but I force myself to pay attention now. I refuse to let Connor ruin even more of my night.

"—and we're thrilled tonight to be graced by the presence of two extraordinary brothers. Both who had to endure the ridicule of a rising Karen, and then legal bullshit by her racist-ass father. Let's give it up for Noah and Damon!"

It's only then that I notice Noah and Damon are on the stage with Orlando. They wave at everyone as the crowd cheers them on.

"Yo, it's an honor to be here," Damon says into the mic that Orlando hands him. "And don't worry, we didn't run into any issues in the parking lot."

The crowd laughs and my heart hiccups. Now I know why they looked so familiar. Sounded so familiar. These are the guys in the video with Kylie. The video that started the mess I'm in with her and the Brookses.

"Scott Brooks is a crook," Damon continues. "And he's raising little racist mini-mes. But I say it's time to stop giving him our money. Stop giving him our power. Let's boycott all King's Pin Bowling Alleys!"

The crowd whoops and hollers, and I feel dizzy.

"Fuck Parking Lot Becky!" some guy from the back shouts. The crowd makes it a chant.

"Fuck Parking Lot Becky!"

"Fuck Parking Lot Becky!"

The floor shifts, and I bump against Faith. She steadies me.

"Did you know they were going to be here?" I ask her. She shakes her head, dumbfounded. Keeps her hands on my arm to hold me up. I look over at Cleo, who smiles like a madwoman as the chanting continues around us. "Did *you*

323

know they were going to be here?"

She grins even wider. Her cheeks are getting a workout. "Isn't it great?" She holds up her phone and shows me her Instagram. She just posted the picture with me, her, Damon, and Noah and has already received over two hundred likes. "Now the people know you're with us."

With them? I never said I was with anyone. I came here to learn. To figure out my own way. But now, Cleo's thrusted me into the middle of a war I didn't even know if I wanted to fight yet. Just like Kylie with her apology video. Kylie and Cleo—two sides of the same damn coin. I try to step back from her, but Faith's still holding on to me. I shrug out of her grasp and shuffle backward. Cleo pumps her fists and chants with the crowd. Faith stares at me, wide-eyed. I want to escape, but the crowd is too tight. Too closed in. And even if I did find a way to wiggle through, I wouldn't even know where to go. I have nowhere to go.

TWENTY-TWO

[FRENETIC JAZZ INTRO MUSIC]

DANIEL CREWS: Hello, hello, my right-wing warriors. Daniel Crews here with a special episode of *Crews Control*.

NOW IT'S NOT TOO OFTEN THAT I REPORT ON ANYTHING IN MY OWN BACKYARD—SEPARATION OF CHURCH AND STATE, AND ALL THAT. BUT I WOULD BE REMISS TO NOT ADDRESS THE TRAVESTY OF WHAT HAPPENED IN MY VERY OWN COMMUNITY THIS WEEKEND. FRIDAY, SEPTEMBER 30, STARTED OUT NORMAL ENOUGH. AN UNREASONABLY COOL FALL DAY, AND MY SON AND HIS FRIENDS WERE HEADING OUT TO ENJOY A GOOD OL'-FASHIONED FOOTBALL GAME. NOT JUST ANY GAME, BUT HOMECOMING. A LONG-HONORED TRADITION HERE IN WINDSOR

WHERE YOU CAN FIND EARL JENKINS SMOKING A WHOLE PIG IN THE SCHOOL PARKING LOT, AND THE PTA SELLING BAKED GOODS NEXT TO THE TICKET BOOTH. YET, THIS GAME DIDN'T END LIKE ANY OTHER GAME. IN FACT, IT NEVER OFFICIALLY ENDED. INSTEAD, CANCELED DUE TO A VIOLENT RIOT THAT, WITHOUT A DOUBT, STOLE THE YOUTH OF THE STUDENTS IN ATTENDANCE. HERE TO SPEAK ABOUT THIS TRAVESTY WITH ME IS RESPECTED LOCAL BUSINESSMAN SCOTT BROOKS. SCOTT, THANKS FOR BEING HERE.

SCOTT BROOKS: Thanks for having me, Dan. I just hate that my first visit to your podcast has to be under such dire circumstances.

DANIEL: Agreed. Now, Scott, you've been a longtime resident of Windsor. Even attended Windsor Woods High yourself back in the day. What do you make of what went down over the weekend?

SCOTT: (sighs) First of all, Dan. I'm grieving. Windsor has been my home. *Is* my home. That's why I never ventured far. Virginia Tech for my undergraduate degree, William & Mary for my MBA. I wanted to be able to drive home on the weekends to be embraced by my townsfolk. Sadly, though, I haven't felt that same warmth in a long time.

DANIEL: Ah, you're referring to your lawsuits, I assume.

SCOTT: Sadly, yes. I can't talk about that too much, of course. But here's what I will say—I have long been an advocate for equality. I don't hire people based on any physical characteristics, but rather based on merit. And with that system, I've hired just as many individuals of color as white individuals. If you got the skills, I have a place for you.

DANIEL: Absolutely.

SCOTT: In the wake of some of the radical movements of the far left, my business practices have been scrutinized under a magnifying glass. People try to find holes where there weren't any. If anything, there were just a lot of individuals who were jealous of my success and blamed factors outside my control for their misfortunes.

DANIEL: I see. And you believe this might have trickled down to the high school?

SCOTT: How couldn't it? Our kids can't escape these ridiculous messages. It's practically at their fingertips. What we saw was a community frustrated due to the wacky philosophy of critical race theory. We live in the greatest country on earth—and some of us have worked really hard to get a larger slice of the pie. Now everyone wants to bring a plate for dessert without supplying the ingredients. As a result, chaos at a homecoming game that left my children mortified. Absolutely mortified. Can you blame them?

∗ ∗ ∗

When I get to school on Monday, one of the teachers on duty reminds me to take off my shades while I'm in the building. I feel hungover, and I didn't have a drop of alcohol. More like a drama hangover. I listened to Jared's dad's podcast this morning on the bus ride to school. It had been uploaded on Sunday and was already trending online. It was all pretty quick, but if the devil works hard, Mr. Brooks worked harder. The halftime rumble was the perfect opportunity to save face and to point the finger elsewhere. And his kids were *mortified*? That word must have an entirely new meaning. I still remember Kylie's smug shrug as the booing began. Connor's glee as the town fell apart all around him. But this is the family we're supposed to feel bad for. The Brookses were the victims.

I survive my first block of AP English with a series of head nods and pen scribbles and looked convincing enough for my teacher to believe I was about that Brontë life. I barely take two steps into my physics classroom when Drew intercepts me.

"Bish," he says, his eyes about to pop out of his head. "Tell me we're about to find Connor and string him up by his family jewels."

I turn up my nose. "I don't care about Connor or his jewels."

"Why not?" Drew whines as he follows me to my lab table. "I dressed down and everything in case he got squirrelly." He tugs at his cotton track pants.

I raise my eyebrows. "*You're* wearing athleisure wear? I

thought you wouldn't be caught dead in joggers and a running vest."

"Hey. To see Connor get his ass handed to him, I would gladly sacrifice style." He stops when he sees Xavier Moore walk over to us. "I typed up our lab notes last night and was about to hand them in," he says to Xavier.

"Naw, you're good," Xavier says, then turns to me. "Much respect, sis. Way to take a stand." I frown at him, and he holds up his phone to clarify. "You're trending across the state."

I look at his phone. #FuckParkingLotBecky is the number two trend, right above Mr. Brooks's podcast appearance—and my picture with Cleo and the guys from the Target video is right next to it. I groan. *Dammit, Cleo.*

Xavier gives me a gentle slap on my shoulder before walking away. Too bad the only way to get him to speak to me after all these years is to get roped into a movement I didn't sign up for. Kennedy even raises her fist at me when she enters the classroom. Suddenly, I'm liked by the Black students again.

"So." Drew rests his elbows on top of my lab table. "If we're not getting Connor, please say you got tricks in mind for that treacherous heifer, Kylie."

I tilt my head. "What for?"

Drew raises his eyebrows, surprised. "You haven't been online this weekend?"

I shake my head. I muted all alerts after I saw the porn

that was Connor and Serena's coming-out pic. Didn't unmute until the bus ride this morning, when I found out about Mr. Brooks's insincere interview. Drew's all too happy to show me what I'm missing. He pulls out his phone and begins reading:

"Fake-ass advocate. Louis Fake-akhan. Not woke, just mad tired." He looks up at me. "I can keep going if you want."

"What is all that?"

"People hating on your newfound activist status—and your girl Kylie's leading the charge." He shows me his phone. Kylie's posted an old pic of us on Halloween when we were around eight. She was Elsa, and I was Anna. Kylie put white powder on my face to make me look even more the part, and I grinned and let her do it like an idiot. But I was a kid. I didn't know better then. *She* knows better now.

I read her caption: *DAB's new fearless leader y'all. *gags** That. Bitch.

I'm thrilled when the bell rings after third block for lunch. Not because I'm hungry. I don't need anything to eat when I'm full of rage. I push past my classmates strolling into the cafeteria and make a beeline to the table near the back corner. My former squad's table. Kylie's table. And a few seats down from Kylie is Connor, with his arm draped around Serena Warren's shoulder. Since when did Kylie and Serena eat lunch together? I roll my eyes. Who cares? Three birds, one stone.

I pull out the empty chair across from Kylie and Jared

and plop into it. The table quiets and looks at me like I'm an uninvited guest to their intimate party. Maybe I've always been but I'm just now noticing it.

"Naomi," Kylie says, breaking the silence. Her voice seems less than enthusiastic to greet me. "To what do we owe this pleasure?"

"We don't need to engage in any pleasantries. I just wanted to tell you to stop posting shit about me without my permission." I almost fold my arms across my chest but stop myself. I don't need to protect myself. She does.

Jared rocks back in his seat. "Whoa. Hello to you, too, Naomi."

"I'm not talking to you. And this isn't your dad's podcast, so your asinine input isn't needed." I don't even bother to look at him. He's a nonfactor. Most of the table starts laughing. They're mocking me. These people who were supposed to be my friends now find me a joke. But I don't flinch. I won't allow them to see me break.

Kylie's face lifts like a light bulb just clicked on above her head. Her acting is mediocre. "Oh. You're talking about our Halloween picture? The one that I own because it's in my phone?" She shrugs. "I just figured you were all about photo ops this weekend. What's one more?" She leans against Jared, as arrogant as she wants to be. I imagine all the places I could hit her. I'd go for the mouth first—knock that smirk right off.

"I just figure you'd want to take it down," I say. "Given

that was the time period when everyone called Connor the pretty twin. I wonder what that made you." Her move.

Kylie's lip twitches, just a little. But she fights to keep the tiny smile on her face.

"Somebody's big mad," Serena says. She nuzzles her face against Connor's neck in case I forgot they were together now.

I turn to her. "I don't remember asking for input from the perpetual side piece."

Someone at the table snickers as Serena pinches her nose up at me. She looks to Connor to defend her honor, but Connor has removed his arm from around her shoulders and pokes at his chicken sandwich. I just saw him on Friday, but he looks thinner. Like something's eating away at him.

"This is a cute visit and all, but we're trying to eat so . . ." Kylie flicks her wrist at me, shooing me off.

"I'm tired of playing your games, Kylie."

"*My* games?" Kylie scoffs. "I'm not the one who abandoned ship on a decade-long friendship because some losers on the internet gave me a nickname. I'm not the one who became besties with the people who started the whole Becky bullshit. And I'm not the one who now hates everyone because I suddenly remembered I was Black!"

At that, Connor looks up. He leans over to lock eyes with Kylie, but she's too caught up in me.

"Oh, I just remembered I was Black?" I cough out a laugh

and look over at Ava. Wait for her to read Kylie the riot act for treating my color, my identity, like a nuisance. But Ava just sips on her Gatorade and avoids eye contact with me. I guess when the going gets tough, she's going to side with the majority. "Go to hell, Kylie."

"Why?" Kylie throws her hands up in the air. "You can't get mad at me because you decided to make this whole thing about race."

I leap to my feet before I reach across the table and smack her. "It's always been about race! The fact that you pretended like you didn't see my race says more about you than me. You're lucky you didn't get outed as a Becky sooner!"

"Whoa, whoa, whoa." Roma walks over to the table, tray in hand. She looks at me, then at her friends, sitting. We're all stewing, and she just stepped into the fire. "What is even happening right now? Naomi, are you eating with us?"

I let out another laugh. *I'd rather eat razor blades for lunch.* "Don't post any pics of me. Don't tag me. Don't anything with me." I scan this pathetic group of people who used to be my everything. "That goes for all of you. Forget I even exist." I turn on my heel and rush toward the exit.

"Naomi? Ny!" Roma calls after me.

I bite my lip and keep moving until I push through the cafeteria doors. That's when the tears come. Long, sloppy streams of them pour out of my eyes and won't stop. I glance back at the cafeteria door, but Roma doesn't follow me. She acted like she was concerned, but she clearly made her choice. I pull the collar of my shirt over my mouth and sob into it even more, so much that I choke.

I can't be here. I want to go home.

I take in a shaky breath and pull my phone out of my pocket, dial Eric's number. I lean against a random locker to keep me steady and get me through this call.

"Ny," Eric says, his voice thick with sorrow.

I push off the locker. I can't see him, but I can feel him. There's a cloud over his head about to pour down on him. "What's wrong?" Alarms ring in my ears. I'm not sure if they're real.

Eric waits a beat, then: "I'm with your mom."

The alarms start blaring. I press my hand against my free ear to drown them out. "Is she okay?" My limbs shiver as I wait for an answer. The hall gets colder as I wait for possibly my whole world to change. Again.

"Physically yes, but . . ." Eric takes a deep breath. "Someone hung a noose at her day care."

TWENTY-THREE

WHEN I GET TO MY MOM'S DAY CARE, SHE'S PUTTING ON A BRAVE FACE while she makes the rounds through the toddlers' classroom. She smiles as one of the kids successfully inserts a triangle into his shape sorter.

"Wow, look how well you did that, Manning! Such a big boy!" She spots Eric and me lingering in the doorway, then says something to one of the teacher assistants. She keeps the smile on her face as she leaves the classroom, and we follow her into her office. As soon as Mom closes the door, she spills into my arms and cries into my shoulder.

"Oh, baby," she says in between tears. "I'm so sorry. We didn't mean to scare you."

"It's okay." I rub her back, even though I know it's not

okay. It's far from okay. But for this moment, our roles needed to be reversed. All these years, she's held my hands when I needed a shot and scared off the monsters under my bed. Now I need to be the protector, and she needs to feel safe.

Eric leans against the closed door. His whole body clenched like a fist, both grief and rage muddled across his face. He'd been comforting Mom all morning. Now that I'm here, he can have his moment to fume.

Mom pulls away from me and grabs some Kleenex off her desk. "I'm sorry," she says again, dabbing at her eyes.

I shake my head. "You have nothing to apologize for."

"Damn right," Eric adds. The words must've come out angrier than he intended, because he then takes a deep breath and puffs it out of his mouth.

"What did the police say?" I ask.

Mom scoffs and crumples the Kleenex in her hand. "They asked me questions. Lots of questions. 'Who would want to do something like this to you? Where were *you* last night?'"

"What? Like this was your fault?" I ask. Eric's rage is contagious. "Why the hel . . . why in the world would you hang a noose on your own property?"

Mom clicks her tongue at me: *Don't get me to lyin'.*

"She didn't even get to the good part," Eric says.

I look at Mom. She sighs and takes a seat behind her desk.

"They demanded to know why I didn't have an exterior camera to see who might have trespassed last night. I told them every classroom has a camera. Even inside the front entrance, so I can keep tabs on visitors. I was waiting until the next quarter to see if we broke even to secure the perimeters with cameras. I offered to let them review the front-entrance camera just to see if they noticed anything, but they dismissed me. Said it wouldn't be helpful before they even tried to take a look. It's like they were blaming me for not having a high-tech security system in place."

"That's ridiculous," I say. That's all I can say without cussing in front of my mom. Cleo mentioned this to me before. There are systems in place to keep us down, and then we get blamed for not excelling or living up to certain expectations. *White supremacy at its finest*, Cleo had said.

I never truly knew what she meant until now, watching my mom fight back more tears. She wanted to start this day care to help low-income families and families of color. She used her funding to give these kids the best toys, the cleanest facility, the best learning resources. She made sure that these families didn't have to pay the same outrageous prices as at other day care centers—just whatever they could. Those things are what's most important to her—but she still gets scolded for not being able to afford better security equipment. What in the actual hell?

"I'll take a look at the footage, babe," Eric says to Mom.

"I might be able to see something."

Mom wrings the Kleenex in her hand. "They might be right. It'll probably be a waste of time. Those cameras aren't the clearest. I wanted to go with high-definition ones, and I meant to upgrade them but . . ." Her bottom lip trembles.

"The cameras are fine, Mom," I reassure her. "They do exactly what they're supposed to do."

Mom shakes her head over and over, and with each shake, I know I'm losing her. "Not enough, though. And he knows that. He's clever."

I almost ask who "he" is. Almost. Eric and I exchange a look. Mr. Scott Brooks.

"That whack job had to go and do an interview that villainized everyone but himself," Eric says, his mouth working overtime to not speak through gritted teeth. "He's making the whole town scared of Black folk succeeding at anything. I'd be surprised if no other Black-owned business was targeted too. It's MAGA bullshit all over again."

Mom shakes her head three more times. "No, I don't think this is any groupthink situation. This has Scott written all over it. But he knows how to cover his tracks. He's not going to do the dirty work on his own. He probably hired some down-on-their-luck sap to take the fall for him."

I chew the inside of my cheek, trying to connect the dots. She thinks Mr. Brooks did this to send a message: play ball. Help him drop this lawsuit. Mom said he hinted that he'd take the day care center away from her. Maybe this was his way of scaring off the families who enrolled their kids here. Making them think this isn't a safe space.

"I don't get it," I say when the dots don't connect soon enough. "If he wanted to take back the day care, then just go to a bank or lawyer or something. Why jump through all these hoops?"

Eric scoffs. "And look like the bad guy? Please. He's all about appearances. Your mom of all people knows that."

I turn to Mom, confused. Mom lets out a slow sigh. "There was someone who worked for the Brookses before me. Gloria," she says. I nod for her to continue. Gloria's name has come up more than once over the past few weeks. "We'd known each other through the pork-packing plant. Worked the same day shift and formed quite the bond. Told each other everything. Had our own inside jokes. Everyone started calling us the Bobbsey Twins, even though we didn't look a thing alike." She smiles like she's back there, in a break room with Gloria kiki-ing through lunch.

"One day, she tells me that she's been picking up part-time hours with a family. Watching their kids a few afternoons a week. Touching up the house and whatnot. She was doing such a good job that they wanted her full-time. Scott comes by at the end of our shift to give Gloria a lift. Gloria left something in the break room—her lunch bag maybe. So she runs back in, and I start making small talk with Scott. Just to waste time, you know?" Mom wrings her hands together so tightly that her knuckles look white. "I made a comment about how it's good that there were people in the world still willing to give Gloria a chance. She had done time. Check forgery to help pay some medical bills for her mother. But . . . she was a good person. A great person. She was doing what she had to do to help her family. I had just assumed the Brookses had known. . . ." The tears start to spill from Mom's eyes again.

"I didn't mean to." Mom grabs more Kleenex and pats her cheeks. "I wasn't trying to rat Gloria out. I was thrilled for her. Next thing I know, she was out of the job. Then Kristen and I met during a parent-teacher conference. You and the twins were in the same kindergarten class, Ny. Remember? Next thing I know, she offered me the job. I couldn't say no. The pay was better; the hours were better. Best of all, though, is that you could be with me. I didn't need to worry about childcare. And I fell in love with those twins. I really did. But there was always this nagging feeling, like a stomachache. I felt so bad about what I did to Gloria. And now he wants me to throw more stones at her. I can't. I won't."

"You don't have to, baby," Eric says. "We understand."

"I'm just glad that I was the first one here this morning. The noose was right there. . . ." Mom points a shaking finger toward her closed office door, and I know she's referring to the main doors. "Just right there, for anyone to see. If any of

340

the parents saw it . . . if any of these babies saw it . . ." More sobs begin to tremble out of her. "I just don't know what I would've done. How could he do this? I don't care about me, but why wasn't he thinking about those babies? Why do they need to get hurt?"

Her cries fill the whole room until I'm choking from them. So is Eric. He grips the doorknob like he wants to escape, but I know there's more to it. He wants to find Mr. Brooks. Hurt him. But Mr. Brooks has enough sway to get Eric buried under a prison. Mom needs Eric more than she needs vengeance.

I grab Eric's hand and he flinches, almost like he forgot I was here. I guide him over to Mom and place his hand on her shoulder. Eric looks at me, then nods as if he understands. He crouches next to Mom and wraps her in his arms.

I watch as they cling to each other, but this does nothing to douse the fire building inside me. I slip out while they lean on each other. Eric can't afford to get crooked, so that leaves it up to me to set things straight.

Kylie's already at the natural playscape, sitting on one of the tree stumps surrounding the sandbox, when the Uber drops me off at Castle Park. She scrolls through her phone like she doesn't have a care in the world. And she doesn't. Not the same as I do. Weeks ago, she came over to my apartment boo-hooing because some people called her a name. A *name*.

But she still gets to drive her Audi to school. She still gets to go home to a house with a three-car garage and formal dining room. Her father can go to any one of his businesses without the fear of someone hanging a noose there.

She has everything. She's always had everything—I just never could see that before. She always made me feel like what was hers was mine. Her gifts were my gifts. She let me name her pet hamster in third grade. Let me try out her Kylie Jenner Lip Kits in middle school. Let me test-drive her brand-new Audi last year. The thing about "letting" people do stuff, though, is you never mention that nothing is truly theirs. That you can take these things back at any moment. Like Mr. Brooks and Mom's day care. Like Kylie and her friendship with me. She sits here in all her perks and laughs at something off her phone. The audacity.

Kylie looks up at me and shoves her phone into her jacket pocket. "I hope you have a good reason to drag me out here in the middle of the night. Me and Jared have dinner plans."

I no longer feel fire in my chest. I am the fire. "Stand up."

Kylie scrunches her face at me. "Why?"

I think about all those years when Kylie and Connor and their parents sat at their dining room table for dinner, and Mom stayed on her feet, serving them. I wasn't going to give Kylie that power anymore. Another Henry woman was not going to stay on her feet while she got to chill out. "Stand. Up."

Kylie frowns at me but slowly rises to her feet. Something in my voice told her I had no patience for foolery. She spreads her arms and raises her eyebrows at me: *And?*

"Tell your dad no more," I say. My teeth beg to clench, but I fight it. Kylie needs to hear every single syllable I deliver. "My mom doesn't have shit to do with his lawsuit, but if he comes at her, at *us* again, he'll be dealing with more than just another lawsuit."

Kylie blinks at me. "What in the hell are you talking about?"

"We're going through the security footage. He'll get caught sooner or later. Even if he wasn't the one who actually left it there, he's not that clean. The crumbs will lead back to him."

"Left what where?"

I throw my hands in the air. "Stop playing dumb, Kylie! I know you ear hustle on your dad's calls. Hell, I've done it with you before. And if you guys think we're going to sit there and let him leave a noose at my mom's place of business—"

"There was a noose left at Itsy Bitsy?" Kylie clutches her chest like she has a right to be heartbroken. "Is everyone okay? Is Mama Nina okay?"

"She is *not* your mama!" I cram a finger in her face. "There is no way that she would claim someone as clueless and entitled as you as her child." I turn on my heel and storm away. I said what I had to say. I hope Kylie brings every word of it back to her father.

"Really, Naomi?" she shouts to my back. "I'm the entitled one? Bitch, anything I had you had. My parents made sure of that!"

I spin back toward her. "I *never* had what you had! I was a fucking charity case for your family. Just a token to prove you guys had Black friends. But guess what? I'm done! And good luck finding another sucker, because now the whole town knows how full of shit your family is. Your dad can give all the phony interviews he wants, but we all see through him."

Kylie crosses her arms across her chest and juts a chin at me. "You never had what I had? Well, then you sure did try to get it. Is that why you went after Connor? So you could trap him into having some mutt-ass baby with you?"

My entire body recoils as I shove her. Hard. Kylie's arms flail out to try to gain her balance, but my fury is no match. She tumbles onto her butt right in the sand. "Guess I know how you really feel, huh?" I kick sand at her. "Hiding in plain sight."

I don't even get to turn around before Kylie scrambles to her feet and pushes me back. I dig my heels into the sand to keep steady and grab onto her arms. I try to pin them down, but Kylie's too wiry. She wiggles out of my grasp and swings her arm, and her palm connects with my left cheek.

That bitch.

I swing back, and my fist grazes Kylie's ear and soon we're hugging and grunting, sand kicking up at our heels as we try to attack each other. But we know each other too well. I know what Kylie wants to do before she does it, and she knows any strike I try to take. We both lose our footing and fall into the sandbox. That doesn't stop us. Kylie climbs on top of me and raises her hand to slap me again, but I grab her by the wrist and squeeze her between my thighs until we rotate, and now I'm on top. I grab her by the shirt and slam her back into the sand.

"Hey!" A man walking a small dog stands on the trail near the playscape. He beams the flashlight from his phone right at us. "You stop it before I call the cops!"

It's dark, but I can tell by his voice that he's white. And with his flashlight, all he sees is a Black girl pinning down a white girl. Of course he wants to call the cops. I'm so distracted that Kylie manages to push me off her, and I land on my butt across from her.

"Are you okay, miss?" I see the man clearer now, and yep, he's white. He's speaking to Kylie. Only Kylie.

"Yeah," Kylie calls out.

"Are you sure? Because I can—"

"Ugh! Kindly go the fuck away!"

The man mumbles something harsh at Kylie before tugging at the leash and dragging the puppy. The pitter-patter of their steps fades away, and soon all I can hear is me and Kylie both heaving for air. After a few more seconds, Kylie climbs to her feet and swats sand off her jeans.

"Tell Mama . . . Ms. Nina that I'm sorry," she says, her voice tiny in the night. "And tell yourself to go to hell."

I roll my eyes, but I figure she's too tired to deliver a cleverer burn. She stomps past me and disappears into the night. I stay seated in the sand and remember the last time Kylie and I were here. The last *times* Kylie and I were here. None of them ever ended like this, with Kylie leaving me in the dark. This place had always been our sanctuary. The place where we could peel everything off and let our secrets spill out. I run my fingers across the sand and almost feel ten-year-old Kylie's hand on top of mine, stopping my fingers from roaming.

"Can I tell you something?" Kylie had asked me. Her two French braids were a rumpled mess after an afternoon of horseplaying.

"Always," I said to her. And meant it.

She let out a dramatic sigh. The same one Mrs. Brooks would give when the waitstaff at a restaurant moved way too slowly. "I don't want to go to middle school."

I tilted my head in confusion. Middle school was all we

talked about. We couldn't wait to switch classes and have lockers and get invited to parties where we could have our first kiss. "But we love middle school."

"I thought we did, but . . ." Kylie bit her bottom lip, wrestling with how to get the rest of her thoughts out. "I'm scared. They'll be kids there from other schools, and what if they don't like me?"

I shrugged. "I'll make them like you." It was as simple as that to me. Kylie was pretty and funny and did the best impression of Britney Spears that I had ever heard in my life. Who couldn't like that?

Kylie shook her head, not convinced. "But what if they don't? What if they all hate me and I'll have to be home-schooled and my dad yells at me because I don't have a lot of friends?"

I smiled at Kylie. She spiraled like this often, and I knew it was best to grin and give her the space she needed before I interrupted. Kylie let out another heavy sigh and gave me permission to speak. "You don't need a lot of friends. You have me."

"Yeah, but what if you stop liking me in middle school?"

"Never." I pulled the bubblegum I'd been nursing out of my mouth and glued it to my palm. "You're stuck with me!" I grabbed Kylie's hand, and she squealed in disgust. But the squeals soon turned into laughter, which was the goal.

Making Kylie happy had always been the goal.

Not anymore. I pull out my phone and dial Cleo's number.

"Yeah?" she says after the first ring.

"A boycott isn't enough," I say into the phone. "We can't just stop bowling at King's Pin. We need to shout about it. Mr. Brooks needs to go down. Loudly."

NOW

"WE RAN OUT OF HOLDING SPACES." DETECTIVE SUMMERS'S VOICE IS gruff as he nudges Cleo into my interrogation room. "Stretch, you have a phone call."

"Take a message," Detective Stretch says back to him.

"No. You need to take this one." He gives her a look. Something quiet but stern, a lecture between two old colleagues.

Detective Stretch nods and pats my lap. "I'll be back," she says. She nods at Cleo before following Summers out into the hall and closing the door behind her, leaving me and Cleo together. Alone.

Cleo falls into the seat that Detective Stretch previously occupied and crosses her legs. Her foot tremors. She chews on her thumbnail and stares down at her foot, watching it flip and flop like it's detached from her. I've never seen her like this. The Cleo I know is cool, calm, and commanding. She stares danger in the face and smirks. This Cleo, though, looks like she's cold and can't remember how to keep herself warm.

"You okay?" I ask.

She flinches and looks up at me, as if she's just remembering that I'm in the room with her. She nods and continues chewing.

"Did you want a Twizzler?" I push the package of candy across the table toward her. "You can have as much as you want. I don't really like them."

She doesn't answer me. Just chews, chews, and chews.

"Cleo." I tilt toward her. "What happened? Did they . . . do something to you?"

"Be quiet, Naomi."

I blink, confused. "If they did something, you can tell me. I asked for a lawyer, and my mom should be here any minute with one. We can let them know if somebody threatened you or touched you or—"

"Jesus, Naomi! Shut the fuck up!"

I jerk away, and my back knocks against my chair. Cleo's not fazed. She squints her eyes at me as if she's trying to blink me away.

"What the hell is wrong with you? Don't you see what

they're doing? Do you think that heifer really had a phone call? That they really didn't have anywhere to put me? They're *list-en-ing*." She stretches out the word so that it comes out like a hiss. "You of all people should know when to keep quiet."

Me of all people? What the hell does that mean?

Cleo shakes her head as she reads my expression. "If you say too much, then it'll be harder for your Brooks in Shining Armor to get you out of this mess."

I let out a dry laugh. "Are you serious? You really think Mr. or Mrs. Brooks is going to save me? After what happened?"

"Maybe. Saving you is on-brand for them. And the rest of us get to go down after you dragged us into this bullshit." Her eyes shift somewhere over my head. I turn around and notice the camera hanging high in the corner of the room. Wow. She's trying to make me out to be the mastermind and her just a pawn. As if Cleo could really be some mindless follower.

I swivel back toward Cleo and lean back in my chair. "I've never dragged anyone to do anything. Last I checked, this was *your* operation. If anything, I have the most to lose of either of us."

Cleo propels forward in her seat, like she wants to jump on me. "I have nothing to lose? I don't have a future now? Girl, you didn't know how to wear a crown, let alone lift your own goddamn head before you met me! Let's not forget."

"I can't forget! I can barely remember my life before you came and twisted it all up!" I'm shouting now. All the anger and fear and grief bottling up inside me erupting all over her. "And the memories I do have all seem dark and stormy after you came and rained all over them. So, I'm sorry if you lost this battle—but I lost my goddamn best friend! I lost . . . I lost my *family*." I barely get the rest of my thoughts out before I'm choking off them. The reality of it all hits me head-on, and I don't even have the cushion of an airbag to protect me. I feel the loss. All of it. Crushed metal against my chest. Shards of glass slicing through my skin. And I don't know how or when the collision will end.

I rub my chest. Practice the deep breathing I did with Detective Stretch not so long ago. Try to fight off the panic before it settles. After a few breaths, I look up and Cleo's back to chewing her thumbnail. Legs still crossed but foot no longer dancing.

"Maybe that's not on me," she says. "Maybe they were already gone long before I came into the picture."

Now there's a thought. But I don't want to chew on it. I don't want to think back and add soot to the few lingering memories that make me smile. I pull a Twizzler out of the pack and shove the whole thing into my mouth. Keep my mouth occupied while the camera stares down at us.

TWENTY-FOUR

"I STILL DON'T KNOW ABOUT THIS," FAITH SAYS TO ME OVER THE PHONE.

I stop tying my shoe and frown at my phone on my bed beside me, even though Faith can't see me since she's only on speaker. "How can you still not know? Cleo and I planned everything down to a T." I'd waited all week for Operation Call Out Mr. Brooks, and finally, the time had come. I told Cleo I wanted to hit him where it would really hurt—and that's his wallet, since it's clear the man doesn't have a heart. Peak business hours for his bowling alleys are on Thursday nights—when the bar's happy hour lasts for four, and wings are only a dollar. So that's when Cleo said we needed to strike.

"About that . . ." Faith pauses, and I think she sighs a

little. "I know you and Cleo are getting close, but she can get really intense. It's a running joke in our family. You tell Cleo that someone accidentally stepped on your shoes, and she's off finding an axe to cut the old dude off at the ankles."

I shrug. "Sometimes old dudes need to be cut off at the ankles."

"Naomi." She sounds like a teacher scolding me for talking to a friend instead of taking notes. "I just want to make sure that what we're doing tonight is legit. Neither of us can afford to get into any trouble, especially with college application deadlines looming. I haven't even heard you talk about Howard in a minute."

I stop fluffing out my hair in front of my vanity mirror. She's right. I had all these reminders in my phone calendar to work on college applications. Requesting letters of recommendation, drafting a personal statement, the whole nine. Mrs. Song even stopped me a few times in the school halls to follow up with our game plan. But I've been too busy putting in work with Cleo. Plotting ways to bring down all the Mr. Brookses in the world. Advocating for my people. That kind of education has to count for something. Once I let the world see Mr. Brooks for what he really is, I'll get back on track with the admissions process.

"Does that mean you're not coming to get me?" I ask.

Faith sighs again. "That's not what I'm saying. Just . . .

never mind. I'm on my way now. I'll be there in ten." She hangs up.

I'm not sure what all the fuss is about if she's still rolling through. I add a little more moisturizer into my hair, then head toward the front door. Mom and Eric are snuggled up on the couch, watching something on Netflix.

"Later, y'all," I say, reaching for the doorknob.

"Excuse me?" Mom lifts her head from Eric's shoulder. "Where are you going, and who are you going with?"

"Me and Faith are just going for a drive. You remember her? From the Wolverines?" I keep my answer as vague as possible. Lying by omission isn't full-blown lying.

Mom studies me, searching for a crack.

"Leave that girl alone," Eric says. "Ny's solid. She knows better than to get into trouble." He eyeballs me—his words more of a warning than a declaration.

I nod. "Of course."

"Fine. Text me updates. And you know what time I expect you to be home." Mom rests her head back on Eric's shoulder. "Love you."

"Love you too." I'm out the door before more questions are asked. I decide it's best to wait for Faith outside. She seems on the fence about tonight, and I wouldn't want her slipping up and saying anything she shouldn't in front of my people. I take a seat on the curb in front of my building and tap my feet over and over on the asphalt. I hope Mr. Brooks will be there. I just want to see his face. I told Cleo we should hit the King's Pin on Highway 17. That's his biggest spot and by far the most popular. Even more popular than the one on Windsor Boulevard. He likes to pop through there from time to time just to see how his money is looking. I hope he's looking tonight.

Headlights spill across my face, and I squint to see who it is. I stand just in case it's Faith already. The car pulls two parking spaces away from me, and out pops Roma from the back seat. She says something to the driver, some Indian man I've never seen before, then heads toward my building as the car pulls out again. She slows her pace when she notices me standing there.

"Hey," she says, and hugs herself like she just caught a chill. "I came to see you." She taps her head and smiles. "Duh."

I watch as the car continues to peel out of my parking lot. "You caught an Uber here?"

"Yeah. I couldn't ask—" She stops short of saying Kylie's name. "Nobody else knew I was coming."

I nod and keep my cool. Inside, though, I'm spinning. It's been forever since I talked with Roma. Since we've been alone in a space together and not just giving quick glances to each other in the hallways or cafeteria. I want to ask her what she's been up to. If she has plans for her birthday. I want to hug her as she rolls her eyes and makes a sarcastic joke while hugging me tighter. But there are important things to be done tonight. Things that Roma may not understand. "Well, I wish you would've called. I'm dippin' out soon."

Roma frowns like she's never heard me use slang before. "Where are you going?"

I can't tell her. For all I know, Kylie sent her to spy on me or something. Her timing is just a little too perfect. "What's up?"

"Not us, apparently."

"What do you mean?"

"You have plans, and I don't know about them. That's never happened in the history of ever. You, me, and Kylie used to sync up our calendars so we'd know each other's schedules. Remember that?"

I almost flinch at the mere mention of Kylie's name, like there's an ache that hasn't quite healed since our tussle in the sandbox earlier this week. But again—I'm no longer giving away my power. "Well, there is no you, me, and her anymore."

"And how is that fair?" Roma returns to hugging herself. "You and Kylie have a falling-out, and that means I'm kicked to the curb too?" She brushes her hand toward the parking lot. "Literally. You haven't even invited me in."

She's right. I lumped her in with Kylie and the rest of the cheerleaders. Drew a line in the sand, and I wouldn't let her step over it. But it's not just me. She could've tried. Communication works two ways, and her silence about everything told me what I needed to know about her. About our friendship. "I told you I was heading out. Besides . . . you made your decision the other day in the cafeteria."

Roma blinks before the memory washes over her face. "I called after you. And I tried calling you when I got home."

"Yeah, but you didn't follow me. Right then and there. You didn't follow me. Then I called my mom and—" I stop myself so I won't remember my mom's tears. Eric's quiet rage that he couldn't stop my mom's tears. My loud rage at the Castle Park later that night. Thinking about all of it leads me to an ugly cry, and I can't get thrown off my game. Not tonight.

"You get pissed when I don't give you your space when you're that angry," Roma says. "Or did you forget about Prom-mageddon?"

I exhale through my nose. Our final dance in middle school. The eighth-grade "prom." I got mad at Drew for dancing all night with Phil Townsend III even though Drew and I supposedly went together. This is when I still had crumbs of a crush on Drew. Me and my stupid crushes. I sure know how to pick them.

"I think what went down between me and Kylie is heavier than drama at an eighth-grade dance."

"I know it is." Roma kicks at something on the sidewalk.

"Just like I know Kylie isn't perfect. But I think you some-times forget that you're not either."

I click my tongue. "So, I'm the bad guy?"

"No. But why does anybody have to be the bad guy?" She takes three steps and closes the space between us. "You had this beautiful transformation this year, Naomi. You're amazing out there with the Wolverines. When I watch you dance with them, it's like I'm seeing you for the first time. And I love what I'm seeing. I love watching you love yourself. And don't even get me started with your hair." She smiles and looks up at my coils. "But just because Kylie's in her cocoon a little longer doesn't mean she'll never find her wings."

I look down at my feet. If I look at Roma any longer, some of her words might find a place in my chest. Roma sees my joy. She respects it, maybe even accepts it. But as much as I grouped them together over the past few weeks, Roma isn't Kylie. Roma is open arms, and Kylie is clenched fists. Kylie didn't need my empathy. The whole world kisses her ass—she doesn't need my lips any longer.

Faith's car inches up to the curb next to us, and I breathe a sigh of relief. Cracks were beginning to show in my armor, and I needed to keep my strength.

"You don't know the full story, Roma," I say. "But you will tonight."

Roma's eyebrows stitch together. "What does that mean?"

I walk to the passenger's side of Faith's car. "Thanks for

stopping by," I say to Roma. "Get home safe."

I slip into Faith's car before Roma can say anything else. Faith looks at me, then at Roma, then back at me. "Ain't that your friend?" Faith asks. "Is she coming with us?"

I shake my head. "It's just us."

Faith shrugs and pulls out of my parking lot, leaving Roma in the rearview mirror.

We park at the Food Lion across the street from King's Pin Bowling Alley, along with everyone else. Students from Hampton University, activists from Don't Attack Blacks, and any other person of color or ally from Windsor Woods who caught wind of what we were doing. Cleo and I used discreet methods to loop everyone in—word of mouth, secret rooms on Clubhouse. Cleo even suggested starting a private Facebook group to reach out to the millennials and Gen Xers. We told everyone to park across the street, not at the King's Pin. We didn't want Mr. Brooks or any of his employees to get tipped off before we did what we wanted to do. Good thing. The Food Lion has more parking spaces, and we fill almost every single one of them. Every. Single. One. Faith drives through the parking lot twice before finding a free spot.

"Wow," I say as we leave Faith's car. That's all I can manage. There's a sea of people here. Okay, maybe not a sea, but a large-ass lake. Wearing hoodies. Holding signs. Rallying with and for each other. Pretty much every shade is out here representing too. I'd assume that Black people would mostly show up. We're always the ones who step up when one of our people is wronged. For us, by us. Tonight, though, we're not alone. Other people came to help us carry some of the burden.

My eyes land on two white girls. Around my age, wearing pressed khakis and cashmere sweaters. The type of girls you expect to see more at a country club than a rally. But they're here, both holding signs that read *BROOKS IS A CROOK*. They chat it up with some Black girls next to them, and there's something casual about their mannerisms. Relaxed, even. Like standing up for Black people is something they do in between their tennis and piano lessons. You love to see it.

Faith nudges me with her elbow. "You did all this, you know?"

I take a deep breath, take it all in. Maybe I did, a little. At least with Cleo's help. A finger pokes my side, and Drew's next to me, beaming. My Eternal Lab Partner. And he didn't come alone. Phil is at his side, wearing a Don't Attack Blacks tee over his thermal shirt.

"Hey, bish," Drew says, teeth flashing at me. "Are refreshments going to be served at this thing? Because in about ten minutes, the hangry's making an appearance."

Phil sucks his front teeth. "Yeah, right. The hangry arrived an hour ago when I skipped a song in the car."

"It was Lady Gaga. Who skips Lady Gaga?"

I don't laugh at their banter like I normally do. The knot

lodged in my throat won't allow it. Before I think about it, I pull Drew into a hug. "You came," I choke out. "I can't believe you came."

"And miss history in the making? No, thank you." Drew lets me continue hugging him. He even squeezes me back just as hard. The knot loosens, and streams of tears make their way down my cheeks. Not hot ones, but happy ones. I have this strange sensation of laughing and crying at the same time, and I thought that was something only old people did at graduations or other joyous occasions. Phil smiles at us, and I catch him dabbing his eye behind his rimless frames. I reach out to him and pull him into the embrace. He deserves the hug just as much as Drew.

"Okay, you guys are messing up my hair," Drew muffles over my shoulder. We all pull apart, and I catch Drew wiping at his eyes too. I knew he was a big ol' softy.

"Sorry," I say to Faith, straightening out my shirt and getting myself together. "Faith, this is Drew and Phil. Drew and Phil, this is—"

"Naomi, I'm in the same physics class as you and Drew. And Phil and I go back since like fifth grade," Faith says. She raises an eyebrow to Phil. "Excuse me, sir, would you like some salt with that?"

"I got enough salt, but I can take a small shake." Phil begins to sway his hips to a phantom beat, and Faith pretends to throw money at him, strip-club style. Seconds later, the two erupt with laughter. Drew and I glance at each other, amused. Apparently, we live in a world where Faith and Phil have inside jokes.

Cleo and Butter make their way over to us. Cleo and I grin at each other, our smiles letting each other know that we did the damn thing, then embrace.

"You did your thing, sis," she says in my ear.

"*We* did our thing," I correct as I pull away and make sure to look her in the eyes. I want her to know how much all her help means to me.

Cleo shrugs. "I was following your lead."

I peek over at Butter and give him a small wave. He's rocking his full 'fro, just like the first day I met him. The fluorescent lights in the parking lot hit his skin just right to give him a majestic glow. Combine that with his mane, and he looks damn right kingly.

"What? No hug for me?" he asks.

"Sorry." I inch over to him, and he envelops me with his long arms. I ease up and bury my face into his chest for a second. He smells woodsy, like that mahogany teakwood candle Mom and I love. It takes everything in me to not take a deep whiff and melt.

Drew clears his throat behind me and snaps me back to reality. I pry myself away from Butter and make the introductions between my HU friends and my Windsor Woods friends. When I introduce Butter, Drew gives me a slick side-eye.

"Mm-hmm," he says under his breath.

I elbow him on his side and turn to Cleo. "I don't think we have enough stuff," I say, still taking in the crowd that seems to grow by the minute.

"Don't worry. I told Neesa and them to hit up Lowe's to grab some more rope. Just in case. We're good to go."

I don't get to ask who "and them" are, because Orlando bops on over carrying a cardboard box filled with supplies.

"Just the people I was looking for. The Bold. The Black. The Beautiful." Orlando smiles, pleased with his nickname. Butter, who's found his way next to me, exhales loudly through his nose. He doesn't even try to hide his annoyance.

"Okay, we're about to get this show on the road," Orlando continues, ignoring Butter. "Naomi, I think it's only right that you say a few words to the people. Get them nice and amped up."

I blink. "Me?" It's one thing to work behind the scenes, but another to be front and center. I know my strengths: I hold the light and allow others to shine.

"You think that's a good idea?" Butter asks, and I want to squeeze his hand in gratitude. "Naomi's got enough heat on her since her family used to be tight with the Brookses. People are out here filming and streaming left and right. She doesn't need the Brookses to come after her like she started all this."

"But she did," Orlando says, cutting his eyes at Butter.

I shake my head. "No, *they* did." It's true. Mr. Brooks hasn't been convicted of anything yet, but he was scared enough to threaten my mom to get out of the lawsuits. Which means someone's got something solid on him. And nobody forced Kylie to freak out at Target, or Connor to film himself being a jackass. This is all on them. My head jerks into a nod now. "I don't mind saying a few words to remind them of that."

Butter and Faith both look at me like I'm wearing a pair of underwear on my head. Cleo and Orlando hold up their fists at me.

"Right on, queen." Orlando hands me his megaphone. "Showtime."

Phil claps his hands in pure excitement while Drew squeezes both my shoulders to amp me up.

I take a deep breath and press the megaphone to my lips. "Hello?" The megaphone screeches at me, and I jump. Orlando adjusts the volume, then nods for me to continue. "Hey, everybody," I try again. The crowd quiets down, searching for the source of the voice. Orlando takes my hand and helps me climb onto the hood of a random car. I hope the owner doesn't get pissed at me.

"Thank you for coming out here tonight," I continue. "I look out and see all these faces, all hues of faces, ready to be heard and make changes. *Big* changes and, I don't know, I feel good. I feel better than good. I feel proud. You all care. Too often, the Mr. Brookses in the world think they can get away with doing foul stuff. That just because they hire an appropriate amount of people of color to work under them or invite a Black face to dinner so that we can call them woke or a friend . . ." My voice trembles. I look down, and Butter peers up at me. He nods and pounds a fist to his chest: *You got this.*

"Well, we don't need any handouts. And we don't need any fake friends. What we need is the basic decency and respect that he affords to everyone who looks like him. And if he doesn't want to give it to us, then, dammit, we'll take it!" The crowd begins to clap and cheer.

At that, I reach into Orlando's cardboard box and pull out a noose. I hang it from my neck. "He doesn't have us by the end of his rope anymore. We're breaking free!" I shout into the megaphone.

The crowd roars and follows suit, each person hanging a noose around their neck from the ropes Cleo and I supplied. Orlando takes back his megaphone and winks at me. Cleo pounds her fist against mine, then waves her arms in the air. Our signal.

We march.

We trek through the Food Lion parking lot, signs high in

the air. Nooses dangling around our necks. We march across Highway 17. We march as we spill into the King's Pin parking lot. Cleo sneaked over earlier—she drew a chalk outline of the area we couldn't cross. That way, Mr. Brooks can't say we're trespassing. Then we spread out and stand in front of the building. That's when the chanting begins:

Cleo: "When I say *Brooks*, you say *crook*! Brooks!"

Us: "Crook!"

Cleo: "Brooks!"

Us: "Crook!"

Cleo: "When I say *Brooks*, you say *bigot*! Brooks!"

Us: "Bigot!"

Cleo: "Brooks!"

Us: "Bigot!"

And on and on we shout. Voices so loud that it sounds like it's coming from one large mountain of a man. Customers trickle out of the bowling alley, looking both confused and frightened. They rush for their cars—as if we came to loot them or something. But we're not here for their money. We're here for Mr. Brooks's money. And the more customers who leave, the less money he'll pocket. What's he need it for? He damn sure isn't paying his Black employees what they're worth.

I'm not sure how much time has passed. Enough that my voice feels raw from all the chanting. Eventually, though, a few employees come out of the building to see what's going on—followed by the man we all want to see, Mr. Brooks. He sneers at us with his fists on his hips. He has a megaphone of his own and pokes a button to make an alarm ring out from it. We quiet down, but only a little.

"Just so you know," he announces through the megaphone, "I've called the cops! Leave now, and this will all be water under the bridge!"

The crowd boos and hisses. I join in. There's no "water under the bridge" when he's trying to sic the cops on us.

"Go ahead and call the cops!" Orlando shouts in a battle of the megaphones. "We've seen the city permits. We're peacefully assembling in a public space!"

Mr. Brooks barks out a laugh. "You call this peaceful? I hear you over pins crashing!"

"That's because most of your customers peaced out," Orlando continues. "And they're going to keep leaving until you provide equitable pay and a culturally responsive work environment for your Black employees! Until you stop threatening your former Black employees. Because guess what?" Orlando tugs at his noose. "We ain't scared of you! We'll show up every damn day until you make changes or step down. When I say *Brooks*, you say *crook*!"

We continue our chant. Mr. Brooks glares at Orlando, and then his eyes land on me, standing right next to Orlando. His face falls in what seems like slow motion, and he blinks a few times, like he's making sure it's really me. My voice cracks, just a little, as a wave of nerves roams across my chest. It jars me, just for a second, seeing the man who was another father figure to me. The lighting from his bowling alley shrouding him like a villain about to commit his final act of crime. Then I remember that he is, in fact, a villain. A villain who fires employees for no reason and incites racism in interviews and leaves nooses for babies to see. I don't break my gaze. I don't stop chanting. If anything, I get louder. Taller. I want him to hear me. No, I want him to *fear* me.

Mr. Brooks looks away only as several patrol cars pull up in front of his building. The cops spill out of their cars, doing that strut with their chests out and their pelvises tilted inward, wanting us to see how big their balls are. One of the cops exchanges a few words with Mr. Brooks, then takes the megaphone from him.

"You do not have a permit to assemble," the cop shouts through the megaphone. "Gather your belongings and leave in the next thirty seconds, or we'll start reading Miranda rights. Capisce?"

We continue our chants. We know our rights. We know where the King's Pin property lines end. We looked at those blueprints until I saw the diagram of King's Pin in my sleep.

The cop smirks, his patience for us razor-thin. He turns to Mr. Brooks and shrugs at him, all: *What do you want us to do?* As if Mr. Brooks runs the police department. Mr. Brooks scans the crowd again before looking directly at me. His mouth moves. I can't hear him, but he enunciates like he wants to make sure I read his lips:

"Arrest them all."

TWENTY-FIVE

CHAOS. SCREAMS. SNEAKERS SCUFFING AGAINST THE ASPHALT. EVERY-thing happens so quickly that it takes my breath away trying to keep up with it all.

"What do we do?" I ask, more to myself than to anyone in particular. There are too many bodies moving, scurrying, to answer me anyway. I crane my neck, searching for Cleo. She was right next to me. Wasn't she just next to me?

A hand reaches out and squeezes my hand. "I got you," Butter says to me. "Come on." He tugs me away from the building when a cop intersects us.

"Too late," the cop says to us, his belly overlapping his belt like melting ice cream on a cone.

"You told us to leave, so we're leaving," Butter says to

him, his hand clinging more against mine. I can't tell if he's scared, or angry, or both. But whatever it is, he holds on to me tight enough to keep me from shaking.

"I also said you had thirty seconds." The cop looks at his Fitbit watch. "Time's up." He reaches for me, but Butter steps in between us.

"Don't touch her," Butter warns.

The cop rocks back on his heels, Butter's audacity knocking him off guard. "You interfering with my arrest, boy?" He spits out the final word with such malice, such cruelty, that it seems like he couldn't wait to get it out. That he's been holding on to it for just this moment.

Butter's jaw clenches. "What arrest? I didn't hear any Miranda rights read."

"Oh, that's not a problem." The cop pulls out his handcuffs, and my stomach flips inside out. This is it. I'm getting arrested. My life flashes before my eyes like I'm about to take my last breath. Me sitting on the floor in between my mom's legs as she combed my hair. Eric handing me my oversize Tigger stuffed animal to butter me up during our first meeting. All the talks Mom and Eric had with me about how to conduct myself around the police. Conversations that I never quite understood . . . until now. I swallow down the lump of tears trying to make its way up my throat.

"It's okay," Butter mouths to me. Or maybe he says it

aloud. All I can hear is my pulse beating overtime. "I got you."

I blink away tears and nod. What will my mom think? All those talks she had with me just gone to waste.

"Wait!" A voice pierces through the air. Mrs. Brooks pushes her way through the crowd, making her way over to me. Her usual precise bun is now lopsided to the left as loose strands of her hair dangle around her ears. "What do you think you're doing?" she asks the cop.

"Making an arrest, ma'am," the cop says, his voice suddenly lighter and gentler.

"No, you're not. This young lady is coming with me." Mrs. Brooks pulls my hand out of Butter's grasp. Butter starts toward us, but I shake my head. I don't want any of his actions to get twisted and used as an excuse for this cop to get forceful.

"I'm sorry, but I've been directed to arrest everyone still on the property," the cop says.

"We're not on the property," Butter and I say at once.

"Directed by whom?" Mrs. Brooks continues over us. "Scott Brooks? Well, I'm his wife and my name is also on the lease. I'm telling you I'm not pressing charges against this young lady. I'll take her home myself."

The cop smirks at me, then looks back over at Mrs. Brooks. "Fine," he mutters.

Mrs. Brooks starts guiding me away when I notice the cop turning his glare on Butter.

"Wait!" I call out. "You have to let Butter go too!"

Mrs. Brooks frowns. "What's a . . ." She notices my gaze on Butter, and it all clicks. She sighs. "Let the young man go too."

The cop purses his lips together. He was looking forward to arresting someone, but here comes Mrs. Brooks, blowing up his spot. He shoves the handcuffs back onto his belt loop. "Get out of here," he grunts to Butter.

Butter looks at me with his eyebrows raised, checking to see if I still need rescuing. I nod at him, let him know I'm okay. But he watches me as Mrs. Brooks steers me through the lingering crowd and toward her car. I can't tell if it's still out of concern, or disbelief. Less than an hour ago, I was hyping the crowd up to make some noise against Mr. Brooks. Now here I am, allowing Mrs. Brooks and her white skin to bail me out when things get rough. But I have to get home to my mom, to Eric. I promised them. Still, my skin burns as if I have the word *TRAITOR* tattooed across it.

Mrs. Brooks uses her fob to unlock the doors, and I hesitate to reach for a door handle. She pauses and looks at me. "Ny?" she asks.

I glance over my shoulder, and Butter's walking away. He looks back at me at the same time, as if he heard me staring at him. He pats his chest and gives me a nod: *We're good.* I exhale and open the back door.

"You don't have to sit in the back like a criminal, Ny," Mrs. Brooks says. "You can sit up here with me."

I shake my head. "That's okay." It's one thing to use Mrs. Brooks's privilege to avoid an arrest, but I didn't have to rub it in everyone's faces by sitting right next to her. I slip into the back seat, buckle my seat belt, and turn toward the window. I can't read the expression on Mr. Brooks's face as he watches us peel away. But with his hands stuffed in his pants pockets and his brows furrowing down toward his nose, he probably isn't too happy.

We drive in silence for a few minutes. Only the voices from some NPR show leaking out of the car speakers keep us company. I go over in my head what I should tell Mom and Eric. I'm sure Mrs. Brooks called my home already to fill them in. I pull at my fingers and think of my opening argument when I realize the noose is still dangling from my neck. I yank it off and shove it under my thighs, then catch Mrs. Brooks watching me in her rearview mirror.

"I'm glad you took that off," she says. "It doesn't belong on you."

"It doesn't belong at my mom's day care either," I say, and look back out the window.

"Is that what this is about? Is that why you joined those . . ."

I wait for her to say it. To take off her mask and reveal the conversations she has in her household when I'm not around.

"Those people," she continues. "You can't possibly think that we had anything to do with that disgusting act at Itsy Bitsy."

I shrug. "I have no reason to think you didn't. It's not like you called to check on my mom."

Mrs. Brooks sighs. "Naomi, things have not been the same between your mother and me for a while. I didn't think she wanted to hear from me."

"Sometimes silence says enough."

We reach a red light, and Mrs. Brooks spins around to face me. "I don't know what happened between you and the twins. And I don't know how it trickled into this . . . weirdness between me and your mom. But you have to know how much you both mean to me. To us. We're always going to be family, and I'm willing to put in as many resources as needed to investigate what happened at your mom's day care. You hear me?"

"You mean money?" I ask before thinking. Maybe this needs to be put out there, though. She didn't plan to use money to hire private investigators or buy security cameras. The money is to keep Mom quiet and drop the investigation. Money to make sure Mr. Brooks's hands stay clean. Once that happens, though, it'll be yet one more thing they can hold over our heads.

"Naomi, if I have the resources—and yes, that includes money—to help out you and your mother, why wouldn't I do that? Why does that have to be a bad thing?"

"Sometimes people use money to do bad things."

"True." Mrs. Brooks sighs through her nose. "But . . . Naomi, I have known you since you were five years old. You lost your first tooth in my house. You learned to ride a bike in my cul-de-sac. You were at my house when I found out my father died, and you squeezed into that group hug right in between the twins to make sure I was okay." Her voice breaks as she pinches her eyes closed, the memory taking her to a painful place. After a few beats, she opens her eyes and continues. "We are family. You can look me in the face and honestly think I'd do anything to harm you or Nina?"

She stares back at me, her wet eyes just as blue as Kylie's and Connor's. Eyes that lit up when Kylie and I showed her a new cheer routine we learned, or darkened when I told her about how Abbas Ali pushed me off the jungle gym. These eyes have praised me, scolded me . . . and even loved me. Which is why I can't stare at them too long.

"The light's green," I say to Mrs. Brooks.

She bites her lip, defeated, then swivels back around to drive. We fall into silence again and stay that way until Mrs. Brooks pulls into my parking lot. Mom stands on the sidewalk in front of our building, wrapping one of Eric's jackets around her to fight the chill of the night. I guess Mrs. Brooks did give my mom a heads-up that we were on the way.

As soon as Mrs. Brooks puts her car into park, I pop out

of her car and head right for my mom's arms. She crushes me so tight that my ribs might crack, but I don't care. She's just passing all her love to me. She finally pulls away and gives me a quick scan for bumps and bruises.

"We'll talk in the morning. Just get some sleep tonight," she says to me. She looks over my shoulder at Mrs. Brooks, who climbed out of her car at some point during our embrace. "Thank you. Ny, did you say thank you?"

I turn toward Mrs. Brooks but look down at her feet. "Thank you."

"Of course, sweetheart," Mrs. Brooks says.

Mom takes my hand, and we head for our building.

"Nina, if you have a minute," Mrs. Brooks calls out.

Mom stops walking and takes a breath. "Go on in and get ready for bed," she says to me.

I look between her and Mrs. Brooks, then trudge toward our building. I don't climb the stairs, though. I wait at the entrance, in the shadows, and strain my ears to catch their conversation.

Mom: "I said thank you."

Mrs. Brooks: "I don't need another thank-you. I just want us to resolve this mess."

Mom: (scoffs) "Then talk to your husband."

Mrs. Brooks: "Listen, I don't know what he said to you or how he said it, but you know Scott never intended to threaten you. We just felt that, after all these years, you might have his back. You know what kind of man he is."

Mom: "I do. And that's why I didn't want to make things worse by involving myself in this case."

Mrs. Brooks: "I don't understand. After all we've been through. After all we've done for—"

Mom: "Kristen, I'm not compromising my soul just because you think I owe you something. That's the only thing besides Naomi I can claim as my own. Now, I appreciate you getting Ny home safely tonight. I'm always going to appreciate how you've treated her. But after tonight, you don't have to do anything else for her. Or me. We're good."

I step away from the entrance as I hear Mrs. Brooks close her car door. I don't hear Mom's footsteps. She must be watching Mrs. Brooks drive away, all her memories fading along with Mrs. Brooks's taillights. I wonder if a part of Mom's chest aches as she watches Mrs. Brooks leave our lives. I know the feeling.

Mom finds me sitting on the bottom of the staircase once she makes it into our building. She doesn't look angry when she sees me here. If anything, she nods like she expected me to still be here.

"So, that's it?" I ask Mom. I'm not even sure what I mean entirely, but Mom doesn't question me. She grabs my hand and helps me back to my feet.

"That's it," she answers. "Let's get to bed, baby." There's a finality in her voice that makes me want to cry. I wonder if she feels it too. The pain of closing the door on such a major part of our lives. But Mom had been carrying the guilt of how we've entered the Brookses' home for far too long. She must be exhausted from carrying it after all these years. I'm exhausted for her.

We hold hands and climb the steps together. I look over my shoulder, toward the parking lot, even though I know Mrs. Brooks is long gone.

TWENTY-SIX

NOBODY GOT ARRESTED FROM THE PROTEST, SO THAT'S A RELIEF. CLEO
and I had done our homework too well. We understood our
rights and knew how to toe the line without crossing it.

"I was a little disappointed, though," Drew said to me the
next morning in physics. "I was hoping to spend at least an
hour behind bars. I figured it was the only time my parents
would let me get a tattoo before I turned eighteen."

Faith and I stared at him long and hard before he got the
hint and went back to his own lab table. It's not like I didn't
want to laugh along with Drew. I know that's what he does
when the tension gets too thick, just like Roma. And while I
want to celebrate the triumph of the protest last night, I still
can't get Mr. Brooks's face out of my head. How he sneered

at us with the hopes of throwing us in jail. How he sneered at me like I was some hood rat who sullied his parking lot. Even though we were all safe, Mr. Brooks put the fear in us by getting the cops involved. Just like he told Kylie to do weeks ago at Target. When you put that fear into the equation, Mr. Brooks won. Again.

I use my anger as fuel. At the football game that evening, the pulsing beat of the marching band's percussion section only amps me up more. I'm out on the field with my fellow Wolverines as we finish up a new routine. We step kick in time with the bass line, each kick getting higher and higher as the beat builds. We end the routine by whipping our hair and snapping our hips to the side. Then strike a pose, one hand extended high in the air, and wait for it.

The crowd starts to clap and cheer. If there's jeering, I don't hear it. Police officers patrol the stands, making sure nothing and nobody gets out of hand. Principal Hicks even stepped out onto the field at the start of the game to nip potential nonsense in the bud, holding a stuffed Windsor Woods wolf to build morale and show unity. Really, though, it looked like he was gripping a security blanket. Ms. Denita also warned us to keep it cute and keep it moving if the crowd lost their minds again. Don't let them ruffle us like during the homecoming game. "It's a miracle they're letting us perform tonight," Ms. Denita said. As if we were the ones who started the rumble last weekend.

We sashay off the field and return to our seats in the stands. It's not until my butt parks on the bleacher that I let out the breath I'd been holding since the routine ended. Like if I breathed too loudly, too comfortably, I'd piss someone off and World War Three would get started right on our field. But the cheerleaders kept quiet on the sidelines, and we strutted past them like they weren't even there.

I take a gulp from my water bottle and watch as the cheerleaders get the crowd hyped before our football players return to the field. Their voices tiny compared with the heat we just brought to the field. I shake my head in annoyance.

"Who's the recipient of that stink eye?" Faith asks next to me.

"No one in particular," I say. "But definitely all the heifers out on the field right now." I let out a small laugh.

Faith smirks, unamused. "You're doing too much."

"I didn't even say anything to them."

"Your face says it all. You remember what Ms. Denita said."

I wave my hand in front of my face, and my cheeks lift. "There. See? I'm smiling."

"You're hopeless," Faith says. "But I'm still willing to give you a chance. We're rolling through to the movies after the game to catch that new Michael B. Jordan joint. You riding with us?"

I shake my head. Michael B. Jordan's definitely appealing, but I have more important stuff to take care of. "Cleo and I are meeting up with Orlando a little later."

Faith just stares at me.

"What?"

"Didn't we all almost get arrested last night?" Faith cocks her head at me. "And you're kicking it with Orlando why?"

"The keyword is *almost*. We're having a strategy meeting to figure out next steps."

Faith rolls her eyes. "Lord, Naomi."

"'Lord, Naomi' what?"

Faith's mouth swishes back and forth, like she's rolling the words around on her tongue before settling in on the right ones. "When is enough going to be enough? We showed up. We made our point. Trended on social media. Everyone knows Mr. Brooks is a clown—and that they'll look like a clown if they go to any of his spots."

"Yeah, but what about his Black employees not being paid their worth?" I remind Faith. "What about him being a snake and doing what he did to my mom? Change doesn't happen in one night. If we want to move mountains, we have to lay the groundwork."

Faith frowns at me.

I sigh. "Why do you keep staring at me like that?"

"I'm sorry. Just making sure it's you sitting next to me and not Cleo. You're spewing the same nonsense that she says all the time."

"It's not nonsense if it's the truth," I insist. So what if I borrow a few lines from Cleo? When they mean something, they're worth repeating.

"You want to know the truth? The truth is, Cleo ditched us as soon as the cops started pulling out handcuffs."

I blink. Shake my head. "No . . . no, we all scattered." I do remember not being able to find her, but I didn't really see anyone. No one but Butter, at least.

"Yeah, and she made sure she had the one car parked at King's Pin so she could have a quicker getaway. That heifer didn't even call to see if I was okay last night. Had my dad heated too."

Was that true? If it was, there had to have been a reason. Maybe Cleo wanted to stream what was going down for the whole world to see. It makes sense that she'd need a safe spot to do that—like a journalist in a war zone. I want to ask Faith more, but she turns to Jordan, who sits on the other side of her. Ends our conversation without a goodbye. Okay, then. If Faith isn't down for the cause anymore, she'll never understand what I'm trying to say anyway. I sit on my hands to keep them warm and wait for the game to end.

We lose.

We plan our next moves at Orlando's home, a small house in downtown Hampton. I'm talking deep downtown, where you can find the good Chinese restaurants and a beauty-supply shop on every corner. Though he lives in an actual house,

Orlando's home probably has the same number of square feet as my apartment, if not fewer. And instead of sofas and coffee tables, he has gaming chairs, dinner trays, and plastic patio furniture substituting for the real thing.

One cool area, though, is the window seat in Orlando's kitchen. It was probably intended to be a breakfast nook, but Orlando uses it to store his paper plates and cutlery. I set them aside and pop a squat, watching a few guys play dominoes at the small round table next to Orlando's fridge.

I scroll through my phone as I wait for Orlando or Cleo to talk about why we're here. I avoid IG and TikTok, since all either platform has done is cause drama for me the past few weeks. Instead, I delete spam emails. Text an update to Mom. Look through my photo gallery. A memory pops up as soon as I open the Photos app. It's from the last day of my junior year. The start of the summer. The end of my innocence. I sit on the grass in the Brookses' backyard, Kylie to my right and Connor to my left. We squeeze in real tight for the selfie; Connor extended his arm to make sure he captured each of us. My hands are wrapped around their necks as we smoosh our faces as close together as possible, almost like we're the same person. Kylie's face is tilted toward mine, lips poked out and ready to plant a wet kiss on my cheek that Connor's quick finger missed.

I study my face. My cheeks lifted so high that I can feel them now. My eyes squinty from the sun or all the joy. And

Kylie and Connor look just as stoked to be with me as I was with them. I survey their faces, try to find the seams of their masks. But I don't see any creases, just grins. Just bliss. God, could this be from only four months ago? We all look so much younger. Especially me. And happy. How could I have been that happy then? This is right before I went natural. Before I spoke to Mrs. Song about HBCUs. Before I even thought that being a Wolverine could be a reality. Now all these things have happened. I felt freer, but . . . I haven't smiled that wide in a long time. Almost like those two feelings are mutually exclusive. I can either be happy but ignorant or woke and weighed down with rage. I wish I could find a balance.

"You found a quiet spot, huh?" Butter stands over me, sipping on a can of Sprite.

I quickly put my phone to sleep and smile up at him. "You are forever thirsty. Every time I see you, you're sipping on something."

"I'm a growing boy. Gotta stay hydrated to keep up with this physique." He flexes one of his arms, then nods at the space beside me.

I scoot over, and he folds his long body next to mine.

"Okay, I didn't think this through," he groans, then shifts to get as comfortable as possible.

I laugh. "I'm surprised you're here. I didn't think you were Orlando's biggest fan."

Butter rolls his eyes, proving my point. "He's a joke. But

Cleo wanted me to come, and you know how convincing Cleo can be."

I know exactly how convincing Cleo can be. She could make someone follow her headfirst into oncoming traffic. I wonder how far Butter has gone for her. Or with her. "You and Cleo ever . . . ?" I let the words dangle. For some reason, I can't bring myself to say them aloud. Something about Cleo and Butter being *together* makes my throat dry.

Butter chokes off his Sprite. He bangs at his chest to get the coughs out. "What? Naw. That's sis right there," he says once he gets himself together. "You didn't let me finish. I also knew you were going to be here."

Okay, I know I'm in Orlando's kitchen, but when did it get this hot? My face flushes, and I wipe my palms across my jeans. I don't get Butter, and that drives me crazy. He's one of the few people in my life right now who I haven't known for eons. And maybe the mystery of him is what makes me search for him when I know he might be around. Think about him when he's not. But this mystery also makes him hard to read, which is frustrating as all hell. I didn't know how to act around someone with such a clean slate.

"I'm not . . . seeing anyone actually." Butter keeps on like he's listening to every thought in my mind. He looks me right in the eye, waiting to see what I have to say about that. And there are things I want to say. So many things. Like how the color of his eyes reminds me of the gingerbread cookies my mom bakes every Christmas. Like how he always smells like my favorite candle. Like how when I talk to him, it feels new but safe. But I've been wrong about boys before. Super wrong. So, I swallow down those things and keep it moving.

"Thanks for looking out for me last night," I say, looking away. "Did you get home okay?"

Butter waits a few beats before answering. Probably trying to follow the tangent I just took this conversation. "Yeah, I was cool. Old boy with the badge gave me a few nasty looks as I left, but I'm Teflon. Stink eye from cops bounce right off me."

The guys at the round table next to us explode in jeers. They must not be too happy about whoever won that round, if they're even called rounds in dominoes. Regardless, the guy who won gets up and busts out moves that he looks like he learned from a TikTok challenge.

"Last year I was pledging a frat," Butter says over the jeers and laughter. I turn to make sure he's talking to me, and his body has twisted in my direction. "One of the things we had to do was eat a whole stick of butter without throwing up. I was the only one who scarfed it down like a champ." He shrugs. "The name stuck."

Everything clicks together, and I smile at him. "*That's* why you're Butter? I should've known you were in a frat. Let me guess . . . you're an Alpha. I heard those guys are no joke."

Butter shakes his head. "Naw. I never finished pledging."

"Why not?"

He gives me a side eye. "Those niggas made me eat a whole stick of butter. Weren't you paying attention?"

I crack up laughing.

"But," he continues, "I guess Butter has a better ring to it than Aidan. Apparently, that was a popular name back in the day."

My laughter dies, and I study him. Wow. There must be some truth serum in that can of Sprite. "Aidan." I repeat. "I like it. It's . . . you."

Butter smiles. "And Naomi fits you. 'Above all' and 'beauty.'" He looks down at his legs as he stretches them out. "I looked it up."

He looked it up? That means he thinks about me enough to find the meaning of my name. That means he *thinks* about me. Period. I take in a shaky breath. I've been fighting whatever this was between me and him, but maybe it's pointless. He feels what he feels, and I definitely feel it too.

I want him to look up. I want him to look back up at me so I can lean close and let him know he can kiss me. And if he doesn't make the first move, maybe I can touch his chin and guide him.

"Power to the people," Orlando calls out, swaggering into the kitchen with Cleo right next to him.

My shoulders deflate, and everyone pauses what they're

doing to give Orlando and Cleo their full attention. Even Butter.

"Thank you all for making it out tonight. As you can see, there's only a few of you here. But don't let the quantity fool you. Cleo and I hand selected you all for a very special reason. First, let's give it up to our Nubian queen, aspiring empress, Naomi Henry, for orchestrating the first attack against the Brookses' monopoly."

Cleo raises her fist, and everyone in the kitchen claps their hands for me, including Butter. I give a small smile and look down at my feet. I don't know what to do with all that adulation when I'm not cheering or dancing on a football field.

"But, as we all know, there are many battles to be fought before we win the war," Orlando continues. "Brooks thought he had the upper hand by calling the cops on us, but that's what white folks do. Abuse their power and abuse the system, but nobody calls them out for misusing 911. For breaking the damn law. Two can play that game." Orlando rubs his hands together, getting geeked out for what he's about to say next: "We're planting a bomb."

The oxygen vacuums out of the room, and the change in pressure clogs my ears. I can't hear anything. I tug my ears to clear them, but it's not me. The whole room has gone silent. And it's so still, so quiet, that the drips and drops of the leaking faucet in the kitchen sink seem supersonic. A bomb? An actual bomb? I look to Cleo for clarity in this fog, but she stands with her hands on her hips. A small smile on her lips. She's eating this idea up like lo mein from one of the Chinese restaurants around here.

"Huh?" Neesa's voice pierces through the silence. "Like a *bomb* bomb?"

I didn't know any other types of bombs besides a *bomb* bomb, but I totally get Neesa's question. I lean forward and wait for an answer.

"Yeah." Orlando shrugs his response. As matter-of-fact like Neesa just asked him if he watches horror movies.

The room erupts in chatter. Everyone has a question. Everyone has a concern. But they all get jammed together into a clog of confusion.

Cleo flags both arms in the air. "Hey, hey, hey!" The room slowly settles. "Don't worry. We thought this through. We're going to plant the bomb on one of the slower nights. It's going to be a dummy. It won't even go off. But it'll look convincing enough to leave Brooks shaking in his patent-leather boots and turn the business over to someone who knows how to treat their Black employees."

This pleases some of the people in the room. Heads nod, and mouths circle to form a couple of *oh*s. They get it. It makes sense to them. But no. *No.*

"No." The word comes out so sharply from my mouth that it lifts me from my seat. All eyes are on me now. I take a breath to fill my lungs with courage. "This doesn't sound safe at all."

Cleo's head tilts. She stares at me like I just stuck a shiv in her back. "Are you kidding me? You of all people should be on board with this. You know what he left on your mom's property."

"I know." My jaw clenches at the memory. "And it was terrible. But nobody was inside the noose. Nobody got physically hurt. A bomb . . . a bomb could hurt a lot of people. A bomb could *kill* people."

"I'm sorry. I know you're in high school and all," Orlando begins with a laugh, "but I assumed you were following the conversation. The bomb's not going to be real. Which means nobody's getting hurt." He lifts his eyebrows to me in this patronizing way that makes me feel like I'm a toddler getting caught eating a crayon.

"But fake weapons can cause real damage," Butter says, standing right beside me. "That shit happens all the time on movie sets, and they even have experts overseeing everything. And you damn sure don't look like an expert on anything."

Orlando gives Butter a glare that would make a weaker man sob, then turns and smirks at Cleo. "I told you not to invite any soft-ass niggas tonight."

"Soft?" Butter repeats. "I'd rather be soft than a bubblehead. Because only a bubblehead motherfucker would plant a bomb on a property that we all just boycotted. Who do you think the cops would point the finger to first?"

"We're not the only enemies that Brooks has, or are you too unenlightened to pick up a newspaper, brutha?"

"You could always enlighten me outside," Butter says, tucking his silver chain inside his shirt collar. *Brutha.*

"You ain't say nothing but a thing." Orlando starts toward Butter, but Cleo grabs Orlando's arm. I pull at Butter's hand. He's been trying to keep me out of trouble; now it's my time to do the same for him.

"Look at us," Cleo shouts. "We're not supposed to be fighting each other! That's what people like Brooks want! Remember, we can't give them our power."

I look down at Cleo's T-shirt. She has the exact same phrase across it: *We can't give them our power.* Is this what she does? Speaks in catchphrases and bumper stickers to try to prove her point? How many other lines has she stolen?

"But aren't we doing that by planting a bomb?" I ask. "No matter how much you plan, one of us will go down for it. And it's hard to make noise and change when you're locked behind bars." Or even when you get out. I think of how long it took Eric to find a job once he was released. The way that people automatically snubbed their noses at him for something he did years ago. Eric has a way with tools. He could take apart anything and put it back together like it was brand-new. But he uses his skills to install satellite dishes during the day and clean hospitals overnight. Not that there's anything wrong with either—except that Eric could design and construct bridges if someone would only give him a chance.

"Sometimes someone has to be sacrificed to make waves," Cleo says. "Think about Martin. Malcolm—"

"They were assassinated, fam," Butter says. "And for less than threatening people with a bomb."

"Nobody needs to be 'sacrificed' for this," I continue. "Not even Scott Brooks." Yes, he's a wolf in sheep's clothing, but when I try to think of Kylie and Connor and even Mrs. Brooks sitting at their dining room table without him, something inside me aches for them. Like I remember that, even with their flaws, they're still human.

"Well, if you're not down for the cause, you can dip." Cleo hitches her head toward Orlando's front door, as if she wasn't my ride here. "Maybe you can call Mrs. Brooks to pick you up." At that, Orlando coughs out a laugh.

I look at her for what she really is. For what Faith has been trying to tell me about her all this time. She's the same person who roped me into taking a pic with Noah and Damon without telling me who they were. The same person who scoffed at me for leaving the protest with Mrs. Brooks but hightailed it out of there quicker than anyone else. The chick who used me for clout to rub elbows with Orlando and DAB. The same thing her first boyfriend did to her all those years ago, she was regurgitating with me. My rage toward the

Brookses blinded me from all of this. From seeing the creases of *her* mask.

"Fine," Butter says on my behalf. He grabs my hand and guides me toward the door.

"And you know what happens to snitches!" Orlando shouts to our backs. I wait for Cleo to shut him up, to stick up for us. But she never does. Butter and I leave the house with targets on our backs.

NOW

MEDICAL EXAMINER AUDIO RECORDING EXCERPT
"THIS EXAMINATION IS BEING CONDUCTED BY PATRICK RYAN AT APPROXIMATELY 0215 HOURS ON OCTOBER 13. THE DECEASED IS A SEVENTEEN-YEAR-OLD FEMALE, THOUGH OFFICIAL RECORDS HAVE NOT BEEN YET OBTAINED. ADDITIONALLY, PREVIOUS MEDICAL HISTORY INFORMATION HAS NOT YET BEEN RECEIVED. THUS, THIS IS A RECORDING OF MY INITIAL OBSERVATIONS. FURTHER AND PERTINENT FINDINGS WILL BE INCLUDED IN MY FINAL WRITTEN REPORT.

"UPON FIRST EXAMINATION, THE DECEASED APPEARS TO HAVE EXPERIENCED FATAL BLUNT-FORCE TRAUMA ON THE BACK OF THE SKULL. IT IS NOT CLEAR YET IF THIS TRAUMA WAS FROM A FALL, OR IF AN OBJECT FELL ON TOP OF THE DECEASED. THE

397

DECEASED WAS FOUND UNDER A PILE OF DRYWALL AND DEBRIS FROM THE EXPLOSION AT KING'S PIN BOWLING ALLEY AND WAS UNRESPONSIVE AT THE SITE. A FULL AUTOPSY WILL NEED TO BE CONDUCTED TO FIND SIGNS OF POTENTIAL SMOKE INHALATION. HOWEVER, THE AMOUNT OF BLOOD LOST AT THE SITE AND THE PENETRATION OF THE SKULL FRACTURE INDICATES PROMPT EXPIRATION. IN OTHER WORDS, THE DECEASED DOES NOT SEEM TO HAVE SUFFERED."

TWENTY-SEVEN

It's off.

That's it. That's the text Cleo sends to me on Sunday evening. Maybe Butter's words reached her. He told me when he dropped me off that he'd talk to Cleo away from the noise. Away from Orlando.

"Sometimes she thinks she needs to prove something," Butter said to me while we idled in his car in my parking lot. "Like if she ain't angry, she ain't Black enough. But I'll catch up with her later."

I wonder what he said to make her change her mind. Whatever it was, I want to kiss him—or at least more than I already wanted to. My stomach ached all Sunday before the text. I had too much knowledge that I didn't want, but

I had no clue what to do with it. If I talked to Mom and Eric, I'd get them tangled up in this mess—and they had enough of their own problems. If I told the Brookses, I'd be a traitor to my people. I toyed with the idea of calling one of the King's Pin locations and leaving an anonymous tip. I'd even researched voice-changing apps when Cleo finally texted those two words that made me breathe easier. I wrote her back immediately:

Thank you. We can think of a better way.

She didn't answer me that night. She didn't answer me Monday or Tuesday either. By the time Wednesday rolls around, I've stopped expecting anything from her. That's okay, though, because I have other things to keep my mind busy—now that I have room in it for anything besides worry. I wait by Roma's locker before the first bell. When I see her strolling over to it alone, my stomach tosses—bouncing between relief and disappointment. Happy to see her by herself because it might make this easier, but also wishing others were there so I could make things easier with them. Cleo had shown me that everyone has gray areas, and I was tired of seeing my old friends in black-and-white.

Roma stops in her tracks, and her shoes squeak against the floor. I give her a tiny wave.

"Happy birthday," I say.

Her eyes shift, waiting for something or someone to pop out and scare her. Finally, she takes timid steps toward me.

"Thanks. I didn't think you'd remember."

"As if I'd forget after eight years. Plus, you made sure to post a countdown pic every day for like the last month. If none of your followers remembered your birthday, they're missing a brain cell or two."

"You know me. Subtle with a capital *S*." Roma gives me a smile.

"Spoiled with a capital *S*," I correct. I reach into my shoulder bag and pull out a box. "For you."

Roma raises her eyebrows, then takes the box and shakes it next to her ear. I push the thoughts about the fake bomb at King's Pin out of my head. It's time to move on. Roma opens the box and pulls out a pair of white cheer shoes.

"They're not necessarily the best," I explain. "I found them on sale. But I remember how you looked when Kylie gave me a pair of new shoes and not you. That wasn't fair. Plus, they look like they'll get the job done."

Roma inspects the shoes and smiles again. "I love them," she says. "I love *you*." She tilts her head forward like she's trying to toss the sentiment at me.

I catch it, right in my chest. "I love you too." My throat's too tight to keep speaking, so I grab Roma and pull her in for a hug. She squeezes me back, and just like that, I know we're okay. Almost.

"I'm sorry," I say in her ear. "I never meant to cut you out. I've just been trying to figure things out."

"I'm sorry too." She pulls back and wipes a tear from her eye. "I should've been helping you figure them out. Or at least stood by you while you figured them out on your own."

"Does that mean I can start liking your pictures again?" I ask, smiling through tears.

"Bitch, I don't know why you stopped." She wipes away the trails of tears on my face.

"Okay." I take a deep breath and shake out my limbs, get all the sadness out. Roma does the same. It's something we always did when things got too mushy. "How are you celebrating?"

Roma makes a face. "With some Ben and Jerry's and a Dylan O'Brien movie."

I groan. "You can do that any day. Come on. You're eighteen now. You're an adult. Don't you want to join the military? Play the lottery? Get married?"

"Maybe next year. I haven't been a celebratory mood lately." She holds up her shoes. "Until now, that is."

"That's sweet, but it's not going to work. We're not waiting a whole year to commemorate this major birthday. Let's get into something this weekend." I clasp my hands together and add a pout for good measure.

Roma sighs, then shrugs. "Fine. Question—will it just be me and you partying, or . . . ?" She does it again. Leaves Kylie's name out of the conversation like the mere mention of it will set flames to this happy reunion.

It's my turn to sigh. I lean against her locker. "How about baby steps?"

"So you're saying there's a chance!" She bends over and does her giddy booty-popping dance.

I laugh and shake my head. "I'm leaving before you make me late to class. Careful, don't pull a muscle."

"Please. This is the reason why I do squats."

I continue to laugh as I head toward my first block and feel like the huge boulder that I've been carrying on my shoulders for the past two months has lifted. My head is lighter, my spine is a little straighter, and I'm softer on my feet. All this time I thought I couldn't have it all. I couldn't have natural hair and the Wolverines and HBCUs plus keep my old friends at the same time. But maybe I just never gave it a chance to work.

I test this theory out during second block. As soon as Faith sits at our lab table, I pivot in her direction. "What are you doing this weekend?"

Faith flinches from my question. "Whoa. Good morning."

"Good morning. What are you doing this weekend?"

"I'm not sure." She slowly pulls out her notebook while keeping a skeptical eye on me. "Why?"

"One of my friends just turned eighteen, and I wanted to do something for her. Maybe hit up that steak house on Brewers Neck?"

"Isn't that the place with the mechanical bull and the country line dancing?"

"Yeah. My friend Roma used to be super into line dancing before she discovered booty popping." I lower my head. "Is . . . is that a problem?" My voice gets small as my palms start to sweat. Here I was talking to Roma about baby steps this morning, and now I was doing a full cannonball with Faith.

Faith smirks. "Girl, please. My Spotify playlists have both Kacey Musgraves and Kendrick Lamar. I'm 'bout that life. I'm just surprised you weren't going to be up under Cleo this weekend."

I remember my unanswered text. Then remember how I haven't checked to see if Cleo's responded to my unanswered text in almost twenty-four hours. Not because I forgot—I'm just not too pressed about it anymore. "Cleo has enough groupies." I wince, remembering who I'm talking to. "No offense."

Faith smiles at me like she just watched me take my first steps. "None taken. I mean, I love her and all, she's just Team Too Much sometimes."

She doesn't even know the half of it. "Yeah. I get that." But we've done enough talking about Cleo. I wanted Faith to chill with me for me, and I wanted her to know that Cleo or Ms. Denita didn't need to be around for us to kick it. I think about our moment at the college fair. We started something promising, and I wanted to see it through. "What time will you be free on Saturday?"

I frown as I flip through my physics book later that night. The labs were one thing, but reading the concepts without the hands-on engagement was like starting *Grey's Anatomy* on season sixteen. But we have a test tomorrow, and I need to get cracking on my college applications. I don't want to send off a transcript with a C in Honors Physics, or worse.

I look at the clock on my phone. It's just a little after eleven. I've been at it for at least the last two hours trying to digest all things physics, but the laws of thermodynamics are giving me heartburn. If anyone is going to get me through this test, it's my Eternal Lab Partner. And knowing Drew, he's awake streaming episodes of the *Gossip Girl* reboot on his laptop.

I run a hand through my hair as I open the contacts list on my phone. "Ugh," I mumble. My curls feel as harsh as the skin of a pineapple. I call up Drew and put my phone on speaker as I head to the bathroom to begin the process of getting my hair satin-bonnet ready.

Drew doesn't pick up until the fourth ring. "Huh?" His voice is muffled by a pounding bass line in the distance.

I frown at my phone as I rub Carol's Daughter Hair Milk through my curls. "Why do you sound like you're at a rave?"

"What? I can't hear you?"

"WHY DO YOU SOUND—"

I groan and pick up the phone before I can properly wipe my hands. "Where are you right now?"

"Naomi, is this you?"

"Yes." I speak to him slowly like he just woke up from a coma. "Where are you right now? Shouldn't you be studying for your physics test?"

Drew doesn't answer. An EDM song streams through my tiny speaker. Sounds of laughter rip through it.

"Hello?" I ask.

"Okay, don't be mad at me," Drew finally says.

"Why would I be mad at you?"

"Kylie wanted to throw a surprise party for Roma. She invited a few of us to the bowling alley."

My fingers curl around my phone, and I clench my teeth. This is a classic Kylie move. King's Pin closes early Mondays through Wednesdays, so every now and then she and Connor like to sneak friends in after-hours to dip into the alcohol supply. These parties are like an urban legend in Windsor— everyone scrambling to get an invite. Except for me. I was always on the VIP list. Always the first to know when these covert gatherings were happening.

But not tonight. Tonight, I'm standing in my bathroom, taking a break from studying to moisturize my hair, while Kylie invites my Eternal Lab Partner to a surprise birthday party for our shared best friend. Kylie doesn't even like Drew.

And Drew was out there with me last week protesting that very same bowling alley.

"Why would I be mad?" I ask, finally separating my jaw.

"Because. I know things are . . . weird between you and Kylie."

"Who's weird? I'm not weird. Your face is weird." Okay. I'm definitely being weird.

"Drew! Get off the phone and take a shot of Fireball!"

Even through all the noise, I know that voice. My entire body tenses in response, sending my phone flying into the air. I scramble to catch it, but the damn hair milk makes it impossible. My phone makes a sickening plop as it lands directly in the toilet.

"Shit," I hiss. I curl my lip and try not to gag as I reach my hand into the toilet. The phone slips from my fingers every time I think I get a good grip on it, as if it's playing tag with me. Finally, I chokehold that little bastard, shake it off, and then use a hand towel to pat it dry. It hasn't been in the water *that* long. It shouldn't have too much damage, if any at all. I touch my screen, and nothing happens. New waterproof model, my ass.

"Shit!" I wince and look at the closed bathroom door behind me. I hold my breath for a few beats, but thankfully, Mom and Eric are still asleep. At least I have that going for me, since Kylie ruined the rest of my night. First, she hijacked my friends, and now she obliterated my phone.

I make my way to the kitchen to grab some uncooked rice, then head back to my room for more studying.

I wake up with my face buried inside my physics textbook. On impulse, I reach for my phone, but then I remember it's drying in a bowl of uncooked white rice on my nightstand. The image of it taking a deep dive into the toilet floods my brain, and I scowl. Fucking Kylie.

I retrieve my phone and attempt to cut it on. It lights up, and I breathe a sigh of relief. My clock shows that it's a little after midnight. I'm sure everyone's still living it up at the bowling alley, laughing like they have no tests to study for and no soggy phones to dry. They're probably posting all their shenanigans online. Makes sense since Mr. and Mrs. Brooks never check out Kylie's or Connor's social media. *White-people shit*, Eric always says.

I hover my thumb over the Instagram icon on my phone, ready to torture myself with a serious case of FOMO, but a barrage of texts and missed calls attacks my screen at once. Apparently, all this has gone down during the past hour I was off the grid. And apparently, all the missed texts and calls are from Butter.

My heart skips a beat. I've been wanting to talk to him since he brought me home from Orlando's house last weekend, but the timing never seemed right. Not after we both were almost involved in a domestic act of terror. But I know there's something there between us, and maybe he was finally ready to talk about it.

I take a breath and call him back.

"Naomi." He sounds like he's out of breath. Maybe he's just as nervous as I am. "I've been trying to call you."

"I know. My phone died. I was doing my hair and . . ." I almost tell him about the toilet. Why would I tell him about the toilet?

"Look, I'm about five minutes from you. Can I see you?"

I sit upright in my bed. "Yes," I say too quickly, then look at my bedroom door. Remember that Mom and Eric are sleeping in the bedroom right across from mine. "I mean . . . my mom's home and it's after midnight. . . ."

"Shit. You're right. I'm sorry."

I'm losing him. "But I can meet you outside." I grip the phone like I'm gripping onto him.

Butter pauses for a second, then: "I'll be there soon."

He hangs up, and I leap from my bed. I rummage through my purse and find a tin of mints and a tube of ChapStick. I pop an Altoid into my mouth and get my lips nice and moisturized. Butter is on his way. To see me. Like he couldn't wait another possible minute to be near me. I understood the feeling. I haven't been able to stop thinking about him.

I slip on some Ugg boots over my flannel pajama pants. I think about changing into jeans or something cuter, but then Butter might wonder why I'm dressed to the nines after midnight. I scurry to my door when I catch my reflection in my vanity mirror. Dammit, I still have on my satin bonnet. I yank it off, toss it on the bed, and fluff out my curls.

I make sure to keep the doorknob to the front door turned downward so it won't click loudly and wake up Mom. Last thing I need is her coming down in her silk scarf and faded Jodeci T-shirt, messing up my chance with Butter. Just as I reach the sidewalk outside my building, headlights swim across my face. Butter keeps his car running as he jumps out of it. My God, this is just like a rom-com. I run over to him.

"Naomi—"

I don't let him finish. We've been doing this song and dance for too long, and I don't want to do or say anything that will ruin yet another moment. I hop up on my tippy-toes, wrap my arms around his neck, and kiss him. I kiss him hard, then I kiss him soft. I take in his smells, his skin. The ends of his cornrows ticking the top of my hand. He's frozen at first, taken off guard by my assertiveness. But eventually his shoulders soften and he rests his hands on my hips, bracing me so I don't fall. Too late. I already fell for him. Hard.

I pull away so I can see Butter smiling down at me.

Only he's not.

He has a crease in between his eyebrows that forms a question mark.

My heart drops. "Oh, God." I step back. "I'm . . . I'm sorry. I thought that's what we both wanted."

"No." He flinches. "I don't mean that. It's . . . Naomi, the plan isn't off."

I frown at him. "What are you talking about?"

"Orlando's plan." Butter takes a deep breath. "There's a bomb at King's Pin tonight."

TWENTY-EIGHT

"PICK UP, PICK UP, PICK UP," I MUMBLE INTO MY PHONE AS I LISTEN TO Roma's phone ring nonstop. Butter's zipping through red lights, going about twenty miles over the speed limit, all to get us to the King's Pin on Highway 17. We weren't sure if that's where Orlando planted the bomb, but it's the biggest location. The site of the protest. If Cleo and Orlando wanted to leave a message, that's where they would go. And that just happens to be where my former friends are partying for Roma's birthday. Kylie and Connor always picked the bowling alley on Highway 17 for their after-hours festivities. It was grand, more impressive—and they're all about impressing people.

I groan as Roma's phone goes to voice mail. "Roma, it's

Ny," I say after the beep. "You all need to get out of the building. Now. Call me after and I'll explain." I hang up the phone, and my leg bounces up and down. Even with Butter driving like a NASCAR racer, this ride takes forever.

"No luck?" Butter asks as he whips a turn.

I shake my head. "I've tried pretty much everyone." Roma. Drew. The girls from the squad. It's like everyone agreed to ignore my calls. "What about you? Cleo answer?"

Butter sighs and shakes his head too. "But I reached out to Faith when I couldn't get to you. I figured Faith might have better luck getting through to Cleo."

"Good idea." My leg won't stop bouncing. "I can't believe Cleo told you it was still going down."

"She didn't. I thought we were cool after I hit her up on Sunday, but for the last two days she's been acting squirrelly. Difficult to get ahold of. So, I hit up Neesa, and she broke."

I rest the back of my head on the seat. Cleo was trying to get me and Butter off her trail. That's why she texted me. That's why she pretended to be cool with Butter. *Soft-ass niggas.* That's what Orlando called us. Cleo did what she had to do to pop pacifiers in our mouths and keep us in the dark.

"Hey." Butter reaches over and grabs my hand. "We're almost there, okay? Did you try calling the twins?"

Kylie and Connor. I can't believe I was letting our tension—my stubbornness—get in the way of something as urgent and dangerous as a bomb, prop or not. I take a breath and call Kylie. Her phone rings once. Twice. And it keeps on ringing just like everyone else's phone tonight. Kylie's voice pops up on the line, but it's her voice mail greeting: *Leave a message, I guess. Not like I'm going to listen to it!*

The phone beeps and I pause. Her greeting is right. She never listens to messages. But maybe seeing something from me after all this time will make her think otherwise. "Kylie," I begin. "Please. It's not safe there. Get everyone out ASAP." I linger for a few seconds as I consider how to end the message. Do I tell her to call me? Apologize for the past few weeks? Say that I love her? None of them feel right in the moment, so I hang up.

"She didn't pick up," I say to Butter, staring down at my phone in my hand.

"It's cool. We're here."

I unbuckle my seat belt before Butter turns into the parking lot. I don't want any other obstacles in my way. The King's Pin signs aren't lit up. Kylie and Connor try to be as discreet as possible for these gatherings, even though the sprinkle of cars in the parking lot blows their cover. Butter's headlights float across three bodies standing in the parking lot, arms swinging around in the air as if they're arguing not just with their words but their limbs. Butter doesn't bother with finding a parking space. He just stops his car next to the arguing bodies, and we hop out. Faith and Cleo scream and shout, their words toppling over each other's. Orlando stands in between them, trying to get them to quiet down with no success.

"Cleo!" Butter barks, running over to them. "What the hell are you thinking?"

Faith throws her hands in the air in relief. "Finally! Somebody else is here with some common sense!"

I don't hear Cleo's rebuttal, because I'm already running toward the building to warn everyone.

"Hey!" Orlando's meaty hand grabs my arm and snaps me backward. "The fuck you think you doing?"

"Saving my friends!" I try to wiggle out of his grasp, but he has a firm grip.

"Back off!" Butter shouts to Orlando, ripping his hand off me. He then pushes Orlando to make sure he keeps away.

"Stop it, B!" Cleo says, stepping in between them. She looks over at me. "Nobody needs saving, Naomi. We told you. The bomb is a dud."

"The charges placed against you won't be duds!" Faith snaps.

"This is what we get for bringing babies into the fold." Orlando glares at me and Faith, then turns his malice toward Butter. "Babies and this big, doofy motherfucker here."

Butter pushes Orlando again. This time, Orlando pushes back. They start going at it. Fists flying, scuffing sneakers. The whole nine. Faith and Cleo scream and try to pull them apart from each other. This is my moment. I run toward the building and head right to the side door. The employee entrance. This is the door Kylie and Connor unlock to get us all in after-hours. To my relief, the door is still unlocked.

The floor vibrates against the bottom of my Uggs, in time with the music blaring through the PA system. No wonder they couldn't hear their phones or all the commotion going on in the parking lot. I rush past the bathrooms and employee lockers and make my way to the main area. There they are. Drew, Phil, and Jared are bowling at the lanes. Shauna, Brittany, and a few other people are dancing to the music near the tables. Roma sits with Ava and Serena, laughing and chowing down on pizza. And I spot Connor with Brian and Weston behind the bar.

"Hey!" I call out, but the music is too powerful. Nobody has even noticed that I've entered. I run over to the closest area, the bar.

"Hey!" I shout again, leaning over the bar top.

Connor turns and jumps when he sees me. "Naomi?" He frowns like he wants to make me clearer.

"Bro!" Brian cackles when he notices me too. "What the hell is she doing here?"

I don't have time for his foolishness. "Connor, we have to get everyone out of here."

"What?" Connor asks, still frowning.

"It's not safe! We have to go!"

Connor looks me up and down. "Are you on something?

What are you talking about?"

I sigh and try to repeat myself, but Brian and Weston hooting on and on like owls isn't helping my case.

"Who the hell invited you?" I don't know when she gets here, but Serena slinks up behind Connor and wraps her arms around his waist. Even now, she's claiming her man. As if Connor and I have uttered a single word to each other in forever.

I roll my eyes and hop on top of the bar.

"Ny, what are you doing?" Connor asks me.

I snatch the microphone that's kept on the floating TV stand over the bar and cut it on. "Everybody needs to leave. Now!" I say into the mic.

All the chatter dies down, and everyone in the room peers at me. I hear my name escape out of a few mouths. One or two: "What is she doing here?" and related questions.

"This isn't a joke," I continue. I grip onto the mic, knowing what I have to say next. "I have reason to believe there's a bomb in here—"

The chatter erupts again. People cussing at me. Jeering me. Just like at the homecoming game. I try to talk over them, but they overpower me. Even with the microphone.

I feel a hand on my calf. I look down and Connor stares up at me, his entire face scrunched in concern. "This isn't funny, Ny," he says. Not out of anger, but out of fear. Not for himself but for me. Like I've fallen off the deep end and he

417

doesn't know how to reach me.

"Get this lying bitch out of here!" I don't recognize the voice.

"Why the hell would she lie about that?" Drew asks, heading closer to me like he's trying to dodge the jeers on my behalf. "Maybe we need to listen to her!"

I spot Roma staring at me, wide-eyed. "What's going on?" she mouths.

I don't answer. In my scanning of the crowd, there's still one person I haven't seen. "Where's Kylie?" I ask Connor.

"Bitch, just leave," Serena demands.

"She's in the kitchen," Connor answers, stepping out of Serena's arms. "But why are you—"

I don't hear the rest of Connor's question. I jump off the bar top and run straight toward the kitchen. The chaos continues behind me. Drew and Roma arguing on my behalf, defending me against claims that I'm "crazy." I hope they listen to Drew and Roma. I don't know how much longer we all might have.

I push through the double kitchen doors and Kylie shrieks, dropping two-gallon bottles of ranch dressing onto the floor. Some of it spews back up at her, splashing the bottom of her jeans.

"What in the world, Ny?" she snaps at me. She then pauses and blinks at me. As if she's just remembering that I wasn't supposed to be here. Even after this mess of a school year, she's used to me being right next to her.

"Kylie, we have to go."

Kylie smirks at me. "Go where?"

"Leave!" I pause and try to turn my volume down a few notches. I don't want her confusing my concern for anger. "I know you have no reason to believe me after everything we've been through the past two months, but I think someone's planted a bomb somewhere in the building."

I actually see the color leave Kylie's face. "That's not funny."

"You know me. You know I wouldn't joke about something like this. I wouldn't come out here looking like this"— I wave a hand at my pajama pants and Uggs—"if I didn't think you were in trouble. So please. Leave with me." I reach out my hand to her, and Kylie looks at it. Her hand moves up an inch just as the kitchen doors burst open behind us. The noise sends me leaping out of fear that I'm too late.

"Look, I don't know what shit you're trying to pull tonight," Serena begins as she storms toward me, "but if you think you're getting Connor back looking like *that*, then you truly must be on something."

This bitch. "Serena, getting with Connor is the furthest thing from my mind. I'm just trying to get everyone out of here safely."

Serena rolls her eyes. "So, the first party you're not invited to is suddenly not safe?"

Roma jogs in behind Serena. "Drew and Phil left," Roma says to me. "I tried to get the others to listen, but . . ." She looks between me and Serena. "Did you come in here just to start shit?" she asks Serena.

"Yes," Kylie answers, retrieving the bottles of ranch. "Per usual."

Serena sucks in a breath, like she has a right to be offended. "Forgive me for saving you all from falling for Naomi's shit again."

Enough with her drama. I spin back toward Kylie, who's casually placing the bottles back into the oversize pantry as if I didn't just warn her of imminent danger. "Look, if I'm lying, I'm lying. But wouldn't you rather be safe than sorry?"

Kylie sighs. "The sad part is, I can't even tell when you're lying. Not anymore. But maybe you've been lying to me all this time." She slams the door behind her.

The slam causes a tremor in the room. Subtle, like maybe I catch a dizzy spell. But as I stare around at the confused faces of Kylie, Roma, and Serena, I realize that they feel it too. Our arms and legs spread out, bracing ourselves as the floor continues to rumble. Then, as quick as it started, it stops. We stare at each other, too stunned to speak.

Finally: "The fuck was that?" Serena. Always the eloquent one.

Kylie and I lock eyes. Even now, we speak without speaking. *I'm scared*, her eyes tell me. *Me too*, mine say back. I swallow, as slowly and quietly as possible. Worried that any sudden movements could trigger something.

"Okay," I say in a hushed voice to everyone. "Let's tiptoe to the side entrance and—"

The building bellows at us. A vicious boom that causes not a tremor this time, but a quake. The floor splits from under us and the walls cave in all at once, like the earth cracks open.

Kylie's blond hair whips around her face. Someone screams behind me. I'm flying across the room, as if gravity doesn't remember how to function. My back slams against a remaining wall behind me, and I plummet, facedown, onto the floor. My finger twitches. Then my hand. Next, my wrist. I can move. I raise my head, search for Kylie. Plaster from the ceiling topples on top of me, burying me alive. I can't breathe. I can't breathe. I can't breathe.

I can't . . .

NOW

THE FLUORESCENT LIGHTS IN THE INTERROGATION ROOM BLIND ME, SO I press my head against the metal table. The metal no longer feels cool against my skin after baking so long under the lights, but still, I don't move. My head's too heavy to lift. This whole night's too heavy to lift. The base of my neck and my shoulders scream in agony. Probably from the blast. I never had a chance to get fully checked out before the cops whisked me away.

But the pain feels deeper. Somewhere buried that clawed its way to the surface after Detective Summers showed me those horrific pictures from the scene. Even through all the smoke, the soot. The blood. I recognized the body. And now that's all they'll ever be. The body. All the years they lived before now don't matter, because they'll always be known as the victim, the body, from this horrific night.

And now that's the only way I'll remember them.

The door opens and the light from the hallway spills into the room, as if there aren't already too many lights in here. I slowly lift my head, every bone in my neck aching, and my mom comes barreling into the room.

"Mom!" I cry out. I jump from my seat, forgetting the pain, and my mom scoops me into her arms. Almost knocking me off my feet. I cry into her shirt, and she rubs my back. She doesn't try to shush me. She wants me to get it all out. I do. I cry a river through the cotton of her T-shirt. After what feels like hours, someone clears their throat. I look over Mom's shoulder, and Detective Summers leans against the doorframe with his hands in his pockets.

"All right, Naomi. You're free to go," he says with the enthusiasm of a sloth.

Mom keeps an arm around me. "Well, then you best get out of our way," she snaps to the detective.

Detective Summers throws his hands up, all "my bad" as he steps out of the doorframe.

"Wait," I sniff. "What about Eric?" I remember the knee in his back. His face in the asphalt. Even though they pulled him back to his feet to arrest me, that doesn't mean he was in the clear after I was taken from the scene.

I don't have to wonder much longer, because Eric waits

for me and Mom as we step into the hallway. I pull away from Mom and run right into Eric's arms. He tries his best not to squeeze me too hard, remembering what I've been through tonight. Or last night. I have no clue how long I've been in that interrogation room.

"You can't get rid of me that easily," Eric says to me. I laugh and pull away to inspect him. He does the same to me. "You good?"

I nod. "You?"

"I am now." We do our handshake. Then he keeps hold of my hand as Mom grabs the other one.

We walk through the precinct just as Cleo leaves one of the rooms. Her eyes are puffy as she pats them with a balled-up tissue. The whole image is so jarring, so wrong, that I stop in my tracks. Since when does Cleo cry? Especially after our argument earlier.

She pauses when she sees me, then quickly looks down at her feet as Detective Stretch leads her to another room. She seems so small. So fragile. Nothing like the queen who was proud that I was being thrown into the back of a squad car. Sacrificing myself for the cause, just how she wanted.

Detective Stretch looks at me sandwiched between my parents and gives me a small smile. She nods at all of us, then disappears into the room with Cleo.

"What's happening?" I ask.

Mom gently tugs at my hand. "Let's go home, baby."

I let her and Eric guide me out to the parking lot, but too many questions pile up in my head. Where was everyone else? Why was Cleo so devastated? Why did they suddenly let me go?

"What happened?" I repeat as I climb into the back seat.

Eric gets behind the steering wheel, and Mom slides into the car next to him. They exchange a look that I can't read from back here.

"That's not fair," I say. "I deserve to know what's going on. Especially after everything."

"She's right," Eric says to Mom. "She's going to find out eventually. Might as well be from us."

Mom rubs her forehead, then turns around in her seat to face me. "Scott—Mr. Brooks—he planted the bomb himself."

It's not until I see Eric turning the steering wheel that I realize I'm not imagining us spinning. We're actually moving. Even though he goes the normal speed limit, I grip my seat belt to keep me stable.

"I don't . . . I don't understand," I manage. "Why would he . . . ? How did he know . . . ?" I can't complete the questions, because I can't comprehend anything at the moment.

Mom just nods like she's following my stream of thoughts. "He was working with someone. Somebody named Orlando Jones or something."

I stop breathing. Orlando? Orlando from Don't Attack

Blacks? There had to be a mix-up. Orlando called us into his house to plot this out. He even showed up last night to see it through. He was determined to see it through. All this time he made us think he wanted to make a statement . . . but was he in it for something else?

"He wanted Orlando to plant the bomb. Thought it would make sense if it came from an 'extremist group.' He and Orlando were going to pin it on somebody else from DAB. But apparently the cops had too much on this Orlando guy, so he spilled all the secrets. Something about Scott needing the insurance money. I guess these lawsuits are costing him hundreds of thousands of dollars. Who knows?" Mom turns back around and leans against her headrest. "All of it just so sick."

"Damn right," Eric says. He doesn't boast about being right about Mr. Brooks all this time. He just gives Mom her space. Gives me my space.

We ride along in silence for a while. Good. I couldn't stomach discussing much more of this right now. Mr. Brooks put all of us in jeopardy just so he could make money. Of course, he never knew about our secret parties, but anyone could've been in that building. A janitor. A maintenance worker. They're human, too, but it didn't matter to Mr. Brooks. Anyone could've been sacrificed to make these lawsuits go away. I remember Mom's words at Itsy Bitsy: *He probably hired some down-on-their-luck sap to take the fall for him.*

Orlando was willing to be that sap. With his highfalutin comments about Black power and community. All this time he was selling out to make a quick buck. He pulled Cleo and the rest of us into his BS. Convinced Cleo that doing something so radical was key for the movement. For the cause. No wonder she was in tears at the precinct. He betrayed her. For all I know, he probably was going to pin everything on Cleo.

"Seriously, Naomi." Mom's voice breaks through the silence. "How are you, baby? I . . . I know that was your friend who passed. Right?"

I think about the word *friend*. How six simple letters can't match the complexity of the meaning. How people who I thought were my friends shed their skin and revealed something ugly underneath. How I yanked masks off friends and saw only the flaws but not all the beauty in between.

How I forgot how to be a friend. Period.

I sigh and lean against the window. "No. Not really," I answer, and the tires eat up the road underneath us.

AFTER

IT'S WEIRD BEING AT WINDSOR WOODS HIGH AFTER DARK. SURE, I'VE been to games, but this is different. There's an eerie calmness in the air that's par for the course at a candlelight vigil, but there's something else going on. We all walk on eggshells so that one of us won't crack. Especially for a death like this. Correction, for a *murder* like this. It was a culmination of all the racial tension that has bubbled up to the surface in our school. In our town. But it's sad that something this dark, this tragic, had to happen for us to hold a mirror up to ourselves.

"I feel weird," Roma says as we climb out of Eric's car. "Are we even supposed to be here?"

I take a deep breath. "We're here to honor a fallen

classmate. It's only right." I look over my shoulder, and Eric gives us an encouraging nod.

"I'll come back to get y'all in about an hour," he says. "Unless you want me to stay."

The offer's enticing, but I shake my head. "We need to do this alone."

Roma and I join the others in the courtyard. Many of them already have their candles. They cry into each other's shoulders. Snap pictures of the vigil on their phones. Some of them even pose next to the stuffed animals and flowers people have left by the flagpole, as if it's there for a photo op and not to commemorate Serena.

Wow. Serena.

It still feels strange knowing that she's gone. Knowing that I will never see her sashaying through the halls, or smirking at me, or rolling her eyes at a joke before breaking into a fit of giggles. A few years from now, I probably won't even remember what her laugh sounded like. What her voice sounded like. She'll be a footnote in a dark chapter of my life, and that doesn't seem fair. She's supposed to have so many more pages to complete of her own story.

Faith stands next to Nevaeh, Amari, Mercedes, and Jordan near the back of the crowd. She waves and walks over to me and Roma.

"I grabbed two for you guys before they ran out," she says as she hands us each our own candle.

"Thanks," I say.

Faith tilts her candle forward and lights our wicks one at a time. "I feel bad. I didn't even know the girl. I had a few classes with her, but we never really spoke. But . . . I was *there*, you know? Seems only right to pay my respect."

Roma and I nod, completely understanding. Even though we were in the building, Faith later told me that the parking lot rumbled and made everyone out there lose their footing. She couldn't even verbalize the fear she felt when the bomb went off, knowing that I and others were in there. She didn't have to, though. It was all in the relief I saw in her eyes the next day when she checked on me.

We meet up with Nevaeh and the others, and they wave at us. Give us respectful smiles. Happy to see us, but not happy to be here. I can't imagine who is.

Principal Hicks and Ms. Guy step onto the portable stage in the center of the courtyard. Serena's parents stand behind them, next to a few oversize pictures of Serena on easels. You can see her sassiness in most of them, especially one where she couldn't have been more than five or six years old. She stands with her hips cocked to the side, hands on each one, and gives the camera severe duck face. I tattoo that picture in my brain. This is the way I prefer to remember Serena. To see Serena. And not the battered body Detective Summers displayed to intimidate me.

"Thank you for this beautiful showing of love and

support for Serena and the whole Warren family," Principal Hicks says into a microphone. He looks back at Serena's parents. "Mr. and Mrs. Warren, you are a picture of grace under tragedy, and I hope this vigil tonight offers you just a small glimmer of how much Serena meant to this school and community."

Serena's mom squeezes her eyes shut and nods. Mr. Warren wraps his arm around her shoulders and bites his bottom lip. But I see it trembling underneath his front teeth.

Principal Hicks says a few more words, but they get eclipsed by the sound of muffled crying. Lots of people are crying in the crowd, but this one is so distinct, so painful, that it stands above the rest. I scan the crowd and find the source: Jared. His head hangs low, and his shoulders bob up and down in grief. His friends are next to him, patting his back and squeezing his shoulders, but it's pointless. He just needs to let the tears flow, and they need to let them.

"Jesus," Roma says, sucking in a breath next to me. "I never thought there'd be a day when I actually felt sorry for Jared Crews."

"You and me both," I say, watching him and wondering if I should go over there and tell his friends to give him a moment. But that's not my place. It dawns on me that Kylie's not close by, offering him comfort. As far as I knew, they were still dating. But I can only imagine how strained things had to be between them. Kylie's dad is the reason we're all here, memorializing Serena. Neither Kylie nor Connor has been back to school in the week since they've arrested Mr. Brooks. I don't blame them. How can you recover from that?

I search the crowd, seeing what other faces I recognize. I spot Drew and Phil near the flagpole. Phil has his head resting on Drew's shoulder as Drew watches Principal Hicks speak without a hint of irony in his face. He finally senses me looking at him and glances my way. Gives me a soft smile. I return it. Drew then blows me a kiss, and I pretend to catch it. I know what it's for. He's told me one hundred times each day that if it wasn't for me, he or Phil could've very well been buried alongside Serena. He keeps thanking me for saving their lives. Thanking me for helping him to not take Phil for granted anymore. They're both applying to VCU and hope to rent a small apartment in Richmond together next fall. Drew told me I better visit them. As if there was any other option.

My eyes roam to the parking lot at the side of the school, the one that's usually reserved for the buses. It's empty now, save for a lone car. Sleek. Shiny. Silver. Someone sits on top of its hood. Far away from the vigil, but close enough to catch some of Principal Hicks's words through the sound system.

"I'll be back," I say to Roma and Faith. I hand Roma my candle, and she doesn't question me as I trudge through the damp grass in the courtyard and head straight to the parking lot. As I get closer, the figure gets clearer. But I recognized him from the courtyard anyway.

Connor's shoulders slump over as I approach him, but he doesn't move. Almost like he expected me to pay him a visit. He's probably right. I would've found him. If not here, then after. Just to see if he was okay—whatever that means.

"Half of those people don't even know Serena," he says when I'm close enough. "They just came for gossip. To see what else they can learn about how she died." He yanks off his ball cap and tousles his hair. "It's pathetic."

"I agree." I shove my hands into the pockets of my fleece jacket. Autumn's just come into full effect in Windsor even though we're nipping at November's heels. "But it's good that you came out. I mean, kind of." I nod at his car.

Connor huffs air out through his nose. "I don't deserve to be over there."

"Connor, you're not your dad. You're not the reason why Serena's not here anymore."

"I'm supposed to play the role of the grieving boyfriend." He folds and unfolds the bill of his cap like he's doing origami. "But I can't feel what Jared's feeling. I can't feel what her friends are feeling. I mean, I guess I miss her, but only because I'm used to her being around. I don't know how to miss her like a boyfriend should." He laughs a little under his breath. "I'm not even sure I liked her."

I take a step forward but stop. I'm not sure if I'm supposed to touch him, though I want to. Leave a hand on his knee so he could feel how much I'm feeling for him. "Of course you liked her. You two dated. Even if it was just for a little bit, some emotions had to have been there."

Connor looks up from his battered cap. "We both know why I started dating Serena."

I swallow and look down at my shoes. I didn't expect him to admit it, even if I knew it was true. My face gets warm, but not like before when I was around him. Now I'm trying to find the right thing to say without leading him on.

"Roma told me about the college guy," he continues. "He's been checking in on you?"

"Um. Yeah." I leave it like that because I don't know how much Connor wants to hear about Butter. Butter's been amazing, though. He made sure I saw him every day since the bombing, whether it's on FaceTime or just stopping by my apartment. He even brought my mom flowers and endured a year's worth of questioning from Eric. But Eric didn't scare him off. Butter even told me he wanted to take me on a real date sometime before Christmas. He wanted to make sure I felt ready. I told him I'd be ready before Thanksgiving.

"That's good." Connor gives me a soft smile. "You deserve for a guy to check on you. Not that you need it or anything."

At that, I return the smile. Something about this moment feels like old times. Before things got complicated with make-out sessions in the pool or skeletons being exhumed from closets. It's like we're just . . . friends. At least almost.

"Are you ready to go?"

I flinch at Kylie's voice from behind me. She takes timid steps toward Connor's car, not sure whether she should look at me.

"Yeah." Connor slides off his hood. "But I'll give you a minute." He looks at Kylie, then nods at me before slipping into his car and playing music. That's his best way of giving us privacy.

Kylie and I peek at each other, like two old friends spotting each other in a grocery store and wondering if we should speak. She hasn't scurried away into Connor's car, though. That's a good sign.

"I didn't see you out there," I say, jutting my thumb toward the courtyard.

"I wasn't. I stayed here with Connor to listen, but then had to sneak into the school to make a delivery. You know how my bladder is."

On cue, we both hold up our pointer fingers and thumbs, making a "tiny" gesture. It's funny how well we still know each other, but it doesn't feel right to laugh in the moment. Instead, we settle for small grins.

"Can you tell Mama—" Kylie stops herself and shakes her head. "*Ms.* Nina, thank you for dropping off all that food at the house. My mom hasn't been up to cooking much. Or eating. Or pretty much anything." She kicks at a stray pebble.

"I didn't know my mom brought you all any food," I say.

435

It doesn't surprise me, though. No matter what, she's going to feel a maternal bond with Kylie and Connor. She's wiped away too many of their tears to not. "I hope your mom's okay. She's always been incredible to me, no matter how much of a snot I am." I think about her saving me from the protest. How I had to be reminded to thank her. Who even was I then?

Kylie shrugs. "She loves you. We all do." She kicks her foot again, this time at nothing. I wonder if she's trying to figure out how she can lift her foot to her mouth before she says anything else she doesn't mean to. "But we should be heading back. I want to make sure my mom eats something tonight."

"Yeah. Sure."

Kylie walks past me and heads for the passenger's side of Connor's car. My heart skips, panicking at the sight of her leaving already. Not ready to say goodbye.

"Hey, Kylie," I call out to her, and she pauses. I swallow. "Did you submit your NYU application?"

"Yep. I submitted for early decision." She leans against Connor's car. "You?"

"Howard, Florida A&M, and North Carolina Central."

Kylie raises an eyebrow. "No Hampton?"

I shake my head. "I've seen enough of Hampton." Of course, Butter is a perk, but Butter won't be there forever. Besides, if I wasn't going to pick a college because of my best friend, I damn sure wasn't going to choose one because of a guy—no matter how amazing and fine that guy is. "But all the ones I've applied to have amazing prelaw programs. I think I want to become a civil rights attorney."

Kylie drops her bottom lip and nods, impressed. "Watch out, Ben Crump."

My chin almost hits the ground. "Wait, you know who Ben Crump is?"

"I use my phone for more than just TikTok." She adds a smile to make sure I get that she's joking. I smile back, and silence looms over us again. Someone else speaks through the microphone from the courtyard, but I'm more aware of my and Kylie's deliberate breathing as we wait for the other to say goodbye.

I'm not ready for that yet. "Hey . . . what do you think of my hair? Seriously?"

Kylie frowns at first, confused, then tilts her head to take in my curls. "I hate it."

A laugh pushes out of my belly. "Wow," I say once the snickers stop. "I think that's the most honest you've ever been with me."

"I think you're right," Kylie says. There's a tentativeness to her voice, as if she's just made this revelation and is letting it sink in.

I'm not angry, though. Kylie and I have both shared white lies with each other. Not out of mistrust, but out of fear. Too scared that complete honesty would shatter the bond between us—a bond that's been our entire worlds for so long. But neither of us is that fragile. The past few weeks have shown how strong we are on our own.

"Well, sorry, bitch. I'm not changing it," I say, with a mock neck roll.

Kylie allows a small laugh to escape, then shrugs at me. "And you shouldn't." She grabs the car's door handle, then pauses again. "I think we're coming back to school next week . . . maybe I'll see you at lunch?"

I nod. "I'll have some grilled chicken nuggets waiting for you."

Kylie lets out a sigh, almost like she's relieved, then gets into Connor's car. I sigh, too, as I watch them drive away. Yeah, we're tough—but sometimes it feels good to let someone else see your cracks and love you anyway.

I run my hand through my curls. They could use a little more moisture, but they're soft. Beautiful. Mine.

ACKNOWLEDGMENTS

Wow, I can't believe I made it to Book No. 2! There are so many people that helped me get to this point. First, Natalie Lakosil—thanks for keeping my eye on the prize and fueling my drive (especially when I idle a little too long!). You never laugh at my dreams, and help me outline the necessary steps to achieve them.

Rosemary Brosnan and Karen Chaplin—I appreciate the personal phone calls to let me know I was a valued member of the Quill Tree Books family, especially when things felt up in the air. And Karen, I love that you ask me the tough questions and make me really think about characters' motivations and see their stories with different eyes. Thank you also to everyone else at Quill Tree Books and HarperCollins who put their hands on this book in some capacity—your diligence and hard work is *always* appreciated. Andrew Eliopulos— thanks for believing in me and paving the pathway.

To Nic Stone, J. Elle, Christina Hammonds Reed, and

Kelly McWilliams—thanks for your support during my debut year. I don't know how I got so lucky to have you amazing ladies play a part in alleviating some of my anxiety as I navigated through so many unknowns.

Now on to the mushy stuff. To my mom, Tamara Hunt, and my cousin/best friend/sis/roomie, Marquita Hockaday: Thanks for being my village. You both love my kiddos as much as I do, and willingly deal with tantrums and snotty noses just so I can get words on the page. To my sister from another mister, Racquel Henry—thanks for being such a constant light and an avid cheerleader. To my aunt, Pamela "PaPam" Hockaday—thanks for making me feel like a superstar. Once I make a million dollars from this writing thing, a new car will be sent your way! And to my beautiful children, Easton and Brooklyn, thanks for motivating me. Whenever I want to give up, I see your tiny faces and they remind me that maybe I can make this world a better place for both of you through my stories.